ALSO BY NATHANIEL J. RATCLIFF

Into the Mindsai: A Region of Significance Beyond the Veil

The Long Cold Stare

Mind Fissures

Beyond the Mindsai

A Dream Between
Two Eternities

By Nathaniel J. Ratcliff

©2025

Ebony Tower
—Press—™
Springfield Virginia

Published by Ebony Tower Press™

Copyright © 2025 by Nathaniel J. Ratcliff

ebonytowerpress.wixsite.com/ebonytowerpress

ISBN-13: 978-1-7339239-8-9 (Hardcover Edition)
ISBN-13: 978-1-7339239-9-6 (Paperback Edition)
ISBN-13: 979-8-218-74586-8 (Ebook Edition)

Printed in the United States of America
Library of Congress Control Number: 2025916046

This is a work of fiction. Characters, places, corporations, institutions, and organizations in this novel are either the product of the author's imagination or, if real, used fictitiously without any intent to describe their actual conduct.

Interior designs by Nathaniel J. Ratcliff
Book cover design by Haddy Kreie

10 9 8 7 6 5 4 3 2 1
First Edition

Soli Deo Gloria

Then Moses said to God, "Behold, I am going to the sons of Israel, and I will say to them, 'The God of your fathers has sent me to you.' Now they may say to me, 'What is His name?' What shall I say to them?"

– Exodus 3:13

Just as a camera is unable to fully see itself and its innerworkings, so are the limitations of our minds short of transcendence. The interplay of choice and time are impossible to fully comprehend until you are beyond both.

– The Man with Sapphire Eyes

The answers to life's great mysteries are only a heartbeat away and there you will stare into the vastness of eternity. The only problem is, the dead tell no tales beyond the veil. The veil between life and death may be thin, but the gulf is great. For most, it is a one-way trip, and those that do return, they are never the same.

– The Man with Sapphire Eyes

CONTENTS

Beyond the Mindsai

A Dream Between
Two Eternities

Prologue:
A Rare Plot of Dirt

The waters had been rising longer than Ur could have imagined—slowly and steadily encroaching upwards to the top of the fertile plateau. For many years the plateau had dominated the landscape casting its long shadow over the valley and the plains below. With the world slowly slipping beneath the waves, it had fallen low; now only a footrest for the stony mountain in the distance. In what was left of a valley, the tops of trees—which had once stood tall and mighty for many generations—were nearly engulfed by the rising of the murky torrent. Some of the timber's sturdy boughs were still adorned by the foolish few who thought no water could reach such towering heights. Drenched to their bones, with eyes open wide, the men looked more like cornered animals than the strong men he had quarreled with many moons ago. Even amongst the highest branches, the frothing waters had begun to lick their toes like a hungry beast. Seeing no signs of abatement, one-by-one they dropped like falling fruit into the maelstrom, some with mouths open releasing silent screams. A couple of heads reemerged amidst the waves frantically spinning to find the direction of higher ground. But, in the gloom, their place was quickly lost in the splash and foam.

It was difficult to tell how long the curs*ed* water had been falling. Obscured behind the tempest's black veil, there had been no sign of sun or moon to guide—days…weeks…a moon cycle could have passed since it all began. It was hard to even think of a time before the chaos started. Even amidst the wailing wind, he could still remember dry ground and a sun-filled sky. Before the darkness. Before the sky water. Before the world had been tossed into a basket to shake and churn upside down.

Ur closed his eyes for a moment in a vain attempt to go back before the deluge had covered the land. It had begun on a hot eve…The memory was quickly fading from his grasp like the blackening embers of a dying camp fire.

Was this the new state for the world? Some swift judgment for knowledge I now bear? he thought. *No, it must stop eventually; surely, there cannot be so much water in the land. It belonged in the deep low places of the world— the places I had so recently tread—not falling from on high.*

There had been a time of dryness, of comfort, of undisturbed sleep. All he could focus on was that final evening, before this cataclysm had begun…

After arising from the very roots of the world, he had found a brief moment of repose atop a grassy hill. From the vantage, he could finally see the last few steps of a long quest before him down a well-trodden path. It was his usual spot that overlooked the stone city. The city stood large and sturdy upon the low plain— like the sons of Watchers who still garner great fear and renown in lands beyond the mountains. At the city's center, sat a kingly ziggurat structure that towered over the numerous dwellings wrought of stone. Hewn by the hands of man for over nine generations, the towering ziggurat now possessed six terraced levels, oval in shape, one for each lordly Watcher who had provided knowledge to the great city. At the ziggurat's zenith stood the Temple of the Memory made of gold and silver brick and crowned by an ox-sized blue crystal that shimmered a cooling light against the blushing sky. On certain occasions, the blue light would lay upon the land so that divinations of future plantings and sacrifices could be divined by the temple's high priest, Zikaron. For it was known that Zikaron was old and knowing beyond any other man. He alone kept the memories of the world back to the unsighted time; before the first man, and even—it was said amongst the elders of the city—before the birth of the sun and moon.

On this particular evening, the crystal's light was diminished and scattered against the foothills of the watchful mountains in the east. Sitting on that evening perch, he had regarded the unusual position of the moon and sun which both appeared to be setting in unison. They both hung in a robin egg sky that had a touch of red like the blushing cheeks of a young women filled with desire. Joining the celestial balls this eve were strange orbs of white that had appeared at the edges of the world. Yet, the winds were calm and almost sickeningly sweet from the onset of a coming spring. There was no sign or rebuke in firmament or upon the lands—as if all the Watchers and beasts of the field had fallen into a quiet slumber. Now, in knowing, the land was holding its breath for what was to be thrust upon it.

It had come like the glint of a spark. A flash of light fell over the land, bathing it in a white glow. Many heartbeats passed until his sight eventually returned. When it did, he saw the sky ablaze. A great sign had burst through the firmament with the roar of a hundred lions. It glowed orange, like a falling sun with a yellow tail fanning out behind. The sign was joined by the sound of laughter coming from places down below—places he thought he had left far behind him, out of reach of ear nor eye. Outside the stone city's bronze gate, a small assembly of men and women had gathered. The people, in their nakedness, danced and twirled around a carved stone tree in drunken revelry. With arms raised, they pointed and gleefully shouted at Nature's wonderous new display. The ball of fire aroused no such elation in him. From his vantage, it was an ill tiding after his arduous journey—perhaps another fallen Watcher being cast from the heavens.

He had continued to stare as the orange ball crackled across the sky. The wispy white clouds were thrown asunder in twirling whirls as it traveled its resolute course. Once it reached the edge of the horizon, its roars became ever fainter until silence retook the land and then the fireball had disappeared beyond the outer rim of the world.

A few still moments had passed. All that had remained of the ball of flame was a trailing scar in the sky that led back to a gaping black hole from where the fireball had pierced through from the outer heavens. The ring-shaped wound did not appear to heal or diminish as dark wisps of clouds had already begun to form and circle around it like a whirlwind. It was hard to tell if it was sucking the light out from the heavens or spilling darkness into them. Standing alone on the hill, he felt small beneath the dark hole. It seemed to stare into him like the cold dead eyes of so many men and women he had killed before, some for his city and others for himself. Eventually, the pure black void had drawn in his gaze until he drank deep into it. His head felt light and the world seemed to dim all around him. He feared that he just might fall up into that black hole, into pure nothingness.

Having finally wrestled his gaze away from the hole in the sky, strange tones came forth from it. Sounds not unlike blown horns, they were deep and drawn out. Their resounding blast echoed across the land, harkening not of joy, but enveloping the world in sorrowful lamentation. There was little doubt that a great change was being heralded. One not seen in many ages.

Fear crawled into his mind then. *Perhaps the discounted prophecy had been true*, he had thought. Yet, before terror could consume him or prompt flight, a brilliant white light erupted at the edge of the world, where the fireball had fallen. As if a sign had been granted, the white orbs hanging over every corner of the horizon dispersed, vanishing into the distant reaches of the world.

Shortly thereafter, a rumbling rolled across the land like a giant awakening from a prolonged slumber. The very ground began to shake beneath his feet. The convulsion sent up droves of black birds and other large wing*ed* beasts. The creatures poured out from every cave and hidden crevice scattered about the land until their black streams had darkened the sky with their uncountable numbers. Even the band of revelers, now on unsteady footing, had ceased their dancing and rushed back through the gates into the city.

It was then that he had hastened to return to the city to complete his task before the chance was forever lost. The way down the hill was difficult and slow for the ground had shifted in many places. Patches of earth had risen or sunken a foot length or more, while in other places, the ground had fallen away altogether into narrow cracks. When he had reached the bottom, something dropped from the sky that stopped him dead in his tracks. Upon his forehead, a single drop of water had fallen the length of the sky from some unseen spring.

What is this? he had thought. *Water does not fall from like such. It lives in the low cool pools and streams of the land. Has this sign of fire turned the world upside down?*

As he looked upwards to find the source of this new form of wetness, a line of blackness, as deep as burnt coals, appeared on the edge of the land. The blackness crept slowly, rolling across the four corners of the heavens until every celestial sphere had been swallowed by the inky sea of darkness. From some unseen realm within or beyond the darkened sky came terrible growls like that of a cornered beast. Amidst the rumblings, flashes of white fire streaked across the land. He remembered feeling a tingling in the air just before a white flash hit a bush a few paces from where he stood. The sudden burst of white light had briefly blinded him, enveloping him in intense heat and the scent of burning. When sight had returned to him, the bush had become consumed by yellow flames. The fire ravaged the bush until only a heap of darkened ash remained amid the scorched ground, marking the spot where the white fire had struck.

Once his wits had returned, he ducked behind an olive tree in fear. The rumblings continued on without ceasing. It was not long before a groaning could be heard deep under the ground. It was as if some great forgotten beast was clawing its way up from very foundation of the world. Its roar grew until the ground shook violently beneath his feet. The land began to twist and crack with great strain. Fissures formed that stretched their thin tendrils across the land as far as he could see. Thick inky-black smoke billowed out through the scarred earth in tall pillars that reached upwards towards the sky. The wind also began to whirl all around him, carrying with it the foul scent of rotting eggs. And somewhere in the gusting air, he thought he could hear screaming.

It was then that he looked back upon the stone city. It no longer gleamed majestically as the crown jewel of the land. It had become darkened and broken. The once mighty temple, that overshadowed the hills of the flat plain, had nearly cracked in two exposing its once-sturdy innards. And out of the fissure, spluttering like black blood, was a torrent of dark water that rose above the city like a tall fountain. Not quite reaching the sky, the dark waters crashed back down upon what was left of the temple. The torrent poured over the terraced levels of the ziggurat in great falls before rushing into the stone city. The lessor buildings were quickly leveled like a hand passing through a mound of sand. Person and animal alike were carried away down the avenues by the powerful current like tiny clay figurines.

Then, the sky water came raining down. It spewed from the heavens angry and sharp with teeth of a springing serpent without ceasing. In those first early days, the people of the land scrambled to find shelter from the pounding waters. At first, the sky water wettened the land, turning the brown ground to black mud. Mud that pulled and sucked at your feet. Many livestock and a few young herders were abandoned in the growing pits of black muck.

Then, more time passed. The land was covered in the same dull darkness and falling water, making it the passing of days difficult to know. The falling water eventually increased in its violence upon the world. The land became soaked until the ground itself could take in no more. It was then that the waters came up out of the ground like some hidden sea whose black and tumultuous waters had been waiting beneath the land. The waters rose slowly, drowning the low areas. People were forced from their dwellings as the waters overtook their roofs, licking at their heels as they sought higher ground. Eventually, not a dry place remained anywhere to be found...

The early days of torment now seemed far off to Ur as the memories slipped back away to the present. Not much had changed. Only the sinking of the landscape around him. The falling waters continued now, like it had begun on that last dry evening. Drop after relentless drop, added more to the ever-emerging sea that covered almost every corner of the land that the eye could see.

Looking at his hands, Ur saw that they had become pale and shriveled like a dried plum. His once bronze skin had taken on a milky appearance with white scales covering the palms of his hands. The red circle-shaped mark he had from birth on the back of his right hand had almost disappeared entirely. In areas around his legs and feet, sores had opened to ooze blood and yellow pus. Yet, the waters washed away everything—his blood, his sweat, his tears. Even the cries of those who had lost hope were lost in the falling rain. As was the land itself.

Few options now remained as the land sunk away. With each passing, immeasurable moment, solid ground became an ever-rarer refuge. Through the rain and mist, his last hope stood grey and motionless. A rocky ridge led up before him to higher ground where the last remains of land still touched the sky.

Ur trudged along the ridge for some time until he came upon a couple of men wearing nothing but a soaked sackcloth around their waist. The men hurriedly scrambled up a grey rock face about a half dozen reeds away. Before they vaulted out of view into the undulating ribbons of rain, he could see the tiny streams of water running in and out of the red creases of their backsides that had been beaten into them from the pounding rain. Just beneath the path the men had taken, a pair of children with a young woman laid huddled under an overhang. They shivered uncontrollably and heeded him not as he passed up the mountain face, following the path the men had taken. He seemed no more than another tattered bunch of debris blowing by upon the wind in their distant eyes.

A cascade of white water rushed over the rocky path, roaring as it flowed unimpeded off the rock edge. Yet, it fell silently down into the misty darkness below where greater, darker waters were gathering for their slow march upwards. Further on, a different sort of veiled darkness blocked the sky. It was only interrupted by flashes of white fire that cracked through the whirling clouds.

Higher and higher he climbed, through a narrow rocky pass that grew increasingly steep with each cautious step he took. His feet flinched uncontrollably on each jagged stone. He knew that one slip on the rain-soaked rock would mean certain death down into the abyss encroaching below. The weariness of countless days without sleep crept into every movement he took to find higher ground. If not his feet, he feared it would soon be his mind that slipped away. His head had already grown heavy from lack of sleep. The pounding beat of the rain left little space for thinking or resting—each moment was a struggle to focus on the bleary path ahead. But there was little choice now, all the junctures had disappeared and merged into the single soaked grey path that laid before him. He *had* to march forward; there was nothing to his back. In between each carefully laid step, he tried not to think of the things that laid behind him. The groves of fallen trees, the shallow bowls filled with floating little babes next to their pale water-logged mothers, the hordes of rodents scampering up to escape the waters…It was easier to think of it all as a black void, of a world no one would ever see again, nor remember.

Before his blurry eyes could realize it, the narrow path opened up onto a small grey promontory rock that jetted out upon the shoulder of the mountainside. The wind was strong here, at the top of the world. Above his head, the jagged summit of Tannis was obscured by swirling black clouds that flickered with light and fire. Yet, at the center of the whirling winds, there was a tunnel of calm that connected the drenched world with the heavens that seemed unmarred and unthreatened by the dark calamity happening below. Uncountable flocks of birds set forth from the exposed peaks towards the blissful calm but even their wings could not carry them to safe aeries above the clouds. Ur squinted as such he could amidst the rain and wind to see far beyond, a ball of bright white light that shown forth through the darkened tunnel like a beacon of the world as it was before. Unable to gaze upon the light directly, Ur saw other, lessor lights of white that remained steady within the lining of the tunnel. The beings of light were holding the violent winds at bay so that the host of the heavens could see the end of all things. By some power he could not explain, he could see the faces of these benevolent Watchers. Their expressions held nothing short of despair and sorrow for what was befalling the land below.

A multitude of flying creatures had gathered to roost near the crimson peak of the mountain above, perhaps the last remaining eyrie of the world. Many took flight into the bleak skies, but one among them commanded terrible awe. This creature, towering over the others, launched itself from the cliffside on sturdy hind legs. Its wide leathery wings caught an updraft, propelling it swiftly skyward to join the lessor sky dwellers. Large enough to carry several men aloft, the sky dragon's long-pointed beak added to its formidable appearance. The somber flying host rose up as high as their wings could bare them, but salvation was forever out of reach for even the beasts of the air.

An understanding started to wash over Ur with great sadness. He looked beyond to the horizon, hoping beyond hope for some earthly sign of deliverance. *Man is too clever to perish like the salt upon the sea. And to be struck from the Earth now when knowledge is yet to fulfill itself*, he thought in earnest.

No salvation was to be had. Only mud, smoke, and more beating rain as far as Ur could see. Stretching forth from the whirlwind's heart, a thick ebon veil stretched out to all corners of the firmament. It hid any sign of celestial lights beyond. The only luminance came from the soft red glow of liquid fires that still burned upon the last vestiges of land. These last solid refuges projected up through the waves like stony outstretched fingers of so many Ur had seen slip under the waters. Even the waters themselves seemed to glow in places where the liquid fire had become covered by a rising, raging sea. Above these smoldering waters great plumes of steam swirled aimlessly.

Nearly fifty fathoms below from where Ur now stood, a few bare spots of stone remained. These rare plots of redden earth had once been two of the three mighty peaks that comprised the Dragon Spears: Tannis, Tyr, and Dur. For the tales of old had spoken of a great dragon who made a dwelling upon these high places so that it could touch the heavens. The terrible beast had eyes that glowed red, teeth as long as swords, a neck with the girth of the widest tree, and a breath that could still anything living. It had reeked terror on the cities in the valleys below, often swallowing oxen whole. At least until the day, when a great hero of renown, a giant among men, came and cast the dragon down upon the mountain side. It was said that the beast's blood ran across the three peaks soaking them a deep crimson that neither wind, water, or time could sway. But now, these bloodied peaks were cast low at the edge of dark waters whose white frothing pulled the flesh from the land down into an unseen abyss.

Constant falling water had dulled the once jagged peaks below. The two areas that now remained were flat enough for survivors to gather in large numbers. The first and flattest plot of earth was closest to the advancing sea. A desperate throng of people and beasts had amassed across its slippery surface, covering every bare spot like a swarm of ants on a recently fallen morsel of food. There were mothers carrying little ones still suckling at their breasts. Wolves laid next to sheep for warmth amid the frantic people. Near the center of the rock, a child dragged a basket of moldy fruit while another man had just spilled his earthen jar of golden coins that dully gleamed in the gloom.

Those less fortunate cleaved to every spot along the rock's edges that had not yet succumbed to the lapping waves. Men and women gripped tightly; their bodies battered bloody with each new onslaught of waves. Surrounding them, the lifeless bodies of the young, the old, and the broken floated like pale trunks of a fallen forest, while above them, Watchers silently mourned and tallied the countless losses. Those still with blood coursing through them were too distraught to heed these unearthly beings. Weary souls scrambled up the rocks, seeking sure footing, some kicking away others that sought to follow to what little space remained. Yet others, in their final acts before slipping beneath the waves, pushed up crying babes to those that could would receive them. And amidst the chaos, all sorts of serpents and small dragons skittered up the rock face, while a waterlogged lioness paced restlessly, clutching a cub in her mouth. She made frantic leaps up the sheer rock face, searching for any new signs of higher ground.

The second area sat higher up the mountain, approximately twenty fathoms above the first. Here, the rockface slanted upwards like that of a long, tilted table hewn of red stone. Like the rock slab below, no other routes seemed available to man nor beast as many screes prevented ascension. The outcropping was separated from the first area by a rushing torrent of white water that cascaded down the mountain's face with great haste before disappearing into the murky gloom below. Many who attempted to ascend from the lower area were quickly swept away by the ferocious currents.

Upon the higher rock, a smaller gathering, perhaps a single tribe, huddled around what appeared to be their elder. The young screamed in vain, while those of older years simply moaned, lamenting their plight. Once strong and proud, their bodies now trembled uncontrollably beneath tattered garments caked in mud and blood. Their heads hung low, unable to even look up into the sky, as if cowering like dogs before an angry God. Only the elder man remained stoic, casting a scowl skyward through his tangled mat of white hair.

BOOOOM!

The jolt sent everything upon the rock low to their knees as the sound shook through stone, fur, and flesh. The wolves that had found refuge inexplicably abandoned their snug position, jumping headlong into the waves as if the molten fires were at their feet. No one could guess as to where they might go as there was nowhere left as far as an eye could see.

Yet, a shape had begun to form many leagues in the distance at the edge of the world. Tall and dark it seemed from afar, but as it neared, it seemed to be yet another wave, wide but not too dissimilar to what had been crashing against the rocks tirelessly. Slowly, it seemed to gather speed and ever-greater height as it approached. A hum could be heard that grew into a roar that rose above gale and water-pour. Soon the wave entered into what light remained within the world and only then did those below recognize it for what it was—a wave of their doom. At its peak, the wave bore foaming white teeth ready to devour those sojourned against the rockface and to pull them asunder. The people in its shadow could only tremble and fret in vain for there was no route of flight away from the impending wall of water.

For Ur, the crest of the towering wave loomed menacingly close, yet it would ultimately crash and break but a few fathoms short of reaching his precarious perch. When it crashed against the mountainside, it did so with a great *CLAP!* and burst into a million streams that swept away rock, beast, and man just the same. The impact of the wave dislodged a giant boulder which bounded down the mountain, splashing and crashing as it went. It landed on the lower platform, splattering a man and a goat who were scattering to seek new footholds from the wash. A red and pink mush flung in all directions and once the stone completed its roll into the sea, neither the remains of goat nor man could be discerned from each other.

After a time, the waters receded into the steady marching swell of the sea. The people that remained upon the rock regathered themselves, finding what secure positions they could. Of those who had clung to the lower rock, only a quarter remained. The rest had been swept out deep into the waters with some adding their bodies to the growing pale flotsam that bobbed and swirled within the foul black waters.

Yet, there were a handful of those swept out in the raging waters who persisted. Their limbs moved vigorously as they frantically attempted to keep their heads above the waves and return to solid ground. Without a sign or warning, the head of a giant milky serpent shot out of the sea from betwixt the swimmers. The creature's head was drawn out with size enough to engulf a wolf whole. Water emptied steadily out between rows of needle-like teeth that the most slippery prey could not hope to escape once caught up in their pointy grip. Two lidless black eyes stared coldly behind a raised snout the seemed to froth with steam. Its head rested upon a snake-like neck that towered over the swimmers to the height of a gopher tree. It bent and curled searching for prey. Barely visible at the surface, a bulging elephant-sized body held the creature steady with massive flippers that beat back the turbulent waters.

After cocking its head a few times side-to-side, the sea dragon grabbed a woman, naked in its mouth. The woman writhed vainly with her final strength before being pulled down into the murky darkness.

A young man looking not to suffer the same fate, made haste towards the bough of an overhanging arcadia tree. The tree was weathered to but a stub, nearly barren of leaf and branch. Along its gnarled trunk many branches had broken or splintered under the unrelenting rain. But its roots, to the moment, remained strong and firm, anchored deep into the mountain beneath the rushing waters. Though even its strength was failing under the weight of a dozen forlorn souls who ladened its grey length. The young man reached out with a withered hand to grab hold the sole branch that skirted upon the crests of the waves. But even in his haste, he could not outrun a thing borne of the deep. In little time as there was, the pale monster had returned to grab him by his side, and before his face filled with fatal understanding, was dragged beneath the waves. This time, the sea dragon was accompanied by unnamed others who joined in the feast until, one-by-one, not a living soul moved across the waters.

The sea then took an unexpected turn. It began to recede slowly back, relinquishing its progress up the mountain. In its retreat, eddies and pools remained, filled to the brim with every sort of rotting debris. Those that remained upon the rock let out a weak rallying cry for the apparent change in fortune. A brief cheer rose in Ur's own throat until he looked onward…

The horizon had darkened again once more. Only this time, the darkness was complete. It had spread across the length of the sea and nearly four lengths higher than before. The dark shape was so black, that it blocked out every trace of sea and cloud beyond it. It moved slower than the first with many leagues to cross. It would be some time before it fell across the shores of the world's last refuge.

The cries were quickly caught in the throat of all who still clung to the rock. The roaring wave was approaching and it would have its due. Nothing would be left save rock and sea.

The realization that had begun in Ur's mind had reached a final resolution. The waters, it seemed, would not be satisfied until all that were living were cleansed when the world sank beneath the waves and the sea met the sky—everything sunken, washed away, erased. Not a vestige would remain to recall the great makings or deeds of those who once thrived under fairer skies. An impulse, dormant within him for days, now took a stronger foothold. For it was painfully evident that there were no esoteric incantations of words or arcane chants that could halt the relentless advance of these unforgiving waters. Thus, Ur regarded the jagged rocks many lengths beneath his vantage with a new yearning interest. Their teeth beckoned as a quick respite from wind and rain.

But he held back his foot that hovered above the edge. As the cries below grappled back his focus. He gazed earnestly downward to see what choices others were making in these precious few moments that might remain. Some had begun to clasp their hands with hastily dusted prayers upon their lips while others thrust themselves against the sheer rock face to make one last effort of flight. Yet, the clan's elder stayed firm and resolute with his huddled family.

One man, apart from the huddled group, had arisen with a strong intent, walking with purpose across the stone. Under a drooping mop of rain-sodden black hair, his dark eyes were intent and fixed. After a few steps, he reached a woman who had been huddled in a crouching position on the outer edge of the elder's group. In the storm it was difficult to see, but there was a brief struggle of sorts on the slippery stone. The woman was easily dispatched by the big man and no one came to her aid because their own plights were laden heavy upon them. It was a little thing that the dark-haired man had snatched out from under the woman's protective bosom. Once it had begun to squirm it was plain that it was a child, not more than eight moons of age. The woman sobbed in a wet puddle trying to entreat the man to return the child back to her protection, but he paid her little attention as he marched steadily towards the very edge of the outcropping.

When the dark-haired man reached the edge, he looked over it at the swirling waters underneath. His satisfaction seemingly fulfilled, he then lifted the naked little thing high and aloft over the edge. The babe opened its little mouth wide without a tender ear to hear its muffled cry. It wriggled helplessly as it teetered amid the unforgiving storm; its tears fell aimlessly downward to add their small part with the rest of the world. The man, now clearly enraptured with desperate deliverance, was unmoved.

Then, after an unheard command or perhaps a plea to sky or sea, there was a flash in the sky and after, his hands had emptied. The tiny tot had been tossed down into the abyss. The waters seemed not to take any notice of its passing beneath their dark screen, but a small orb of white light, marked where the child had been swallowed up not to be seen again.

By this time, the woman who had harbored the child from the elements had become distraught at the sacrificial act. She crouched away from the huddled group, slowly towards the man at the edge. The others from her group reached out to her, pleading for her to return. Their protest went unnoticed. The distraught woman, heavy with anguish, met the man who turned and grabbed her at the very edge. However, his footing failed him under a rubble of loose stone. In another flash, he too slipped and fell for a length of time before splitting upon a pointed craig below. No orb appeared over his broken body.

The woman received little relief from her vengeance and could only wail uncontrollably into the wind with her small fists clinched at her side. She showed little care for the approaching doom that now loomed larger in the near distance. There was another flash of light and then she too had left the cliff and disappeared into the waters below.

Having apparently seen enough, the elder patriarch of the group rose quietly from his hunched position. His shriveled legs shook like spongey reeds as he took to his feet. His frail frame teetered side-to-side requiring the support of two shoulders of younger kin that had diligently been by his side. As he rose to the fullest that he dared, he planted his right foot firmly in the ground and raised a thick arm up above his head with outstretched fingers towards the last light in the world. The light that, with every approach of the great wave, had slowly begun to shrink and fade. No longer guarded, the eddying winds blew back white hair and a thick snowy beard revealing the old man's face in full in the greying gloom. His muddied white garments flew about from whence they had been wrapped. Even from the great heights of his perch, in the flashes of the storm, Ur could see the stern face of a once strong and proud man. A man that had seen the weathering of years in the dozens of scores. Years filled with many bloody victories and few defeats, for few lived to see such ancient years in that age of violence. That fighting malice to survive and steal away comfort burned hot in the elder's eyes but so did something that had not shone across the expanse of all those years—fear and the foreboding of an utter defeat. Despite his brazen stance against the ending of the world, his eyes betrayed that no strength of arms, no riches, nor wit could deliver himself from doom.

Then, as the last light faded from the rock, a change came over the old man's face. With his outstretched hand, he closed his fingers tightly into a clinching fist pounding upward towards the hallowed light that refused to witness the ending of the world. The man's last act of defiance moved an answer from neither sky, mountain, nor sea—salvation was to be denied to all on this day.

The wave was imminently upon him and a new resolve rekindled in Ur's heart. A primal burning determination to survive moved through every part of him, for who would remember this generation, their great deeds and accumulation of knowledge and, what about the secret things? Who would be left to remember anything as the world was being wiped away into a watery abyss? Who had the right to deny the world's progress on a whim? With enough will or favor from the gods, someone must.

As the great wave reached the first low outcroppings, the land began to tremble as if the mountain itself were in its final death throes. The ground shook beneath the feet of all who still lived as the old rock turned against the living like a hound shaking a scourge of fleas. Screams of terror began to rise, but these voices seemed distant compared to the chorus of strangely beautiful voices singing a woeful dirge upon every gust of wind. It was in these last few precious moments that Ur espied a large log resting snuggly upon the ledge beside him. He needed only leap forward to grab it firmly as a means of floating out the incoming wall of water. It would serve as a mighty raft even in the towering waves.

It was now or never to make the leap. His legs coiled in what strength they had left in them. He pushed with great force but felt no recoil from the stone under his feet because it had already begun to slip down the steep slope towards the jagged rocks and violent waves. In those last moments he did not know which divine name to curse or to ask for forgiveness. The memory had long since washed away into dark depths to which he forthwith returned. A swift escape he welcomed with gladness like returning home after an unsettling dream.

) | (

The helpless screams slowly became drowned by a moaning wind. Even the crashing waves and roar of an incessant deluge somehow diminished into nothing more than the faint sound of a whirling fan out somewhere in the unseen darkness. Dr. Sebastian Silva had become quite accustomed to the nothingness. After witnessing life after life across spans of unrecorded time, the blank places in-between were the only ones where the whispers of his own voice could find refuge. The memory of himself was now but a faint dream, there were so many of them now, competing. So many connections. So many voices. So many flashbulb moments that meant so much to those who experienced them. But what a cruel thing it was to gain total cognizance of human experience with no one to share. All he was left with was that forbidden and forgotten knowledge and he found out quickly that Knowledge is a deadly friend with many faces.

There had been many lifetimes to reflect, to trace back each and every stepping stone that lead to his miserable plight. It was a cruel joke that he had to see the grand picture to see how wrong his missteps had taken him. A ruin that could have been avoided if he could have kept good faith. It was clear now what a fool he had been to tug at the veil with his Mindsai machine. A machine that he designed himself to dig deep into the ancestral memories locked away in the back of his mind. *What folly.* For once a mere peek had been glimpsed, the Veil had thus become broken. Behind it, likely with the demonic aid of ZoZo, unleashed a vast storehouse the hit him like a stiff wind. A wind that blew through his mind with such force that who *he* was became lost to flutter here and to there in an endless stream of life, death, and images of those who experienced neither, but yet still *were* beyond time and deep memory.

He could not quite understand how, but he was no longer restricted to memories of his forebears. He could now slip in and out of any memory of any soul or being that had once set foot on the Earth—an endless stream of images to watch in his own private hell.

There was a flash of a beautiful woman with dark hair that fell around a soft face of porcelain skin. She looked familiar, but from his past, or so many others?

The sorrow had long taken him after living so many lives of the countless people who had ever walked the Earth. No history book could come close to so much that had been forgotten or never tended to memory. Living memory is what they called it. To measure the length of a human life is such a short thing compared to the workings of the world which are long and slow. So easy is it for an individual to fade from living memory. It may take a generation, maybe two, before no one, not even kin, will remember even one of the millions of deeds that make up a life. Yet, there were those who never lived that remembered the first beam of light upon still and empty waters or the groans of the earth settling in the deep. Only the Watchers could say.

HA! HAA! HAARRR!

There was laughter in the dark. Cruel and twisted with pure malevolence.

"Shall you bear another?" said ZoZo in a rasping whispering voice enveloping all around him.

The darkness began to pull itself back like the pulling of a black curtain. Soon the crude image from another stranger's eyes began to come into view.

THE FIRST DISPENSATION

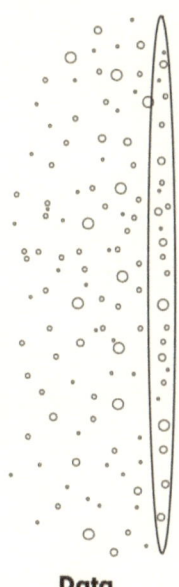

Data

) *Every day we are inundated with a flood of data across our senses. Overwhelmed, we are filled with the false confidence that our understanding is as deep as the information in which we swim.* (

1

The Rooters

Dr. Sebastian Silva's leg twitched out of the thick blanket that had been laid haphazardly across his hospital bed. Outside, the streaks of water droplets meandered down a thick pane of glass that looked out over the city. Under the overcast sky, grey buildings stood silent and dark.

"Will someone turn off that god damn fan? It's cold as hell in here," yelled a young man with a mop of curly brown hair.

"Sure thing, Clayton. Let me find a switch..." replied a man of similar age with buzzed hair of a lighter shade of brown.

CLICK. The fan slowly spun to a stop as a member of the hospital staff entered the room with a fresh bed pan.

"You work here long?" asked Clayton curtly.

"Almost all my life," replied the attendant as he exchanged the bed pans in a single, well-practiced, fluid motion.

"What do you know about this guy?" Clayton continued, not taking much notice of the man's work.

"Well, he's been here about three years I reckon. Some sort of big shot cyber psychologist they say. Not sure what that means but he's been provided this here fancy room. Somebody thinks he's important. Is he a relation of yours?"

"No, he's not, but he is of interest to some people in New Eden, which is why Zack, over there, and I are here. We are agents for the Roots of Unity and we are here to find some known associates of Dr. Silva."

"Is that right…" The attendant gave Clayton an incredulous look over the top rim of his thick glasses. "…well, you won't be getting much from Bash here, that's what people used to call him up at the University, he has been comatose since we received him."

"No friends or family came to look after him?" asked Zack.

The attendant shook his head. "Nope, not a soul has seen the poor man. It's pretty much me, the Brancher-guy, and a few of the other attendants on the other shifts, and that's it."

"Who's the chick, then?" asked Clayton who was pointing to a small picture of a young woman sitting on the bedside table. The woman's dark hair framed a smooth ivory face that smiled begrudgingly towards the camera. It appeared to be the sole article attributable to Dr. Silva amongst the machines and generic hospital décor.

"Ah, the young lady there…yes. One of his colleagues found the frame in the man's office and placed it there. I have never seen her in here. A beauty like that I would be apt to remember," the attendant replied with an assuring nod.

Clayton fiddled with the frame until it fell flat upon the beige nightstand.

"What are you doing?" asked the attendant.

"I am doing my job. And do not question our business here," snapped Clayton.

The attendant took a few steps back from Clayton.

"I think that will be all for now," Zack said flatly and ushered the attendant to the door. With the attendant dismissed, he turned to find Clayton unhinging the claps that held the back of the photo frame together.

"It's been a while since I've seen a real printed photograph," said Zack once Clayton had finally removed the back of the frame.

Clayton paid him little mind. His dark eyes darted back-and-forth until a smirk rolled across his face.

"Well, I don't think The Roots will need to worry about this one."

"Why is that?" asked Zack who had moved from the door to the bottom of Dr. Silva's bed.

"Says here that, this great beauty is Emma Silva…his wife apparently. And, importantly, that she died decades ago. So, like I said, Miss Emma won't be on our list."

Zack nodded his head slowly in understanding. "If the man is not to contact anyone, why is he kept alive?"

Without reassembling the picture frame, Clayton turned with a cruel smile.

"I am told that he is to live in this way as his punishment and no one is to make contact with him save for the properly appointed staff here in this hospital."

"He must have really done something awful, then," said Zack. Hooked up to a nest of tubes and cables, the doctor lying in the bed looked rather pitiful.

"Who knows, and who cares. It doesn't look like he could do much talking or listening in this state, which makes our job easier.

"Besides, you know our mission. We are here to make sure any remnants of old myths and distorted histories are completely stamped out so that none are misled. No one needs to hold on to half-truths and second-hand accounts when Phosos has provided the world with a hyper-detailed revelation of our entire history."

"That's just it," replied Zack. "This isn't like the case we had in Georgia with that woman who was running an old history sim off the provisionary network. Here, I don't see any sign of any books or virtual simulations that have any of the old history…I mean, myths anywhere here."

Clayton snorted not too silently to himself. "Ah, the crazy woman who screamed 'The Holocaust was real!' while the Hands of Provision dragged her away for deep rooting. She had enough banned sims of mythic accounts before Revelation Day to send dozens of people away."

Clayton moved around the bed back towards the door. "It's time we paid a visit to the university to see if any of his associates are still around."

Zack acknowledged his colleague with a nod and without a sound he moved over to the nightstand where the picture frame laid turned over and disassembled. He picked up the pieces carefully and began reassembling them.

"Come on, what are you doing? He won't be seeing that woman again," yelled Clayton from out in the hall.

The comment went unacknowledged and Zack proceeded to piece the picture frame back together. When it was whole again, he set it gently down on the nightstand and turned the frame until the bashful smile of Dr. Silva's late wife was watching over him once again.

Like a beam of focused light, the shy smile shone into a frozen place of Zack's own memory that had not seen light for a long time. For the first time in years—since his calling to The Roots of Unity and long after Revelation Day—the cold wall of ice began to melt and weep. It cracked just enough to allow through images of a woman from his own past. Though he dared not admit in that moment, she had been much more than *just* a woman to him.

Ava! Her name came bursting through the fissure like a beam of light that grew into a constellation of interconnected images. One in particular appeared brighter than the rest. It slowly came forward until it had engulfed nearly every thought in his mind's eye. As the recollection crystalized, the scene of a school dance began to move in vivid clarity. He could almost feel the weight of the hot gymnasium air, thick with adolescent anticipation and the scent of cheap perfumes intermingling with nervous sweat. He swore he would never return, but now he was back in that stupidly backward little town. Yet, Ava was there as well, flashing him a shy smile along with a pair of sparkling bashful eyes. She was handing something to her sister that was in the process of being passed over to him.

A note.

The recognition came upon him like the falling of a curtain in an unused room that had laid in darkness for countless years. Yes, the note was for him. It was the first time Ava had confessed her complete infatuation with him. He remembered his fingers fumbling with the many careful interwoven folds as anticipation grew within him. At last, the broad blue-lined page had yielded itself and he could finally read the message.

Zacky,
We have been dear friends since I can remember and it is
for this reason that I know with all my heart that I love
you with everything I was, everything I am, and everything
I hope to be. I pray you feel the same.

Forever yours, Ava.

His heart had skipped a few beats as he read over the words, again and again as if he did not believe the scripts on the page. When he finally looked up, Ava was standing in front of him. She held out a delicate little hand to dance with a hopeful smile. The cheeks of her round face, were blushed red, full of vitality and all the strength of youth. There was a child-like innocence in her face, yet her hazel eyes sparkled with a fire of emerging womanhood, that knew what they desired. He had taken her soft hand with a crooked smile, like a man who had somehow cheated the universe to snag the attention of someone who shown so bright and pure. They danced that night away as young lovers do who are traveling into unexplored realms of mature love, savoring the moments in each other's arms like there was no tomorrow. A year later they had been engaged to be married.

"Well, are you coming?"

Zack's heart fluttered as Clayton's words hung stale in the air, held aloft by a long-forgotten dream. The innocent love was already starting to fade back into the lifelessness of the sterile room.

Ava, why didn't you receive the mark, you silly little thing, he thought. Such a sweet and innocent thing, if only she had followed what so many others had done. It was only a mark, a mere sign of a new orderly age. Born a century late, she was never made for the modern world. She had very much disliked the virtual reality environments that captivated so many of their peers. She had told him on countless candlelit evenings that VR could not capture the unseen things in the world like the smell of the first warm spring day or the feeling of a kiss with your eyes closed. When Phosos had come with his Provision for the world, her spirit faltered at the thought of the old world being nothing but a collective connection of misconstruals. She would never accept it had all been a myth.

It was her rigid conviction that had gotten her taken away. No one knew what became of her, they were far too busy with their own new provisions, and like many others, she became forgotten. Yet, Zack could not forget his Ava. He knew, like countless others who rejected Unity and Provision, they were taken to be *deep rooted*. The process used intense virtual revelation programs to instill in holdouts the truth of Provision. For the few that somehow persisted through the rooting, only one thing could be done. Zack had never attended a pruning session, but from what Clayton spoke of them, a quick death was more merciful.

Ava had been too strong for all the rooting that she had endured. Her will had been of little surprise to him. He had known from the moment they had taken her what it would come to. Though he wished she would have capitulated in the end, he knew somewhere in his heart that it would have crushed him more to see her spirit broken to do so. When the day of her pruning finally came, he had been there at the Tap Root Complex. She was ushered by two Hands of Provision down a long dark hallway spotted by bright overhead lights. The semi-metallic HOPs (as some called the androids) towered over Ava as they moved in determined strides beside her. A crowd had gathered with Zack against a chain-linked fence in a courtyard. The onlookers had come to cast dispersions against those who rejected the Unity Tree. *"Weed!"* and *"Tree sucker!"* they had called out. It had hurt him to hear such things hurled towards someone who he knew to be as sweet as a flower. She had not been like the rest that had deserved such treatment for their rejection in Provision. It was in a chance instant, that Ava looked at the hecklers and had noticed him there. It was only a brief moment, but he could see her exhausted face that seemed completely drained of the rosiness it had held so fully before. In her recognition, a sad smile swept across her face as the last light danced over her watery eyes. And then, she passed into darkness out of sight to die too young.

"Hey man, come on! You've been in a daze staring at this Emma chick. We need to get moving," cried Clayton who had somehow now moved behind Zack.

"Let me snap a scan of her and we can have some real VR fun with her tonight," Clayton said gleefully prodding Zack in his side.

Zack simply shook his head in dismissal or to shake off the shock. "No, you're right, it's time to go."

) | (

The ride up the streets of Talawanda Springs was silent. Clayton scrolled through mission reports on his ocular display while Zack stared blankly out at the rows of shops and boarded up buildings. They were all but tiny masonry coffins for a world that no longer served any use. In his lap, his hand traced over the Unity Tree branded beneath the skin of his right wrist. The mark depicted a crimson tree, its six branches and six roots connected into each other as a continuous circle. The roots on his mark were black signifying his authority as a member of The Roots of Unity.

Most people in the Tree of Unity, or simply, "Unity," had moved to big cities as directed so that they could be provided and fulfilled. English had been proclaimed the universal, "unifying" language to break down the last communication barriers that had plagued humans for all of their existence. An elect few were invited to take a place in the city of New Eden which resided at the confluence of modern and old civilization, East and West, what was once called Jerusalem. Only those hand selected by Phosos and the Branches of Unity were invited to reside there. It was a true privilege even to set foot in the newly renovated city, one that neither Clayton nor Zack had yet to partake, despite their good work in in the Western Lands of Old America.

When they reached the top of the flattened mountain, they found a shuttered university where not a soul crept the grounds. The tall brick edifices stood in solemn silence atop the numerous bluffs that formed the foundation of Hightower University. The buildings were scattered about like large mausoleums to a pagan form of thought now clouded in a revised history. Like the town below, which laid in a bed of thick white fog, everything was laid to rest in a forgotten slumber.

The car dropped Clayton and Zack off at the foot of Old Main as the sun neared its zenith overhead. Supported by stout columns, the ivory steeples glistened in the midday light as they towered over the front lawn without a shadow. The windows of the grand building were nearly all darkened save for one on the first floor. And everywhere you looked there were visible signs of structures falling into disrepair. Climbing up the front steps, Clayton slipped on the crumbling stone and fell, bruising his knee.

With closure of the University, there had been little need for maintenance these past few years. Since Phosos's provisioning of complete knowledge, no student or faculty member would ever need to walk the sidewalks or climb the steps again. All that remained were the appointed caretakers of this crumbling corpse to ensure that no one wondered into the buildings—for safety of mind and body.

Reaching inside Old Main, the two men found a dimly lit marbled hall. Many rows of darkened closed doors stretched off into the gloom. There was one door half open, however, in which a splash of yellow light was poured out into the hallway. The pair entered the room to find it was filled with various assortments of boxes and racks of old computer servers. Crude by comparison to the network established under Provision. The front desk sat unattended, its surface covered in a tater of papers and loose electrical cords.

"Well, where is she?" Clayton said, peeling his eyes behind the desk into the dark rooms that laid beyond.

"Did she know we were coming?" asked Zack.

Clayton gave him a scowling look. "Did she know we were coming…" he started mockingly. "Yes, she knew. No one can escape a summons for Unity business."

The two of them stood by silently as several minutes stretched with little indication that anyone was presently about. Zack continued to study the mess of equipment as Clayton clamored on the desk impatiently listening to his ancilla "Taproot" intently. Taproot or "Tappy" for short, was an artificial intelligence created by Phosos himself to provide users the ability to access accurate information in both real and virtual environments. The AI was so sophisticated that it could even help augment and correct information being viewed in real-world environments that had yet to be addressed by the Roots of Unity. In the early weeks after Revelation Day, the Hands of Provision modified many of the networked systems around the world so that all could receive Provision equally. Thus, everyone taking the Unity Tree mark received an accurate account of past history and all historical simulations were updated to the truthful record. Acceptance was widespread and quickly adopted for many did not have faith in the veracity of many records going back before their lifetime, typically no more than fifty years before Revelation Day. There had been some "disaccorders" who resisted initially, but besides some enclaves scattered around the remote parts of the world, many of these groups had been rooted out and brought into Unity.

"All right, time to call in a HOP," Clayton said, losing the last ounce of his patience.

"There will be no need for that!" cried a raspy voice far away in one of the backrooms. Uneven steps could be heard approaching and then an old woman emerged from the shadows of the office.

"By Unity, how can I help you boys?" the woman said, her words hollowed out of any sincerity.

Already impatient, Clayton ignored the tone. "We are here on Unity business," he began, pulling up his sleeve to show his tree mark.

The woman paid the gesture with little impression.

Clayton nodded to Zack.

"Yes, our records of this university are not fully complete. We are looking for any known associates of Dr. Sebastian Silva, he used to be a faculty member here until an accident around Revelation Day a few years ago. We ask you to transfer anything you have to us as quickly as you can."

"Records not complete, eh? I thought Provision provided it all; lock, stock, and barrel. Why do you two Rooters need my help?"

Clayton made no verbal response, but Zack saw a smile slowly move up the side of his face like a snake's curling tail. Having served as his partner for many months, he had seen that smile enough to know what might come next.

The old woman stood resolute behind the desk making no signs of movement. It was her eyes that faltered as they crisscrossed the room in quick motions to Clayton, then to Zack, and back to Clayton once more.

Clayton's demeaner relaxed. He then raised his hand in a beckoning gesture for the woman to come closer to the desk that divided between them. The woman leaned forward ever so slightly until both of them were leaning against the old weathered wooden desktop. Then, before the old woman could react, Clayton pulled something out of his pocket that quickly wrapped around the woman's arm. She immediately tried to pull back, but the two tentacles that had sprung from the device had dug into her flesh with thorny barbs. She let out a faint cry before yielding to the pull across the desk.

"Now, you are entangled in my roots, you will tell me what we would like to kn—"

Clayton stopped as he noticed the Unity Tree mark on her arm was defaced by a raised jagged scar caused by what could only had been the searing of flesh.

"Oh, my dear. What is this?" Clayton said with gratification. "It looks like you have tried to remove your mark. You know what consequences that means…Zack call in a HOP, we have someone who has defaced the Tree. The edict of Phosos demands a rooting!"

The woman's eyes bulged at the command. "NO! NO! PLEASE GOD! NO!"

"OH, YES! And lady, you will tell us all that we need to know before the HOP gets here, now, won't you?"

The woman nodded.

) | (

Before they knew it, Clayton and Zack were in the car headed back to the hospital. The Hand of Provision had arrived quickly and taken the woman away, sobbing, to be processed. Before she had been taken away, she had provided them all the information they needed. It turned out that Dr. Silva had several associates at the university that were no longer accounted for. A Dr. Christopher

Irving, a psychology professor at the university and colleague of Dr. Silva. The records showed that Dr. Irving had an extensive history of nonconformity with the administration and several documented accounts of him speaking about his esoteric religious beliefs on campus. His whereabouts were listed as unknown by the university staff since Revelation Day. There was also a Ms. Aliyah Woods and Mr. Craig Nosek, both graduate students of Dr. Silva's. Mr. Nosek was quickly crossed off their list as his dead body had been pulled from a sulphur pool around the same time as Dr. Silva's accident. However, as it turned out, Ms. Woods and an undergraduate lab assistant of Dr. Silva's, Gabe Coleman, had mysteriously disappeared after their brief admittance to the local hospital. To find some answers, and pick up a trail, that was their destination.

The hospital was just as calm and quiet as it had been before. Upon Phosos's arrival, most severe physical illnesses had been cured and so hospitals were mostly centers for recovery of the mind rather than the body. Those not quite afflicted enough to require a rooting were often sent to these places for various virtual treatments. Others simply came to be cared for by officials heralding from the Branches of Unity. Whereas the Roots of Unity focused on cleaning up distortions of the past, the Branches attended to the needs and desires of the present so that all could find their inner bliss. At the hospital, the Branches offered those suffering from an assortment of maladies—from anxiety, depression, to disorders of personality—carefully curated virtual delights to fulfill any patient's imaginable pleasure.

Their contact at the hospital was on the third floor and down a long corridor with many rooms. They walked past the rooms, one-by-one, each with a silent patient laying docile in their bed. Unseen images flashed before their eyes behind a pair of goggles connected to a commercial Mindsai machine. The technology had actually been developed by Dr. Silva, winning him a Nobel Prize, no less. The breakthrough had come in its utilization of the mind's innate capabilities. The mind-body interface constructed virtual environments that seamlessly blurred the line between reality and simulation for the user. What was previously dependent on a graphics processing unit was now autonomously generated by the brain itself through its specialized quantum programming and physical interfaces. It was almost overnight that people all around the world came to own the devices that were hailed as portals to infinite delight. Some used it for learning, others for traveling to far-off places around the world or in the past, but the lion's share of users used the devices for self-indulgence. For the first time in history, the highest societal steward down to the lowest drudger kid bussing tables could play out any fantasy that could be imagined. The allure to be a king of your very own virtual kingdom was strong, even if it was truly a kingdom of one. The freedom from reality the devices offered had pulled society to the brink of collapse. Basic industries became vacated as more-and-more people began to slip away into their digital realms rather than face the painful truth of reality. It would not have been long before the world died a death by decadence. At least, that was the trajectory until Phosos had arrived with the gift of Provision.

When Clayton and Zack arrived at the end of the hall, they found a tiny service desk sitting at the confluence of two splitting hallways. A middle-aged man reclined behind at desk littered with candy wrappers. Behind cold grey eyes he appeared to watch attentively at a bank of flashing video feeds.

Clayton walked straight up to the desk and gave the top two quick taps. "Are you Dr. Mordechai?"

"By Unity, that would be me," the man said, combing a finger through his hair and curling it behind his right ear. The hair was grey with black streaks, and thinning, falling to either side of his cheeks that had sunken in at several places. His wrist revealed the crimson limbs of the Branches of Unity clearly.

Zack positioned himself next to his partner. Now closer, he had a better view of the miniature telewindows the man had been watching. Like staring into a window into a real space, each displayed all sorts of activities from what were presumably the numerous patients that he and Clayton had only just passed by.

Many of the screens displayed all sorts of explicit activities—an elderly man mounting an attractive woman while two other women lathered his chest and back in melted chocolate, a grown woman dressed as a school girl could be seen groping under the blouse of a teacher in a twentieth-century classroom. Other screens chronicled the fulfilment of power fantasies. In one, a young man wore a tapestry of socks from top to bottom as he sat high up on a dais whilst a throng of virtual entities bowed before him. Adoration that was once only the privilege purview of the Pharaohs was now within the grasp to all lowly souls who desired to rule their virtual subjects. Less numerous were telescreens depicting people enjoying more pedestrian pursuits whereby they acted out the roles of great, tragic, and misunderstood heroes of Dracula, The Joker, Sauron, and Gaston.

But one screen remained noticeably inactive on some sort of grey curtain-like standby screen. It carried only the marking: "Room T343 – Doe/J. [Redact: Silva/S.]."

Dr. Mordechai's steel-cold eyes had traced Zack's gaze to the array of screens. The realization startled Zack. An uncontrollable flinch surged up and down his body upon where he stood. He did his best to hide the reaction and Dr. Mordechai gave no outward signal that he had noticed the jolt at all.

"In truth, the experiences patients receive here is not much different than what they can get at home. But I give'em what they need. And they certainly are needful little things."

The doctor's eyes gleamed in a manner that they seemed unaccustomed to as he tossed a butterscotch candy into his mouth. The man's thin lips did little to hide a receding gumline and rows of worn square teeth that were now smacking out the ooze of the melted brown square.

"Sure…" Zack replied with a half nod. "We are here because you might have a lead on some associates of one of your patients, Sebastian Silva."

"Mmhmm…I got your pre-notice," Mordechai replied flapping his hands lightly in unison as he turned to pick up a spare tablet. The tablet screen lit up in a dull blue glow and after some hurried swipes of a finger, Mordechai handed it over to Zack.

"That should be what you're looking for, sonny."

The screen showed several groupings of images. In one set, there were hospital logs showing the admittance of undergraduate researcher, Gabe Coleman. Records indicated that he had come in for the treatment of a severe hand wound—signed in by...his eyes twitched hurriedly.

An Aliyah Woods.

Records also indicated that Gabe was never officially discharged, he had left his room and the hospital before the attending physician had approved.

Zack's eyes moved to an adjacent set of images

Attached to these records were several video recordings of a young man lying in a hospital room not too unlike the one Dr. Silva now rested in. The kid had a mop of brown hair that nearly fell over his eyes. A stubble of a beard did its best to obscure the roundness of his pale baby-facedness. Sitting in a chair next to the bed was a young woman, though slightly older than the man in the bed. Her jet-black hair cascaded down over the low back of the sturdy chair in thick half-curled waves. But there was no trace of repose on the woman's heart-shaped face. Deep lines had plowed their way through her golden-amber complexion.

"Is that Aliyah Woods?" asked Zack, tilting the tablet towards Mordechai.

"Yep, that's the lady you're looking for. She must be the brains of that operation. They both left pretty quickly after seeing that letter there next to their advisor's bed." The end of Dr. Mordechai's chipped fingernail pointed to another image on the tablet.

Zack touched the image until it filled the full screen. The letter had been hand-written and scanned in.

Clayton leaned closer to Zack's shoulder to get a look at the letter that had been addressed to "Bash," a known alias of Dr. Silva. The pair of them stood silently as their eyes rapidly scanned each line of handwriting. The script had an elegant flow to it that was not seen much outside of historical documents. Few people even wrote letters, let alone in curving ink. As they read through, words and phrases began to pop.

"*New Eden.*"

"*Fight.*"

"*…might head westward.*"

"*Some good old self-reliance…*"

"*Alien overlords.*"

Clayton stopped reading abruptly.

Zack took his partner's cue and ceased reading as well. He watched his partner fidget with his root-snare device in the deep pocket of his jacket. Clayton's eyes bore an unmistakable intensity that flickered with a gleam that any moment he was poised to strike.

"Looks like we have a big-time weeder here, haven't we?" Clayton said at last, nudging Zack with his elbow.

"Uh huh. Seems like there is a whole group of weeders out west," replied Zack. He motioned for them to continue reading the final paragraph.

"*Going to Montana.*"

"*Resistance Group. Wayward Sons and Daughters.*"

Signed, "*Christopher.*"

After a few re-reads of the note, Zack turned his attention back to Clayton. "So, what do you think?"

Clayton did not reply, but instead turned to Mordechai.

"So, you say that after Aliyah read this note that she and Gabe took off?"

The man nodded. "I watched them run straight out to their car without checking out. Last I saw of them, they had turned on to Route US-50, headed west."

"Excellent!" Clayton replied, tapping on his earpiece. "Tappy, I'm going to need a HOP to assist us. Send one to my position ASAP."

Clayton finally turned back to his partner. "Who knows how thick of a bramble we might have to clear out once we get west.

Looks like we might get Aliyah, Gabe, and Christopher Irving in one go!"

A few minutes passed before the distinctive gait of a Hand of Provision could be heard coming down the hall. Its evenly-placed footfalls were devoid of any unnecessary sound or weight. The HOP almost seemed to glide effortlessly towards them over the rubberized floor. Its eyes stared forward like two pale blue flames, intense and unwavering. Only Phosos's eyes of fiery amethysts could rival that of his unwavering stewards.

The HOPs were the sturdy trunk of the Tree of Unity and Provision, connecting the branches and the roots into one endless circle. Their untiring labor and services had made the work of those in Unity obsolete and forbidden. Provision had ushered in a new golden age where anyone who took the Mark of Unity could freely focus on leisure and one another without worry of money, food, or social stratification—all were equal parts of the tree in Unity.

The HOP stopped a few paces short of the service desk. Zack stole a quick glance at the android that stood tall above them at more than three meters in height. A strange sensation then came over him. Something more than mere robotic directives seemed to flicker behind the glowing blue eyes of the android. It was as if the machine sensed he was unraveling it with his eyes, trying to figure it out.

And, perhaps, maybe it was. It had been said that when Phosos adapted the android for humanity in his own visage, he instilled in them an image of his own advanced mind to augment their artificial intelligence. It had never been confirmed, but some even speculated that Phosos himself could connect to the minds of each individual HOP, allowing him a measure of omnipresence from New Eden. Like the HOP's true origins from whence they came, people could only speculate about in whispers.

"What is your destination?" the android asked, plainly.

"Looks like we are headed to Montana," Clayton replied, glad to be moving again. "Let's go!"

The three of them then walked out of the hospital to find their ride west. But every step of the way, Zack could not help to feel that the HOP studied him a little bit more intently.

2

The Councils of Wayward Children

The meeting had started and she was late. What had kept her, she planned to keep to herself. It was senseless to speak more power to such things. Besides, despite all that had happened, there were those who still might not believe it. Gabe would, surely, after all they had been through since their Hightower University days.

Now, where is he? Aliyah thought to herself as she reached the outer edge of the gathered crowd. She began to scan for a familiar face amongst the many faces that seemed to dance in the torch light.

It appeared that the entire camp had assembled around the friendship circle this evening. Nearly 12,000 people had gathered around a small wooden platform at the circle's center. The circular platform was weathered from many years of use and many more left forgotten after it served as a scouting jamboree site. Several decades of hot summers and bitter winters in the heart of Montana had been enough to split the sturdy grey timbers apart.

Aliyah slowly pushed her way through the throng towards the center of the ring. A sea of eager faces flowed by her. A discordant murmur hung low above as the crowd awaited the speaker to climb the platform.

But higher, over the assembly, the first twinkling of stars had started shining through the soft velvety blue curtain of an early evening sky. And somewhere, in the growing dark, a light breeze carried the faint scent of pine needles up from the lake not far below. The lake, shaped liked a pinecone, lay in a valley at the feet of two mountains whose peaks still bore the white snows of a winter that had yet to yield to the oncoming spring. The lake's waters were still and dark. Only the pale shimmering reflection of a rising moon broke its black surface. Tonight, it served as a mirrored backdrop to the torch-lit council meeting happening only a short walk above.

An outdoor speaker began to crackle in the cool evening air when, at last, Aliyah reached the inner circle. A middle-aged man with bushy grey eyebrows had climbed the platform, which now creaked under the weight of his heavy boots. He wore a red and black flannel shirt and a pair of blue jeans covered in dirt from a day of light use.

The crowd let out a great cheer that echoed off the lake and mountainsides in eerie response.

"Good evening," the man began.

"Good evening, Dean!" the crowd replied in unison. Then a hush fell over the assembly as the final murmurings were swept out onto the lake by a rising gust.

"Thank you for gathering with me tonight. It has been almost four years since we have made this little spot of earth our home."

He paused to rotate around the platform and look upon all who had come. Under the bright yellow solar-powered lights, a bead of sweat trickled down from the top of the man's smooth head. His balding was near complete except for short salt and pepper patches of hair that crested around the sides and back of his head.

When he had completed a full rotation, he continued. "Over those years, we have pulled together in hardship, labor, and faith. Left behind were many comforts and the promise of everything more. Though we know that it is not through comfort that we stay vigilant; discomfort keeps us attuned to life and not to be numbed by decadence.

"However, together, we have made this place a home, built by our own hands and the grace of God so that we might endure here until an appointed time."

Another pause came. The crowd was silent. As if each member were collectively holding their breath. The feeling of electricity was in the cool evening air like a summer storm rolling over the horizon. Harkening at any moment, a flash of light to hit the ground.

The lines on the man's peach-colored forehead relaxed, letting go of an apparent tension that had been coiled up on his face since he started. He went on.

"It is with heavy heart to acknowledge that the time has now come. I am afraid our secret hidden valley is out."

There were gasps, some tears, and many cries of anger, but Aliyah stood in silence.

"I have received word from an operative out east that the Rooters have become aware of our presence here in Montana and intend to root us all out."

"How could we let them find us? We should have never sent any spies amongst those people."

The lone voice pierced through the rumblings of an uneasy assembly. The voice was strong, yet tinted with a tinge of disappointment. It was a tone that was so familiar. Scoping the sea of faces, Aliyah found a pocket of people who were all staring backwards in the same direction. She traced their gaze to a tall man who stood sternly apart from the people that surrounded him. He held his posture confidently and quietly. A strong jawline showed no signs of wavering as he awaited a response from the stage. A prominent brow hinted at a lifetime of experiences. His skin, a deep shade of mahogany, bore the marks of age with dignity, creased lightly around his eyes and mouth, each line telling a story of laughter and wisdom gained over the years. His eyes, a rich, deep brown, held a quiet intensity that belied the gentleness in his expression. Eyes that Aliyah had stared into many times over the course of her life, for they were the eyes of her father.

As her father spoke, Dean held his eyes closed firmly in thought. There was little expression on his face to betray any clue to his thoughts or possible response.

When her father had finished, Dean's eyes opened with a deep breath and he approached the edge of the platform near the area where her father stood.

"Desmond, you know better than most the reason we could not just pull back into this valley and hope that Time would forget us here. We are charged to do more. We cannot let the world slip towards a false light as we seclude ourselves here. We must help them find the true light and shine on them."

The intensity in her father's eyes then slacked. After a time, he nodded back knowingly, apparently seeing the wisdom in Dean's words. "You are right, old friend. Even with the time we have had it seems we are not ready."

Dean opened his mouth, but before he could respond, an older woman in the very front cried out.

"How did we get to this position in the first place? We've lost the world to a deceiving Santa Claus!" The woman stomped her walking stick to the ground between each wheezy breath.

Dean turned to the old lady and smiled politely. "Is it really so far-fetched that it has come to this? Out of our hubris to think that blind progress meant that our history was irrelevant, we have fallen into the same pitfall that plagued countless generations before us. Only now, we finally succeeded too well. And in that success, we have become robbed of all our strength and resilience. It has been said by those forgotten or ignored in our past that 'good times create weak people, and weak people create hard times.' Without adversity to sharpen our mettle, society became soft and weak. In the end, we were engorged by our apparent techno-social victory over this world and perfectly ripe for those that seek to enthrall us."

The crowd fell back into a discordant murmur once more. People turned to their partners to mutter and nod their heads— some up-and-down and, others, side-to-side. Aliyah began to feel that it was a brief glimpse of the possible chaos that might ensue upon the group if order could not be found to face the grave threat. But before things could unravel too far, Dean raised a solitary hand high above their heads.

"My friends! My friends! Our fellowship can either become frozen in despair and be resigned to our fate…or we can seize what freedom remains with all our chips on the table, to win or lose. But we must act!

"Like the rowdy colonists who *spontaneously* dumped tea into Boston Harbor to ignite a revolution, we must fight against all forms of oppression."

Many in the crowd cheered. If the true account was off, it was lost on all save for a strange-looking man that Aliyah noticed sitting just off the edge of the stage. He wore a yellow scarf with small navy crescent moons and stars around his neck. But it was his deep blue eyes that had caught her attention. Like two sapphire gems whose facets drew any onlooker in, but no one had quite plumbed the depths behind them. Even with a moment's glance one could tell that they held within years of experiences that seemed somehow at odds with the man's youthful, thirty-something appearance. He had only arrived to the camp a couple of months back and the few times she had seen him he had been conversing with the elders. She had always felt that they had met sometime in the past but could never place it. She had thought it strange to misremember someone with such a striking appearance. How could anyone forget those eyes!

No one knew the man's name either. Some referred to him as The Man with Sapphire Eyes and others simply called him "Joe," but if that was his true name, few believed so.

Joe was presently smiling up at the stage, his blue eyes danced in the evening light.

Dean continued speaking. "In this high country of a fallen land, we find ourselves alone but strong in faith and determination. Though the people of New Eden's Unity may not remember it, there were once sons and daughters of a revolution who fought for the ideals of freedom and self-governance. As

Wayward Sons and Daughters, we carry that same spirit. But, what does it matter what we call ourselves? The Tree of Unity grows ever bigger, soon it will rise over those mountains and find us. We must act quickly, but to what end, I am not sure. I ask for your wise counsel."

A period of quiet settled over the assembly. Not even a whisper could be heard amongst the many that had gathered. Only the faint hum of lights and the distant crackling of camp fires kept absolute silence at bay.

Aliyah was not as surprised as the rest when the Man with Sapphire Eyes began to speak. Over the course of minutes, the man's face had shown an intensely as if, behind those shimmering eyes, he was barely holding back a greater illumination.

"There is much power held in a name…" the sapphire-eyed man began, his voice breaking the silence like a thunderclap on a sunny day. It resonated across the still lake and up into the mountains.

Of those present, not a word was spoken, not even a whisper. Everyone recognized that this was the first time the strange man had spoken in a public forum. All anyone could do was watch as the man walked slowly over to the base of the stage. He took the hand of Dean who helped him up to join him. Dean held out the microphone in kind gesture. Joe smiled politely but dismissed the offer with a short wave of his hand.

"Greetings to you all! I offer what tidings that I have to submit to your wise counsel." The man's voice projected outward to great effect as if he were some practiced playactor addressing an amphitheater. The soothing timbre swept across the assembly whose attention was enraptured with quiet anticipation.

"I'll start with what I have discovered and learned over many years. In short, names carry great meaning. Though a name might simply be reduced to a formation of sounds, our identities are so wrapped up into them that the mere utterance of them in a crowded room has the power to instantly capture our attention. Names have been passed down across generations and through lineages representing power real and imagined. The first act of a deceiver is to give a false name, to hide the *true name*."

Joe raised up a clenched hand.

"Some even say to know a thing's name is to have power over it—to call it forth and bend it to your will. Though I believe some willingness is a necessary ingredient in the exchange. I am no shaman, for some things are too powerful for mortals to dare to command. Yet, speaking in their good name still can exude great power over things tied and bound unto this world."

He unclenched his hand and paused to search the audience momentarily. His eyes scanned the crowd until their gaze rested in Aliyah's section. She felt a warm push back the air around her as if his coned gaze was actually shining light on her. Joe then raised his head towards the night's sky and his eyes seemed to twinkle with the stars.

Joe went on. "A most sacred prayer hints at this: Our Father, who art in heaven, hallowed be *thy name*. But what is God's name? Yahweh…Elohim…Jehovah…Allah…Brahman? Across all the ancient traditions there could be nine billion names for God, the One who created all that we see and know with a mere utterance of words.

"There is but only one true name…and, like the face of God, that has not been revealed to any who has lived. Even the Patriarch, Moses, at the burning bush, received only an abstract answer of 'Ehyeh asher ehyeh': I am Who I am or He Causes to Become.

"The ancient Jews considered God's name so potent that its invocation conferred upon the speaker tremendous power over His creations and was only spoken by the High Priest in the Holy of Holies. And…the closer you are to true-naming a thing, the more you understand its true nature and reveal its power.

"I believe on the day that His true name is finally spoken, the last bookend to human history will fall into place. With it, a great change will occur, the likes of which the Earth has not seen since its formation from the void. A change great enough to shine a light through the false light of Phosos and all his enticing deceptions."

Dean, like the rest in attendance, stood in awe at the command of words that came forth from the strange man. The truth of the words seemed strangely self-evident. Some in the crowd had fallen to their knees or raised their hands up as a sign of reverence to the truth that had been spoken.

Dean turned to the man with sapphire eyes, flashing a toothy smile while shaking his hand gently side-to-side.

"I…I must say. *Your words* this evening have been powerful. For months we have wrestled with the insurmountable task of how to combat something so far beyond us. A demon in the guise of a benevolent alien with near unlimited power and resources, not to mention the many followers he has entangled to worship him. How do you defeat something like that?

"But, with your words tonight, I now realize…and hope that you all do as well…" Dean gestured a hand to all around him. "…that we have been too busy searching for an earthly means of victory when we should have been thinking about the transcendent.

"My only question is, how would we find this name if no mortal person has ever heard or spoken it?"

Nearly everyone in the crowd shook their head in acknowledgment and then fixed their eyes on Joe, patiently waiting for a response.

Joe smiled shyly. This time it looked like a great weight had fallen on the man's face.

"Therein lies the rub, doesn't it?" He paused briefly to look back into the crowd near Aliyah's section.

"As I mentioned at the onset, I can only give you what I know. But even my knowledge has areas where it draws short. I can tell you that there are those who never lived, the watchers of old, or angels if you will, that were given the knowledge of God's true name in the immeasurable eternity before creation. However, a great impassible gulf of time and space precludes any access to them and their knowledge.

"But I tell you, and this is the hope that brought me to this place; one among you knows a way to surpass this gulf and this knowledge that has been lost to time and memory."

Then Joe stopped suddenly and raised an outstretched arm, pointing directly into the crowd. The same direction he had been attending throughout his speech. The stretch of his arm seemed to shoot over the crowd like a loosened arrow flying to its target.

"It is to Aliyah Woods that we will find our path."

There were some noticeable gasps in the audience. And, in mere moments, all eyes had turned to where Aliyah stood—her mouth agape and eyes wide. The warming spotlight gaze now felt like the warmth of a million suns.

) | (

As night receded, a water-colored sky took hold to harken in a new morning. The big sky filled with gentle bands of light hued with pinks, oranges, and lavenders that seemingly held little concern for the troubles of the people down below. It was not until half-past eight when the sun first began to peek above the eastern line of mountains. Soft beams of light slipped passed the rugged peaks to gradually illuminate the valley that had been shrouded below. As it climbed higher into the sky, more and more of Timberline Lake Camp fell under its warming embrace. Golden rays transformed the lake into a field of sparkling emeralds. Each of the outlying cabins became like golden oranges nestled in their wooded alcoves. As the sunlight reached the A-Frame lodge the bronze eagle perched upon its apex shone with a yellow glow for that could be seen across the mist-laden valley.

When the morning light finally reached Aliyah's cabin, it filtered through a half-cracked window intermingling with falling dust and whisps of pollen of a late spring. Aliyah was only now waking into the surreal haze that existed between dreams and a waking world. She had unexpectedly slept soundly after the events from the night before. There had been many conversations with many more questions that she did not yet have the answers, but hoped to have by the end of the day.

But all that could wait. It was pleasant resting awake beneath the thick flannel sheets as rays of sunshine and sweet, cool mountain air slowly filled her wood-paneled room. For a time, she was content enough to gaze up at the walls and ceiling. She traced around long-disused ski equipment and faded paintings. Her favorite was a painting of a mountain stream surrounded by summer blooms of flowers and thick green grasses that did not show any memory of winter. Her heart yearned to paint herself into the hidden meadow and to find a serenity where all time and people would be forgotten in an everlasting moment of warmth and tranquility. She could almost hear the babbling of the brook and cheerful call of songbirds when she heard the loud creaking of a screen door slam outside. Her neighbor always let it slam as he went to-and-fro from his cabin. When silence fell back in, she returned to the old paining. Despite her best efforts, the tranquil moment had fallen out of reach. It was time to get up.

A half hour later, she had dressed and taken a slice of bread for a morning stroll. With bread in hand, generously slathered with a homemade strawberry jam that her mother had made, Aliyah took her first bite. The crusty exterior of the fire-baked bread quickly gave way to a supple, sweet center. The little seed bits of the jam tingled her tongue as she swallowed each bite. Naturally, some of the jam had oozed onto her hand to stick and pull between her fingers. It was of little concern today, nothing a quick wipe upon her dusty blue jeans could not solve.

When she had finished her morning treat, a smile came to her face slowly. The day had burnt away the morning mists leaving behind a world amidst a rebirth. Small plants were pushing through soft soil in verdant greens and the sky and lake took on the deepest shades of blues. As she strolled down the path towards the main lodge, the rhythmic crunch of gravel beneath her worn-out tennis shoes echoed through the damp morning air.

A gentle breeze danced through her long black hair, carrying with it the greetings of distant wildflowers. If her battery had been emptied from the events of the night before, the morning stroll under a golden sun had more than recharged her spirits.

It had almost shocked her how quickly she had adjusted to this simple life. Thrust into a world devoid of phones, AI, and virtual realities after working with some of the most cutting-edge technology. It was jarring at first—but a necessary precaution to avoid the tendrils of New Eden. The world before Timberline Camp was a complex interconnected stream of screens and algorithms where every moment was documented and augmented to fit a desired state. Yet here, in the mountains of big sky country, life was simple. Even in its surface simplicity, nature seemed to have its own interconnected rhythm. The *beeps* and *bops* of the technological world were replaced by the chirping of songbirds and the fluttering of butterfly wings on a blowing breeze. One grew more attuned to this natural rhythm with every passing day.

She had quickly come to realize that the complexity had always been there. It was there plain to see underneath all the artificial noise that humans had placed on top it, mostly to distract our wandering minds from uncomfortable existential truths. But all the careful constructions of modern society could not diminish the fact that under the thin technological veneer of light and sound, these hidden truths awaited us all. One only need to disconnect to hear the beating heart of the living world. And this was never truer than on quiet fall and spring nights when she would leave her window open to let in a cooling draft. Beneath a starlight sky, she felt a profound connection to the created world. Hanging on the edge of sleep, she almost could feel that the universe was slowly inhaling and exhaling in the quiet. It was on those nights that her dreams had never been more vivid or revealing.

As Aliyah approached the main lodge, a small group of people had gathered near the entrance that was framed by two large totem poles. Nearing the group, she began to recognize the outlines and faces. Her heart and feet seemed to lighten. She could pick out her father anywhere. He had a way of shifting his shoulders as he talked that stood out in any crowd. Next him was her mother, Cindy, who was having a conversation with Gabe. Somehow Gabe thought it had been prudent to wear shorts and a flannel T-shirt in the chilly spring air. With a few more steps she noticed Dean Wilkins who stood straight upright. The way he carried himself and spoke, it was no surprise that he had been a military chaplain before coming out west. Dean was conversing with another man with his back turned to her. He wore a peacoat that had seen many years of use judging by its faded grey appearance from what once must have been jet black.

Aliyah was almost within speaking distance of the group when a peculiar sensation overtook her that stuttered her steps to a halt. In an instant, a wave of familiarity crashed against her. A surrealness then enveloped her as if she were watching a scene play in front of her that she had seen before, but could not recall when. The way that her mom held her hand to her cheek, the slight smile on Gabe's face, the beam of sunlight filtering through the pine trees that made Dean squint; every last detail was exactly how she recollected. In a dream? A prophetic vision? Another life? There was little explanation for it.

But, just as quickly as it had washed over her, the feeling of déjà vu had passed. Gabe had noticed her and waved gently. The rest of the group dropped their conversations and turned to Aliyah. The shining blue eyes of, Joe, the man that had been conversing with Dean, quickly captured her attention.

"Good morning, Aliyah. We have all been eager to speak with you. I hope you had a restful sleep amidst these turning of events." Dean smiled and gestured for her to climb the stone stairs to the wooden deck of the promenade that wrapped around the lodge.

"Hello," she replied without much clue of what else to say in response.

"This is so exciting, Aliyah. Things were getting *real* dullsville until last night," her mom added, trying, in her usual way, to set her nerves at ease.

"I had not expected to be the center of intrigue in the camp at any point," she responded with a half-chuckle.

"Excellent, excellent. Shall we go inside and have a chat. There are many things to discuss…and plan!" Dean said gesturing towards the large wooden doors.

Aliyah noticed that Joe, regarded her deeply for a few moments before turning with the rest of group.

As they walked, she could not help to notice that this was the first time that she had seen the Man with Sapphire Eyes up close. His coat, worn and fraying at the edges, caught her attention immediately. It had appeared vintage from afar, but with a closer look, it downright appeared like it had come from a museum. The use of threaded stitching, the large plastic buttons, and the material that looked, not synthetic, but truly made from animals. The only adornment the man wore was an old, tiny leather cross that hung on a silver chain close to his chest. It looked rather quaint and hewn from genuine cow leather that—like his coat— had not been sold openly for nearly a decade. And as he reached for the brass door handle to the lodge his sleeve rode up his arm slightly. It was just enough that, for a brief moment, she caught a glimpse of a ")|(" symbol tattooed on his right wrist.

Inside the lodge, the high ceiling of the Great Hall towered above them, rising more than three stories above their heads. The floor was covered in stenciled designs of woodland animals like deer, antelope, and bear whose mounted counterparts adorned the wood-paneled walls. These taxidermized relics were older than Aliyah as the ban on animal harvesting had been in place before she had been born.

The centerpiece of the lodge was a grand stone fireplace that had a firebox which was visible on all four sides. Several members of the camp had gathered around the flames that were merely a ghost of the roaring fires that had filled it during the winter holiday celebrations. Aliyah searched the faces of those who had gathered but only found looks of concern and, in her mind, the hints of disbelief.

Aliyah and the rest of her party turned off from the Great Hall down a small darkened corridor lined with thick wooden doors. The doors were all in various states of openness allowing for translucent golden curtains of sunlight to drape across the hall. Over one of the doors hung a dedication plaque. One that Aliyah had always made a point to regard whenever she was in this particular part of the lodge. The plaque was simple. Made of wood, it had large block lettering whose imperfections belied its carving by hand. The plaque read: *Christopher Irving Library Dedicated by W. S. & D.s* The initials standing for Wayward Sons and Daughters which was too long to fit on the short slab of timber.

The plaque—and the room it marked—always drew Aliyah's attention because of its connection to her life when she had been at Hightower University. Christopher Irving, or as she had known him, Professor Irving, had been one of her course professors. A man late in his middle-age with bushy eyebrows and a bald forehead, Professor Irving had been a man filled with joy and optimism. He was known best for pushing his students to check their hubris at the door and question all of the world's assumptions. He often spoke of the true essence of science not as an unassailable body of knowledge but as the process of gaining knowledge to explain an unfathomably complex world.

Professor Irving had also been one of Dr. Silva's colleagues and closest friends, despite the fact that he had warned Bash to stop his development of his Mindsai machine. Even after everything had gone wrong with the Mindsai experiment—which left Dr. Silva in a coma—she had found a written letter to Dr. Silva from Professor Irving left at his bedside indicating the enduring strength of their friendship. And just like his note had said, Professor Irving found the Wayward Sons and Daughters in Montana. But, as not even good men are immune to the tragedies of life, the jolly professor died before Aliyah and Gabe arrived to the camp. The cause was thought to have been an aneurysm that burst some time while he had been kayaking on the lake that the large picture windows of his library now overlooked. His legacy now was wrapped in the small wooden plaque and library filled with his extensive collection of hardback books he had lugged across country with him. Many of the books were first and second editions that none in the camp had ever read in their original form. Fewer still had even read a book in its physical form. Decades had passed since physical books were widely sold outside of second-hand stores. For those that still enjoyed reading, electronic books were the only formats available. And these digital facsimiles had constantly been revised and censored to cater to modern sensitivities long before the provisions of New Eden had altered or erased the stories for consumption.

Walking past the open door to Irving's Library, Aliyah caught a brief glimpse inside. Two of the four walls were lined with floor-to-ceiling cherry bookcases filled with the dusty spines of books of all shapes, sizes, and colors. The library was presently occupied by two teenage girls sitting on a bed of thick flannel blankets and seat cushions. Their eyes enraptured by different *Nancy Drew* novels. Over near the window, in a plush arm chair, an older gentleman had fallen asleep. A pair of oval-rimmed glasses rested on the bridge of the man's nose and a copy of *The Hobbit* laid flat against his chest. The tranquil scene engendered a warmth in her heart knowing that Professor Irving continued to provide joy and intellectual stimulation after his passing.

It was not much further down the hall until they had reached their destination. At length the group arrived at a small conference room that resided at the end of the corridor. A large wooden table with stone inlays of various woodland animals filled the center of the room. Surrounding it were a dozen black leather chairs with backrests in the shape of a bear's head with a pair of rounded ears contoured out in studded black leather. Aliyah was the last to take her seat. Dean took his natural seat at the head of the table. Her father Desmond, sat at Dean's right hand and her mother Cindy at his left. Gabe chose to sit near the middle of the long table across from her and, "Joe," he sat near the other end of the table, but not in the end seat.

Once everyone had taken their seat, Dean began to speak. "Again, I thank you all for coming this morning. Since I expect there is much to discuss, I will try to keep administrative items short."

He turned to Aliyah.

"Aliyah, just so you know, as senior deacons of our Wayward group, your mother and father have been asked to join us and to offer counsel pertaining to any courses of action."

Aliyah nodded in acknowledgment.

"Excellent!"

Dean then turned to Gabe who was presently tracing the outline of an otter-shaped inlay with his index finger.

"And Gabe, I have asked you to come because I believe you also may have an expertise that few possess with your previous university work."

"Well…" Gabe started but could not find anything else to say. Dean waited patiently for any additional response before moving on after a reasonable time had passed.

"So, now all that is out of the way, let's get started, shall we?

"As I understand it, Aliyah…and Gabe…you both had access to an advanced Mindsai machine on loan from the government, correct?"

"That's right," said Aliyah.

"Right, excellent." The leather chair squeaked as Dean leaned back in it. Two fingers tapped the side of his face as he seemed to be searching his thoughts. At last, he seemed to have gathered what he had needed and continued.

"In truth, during my last official duty assignment, I got to see one of these machines in action, up close. But the machine I saw was more geared to some sort of hivemind coordination task of drones, not looking into the past.

"Can you briefly explain what the Mindsai machine you worked on did, so that we are all on the same page of understanding?"

"Of course. I'll do my best to explain it…at least, how it was explained to me by Dr. Silva, himself."

Aliyah looked over at Gabe.

"And Gabe, please add anything I'm missing, as my tenure in the lab was not as long as yours."

For the next few minutes, Aliyah recounted the innerworkings of the machine that her Hightower University professor, Dr. Sebastian Silva, had extensively modified to unlock deeply-buried ancestral memories. She detailed how the machine, powered by a government-loaned quantum supercomputer, occupied a space nearly the size of a small van in the lab. To operate it, users required a set of Structural Extrasensory Extraction and Recollection goggles, or "SEER" for short. These headset apparatuses—bristling with numerous little pins—were crucial for accessing latent memory. The SEER goggles transmitted impulses into the user's mind to pinpoint and activate memories. These impulses were then received and amplified by the pin-like probes before being decoded by the quantum processor. Once the process was complete, the viewing monitors within the goggles would construct a visual environment virtually indiscernible from reality. Aliyah stressed that the final image was not a digital facsimile but, rather, a biomechanical analogue reconstruction of the memory, utilizing the subject's own neural resources. Once only limited to the rare person with a kind of hyperphantasia or eidetic memory, the Mindsai machine unlocked stored images buried deep in the mind. The result was a vivid, true-to-life reconstruction of one's own memories or the inherited memories from any genetic ancestor in one's lineage up until the moment of conception for the next generation in the line.

Having concluded her explanation of the machine, Aliyah's tongue felt like sandpaper. She swallowed hard, trying her best to coax what little saliva remained back into her mouth. As she did so, her eyes darted around the room to see how the others had processed what she had told them. Dean's eyes, unfocused yet intense, seemed to have drifted to the antler chandelier hanging above the center of the table. A shroud of contemplation seemed to have befallen him. Her father's face bore an inclination of doubt and skepticism, evident in raised eyebrows and downturned lips. Her mother's expression mirrored her father's, albeit with more concern than doubt. And at the other end of the table, Joe simply sat silently behind an enigmatic smile and unrevealing eyes.

Before Aliyah could determine whether Joe's smile was disarming or hinted at some unspoken plan that was playing out, Dean broke the silence with a question that he had visibly been wrestling with for minutes.

"Now, correct me if I am wrong…" he started, now tapping the side of the table in uneven beats, "…but as I heard you tell it, this souped-up Mindsai machine that you were researching in Virginia allows a user to see memories of genetic ancestors, but nothing more?" Dean paused until both Aliyah and Gabe had confirmed with nodding heads.

"Well then, if that is the case…" Dean continued, now leaning forward in his seat. Again, it began to squeak like a large tree bough bowing in the wind. "…how can we be certain that Aliyah will have anyone in her lineage that will have access to the Name of God? And for that matter, how do we know if any mortal has ever heard this arcane true name?"

Everyone in the room knew the question to be directed at only one individual sitting amongst them. As if their heads had all been on the same string, they turned in unison towards the opposite end of the table.

The Man with Sapphire Eyes sat silently for a few moments without any visible discomfort of the question hanging in the air. His eyes seemed to glisten and deepen with every ticking moment. Then, with a soft and calming voice he spoke.

"I can tell you that I have it on good authority that our task will only be achieved if we can use this machine to stare into the past."

"On who's authority?" Aliyah's father quickly shot back before any intercession of silence could take hold. The table banged as he lightly pounded it with a closed fist. But, before Joe could offer a retort, Desmond rapidly fired another question into the uneasy air.

"And just who are you, *really*? A lot of people around camp have been wondering that very thing. For all we know, you could be in league with Phosos and this is all a big trap or misdirection."

All eyes were cast upon the sapphire-eyed man. Looking unperturbed, Joe raised a calming hand like a man who had deep experience managing testy debates. His voice started without even a tinge of vacillation.

"Desmond, I assure you, who I am is of little consequence to this matter. I am merely a man with deep experience and a role to play in all of this. I offer you what I know freely and without malign intent. If you must know, I discovered this path through my conversations with Dr. Silva, himself. I do not think even he realized what power he was attempting to wield at the time. He was certainly a man trying to grasp the candle flame. Yet truly, it was not until I read the little laboratory notebook that he had on him when they brought him to the hospital that I knew that he had been seeing memories beyond even his inherited memory."

It was then that a spark of recognition flashed in Aliyah's mind, illuminating precisely where she had seen Joe before. It had been Joe, posing as a hospital doctor, who had pointed out a note on Dr. Silva's bedside stand, Dr. Irving's note! It had been instrumental for it spoke of the Wayward Sons and Daughters and helped direct her and Gabe to venture west to Montana.

Aliyah did not realize that she was now staring intently at Joe. Somehow his face had changed as if he had understood the recognition building in her eyes. The man's deep blue eyes slowly began to provide a profound level of comfort and reassurance. It gave her courage to speak out in support.

"Joe, is right. I would not believe any of this myself if I had not seen what Dr. Silva's machine can do. I saw memories of his mother through his *father's* eyes! It was like a recording, but as clearly as I see each of you now that no camera can capture the same way."

The mouths of Aliyah's parents were both slightly held ajar as they could not swallow what was unfolding in the room.

"There is a real power in that device that I cannot explain," Aliyah added, her eyes wide and hands messaging each other, nervously.

Aliyah's father had not taken his eyes off of Joe. "I still do not like that you seem to be holding all the cards and not showing us your full hand," was all that he could muster before crossing his arms in a silent form of resignation.

Joe gave Desmond a reverent bow of his head before he continued to lay out the truth that Aliyah and Gabe were the only two people left in this world with the knowledge and capability to operate the Mindsai machine. It perhaps came as a shock when he further revealed that Dr. Bash Silva was a key conduit to reaching deep ancestral memories and beyond. That due to the circumstances surrounding his original experiment—which of course Joe did not elaborate further on—allowed Silva access to knowledge and experience that had been held secret since the early foundations of the world.

A length of time passed as the room digested the information that had been put before them. Aliyah's mother was the first to speak.

"I thought this Dr. Silva was in some kind of a coma. If that is true, then there is not any way to see what he is capable of seeing. And surely, none of you should risk what your professor has attempted, it put the man in the hospital!" Cindy sputtered out.

"Not exactly…" Gabe said cautiously.

Aliyah instantly gave him a perplexed look.

"I know it might sound strange, but the operator need not be consciously awake to use the Mindsai. Now, I remember Bash saying that operating the machine while asleep or in an unconscious state would be risky since there would not be anyone controlling the influx of memories or thought. I believe he said something along the lines of 'the lack of a focused mind could cause an uncontrollable cascade of engram imagery likely to result in a seizure or stroke' or something to that regard. In such a situation, one would need two operators."

Gabe turned to Aliyah's mother and spoke reassuringly. "It would be safer than any of us taking on the Mindsai on our own, as the second operator would only be observing and directing the memories through a connected feed."

"Is any of that even possible, Gabe?" Aliyah replied.

"Possible, I hazard to believe so. Now, is it plausible in the present set of circumstances, I'm not sure.

"We would need a second quantum processor to enable a simultaneous bridge between Dr. Silva's feed and the observer. We already have two sets of SEER goggles but only one processing chip was furnished to Dr. Silva's lab by the military. I imagine finding a chip fitting those kinds of specifications would be virtually imposs—"

"Would the other advanced Mindsai machines have a suitable processing chip?" interjected Dean.

With his mouth still open mid-speech, Gabe's eyes darted from Aliyah to Dean. A flicker of understanding flashed across Gabe's face as he slowly realized the heading of Dean's question.

After a moment, Gabe nodded with a knowing smile and then gave an enthusiastic reply.

"Yes, I believe they would all contain such a chip! Perhaps even more powerful!"

The chair beneath Dean let out another long squeak as its occupant relaxed into it heavily. Though his shoulders and body had relaxed, Dean's face had become overtaken by deep concentration. An arrhythmic finger tapped restlessly against the side of his face once more. Each thump sent his furrowed brows twitching in unison. His lips had come together in a tight line as there were no words ready to offer the group. Behind his grey eyes, a whirling storm of thought raged as he desperately tried to grasp at ideas in the torrent of contemplation.

Taking advantage of the silence and not willing to let things progress too far from where they seemed to be heading, Cindy spoke up again with an air of concern and pause.

"I don't understand why we need to go through all this; shouldn't we wait for God to deal with Phosos?" she asked the whole group.

Gabe, who was also slowly realizing the growing enormity of the unspoken task, added, "Yeah, why can't He wipe the floor with Phosos. Then look around and decide it's time for Judgment Day. End this now."

The turn in the discussion seemed, for a moment, to pull Dean back from wherever his thoughts had wandered. An attentive observer might have noticed the subtle shift: the way his gaze refocused, the slight settling of his posture, as if some familiar mechanism within him had whirled into motion. Years of chaplaincy had carved deep channels into his thinking, and now his mind slipped into them as easily as a truck's tires falling into the worn grooves of a rutted road.

Though silent, Dean's expression betrayed an internal chorus of questions he had heard echoed countless times in hushed conversations and desperate confessions. Why are the wishes in my prayers not answered? Why allow the devil to live? How can a God of love and goodness allow evil? Dean's mouth parsed open ever-so-slightly as the answers waited at the edge of speech, ready to flow freely.

He first turned to Cindy. Wells of water had already encircled around the edges of her eyes. For an instant, a flicker of hesitation crossed Dean's face. He seemed to remind himself that these were different types of people, no longer Soldiers in uniform, at least not in the sense he had known. His resolve softened, and though his voice had yet to break the silence, it was clear he was already weighing each word to come so that they would fall lightly, but not without their weight of truth.

"Cindy," Dean began, stretching out a comforting hand on top of her own. "From the stories of Noah, Abraham, Moses, and

Paul, in words long-written down, we know God calls us to act. Of our own accord, we must go out into the wilderness and be attentive for a burning bush. And when the light is seen, we must act by walking towards it and go wherever its light directs our path before us.

"However, in the absence of guiding light, we must do our best to find the path. We mustn't cower in our own despair but find faith in every step." A winking smile filled the aging chaplain's face. "In other words, pray to God but also be rowing towards the shore."

Cindy's face broke an uneasy smile as the sentiment settled upon her. Aliyah looked across the table and felt the full aurora of her mother's love and concern. A well of emotion began to bubble in her gut and found its way to the edges of her eyes.

Then, Dean cast his gaze further down the table.

"And you, Gabriel. I give similar counsel.

"True, there is no doubting the power of The Almighty. But it seems, in Earthly matters, to preserve the freewill of us all, we must rise to the call on our own. That is the blessing, our gift. We must look to Him to be used as instruments in a plan we cannot hope to fully see from our vantages in this limited form—as it was for all the forefathers that came before us.

"And there is another reason, one that is probably not as apparent due to our limited view of time. The full extent of evil must run its course for mankind to learn its full lesson without any what ifs or but ifs; an absolute rejection like a hand that has felt the burning of a flame.

"Let me illustrate in parable."

Dean sat up straight in his chair, careful not to squeak it. "Say there's a teacher, and he is teaching a classroom full of students how to survive in a harsh world. Then one student becomes defiant and begins accusing the teacher of lying and misleading the classroom. The teacher is aware that this student is lying in an attempt to turn the other classmates against the teacher. The teacher also knows that just kicking this student out of the classroom is not going to put to rest the accusations that were made. But before the teacher sits down, he informs the classroom that the defiant student will certainly prove to be a liar, and that he will be sent away to detention so that he cannot mislead others.

"So, the teacher sits down and tells the defiant student to come up and prove to the classroom that he really knows better than the teacher. The defiant student convinces other students to go out into the wilderness and follow their own will rather than the teachings taught by the teacher.

"The new followers of the defiant student leave to attempt to return and prove the teacher's teachings wrong by trying every unique alternative way of surviving.

"The teacher's pupils also embark following the teacher's commands on how to live and thrive.

"Becoming lost or killed, many who followed the defiant student do not return to the class. Those who do are torn and broken asking for guidance of the teacher and sneering at the defiant one for misleading them. The class, having seen every possible attempt now sees that the ways of the defiant student are folly and wish not to hear from him again. The defiant student is finally cast out of the class along with any who choose to live by their own will despite the self-evidence of the unpleasant cost.

"So, Gabriel, why must Satan endure for a time. Now, I didn't tell you there was going to be a test, did I?" Dean smiled, awaiting a response.

"No...no you did not," Gabe chuckled lightly. "Luckily, I am not too far removed from being a student.

"Well, I think the point is the Devil, 'the deviant student,' offers an alternative that has yet to be fully exposed to convince mankind of its inherent folly. Time has to run every possibility, every disastrous pitfall, every life ruined to make it clear across generations. Only upon complete revelation and acceptance of this truth will the universe be ready and forever remember never to choose the deviant alternative. But, destroy it too soon, before the alternatives have fully played out, and rebellion will continue out of human will, curiosity, and doubt. We must wait until all possible choices are made so that the deviant alternative becomes irrefutably seen as an ill-choice. Only then, when there is no doubt or curiosity left, can the deviant alternative known as Satan be permanently removed. All that would then remain would be inclinations the true original path that was given to us for good."

"Well said," replied Dean. "With freewill others can choose to fall, without it there would be no loving obedience, serving out of fear of retribution as androids are slave to their master. Thus, you learn not by watching, but by experiencing a thing, doing it yourself. A lesson is not learned until one sees why it was the wrong approach."

Gabe leaned back in his seat with a humble smile of satisfaction with his response. However, the smile was short lived as Cindy suddenly began crying uncontrollably. Through the sobs, words became barely intelligible.

"Okay then…Why does it…have to be…our girl that goes? Can we…not fight?"

"I am sorry Cindy; this is the only way laid before us. No machine or weapon made of our hands will have any effect on the devices of Phosos," came Joe's firm but not unkind voice from the other end of the table.

Dean leaned over again, this time with both hands consoling Cindy's hand that tremored.

"Joe is right, I've seen the Hands of Provision fight, there is no use. Too many times, over these years we have tried fighting here and there with no result. Only for fewer good men and women to return to us. These androids can simulate thousands of years of training in a few minutes. Your every move, every possible action has been simulated and noted.

"There is no conventional path open to us. We must seek something no one would think of, even a being as seemingly all-knowing as Phosos."

Joe rose from his seat and approached Cindy, placing his hands on the back of her shoulders.

"Which is why we must seek this unconventional knowledge seemingly lost to the ages and out of reach of all that now live. In the faith that it will bring about the downfall of this demonic scourge on the Earth and lead to a new rebirth."

Cindy's sobs had lessened and her breathing became more measured. She looked up to her husband, Desmond, through a waterfall of tears. It was subtle at first, but he returned her glance with a reassuring nod of acknowledgement.

"Cindy, I see nowhere else to go and we can't give up, not now," Desmond finally said, as a tear had rolled down his cheek.

Dean offered a deferential glance over at Joe who furnished back an unspoken approval with glimmering eyes and a nudging nod.

"It is settled then; our path is laid out before us and now we must walk it in faith that it will grow ever the clearer with each forward step. But, Cindy, Desmond…" Dean held both their hands firmly like in prayer. "…know your daughter will not be going it alone, I will set off for the base in Kansas to retrieve this processing chip. And *you* will be coming with me."

Dean looked directly at Gabe.

"Me?" Gabe croaked.

"Yes, *you*. You are the only one who knows what we are looking for. If I went on my own, who knows what I might bring back, a potato chip?"

A laughter filled the room which lightened the air and dispelled some of the uneasiness that had been building.

"Aliyah, if he will be obliged, I will send Joe with you to Virginia to set up what needs to be done with your professor and his machine."

Joe nodded without hesitation. His blue eyes sparkling intensely.

Dean continued. "I will also send with you Kamil and Petrona. Kamil has proved to be a great pathfinder in case you get lost and Petrona is great with electronics. Given our primitive set up here, I feel she will jump at this mission."

Aliyah nodded as if by reflex.

"Lastly, Desmond and Cindy. Since I will be gone, I am placing leadership in both of your capable hands. Gather the people for a movement east, get to New Eden. That will be the last place that Phosos will expect us to make our stand. God willing, if all goes to plan, we will have a big party to crash."

"A plan...isn't that the only thing that can make God laugh?" Gabe quipped wryly.

"Indeed, you may be right. So let us go with joy in our hearts."

They laughed and then prayed.

) | (

It was not until the sun had dipped low in a blood-orange sky that the events of the day finally began to settle in. The westward mountains stretched their long shadows over the camp as Aliyah made her way back from the northwesterly shoreline. She had been gone since midday, embarking on a long hike around the lake. She had thought the solitude would help her grapple with the day's events and the uncertainties that lay ahead, though now, she could not be sure that she was any closer to truth or resolution.

Her footsteps trudged through old fallen leaves that had only recently become revealed from the receding snow blankets of deep winter snows. The intermittent crunching was the only break in the eerie stillness of the forest. As shadows lengthened and darkness began filling the wood, she became hyper-alert. Her eyes flickered constantly among the trees, scanning for any hint of movement—be it animal, person, or even, though she tried to suppress the thought, the trees themselves. She had the unpleasant memory of witnessing their unnerving motion before, in that waking nightmare at the Old Woodlot near campus years ago. Accompanied by a cold, blue floating orb, the trees had chased her to the very edge of Devil's Leap until she sang a doxology that finally abated the nightmare.

On this evening, she felt as if she was being watched by the trees. Yet, it was not quite the same feeling as it had been back before. The breeze blowing through the wood was cool but it did not carry an icy chill.

She kept moving and rounded another bend of the shoreline. The first warm lights of the outer cabins were now visible at the trailhead a few dozen meters away.

Almost there, she thought. Her pace had unconsciously quickened. She recalled the same feeling she had as a child climbing the last few steps of a darkened basement, worrying that some formless black hand was about to jut out and grab her feet and pull her back down into the darkness.

She had nearly reached the edge of the trees now. The clearing beyond was empty of any sign of others walking about. She was almost at the signpost marking the trailhead when a voice reached out to her from a tree at the edge of the camp lights.

"He is a good leader," said a male voice. Familiar it sounded, but off enough that it could not quite be placed amongst the strange mix of accents.

Aliyah stopped dead in her tracks. A large stick cracked beneath her feet where she had planted them. Then there was a deathly quiet. Her heartbeat noticeably thumped in her chest. She looked over in the direction from wince the voice had come. The lights from the nearby cabins danced admits the trees sending undulating shadows in between their stout trunks and sturdy boughs. Then she noticed a pair of small blue orbs floating in unison about the pale trunk of an aspen tree.

She felt her hands tighten and her leg muscles coiling for potential flight. It would only be a few leaps and bounds before she was in the welcoming glow of artificial light. But she did not flee. As she studied the orbs further, she noticed they did not give off their own light like the one before, they merely reflected what little light reached from the edge of the forest. The fiery blue eyeballs danced in the dim yellow light as a tall figure stepped forward from the shadows. He wore a faded grey coat and a yellow scarf about his neck. *The Man with Sapphire Eyes!*

"Sorry, I did not mean to startle you. I only wanted to catch you when you returned from your hike. I hope it was refreshing. Clear air always seems to help clear the mind," the man said. He took several steps closer so that they both were in easy talking distance.

"What did you mean by 'good leader?'" Aliyah replied looking Joe over as he was now in full light. Despite lurking in the shadows, she did fear him. One look in his eyes and she felt a soothing comfort that put her at ease.

Joe smiled. "I am sorry. I should have been clearer. Wilkins…he is a good leader. He may be unconventional—and certainly no Augustus—but then again, I have seen many in my time."

The man seemed sincere in the manner he spoke. There was a quality that Aliyah noticed in the low light. She had noticed glimpses of it before, but now, with ample time to study his features, she could see something lying beneath the surface that belied the man's middle-aged appearance. Somehow it reminded her of how her grandfather's eyes had looked in his old age, though they were brown and much older than Joe's. In them, a deep well of years and miles of experience could be observed if you looked into them long enough.

"What do you think the true name will be like?" she asked, curiously. It was a question that had been itching in the back of her mind all day.

A change rolled slowly across the man's face. His lips curled upward imperceptibly beneath a short dark beard, betraying a hint of satisfaction. His eyes seemed to soften from a glint of recognition at a question that he seemed to have half expected.

Joe wetted his lips with a quick stroke of his tongue like an artist dabbing in a fresh blob of paint.

"That truly is the question of our time, isn't it?" he paused, looking out over the calm waters of the lake. Its dark waters were pierced now by the silvery streaks of a rising moon.

"It was not action, tools, or thought that created the world, it was *words*. Words defined and brought things into being. A protolanguage was used for communication in that garden paradise, and through it, each plant and animal were named. It was not until the Confusion of Tongues at Babel that this first, Adamic language was scattered and diminished. So, you see, the very structure of our created world is built upon words—orderly sounds and patterns in an otherwise cacophonic chaos of noise.

"That only provides the foundation for the question but does not answer it, I know."

Aliyah nodded, wondering if she might get any hint at all from the strange man who only seemed to reveal tantalizing bits and pieces of information.

"No, it certainly does not. I found in my experience that to speculate on such lofty things is like catching a breeze—you feel it through your fingers but can never fully grasp it or control it. Yet, if I had to make a guess, it would be that our Lord's name is not a noun, that would surely be too limiting into this world. No, I daresay His name is a verb, an action that describes neither beginning nor ending, simply *being*."

Aliyah found her gaze also drawn into the shimmering waters of moonlight. They had a mesmerizing quality to them while speaking of such things.

"And you really think we will be able to find someone who has heard this name?" she asked earnestly.

"No one has heard it since the beginning; it has ostensibly been lost into the sands of time. Only those who have crossed over and beyond the veil might have learned this truth, but they tell no tales to us here.

"All I know is this is the path that we must take and you, Aliyah, are the one that must lead us down it. I can only be but a guide and provide you a place to start," the man said, turning back to Aliyah. His eyes staring deep into her.

"There is a man in Palmyra of central Levant who will be the person where we must begin. The knowledge that he holds will be our trailhead for this great quest."

SNAP!

Jumping at the sound, Aliyah fell back off her feet and hit the wet ground with a thud.

The Man with Sapphire Eyes stood quietly, listening to the now breezeless air. Then shook his head.

"An opossum more than likely," he said, offering a helping hand to pull her to her feet. "Are you all right? You took a quite a spill."

"Oh, I am fine. I've just been on edge lately."

"You, have?" the man replied. The response not seeming cursory but nudging her for more detail. She felt strangely secure with Joe, like an older uncle who was looking out for her.

"Well, to be honest, even before the big reveal last night, I have been dealing with some weird things."

Joe cupped the bottom of his bearded chin and stroked on it lightly. "Weird things, huh? What kind of weird?"

"Well, weird…" she took a deep breath. "It started a couple of weeks back, minor things here and there. A jumping shadow. The slamming of a door. My name whispered on the wind. But then, last night it definitely escalated.

"I was in the outbuilding; you know the one where all the showers and bathrooms are. It was not thirty minutes after sunset and everyone had gone to the dining hall for dinner. I had…umm…some business to take care of let's just say.

"Not sure if it is the same on the men's side, but the women's toilet is one of those old-looking blue porcelain commodes like my grandparents used to have in their house.

"I had reached about a few steps away from it when the florescent light began to flicker above it. I knew that the electricity can be somewhat finicky in camp, so I didn't make much of it at the time.

"I took a seat, and within seconds, the top of the lid clamped down on my back with such force that it propelled me forward, pressing my chest against my legs. All-the-while, toilet water sprayed up from beneath me into my face. I naturally screamed and screamed. Apparently, there was no one around to hear it. I struggled and squirmed to get away but it was no use. The lid was too tight, too strong. In the midst of my panic, I felt a hand emerge from the unseen depths of the bowl. Its twig-like fingers began to touch me.

"It was at that point I summoned every ounce of strength I had to push off with my feet. To my shock, the effort worked! I rolled off the toilet, crying and with my pants down to my ankles. When I turned around the toilet flusher was twitching erratically. The lid was still moving up and down spurting out dirty water and…words! The toilet was laughing at me! And it was growling out obscenities. Suddenly, the whole unit began to rattle off its base and shake towards me, slowly getting closer. Without any hesitation, I got to my feet and ran out of there without daring to look back."

"I see," replied Joe.

A period of silence fell between them in the waxing moonlight. Aliyah began to sway on her feet, not knowing whether her story was believed.

"Do not fear, I believe you," he began after secluding himself behind his eyes. "And from what I hear, this is not the first time you have experienced strange phenomenon?"

"That is right, strange things happened back in Virginia around when the Mindsai experiment took place."

A flicker of understanding flashed across the man's face before becoming quickly covered with a disarming smile.

"You are one of the lucky few who has seen into this strange world-upon-a-world. However, I am afraid once you have seen into it, it cannot be unseen, nor can you become unseen by it. In a way, you have been marked, and these other forces are now keen to see you when their presence draws near."

Aliyah frowned. "Seems rather unlucky to me."

"It can be. But it can also be to our advantage. The presence of the malevolent entity you described seems to confirm that our camp here has become known to these dark powers."

"I guess it is good that we are moving on soon," Aliyah said.

"Yes, the timing is right. But let us get back to camp and muse on these things in the light," replied Joe who extended an arm back towards the center of camp.

It was the best course of action Aliyah had thought of all day.

3

Chasing the Dawn

Two weeks had passed before preparations had been made for the journeys back East. The delay had cost precious time but it was a necessary precaution. The extra time allowed for the spring thaw which would afford passage through the mountains which were hazardous in the best of times between October and April. Now deep into May, Kamil had reported back that the passage was clear enough to travel safely—in both directions. It had been fortuitous that the agents of Phosos were not a punctual lot.

On the day of his departure with Mr. Wilkins, Aliyah found herself on a low knoll watching Gabe fritter to-and-fro to make last minute arrangements loading a truck. The freshly sprouted grass tickled the bottoms of her thighs that stretch out of a worn pair of torn-off jean shorts. Every once in a while, Gabe would look up beneath the strands of brown hair and flash her a wide smile, then reluctantly, turn back to his tasks.

She never showed it, but Aliyah had welcomed the additional time. A postponement meant the delay of taking any first steps down a path without a planned loop for return. And, of course, there was also Gabe. They had grown close in the wake of events at Hightower University and closer still, in the last few seasons. Often, they would abscond out to a distant ledge overlooking the lake to talk about lives that were now as distant as the stars they watched silently together appear above them.

It was on one of these special nights, as they stared out into the vast heavens, when Gabe held her in close to guard against the first chill of autumn. Gabe had looked at her quietly, his eyes growing as wide as the harvest moon rising atop the mountains. He leaned in slowly, closer and closer. She had instinctively closed her eyes anticipating the moment his lips touched hers. When they did, she had no need to see his face to know her feelings. Love, like many of the intangible things in the universe is not experienced in crude senses. No, it lies in the mind where there are no limits to its depth and understanding.

In an alternative timeline, they probably would have become engaged, married, and then settled down in a quaint little stone cottage that would bear the pattering of children. They would have grown old together, watching their children go off on their own life's journeys until a time would come for their own partings from this world and each other.

But all was not to be. The world had forever changed and such a life could only now be lived in memories and daydreams. Aliyah was content enough to see the entirety of those wistful dreams in Gabe's eyes every time they met hers for more than a passing moment.

Helping Gabe was a man and woman of similar age to herself. The man, with shoulder-length dark hair was checking the voltages of the battery on the truck. His name was Kamil and he had joined the camp a year ago after his Cherokee reservation had been "offered" entrance into the Tree of Unity. The offer had been too tempting for most residents of the reservation who had endured decades beyond remembrance of poverty and substance abuse. The provision promised by Phosos was more than a reparation of historical injustice. The Branches of Unity had even provided the latest VR technology so that they could feel directly connected to New Eden and even experience an existence as their ancestors had. Yet for Kamil, and a handful of other families, the changes seemed too easy. So, they had migrated west until they had come across the encampment at Timberline.

Packing food in a pair of large, Army-issued duffle bags was a brunette-haired woman named Petrona. Most in camp called her "Petro" on account that her family had owned the last two gas stations in Colorado before the ban had come down on all petroleum-based products. She was well-regarded around camp as she helped maintain the extensive network of solar arrays and lighting. Without this knowledge, the camp would have otherwise been reliant upon candles and fire light.

As Petro loaded the last duffle bag into the back of the truck, a bustling crowd approached. At its center was Dean Wilkins dressed in his old Army fatigues. Trailing not too far behind were Aliyah's parents. Their faces carrying an uncharacteristic burden.

Before the press of people reached the now fully-loaded vehicle, Aliyah sprang to her feet and trotted own to Gabe who was leaning against an open passenger's door.

"Surprised the old uniform fits the guy," Gabe quipped after offering a peck on Aliyah's cheek.

"Come now, no one has gained weight in this camp, except for baby Daisy," she shot back. Daisy was a three-month old girl born to a young couple who had traveled from Tennessee.

They watched as the cluster of people approach slowly like a drunken Chinese dragon on parade. It was not long before the truck was completely surrounded by the chatter of well-wishers.

Dean detached himself from the crowd and climbed the truck's tailgate. He stood tall above them with the backdrop of a crystal blue sky with a pair of fluffy clouds waving by. He then raised a hand and waited for the chatter to trail off into a wind-swept silence.

Dean began to speak with a vigor that no one in the crowd had witnessed in all his time there. It was a voice filled with astute determination and without a sliver of apprehension.

"Today, we embark on a great mission. Tomorrow, our brothers and sisters leave for theirs. I pray that our paths stay true and cross again. May we find peace when our job is done. For the rest of you, many blessings I place upon you and leave you in the good and sturdy hands of Desmond and Cindy, who will lead you upward and onward. We have all been in darkness, but today we chase for the dawn. Thank you and farewell until we meet again."

"Amen!" the crowd said in unison.

Dean climbed down from the truck bed and passed over to the driver's side door. He gave a last final look at the camp behind them and then to Gabe who was still standing on the other side.

"Let's get this show on the road, Gabriel!" Dean shouted, patting the roof of the truck. "Say your goodbyes and be sure to give your girl a good-long kiss she won't forget." He said the last part with a half-nod and a wink before climbing into his seat.

Gabe turned to Aliyah, his face half-blushing. In her eyes, he had already begun to turn into a blurry kaleidoscope as tears had gathered at the ready. Precious seconds ticked by that she yearned to be stretched into minutes. She shockingly could not find any words to say to the one that now meant so much to her. But perhaps that spoke for itself.

She rubbed the awaiting tears from her eyes to get a good clear picture of his face that was warping into clearer view.

There he was, standing with a sad smile, his kind hazel eyes searching her face.

"No goodbyes or farewells," Gabe began, gently rubbing both sides of her arms. "This is, 'I will see you later,' if I have any power in the matter."

The whirl of four electric truck motors came on like a strong breeze. When the sound had descended into a soft hum, Aliyah only found a few words out of so many buzzing in her head. None of which really seemed to be quite sufficient for tearful partings, such as this.

"I'll see you in Cincy, my love. Then we are onward to Talawanda Springs. I guess we are circling back to where we met, aren't we?" she said, as though reiterating the plan might somehow will it into reality.

Gabe smiled and leaned in close so that only she could hear his soft, sweet voice.

"May our circle go unbroken," he replied and gave her a long kiss that flooded her mind with a loving warmth.

The next moments seemed to flash before her like still frames in a scrapbook.

Gabe climbed into the cab of the truck.

She stepped back from it.

The truck lurched forward down the gravel service road.

The truck became a trail of dust into the distance.

The truck passed out of sight and hearing beyond the mountain pass.

Then, Gabe was gone.

) | (

A jostle of the car broke Aliyah's mid-morning snooze. She tried to open her eyes but immediately squinted against the oppressive white glare beaming through the windows from all around. After a few disorienting moments, she could look out enough to see a grey overcast sky hanging over a muddy brown plain.

A sign flashed by. Its afterimage was of something visibly toppled halfway over. The only word she could catch was "Kirks—"

"Where are we?" she asked, wiping a stray bit of drool that had curdled on the edge of her mouth.

"We just passed south of Kirksville, Missouri," replied Petrona who was driving steadily.

"According to the map here…after hopping between this access road and another, we should reach The Gap in about an hour," added Kamil, buried under several outdated maps in various states of unfolding in the passenger's seat.

Petrona looked into the rearview mirror at the backseat behind Aliyah. "How are you holding up back there, Joe?"

"I am just fine. Been this way before several times, I believe," the Man with Sapphire Eyes called back, absentmindedly.

Chancing a quick glance, Aliyah turned behind her to see Joe staring out the back window. The man's distant gaze was fixed on the horizon, unfocused, as if peering into another world—one far away and long forgotten. His lips were slightly parted and brows gently furrowed bespeaking deep thought. The harsh white light further revealed the faintest of lines etched into his forehead hinting at worries bubbling just beneath.

Aliyah turned back in her seat to watch the unpainted road move under them without any sign of change. If it were not for the odd oak tree and dilapidated barn that rushed by, it would seem that they were not going anywhere.

Yet, time had been passing. They were in the fourth day of their journey eastward. The going had been slow. To avoid the many eyes and agents of Phosos, the main roads and highways had to be avoided. So, taking farm roads, accessways, and sometimes plowing through long-untended fields, they had zig-zagged their way across the northwestern countryside.

It had been easier leaving Timberline than watching Gabe leave the place they had called home for several years. Although there had been a decently mustered group of folks who bid them farewell, it paled to the one that had seen Wilkins off. Now, she could not recall who had been there besides her mom and dad. In parting, her father had given her a few words he must have worked on in his head all morning. He told her, "When you ask for courage, God provides you a situation that affords an opportunity to demonstrate it." The last part of it came out in a croaking voice as the moment must have almost overtaken him. He had to turn away briefly to regain his composure.

Her mother, on the other hand, offered her a story. She revealed to her that when she (Aliyah) had been born, she had screamed and screamed nonstop for hours. She recalled further that even after the wailing had finally subsided, a look of melancholy was on her face for days until it finally passed over her. After finishing her strangely-timed story, her mother gave her a big hug and rubbed her back, like so many times she had done so when Aliyah had been sick or suffered a major setback. Then she whispered in her ear, in between sobs. "After everything that has happened to you Aliyah, I can't help but wonder if you knew then when you came into this world crying and wailing in a terror. Perhaps, like all of us before we are born, you knew the trials that were to be laid ahead of you." She had not thought much of it, but as the car ride dragged on, a nonspecific sense of familiarity began to suggest there might be something to it. She began to wonder: *Maybe every newborn's face is a window into the happiness of the life they were destined to lead.*

"There it is!" Kamil said suddenly, about ten minutes after they had crossed into Illinois.

Aliyah turned to see out the front windshield. They had just crested the top of a hill that gave them a panoramic view of a fertile valley. A few kilometers in the distance a deep black scar carved through the landscape in a north to south bearing.

"It's bigger in person," said Petrona as she let the car coast down into the valley.

Aliyah gazed at the approaching Madrid Gap; a sight she had seen up close a few times in her childhood when her dad took her there. Now, however, it loomed closer like a snarling black gash, filling her with fear. It had been the "Big One" everyone talked about during her upbringing. The tremors from Yellowstone they had felt up to Nebraska were nothing compared to what had formed the Madrid Gap—a massive earthquake, coupled with a meteor strike in the Middle East, had brought it into existence a few years before she was born. In mere hours of these cataclysmic events, the New Madrid fault had crumbled away like a wet graham cracker creating a gap that stretched from the Gulf of Mexico to Lake Michigan. Dubbed by many as "The Gap," it maintained a uniform depth of 200 meters throughout its length and varied in width from 400 meters width to a staggering 1,500 meters at its widest point. The event had been devastating to infrastructure anywhere within 50 kilometers of The Gap, toppling any building taller than two stories at the time. It was for this reason her father had moved to Cincy to help in the extensive rebuilding efforts.

"Where are we going to cross?" she asked.

"Let's see here…" replied Kamil looking at a map.

"We have to make sure not to cross anywhere too populated," stated Petrona cautiously scanning the horizon.

"Well, they don't just put up bridge crossings anywhere. We might need to risk it," replied Kamil who had finally settled his finger in the middle of the jagged black line that ran up and down the map. "Take a left at the next 'T' intersection."

The car turned left onto a road that ran parallel to The Gap. The car traveled down the road for another 15 minutes until they reached a stoplight at a four-way intersection on the outskirts of a small town.

"I don't like this one bit…this town already has one stoplight too many," Petrona said nervously, leaning attentively over the steering wheel.

"Relax Petro, we only need to reach that next light ahead and turn right," Kamil said calmly.

"Come on, turn, green turn green," mumbled Petrona under her staggered breaths.

"I do not think there is much to worry here," said Joe from the back. "I do not believe there is a soul to witness our passing."

The light turned green and they began to travel towards the next light. Concrete buildings lined the street, but all their windows and doors had been tightly boarded up.

"I guess people decided not to stick around," noted Kamil. Then added quickly, "Turn right here!"

Petrona turned the vehicle onto a main road. It was not long before they reached the bridge that spanned The Gap which was around 550 meters wide at this spot. As they crossed, Aliyah looked down into the black trench that fell deep below them. Near its bottom, a small river flowed through it and winded its way as far as she could see.

When they had reached near the end of the bridge, another car emerged ahead of them traveling at great speed.

"Umm...there is a car approaching. What should I do?" Petrona said through gritted teeth.

"Just drive normal," replied Kamil.

"What do you think I am doing?" Petrona snapped back holding the car as steady as she could in its lane. She dared not slow down or speed up to indicate any reaction to the approaching vehicle. Aliyah noticed Petrona's knuckles grew whiter as she held the steering wheel tighter and tighter with each passing second.

When they had finally reached the end of the bridge, the other car shot by them in a blur of motion.

"Did you see that?" Petrona's voice trembled with apprehension.

"I saw three passengers," replied Kamil, his tone tinged with a newfound seriousness.

"But, did you see the one in the back?" Petrona pressed urgently.

"It was a Hand of Provision," stated Aliyah matter-of-factly, her words chilling the inside of the car.

"Out here? Why would any of them be out here?" Petrona exclaimed, her voice mixed with fear and disbelief.

"Let us just hope that they keep traveling west, and then, keep on going until they fall into the sea," replied Aliyah.

They continued down the road heading east, but not much was said in the car for some time after crossing The Gap.

) | (

When they arrived at the rendezvous spot, the streets were empty, the rows of houses darkened; not a soul moved about the old Sharonville neighborhood Aliyah had called home. Cincinnati was not how she had remembered leaving it years ago. Then again, much had changed since departing for graduate school.

"Is this place your house?" Kamil asked hesitantly, slowly pulling up in front of a home nestled quietly in the modest line of houses.

"It is. The blue one," Aliyah confirmed from the passenger's seat. "It does not look like 59 Prospect Street has aged a day," she reflected further.

"Should we get out?" Kamil asked, putting the car in park.

"Are we sure that is such a good idea? It was risky enough to choose a place that could be connected to any of us," protested Petrona from the middle seat, looking over the blue house, examining every window that looked out through its white wrap around porch.

"It is better to find trouble in places you know than to find yourself a stranger with trouble about," said Joe from his spot in the back seat. "Come, let us stretch our legs a bit. Wilkins and Gabriel should be here shortly."

No one argued with the Man with Sapphire Eyes. They each piled out of the vehicle into the street. Kamil and Petrona wandered a half-dozen houses down to a pair of swings in a nearby playground. She watched them pass an old silver maple whose many dead limbs allowed holes in its shady canopy. It had been "The School Bus Tree" when she was in elementary school. It was sturdy back then with a canopy that seemed to cover the sky in a child's eyes. Every kid on the block would wait under its protective branches whether huddling in the cold or avoiding the drenching pours of rain. Seeing its aged state now almost brought herself to tears; it stood on the edge of its purpose withering away.

Wiping the edges of her eyes, Aliyah turned to see what had become of Joe. He remained close to the car, watching the road and not looking much for company. Feeling the tug of curiosity, Aliyah walked up her old driveway daring to get a peek of what had befallen her childhood home. The two-story craftsman seemed the same. It was a typical drudger house, fitting for people who still valued the virtue of work over the ease of sitting at the service of automation. The robin egg blue paint still covered the siding, albeit perhaps a little faded above the windows. The red fence to the back yard still leaned inward. The white pillars, standing on their grey stone pedestals looked as strong as they ever had. Yet, she sensed something had changed.

She crept closer and up the front steps, doing her best to stay out of view of the many single hung windows that stared out in all directions.

The first thing she noticed was that the blinds on all the windows were closed. The only view inside the house she could find was a little crack in the blinds where the they had been pulled down too hastily and got caught on a key hook next to the front door. Several of the blades were bent upwards allowing just enough space to see into the living room.

She moved under the window as quiet as she could. As she rose slowly, she noticed two worn letters "AW" made in red crayon underneath the sill. They were her initials that must have been overlooked for decades now.

Once her eyes were at window-level, she peered into the house. Inside, an oppressive grey gloom left no hint of artificial light. She leaned sideways to see further into the room and stopped. She noticed three pairs of legs that looked to be suspended in air. The feet were still. Stretching the viewing angle to its furthest, she noticed that there were three people in reclined positions on a couch attached to various IV hoses and tubes. Each one had a VR headset on and looked like they had not moved in days.

How can anyone escape the allure of a place where you can have whatever you want, whenever you want it? she thought. From her own studies of the psychological literature—especially the old seminal stuff—people were never the best arbiters of knowing what is good for them. Left to their own devices and endless self-justifications there were not many who could resist the temptation to satisfy the greatest fulfillment of the human ego, to be radical individuals, in their personal virtual kingdoms of one.

She was just about to head back to the car when a sturdy hand fell on her shoulder. She covered her mouth quickly to hold back a shriek. Her eyes opened wide looking to the window to see who stood behind her in the reflection.

"Oh, it's only you," she whispered somewhat shakily.

Joe nodded quietly and hunched down to get a look inside the house. He looked intently for a few long moments. She noticed that his eyes lacked their usual sparkle and his eyebrows were furrowed slightly as if disheartened by what he saw.

"The place where godless people go to become a god," he said, turning away from the window, shaking his head. "This generation has truly drunk deep from the waters of forgetfulness. And now sleep, dreaming within a dream."

She gave a casual nod and motioned that they slip back down the driveway. When they reached the car, she asked Joe a question that had been tugging at her mind for the whole trip.

"If by some miracle we are able to pull all this off, where do we begin to find this man of Palmyra? The vastness of accumulated memories of time, people, and places seems like searching for a needle in deepest ocean, beneath the sand."

A twinkle seemed to return to the man's blue eyes.

"I thought I would wait until we reach Talawanda Springs, but perhaps some opportunities should not be missed when presented in the calm of day." He paused to loosen the yellow scarf around his neck. The day had grown warmer than expected and little glistening drops of sweat had formed on his brow. Unfurling a bit of the scarf, which was set with a host of blue stars and crescent moons, he dabbed his forehead gently.

"Okay, much better," he began again. "No what was it you asked? Ah, yes, the knowledge was passed along to me that there can be found a man in the 40 A.D. city of Palmyra which is in what is now called Syria but then was known as Levant."

Joe closed his eyes to think briefly as a name came to him.

"He went by Atem…yes that's it…Atem of…of Elephantine! That's right. He is the marker at the trailhead for your journey. You will find that he holds an account from his great, great grandsire that chronicles a visit to an ancient city near the Eye of

Africa south of the Atlas Mountains in Western Africa. I believe
in that esteemed city surrounded by myth and legend you will find
the next guidepost backward."

"How did you come by all this information?" she asked,
quizzically.

Joe opened his eyes, and looked up into the sky.

"I was told that this man was a merchant there. Throughout
my life I have built a large network of individuals who have an
expertise in the histories of people and places. I have the utmost
confidence that you will find him there, probably selling an
assortment of vinegars I believe."

Aliyah shrugged.

"I guess that is something to go on. I wish I had the same
confidence I will be able to find *a man*, in *a city*, in *a time* that no
one has seen in thousands of years."

Joe leaned in close and patted her on the shoulder. "Trust that
the future takes care of itself and the past is forever out of our
reach. If you look for a guiding hand, your steps in the present
will be lightened, even if they are treading in someone else's past."
He gave her a wink of encouragement. And before she could say
anything more, he added a warning.

"Do not seek more knowledge than you must. Knowledge is
powerful, but a deadly friend without the wisdom to its proper
boundaries. Let what knowledge you need paint your map, but
allow wisdom to guide you where you need to go."

Before she could utter another probing word, a sound perked
up her ears. It was one she had been unconsciously monitoring
for since she had stepped out of the car onto her old front lawn.
She traced its source down the street. And, just turning the corner,
was the first vehicle anyone had seen all day.

The vehicle, now visibly barreling down the road towards
them was a truck!

Aliyah's heart skipped a beat noticing that it was the same
truck that had left Timberline Camp. But only one person looked
to be inside...Gabe.

When Gabe parked the truck, he did so halfway up on the curb behind their car. His face looked drawn out and sunken in, as if he had not rested in days. After parking, she watched as he gingerly unbuckled his seat belt as if every slight movement was in pain. She wanted to run to him, hold him close but was still frozen by fear as to what condition he was in.

The door swung open rapidly with a stiff kick of Gabe's foot. The now open door allowed her to finally see him for that state he was in. Her eyes were immediately drawn to a dried crimson circle on his left side.

Blood! she thought frantically. Her eyes and mind raced trying to assess the severity of the injury.

"Sorry, I am a few hours late," Gabe said, with some effort. His voice was weak but still carried a glint of humor.

"What happened to you, love?" she cried, lightly placing her hand on the injury site and using her other to wave over Kamil and Petrona who had already started back from the playground after the truck had parked. The wound felt tender and dried with three long gashes that had only just started to solidify into a gummy ridge of fresh flesh.

Gabe gave her a soft smile and climbed out of the cab with her helping hand—noticeably wincing as he reached the ground.

"I guess our circle is still complete," he said, once he found a spot on the side of the truck to lean against. Kamil and Petrona arrived and she could tell by the look in their eyes that they too had noticed the wound on Gabe's left side. But they did not stare too long and took a spot next to Joe forming a semicircle around Gabe with her in the middle.

"Well, Gabe, can you tell us what happened? Where is Dean?" she asked as delicately as she had helped him to his spot.

For a moment, Gabe's face went blank and seemed to stare right on through her, the others, the house, and everything else. His mind seemed to drift off to find an answer or perhaps, she feared, to hide from it.

"Gabe..." she repeated, looking deep into his eyes. A clarity of understanding had begun to fill into them slowly.

"Oh, yes. What happened..." he began, dropping his eyes to the curb and kicking it with his muddy boots. "Well, we arrived at the base and...surprisingly there wasn't anyone about."

Everyone seemed to nod in synchrony to urge him along.

He continued: "It took Mr. Wilkins awhile to remember the bunker location that housed the machine. But we found it. And the processing chip with the SEER goggles, just like he had said we would. I have them in the bag sitting on the front seat."

Gabe motioned to a small olive drab bag zipped tightly and strapped in by a safety belt on the passenger's seat.

"Everything appeared to be going smoothly," he continued. "Until we arrived topside."

Gabe paused for a moment and swallowed as if he had just taken a large horse pill.

He began to speak again, his voice lowering to almost a whisper above the otherwise pleasant breeze passing carelessly between them. "We were near the perimeter fence, about 200 meters from the truck, when we were caught by a crowd of people all bearing the signs of Unity. We must have triggered a silent alarm somehow, at least that was what Mr. Wikins suspected in the moment, but he didn't have time to elaborate. Without discussion, he handed me the bag with the equipment and told me to 'carry on, son.'

"Before I could react, he was running out from our position behind a guard tower, screaming 'I am here, you pieces of deadwood!'

"He kited them away from me back into the heart of the base, leaving a clear path back to the truck. I ran as fast as I could to the fence. As I crossed over the top of it, I guess a few shards of wire caught my side and I fell the rest of the way down to the ground on the other side. When I turned around, I could still see Mr. Wilkins. He had been surrounded by his pursuers and a Hand of Provision emerged from the group, flanked by two, what looked like rooters judging by what they were wearing."

He paused again, lifting up his head to look at his companions and then to Aliyah. Rings of water lined the edges of his eyes.

"The next part happened so fast. The rooters began to approach Mr. Wilkins with an apparent intent to capture him, but, before they could get within ten steps, Mr. Wilkins had pulled out a pistol and aimed at the group. Then, there was a flash of light emanating from the Hand of Provision. And when the light receded, all that was left of Mr. Wilkin's midsection was an empty circle of burnt flesh about as big as a softball."

Gabe closed his eyes tight, trying to hold back tears as his stomach now contracted involuntarily.

"I tried to get back as fast as I could. I drove through the night. I tried…"

"Oh, my love. It's okay. You did what you could," Aliyah said, taking him into her arms.

The others stood in shock at the story that had been told. A slight shaking had taken hold of Petrona's hand as she held it close to her chest. With a somber expression, Kamil merely looked to the sky and whispered an ancestral dirge of nothing living long, only the earth and the mountains.

For Joe, an accepted melancholy had filled his face. After an undermined amount of time, he came up to Gabe and put a comforting hand on his shoulder. In a kind voice he said, "Do not be forlorn by the vicissitudes of life, Gabriel. Dean Wilkins has returned home." Joe then began rolling up his sleeve to reveal the tattoo of a line flanked on either side by two concave arcs—") | (". He began to speak, this time his voice sounded far away, lost in reflectance.

"Our lives here on Earth are like this line, *a dream between two eternities*. The dream is but a clouded lens that will be all the clearer one day when it has ended and we return home to the real-real. Then, our lives as we knew them here will seem like but a fleeting dream when murkiness is shredded away into an all-revealing light."

Aliyah noticed that Gabe seemed to find comfort in the man's words.

"Thank you, I just wish I could have done more for Mr. Wilkins," Gabe replied nodding his head.

"You did precisely what was needed. But, do not dwell on the past, for it has long slipped past your hands to change it. Instead, focus on the moments you have now, enraptured with the infinite potential, utilizing where you have come and where you hope to be." Joe said, giving Gabe another kindly pat on his arm. The Man with Sapphire Eyes did not say anything more. He gave Gabe another kindly smile and rejoined the others.

By then, Petrona had composed herself enough to come forward with some kind words as she took the green bag from the truck and placed it in the car. It was then that the black shape of a vehicle appeared a few blocks down the street. Petrona was the first to point it out to the others. When everyone had turned to follow Petrona's shaking finger, the black car had been joined by a second, then a third—all of the same model and color with the crimson branches of the Tree of Unity stretching across their hoods.

"Oh, God. They followed me!" Gabe cried.

"Get into the car and drive!" yelled Joe, pushing them along. "You have only minutes, now go!"

Kamil quickly hopped into the driver's seat and Petrona took the other.

Joe turned to Gabe. An uncharacteristic intensity of urgency had taken over him. "Are the keys in the truck?" he asked.

"Yes, I think—"

"Good, now go!"

In a few blinks of an eye, Joe had climbed into the cab of the truck and spun it sideways until he had completely blocked the one-way street.

Aliyah ran over to the driver's side window of the truck. By then, the black line of cars was now only a block away.

"Come on Joe, it's time to go!" she pleaded, tugging the sleeve of the man's arm.

The sapphire-eyed man shook his head sharply, side-to-side.

"No, I believe not. Our paths must diverge here I am afraid."

"But…"

He shook his head once more, this time not so sharply and placed a gentle hand over her own which had already begun to loosen its grip.

"Aliyah! Come on!" she heard Gabe calling behind her. She looked over her shoulder to see him standing next to an open car door. When she turned back to Joe, his face gave a quiet resignation, urging her to let go. A tear trickled down her cheek.

"We will be lost without you," she pled, hoping beyond hope that a last effort would change the man's mind.

His eyes shimmered as they always had but she knew nearly instantaneously that he had made his decision. She looked past him, on through the cab. The black vehicles had come to a stop a few houses away and a group of rooters had unloaded. Joe's voice started of softly and measured.

"I know you will find your way. Remember your trailhead."

"Palmyra, 40 A.D., vinegar merchant, Atem of Elephantine," she whispered.

"Yes, you are on your way further than you know…" Joe looked over at the men approaching. "And if you find yourself losing your path, look for the transcendent in the wilderness, for *it* is not found amongst the makings of mankind."

Joe turned back to Aliyah, his face now pleading on its own account.

"NOW GO!"

She turned and ran back to the car, jumping into the back seat.

"He's not coming?" Gabe asked with heavy concern.

"No, he's not," she replied distantly.

Gabe lingered for a moment staring at Joe in the side-turned truck. The approaching rooters were now fanned out a few meters beyond. For a second his body had tightened up as if to make some sort of rescue but, instead, he banged the top of the car's roof and jumped in next to Aliyah. Before he had closed his door, the wheels screeched on the pavement and the car jolted forward. The last sight she could see behind them in the dusty haze was Joe climbing out of the truck and running into the backyard of her childhood home. Following him, in hot pursuit, were nearly a dozen rooters.

THE SECOND DISPENSATION

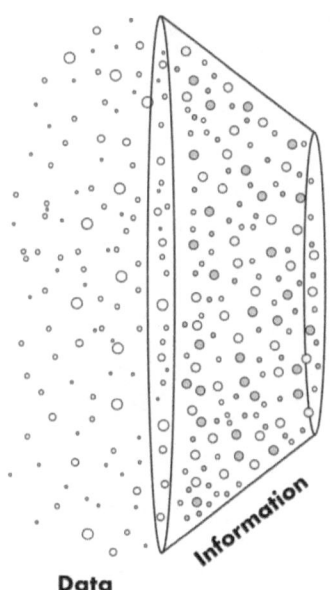

Data

Information

When the complexity of data is sorted you realize
) *from the collective accumulation of information* (
just how much you do not know.

4

The Tap Root

There was a frantic clomping of boots. A whirl of curt conversations. Dozens of voices overlapped each other with an electric urgency. Amidst it all, in the center of a large room, stood two rootmasters, Clayton and Zack. Their eyes seemed fixed on the streaming flows of data and communications being pulled from nodes far and wide.

The Tap Root complex—overlooking the Ohio River in downtown Cincinnati—had been the nearest location they could move their operation. Like many complexes of its type, the room was cast in greige tones of blacks, greys, and beige. The walls were made of mycelium bricks. Black onyx designs of branches and roots were inlayed upon the walls along with proclamations of Unity and Provision. The floor of the grand room was made of white marble and a large polished tiger's eye stone tree served as its centerpiece. Scattered throughout the room were also many plants intended to mimic a garden of sorts. But it was no true garden. The plants were synthetically-derived requiring no tending or care and had no potential to change or grow. The static flora served only for their appearance and represented an idealized vision of perfected provision. Suspended from the ceiling hung numerous telescreens monitoring various parts of the city. A large screen stood from the floor to the five-meter-high ceiling near the head of the room. Without interruption, day-or-night, this screen watched over a large stone courtyard outside the Temple of Unity in New Eden. Almost every building, and nearly every home had a view to this seat of the world where Phosos resided and dispensed his provisions and new proclamations.

"For Unity and Provision, Rootmaster…"

Clayton turned absently towards the more junior rooter, a rootling in rank, who had briskly walked over from a terminal. The young man who was of a short stature had a slightly plump face with sandy-blonde hair styled in the fashion of a bowl cut.

"By Unity we are strong, from Provision we thrive. Now, be quick with it!" Clayton barked.

The junior rooter hesitated a moment before he started speaking again. A quiver of nervousness had amplified in his voice. He had not had need of many direct interactions, especially with a senior Rootmaster of Clayton's station. He continued, "Rootmaster, the…umm…the…we have lost tracking of the weeds."

"Lost track? Lost track did you say?" Clayton cocked his head and then put an arm around the rootling's shoulder to aim him at the wall of telescreens which were presently cycling through countless living rooms, door cameras, street cameras, and sky-view drone cameras. He then stabbed a pointing finger at all the screens, forcefully. "You are telling me that with all our eyes, we cannot locate a single unregistered vehicle?"

"I um…we are trying…their vehicle is…um…not on our network…but let me see." The junior rooter pulled out a tablet and proceeded to tap rapidly at the screen to engage several AI agents. After a few long moments, he looked up from the harsh blue glare of the screen, his eyes wide and watery. He then shook and bowed his head.

Clayton returned a piercing stare and shook his own head in a mix of disappointment and disbelief. "Go back to your station! I could have asked my ancilla 'Tappy' for as much as you gave me. Can't you think for yourself?"

The junior rooter remained mum. He quickly turned heel and slunk off back to his station. Other rooters tried their best not to take notice, poking at their terminals with all appearances of productivity.

Zack also showed little recognition of the interaction. When Clayton had turned back, Zack made no comment. He only continued to stare blankly at the main telescreen.

"They're gone, Zack," Clayton began after quietly muttering to himself. "These incompetent fools cannot seem to clean their own dirty ass without asking an AI agent how, let alone find the *one* group of weeds we have had our sights on since Kansas."

Zack shot a glance over to his partner. He had an ugly sneer to his face and something he had not seen before in the long years of service together—worry. He offered a few collegial pats on Clayton's back and was about to offer some words of encouragement when...

"Rootmaster..." said a soft voice from behind them.

"What is it now..." whipped Clayton.

A different junior rooter now stood behind Zack. She had a shaved head and a set of wooden piercings that extended from the bridge of her nose to its tip. Each piercing took on the appearance of a coiled root.

"This one looks like it's for you, Zachary," remarked Clayton before turning back without acknowledging the woman directly.

Zack turned and gave the woman a smile out of curtesy. "Yes, what do have for me?"

Straightening her posture, the woman replied, "Rootmaster, I wanted to report that we have identified a few onlookers at the old Army post in Kansas. I have instituted a routine rooting with two-hundred cycles of a peaceful gathering of fireworks enthusiasts to be deployed to them during their next VR session on the provisionary network. I even added a nice memory of going for ice cream afterwards, chocolate sea-salt caramel, to which I also have seeded in their entire close social network for reinforcement."

"Nice touch. I see you are using all three pillars of rooting, *digging*, *replanting*, and *fertilizing*."

The junior rooter nodded as if nothing was out of the ordinary and routine.

"And for those who saw the…uh…incident this afternoon…" Zack asked, hesitantly.

"Ah, yes, a ten-year-old boy and a 75-year-old woman.

"The boy was easy; we created a social networking event with his neighborhood friends within an hour of the incident on the network. We had them play a long game of space-soccer. We ensured that each friend attested to the subject that they had been playing the game the *entire afternoon.*

Zack nodded encouragingly.

"The elderly lady, on the other hand…we still have to do a few more cycles of rooting here on-site before she will be able to return home."

"Nice…And good work! Make sure to assign a few dozen of our tireless AI agents to sift through the network to see if there are any others that need rooting in regards to these incidents," Zack instructed and then dismissed the junior rooter.

Zack and Clayton were then standing shoulder-to-shoulder once more, alone in the center of the room. Zack glanced over at Clayton who, frowning, seemed to have taken a keen interest on a telescreen that had been set to show the crossing of the border between Ohio and West Virginia.

Noticing that Zack had returned his attention to the screens, Clayton could not help but to blurt out, "We flippin' had them, Zack. Right within our vines. Now we have no idea where they are, where they are going, or what they are intending to do to disrupt Unity.

"And after what was unfortunately done publicly to the one who split off from their group, I am not sure we will have many leads to go on," replied Zack behind a thinly veiled tone of partnership.

"Don't think I should have taken that blue jewel from him? I did not quite like the way he was looking at me. An eye-for-an-eye, eh?"

Zack made no response. He only stared ahead with his mind now adrift in thought.

"Well...he definitely had a different look to him once I used my root snare device to scoop out that blue gem from its socket," stated Clayton continuing the conversation for himself. "Anyways...what do we have on our blue-eyed tree sucker? Well, I guess one-eyed now." He chuckled, mildly amused with himself.

Zack bit the bottom of his lip and stood silently.

"All right, all right, I know you do not approve. But, seriously...these suckers seem to be up to something big and threatening. It even has the people in New Eden concerned...and they never show concern for any threat we've encountered before.

"So, tell me what we know about this guy..."

"Not much," Zack replied plainly before pausing to order his scattered thoughts that all seemed to be fraying at their ends in unison.

Zack started again, "What we know is that the man has no identification, no markings besides a simple tattoo, and he appears in none of the databases. None of them! If that does not sound strange to you then it should. It is almost an impossibility for anyone living today or even in last fifty years to have no digital footprint.

"What we do have are some public still frames of him. He certainly appears well-traveled, like some nomad, because in the last thirty years we have him captured in what was Jordan, Turkey, Italy, India, Syria, Iran, Iraq, Saudi Arabia, Morocco, Palestine, Egypt, the United Kingdom, the United States, a cruise to Antarctica..."

A right eyebrow raised on Clayton's face as he turned closer towards Zack.

"Weirder still, is that the facial recognition agent did not need to make any adjustments for facial drift. He has appeared as he does now—albeit with both eyes. Which means that across several decades, his physical appearance has seemingly been unchanging."

"I'd like to know what stuff he's taking; I am already starting to get wrinkles around my eyes," replied Clayton rubbing his temple aggressively. Their conversation was immediately interrupted by cacophony of sounds filling the room.

Blip-Blip-Blip!

Blip-Blip-Blip!

Blip-Blip-Blip!

"What the hell is it now?" cried Clayton spinning around on the back of his boots which let out a harmonious pair of squeaks on the marble floor.

"Rootmaster, we are receiving a transmission from…" said a nameless rooter from the back of the room.

Clayton began tapping his foot. "Well, spit it out!"

"…it's from New Eden! It's Lord Throx, Phosos's personal emissary!"

"Ah…Put'em through without delay then."

The large floor-to-ceiling telescreen suddenly flickered away from an empty stone courtyard to an interior chamber lit only by a trio of cold-hued lights. Towering in the center of the screen was Lord Throx, a HOP who was only differentiated from his steely azure-eyed brethren by the amethyst color of his eyes matching those of the Lord of Provision himself. It was a rare occasion that Throx spoke with anyone. He typically was only seen during world telecasts to all in Unity to pass down new proclamations. When he did speak, he spoke with the mouth and authority of Phosos.

The wall-spanning visage of Throx was an intimidating sight to behold. Clayton stood paralyzed. A ripple of anxiety had shot through him as he continued to tap the front of his right boot nervously.

Zack continued to stay silent knowing that any missteps made before Lord Throx were often dealt with severely; at least, so he had heard. He had no intention of witnessing a rebuke first-hand.

As he stared at the screen attentively, he began to notice that there was something odd about the feed. A spherical light anomaly seemed to hover above Throx's left shoulder. *A visual artifact perhaps*, he thought. His eyes continued to focus on the object and then back to Throx's stern face.

"Rootmaster Clayton of The Americas. This comes from Phosos direct," Lord Throx began firmly. "He commands that the prisoner be transported without delay to New Eden, alive and not to be further *blemished*." The last word came out with a hiss as Lord Throx leaned towards the screen until his eyes appeared as twin purple balls of fire. For a moment, everyone in the room feared that he might actually come through it and throttle Clayton in his boots.

"Understood. We will prepare his departure as soon as possible," replied Clayton, mustering what strength he could in the tense moment.

"And…Phosos implores you to accompany the prisoner personally," Throx added. An uncharacteristic pleasure almost seemed to linger on the HOP's lips.

Clayton's face instantly slackened as if it had been injected with a general numbing agent.

"Do you comply?" asked Throx who was determined for an affirmation, and now growing impatient.

"Yes, of course, Lord Throx. My partner and I will—"

"NO! Rootmaster Zack will remain to continue pursuing the untamed growth that has grown seemingly unchecked in our community there. I repeat, do you comply?"

Clayton nodded, holding out his wrist and tapping his Unity Mark with four fingers of his other hand. "I will do as stated, for root and branch."

Throx pulled back from the screen, resetting his posture back to where it had started. "For Unity and Provision. We await your timely arrival," he replied almost mechanically.

"By Unity we are strong, by Provision we thrive," replied Clayton.

The screen then flickered back to the empty courtyard.

"How did he know that we captured someone so quickly?" Clayton exclaimed as soon as the live feed had broken away.

"Information travels faster in this age," replied Zack with a shrug.

"We do not have much time to snag some leads and I fear if we do not track these weeds down quickly, we will all find ourselves in New Eden sooner than we would like."

The pair nodded.

Then, Clayton tapped his Unity mark decisively, "I think it's time to have another little chat with our blue-eye friend."

) | (

The corridors housing detainees were dimly lit. Dozens of darkened rooms seemed to float by Zack and Clayton as they walked through a long empty hall. Hushed auras from the rooting within each root cell shone out the viewing windows in staggered beams of dull bluish-white light. With each opportunity, Zack's eyes darted into the cells as they passed. Some were empty, others were only softly illuminated by monitor screens. He realized that he rarely saw this underside of rooting as a field agent. In the dull glow of these rooms, he knew their unmoving occupants were enduring VR rooting sessions which typically lasted a few days to weeks. Yet, for those undergoing the recoupment process, countless virtual cycles made the experience seem like months to years depending on the severity of their disunity. Growing pains, they called them.

When they came to the end of the long corridor, they came to a T-junction. Without a look otherwise, Clayton hastily veered to the left.

The new passage sloped downward several stories. Zack could feel the air growing cooler and damper with each step of their descent. *This could only be the Harrow Wing,* he thought, rubbing his thumb into his palm. Eventually, the path leveled out and transitioned from grey concrete to a rust-colored pea gravel. The stones crunched loudly beneath their boot steps. The Harrow Wing was darker than from where they had just come. It also had a dank smell of stagnant water mixed with an earthy smell. As they walked on, Zack noticed that they were passing over dark grated portholes which led down to other cells or some other unknown depths of the complex. All he knew of the Harow Wing was that only the most disunified candidates who were unfit for rooting were sent down here. The Harrow was a place for those waiting eventual pruning. It also served as the abode for those who were deemed deformed growths on the Tree of Unity. These "burls" would be cast to such places for an indefinite period exile to sit and ponder in the dark.

After what seemed like a kilometer of walking, Clayton stopped in front of a sturdy steel door. He checked the bronze number near the latch and consulted briefly with Tappy that they were at the right place. The AI ancilla confirmed in his typical jovial tone. Clayton then proceeded to scan his Unity Tree mark which unlocked the door without delay.

The door creaked open, slowly revealing a dusty dirt-floored room. As the pair entered, a solitary light on the ceiling in the middle of the room hummed on. Reaching full brightness, light struggled to entirely lift the dark gloom.

A thick wall of stale air hit Zack squarely in the face almost as soon as he crossed the threshold. It had an earthy stench to it, pungent and slightly sour from long, unabated years of decay. When the light levels had risen enough, he saw that the room was larger than he had expected. It was perhaps four-by-four meters in length and width. Large enough of a space for any unlucky occupant sent to indwell there to constantly feel the unnerving emptiness in the pitch blackness. Zack was not surprised to find the mysterious man huddled naked in a corner where some semblance of structure could be found—even if it was rough stone walls covered in a sticky-looking brown mold.

At first, the mysterious man did not seem to notice the change in his conditions. He simply laid still as a mouse. He might have even been taken for dead if not for the soft rise-and-fall of his muddy rib cage. Zack observed the hair was still matted from the spurting of blood from when Clayton had taken his eye.

What a pitiful-looking creature. The thought seemed to hang aloft for a moment as some distant abstraction of thought in Zack's mind. That was at least until it seemed to fall back down unexpectedly as a growing lump in his throat. He realized, then-and-there that such a place could have been where his sweet Ava spent her last days. Alone, naked, and lying filthy in the dark.

The man finally lifted his head. A solitary blue orb flashed on in the darkened corner. Even in the dingy light, the man's single eye shimmered like a blue jewel, its facets capturing every ounce of light—and more. A strapped patch covered the hollow orbit where his right eye had been. White gauze speckled with crimson droplets protruded haphazardly from underneath the black eye covering.

Clayton began to approach him and immediately recoiled backwards.

"Ugh…it reeks of piss and blood over here!" he exclaimed kicking up dirt at the man. "Come out under the light so we can speak," Clayton demanded.

The blue-eyed man made no attempts to protest. He crawled slowly on his hands and knees along the floor to the center of the room. He then sat up with his legs crossed and covered his manhood with hands folded atop one another.

"See, much more compliant, now," Clayton directed to Zack with a smirk.

Zack brushed off the comment with his own retort, "Maybe it's best that I start the line of inquiry this time."

"Be my guest," Clayton replied without argument. He took a position leaning against the wall near the door.

Zack turned to face the man who had not taken his eye off of him since he had moved into position. Somehow the stare of a single eyeball felt more intense and concentrated than if the he still had both of his eyes.

A sense of vulnerability immediately overcame Zack. He shifted unnervingly in his stance, desperately trying not to avert his own gaze and show inferiority to a gaze that seemed to, with each passing second, be revealing his own nakedness in some way. A pinch of pain throbbed up from his hand where his big thumb had dug a little too deep into his palm. It was just enough distraction to regain some composure. *Time is short and there are many mysteries to solve*, he repeated in his mind. He dug the back of his heels into the dirt and cleared his throat.

"There are little to no records of you in our systems. So, my question is simple and I expect a straightforward answer, who are you?"

The blue-eyed man laughed without hesitation, clutching his chest as he leaned forward onto his crossed legs.

Zack shot a glance to his partner who only seemed to grit his teeth in disdain.

"I don't recall telling a joke," Zack pressed further.

Still chuckling, the man straightened his back. With little apparent effort he arrived to a place of complete calm.

"How does the water ask the rock, 'What are you?' when it is constantly in flux?" the man replied in earnest.

Neither rooter made a response. Their mouths hung agape and eyes were glazed from being unaccustomed to the enigmatic.

Noticing this puzzlement on both rooter's faces, the man continued.

"You struggle to identify *who you are*. How can you hope to define something else when you know nothing of your own state?"

"You are mistaken, stranger. I am a Rootmaster of the Americas. A person of Unity and Provision. I bear the Unity Tree mark of our Lord Provider, Phosos."

The blue-eyed man's lips curled into an expectant smile as if he had known before it had left Zack's lips what he would say.

The man replied, "Provision, you say? It is plain to see that your so-called Provision has made you weak in mind, body, and spirit—what a trifecta!

"You think somehow more is better, do you not? But you would be wrong. The right amount is the only amount that can sustain the human spirit. And having the right amount requires some level of deprivation. Your forebearers knew this. You must suffer in life to know the highest joys and to harken when you run astray.

"But your Provision is an anathema to life. Provision grants only excess. And when you are plump and full, it will dine on your decadence down to your rotten cores. And by then, it will be laid bare that any motivation or drive to the contrary will have died long ago."

The blue-eyed man then raised one of his arms to point directly at Zack. The point of his finger shook unsteadily in the open air, a mere half-meter from Zack's chest.

"Now I ask you, Rooter, why have you allied yourself with the Tree of Unity when you know in your heart not from where its roots drink?"

"I uh…" Zack paused to recall for some personal reason, but none seemed to come to him. He could only grasp at something that laid on the surface of his mind. So, he spit it out as quickly as he could after the delay that felt like minutes had passed.

"I joined because only with sturdy roots and sturdy branches are we unified in the Tree of Unity so that all can be provided for and all can flourish." The phrasing came out confidently, if not sounding slightly rehearsed from repetition.

The blue-eyed man let out a whooshing sigh through his nostrils. "Ah, even a weed like me growing on the outside knows those words come from a proclamation of Phosos. If you cannot articulate *why* you believe the things you do, they are not your own beliefs but someone else's."

Zack felt a rush of blood flushing into his cheeks. All he could do was stare blankly back at the man sitting before him. The man almost looked at ease sitting cross-legged on the dirt floor now. This was not how the encounter had played out in his mind walking down here. The whole conversation seemed to be twisting upside down on him. Not only was it unproductive, but it was irritating him, like a speck of sand that gets caught in your shoe. He needed to wrestle back control.

"Again, I ask, what is your name and who are you?" Zack said firmly.

The man did not hesitate to respond this time.

"I have been called many things across the many chapters of my life," the man replied thoughtfully. "To you, you can simply call me, 'Joe'."

"Don't get smart with me," said Zack clinching his fist.

"Shall I tap in and take swing at him," called Clayton from his perch on the wall.

"No, I can handle this," Zack answered, waving Clayton off. He turned back to the seated man. "We know his type, though they usually start to show more fear by now…are you not afraid of us?"

The man squinted at him, studied him for a few long moments and lightly shook his head.

"Fear you…no. You are nothing, merely vacuous vessels eager to be filled by anything to temper the emptiness inside you.

"What terrifies us is not the nothingness that you have embraced but, rather, what you have forgotten exists beyond the void. You know, the things that your ancestors always warned of, lurking in the penumbra of the forest's edge or out from the corner of your eye. These horrors were once your history but became legend, then myth to fantasy. Now these things that you scoff at in your protected bubbles made of your own hands have returned to whisper from new shadows. Thinking you are somehow superior or different from all those who came before you, these entities fill and lull your minds with all that you might desire. But truly, you are like slumbering flies in the web of a spider, immobilized by blissful euphoria with minds too clouded to awaken and see your own impending doom.

"Yes, you can ignore reality, but when the consequences of its existence eventually strike you square in your face, what will you say then?"

Zack did not venture to say a word. His eyes darted back-and-forth across the dirt floor at his feet trying to make sense of the man's seemingly-cryptic words. Clayton, however, made no effort to hide his thoughts on the matter. A roaring bout of laughter issued from him, slapping his thighs loudly in between quick breaths. Eventually he controlled himself enough to press the man.

"Where have you been, you weed? Or perhaps moss is a better descriptor, as it seems that you missed the past three years under a stone somewhere? Phosos has provided us our history. Every moment of it all in crystal clarity for all to observe. Yet, you stand here and speak of myths and legends."

The solitary blue eye did not blink or move. It only stared intently over to where Clayton stood. Under such focus, the laughter quickly died in Clayton's throat. He even began to shift his weight nervously until the blue-eyed man spoke again.

"Is that so?" he began, incredulously. "And who has corroborated Phosos's account? You all were so willing to accept the alien's testimony. Not because of its impeccable veracity or its breadth, but because you wanted to accept it. Because it meant freedom. The kind of freedom gained from rebellion of truth that is known deep within you. Done so you can then pursue all your earthly delights without fear of higher judgment or the rules formed in a murky past by those long dead and buried."

Clayton scoffed to himself quietly, again fumbling with the device in his front pocket.

Zack now gazed at the blue-eyed man with a slight indulgence of curiosity. He tilted his head and squinted his eyes to study the man. *How does he come about these strange beliefs*, he wondered.

Zack searched his thoughts for something to challenge the man. A point that would be so irrefutable that a concession could be the only possible response. The only things that seemed to bubble to the surface were the virtues of Unity. Which seemed unsurprising. The alien's appearance on Revelation Day had changed the course of the world. Unity had provided unshackled freedom for anyone, from any walk of life to pursue happiness. To not be subjugated to the shackles of the past that had been placed on people by governments, institutions, religions, and tyrants. With all basic needs met, Unity had, for the first time in history, finally allowed for the fullness of freedom and self-actualization. It truly was an Eden made real from myth.

After some more silent pondering, Zack finally posed what he thought was a bullet-proof query.

"Phosos has brought us provision, equality, justice, and unity across the earth. How can that be a bad thing?" said Zack. His question waffling between certainty and apprehension.

The man turned his eye from Clayton to Zack. It rolled in its socket like a tiny blue marble. It then blinked on and off in one long procession. For a moment, while the eye was shut, Zack almost thought the man had disappeared. The gaze had been that intense. When the lid opened again, the icy blue stare bored into him ever-the-more strongly.

The man sighed, "Evil gives voice and tolerates all points of view until it gains power. Once all opposition has been subdued, it is free to silence all that was good.

"Look around you. Look at me!"

The man shot up on his feet like a streak of lightening. He raised his hands to his face, revealing his squalid nakedness for all the rooters to see. He then grabbed the eye patch and threw it down at Zack's feet.

Zack hesitated to look up at the man, but knew he must. He could not risk showing timidness in front of Clayton. So, Zack raised his head and looked at the man in the face. His one blue eye looked like a wild maelstrom, swirling with fervor. Where his other eye should have been was an empty orbit. In its hollow space, red flesh still oozed out a milky-red liquid that began running down the side of the man's face in a viscous syrup. This all seemed to go unnoticed as he continued to speak.

"Remember all those who have been lost to establish this utopia. I will give you a seed of truth, if you will hear it. I hope that with more searching within yourselves that it might grow and uproot this tree of so-called unity that has borrowed so deep within your spirits.

"You have all been deceived. This *alien-being* you revere is not a being from up above, but one from down *below*."

Clayton opened his mouth to interject and a swift swivel of the man's eye was enough to kill the words on his lips.

Unnervingly, the blue-eyed man turned his eye back to Zack and continued. "Phosos is not an extraterrestrial he is interdimensional. He was never born and never lived. He was created like all his brethren when the first foundation stones of this world were laid. He is one of the watchers who were sent to earth to watch over mankind before he abandoned his charge. He was bound for a time, but now he has become free again to sway us all from the natural truth in his many guises. Phosos is a demon and he has taken all of you under his thrall!

"You are only a heartbeat away from all these truths when you will stare into the vastness of eternity. But, by then, it will be too late. For dead men tell no tales beyond the veil."

"Would you like us to make that heartbeat a bit shorter?" growled Clayton who had pulled out at his root snare device.

"For if you could, but this would not be my death. I do not go until the return," replied the blue-eyed man with total conviction.

"Don't be so sure of that," Clayton said as he began his approach towards the man. The man stood unflinching. "You have no—"

The cheerful voice of Tappy interjected. "Incoming priority messages. First from Rootling Sahara: 'We have got eyes on them. Tracking them now, on Route 50 headed due east towards Clarksburg, West Virginia.' Additional message from the front desk: 'A Hand of Provision has arrived to escort you and the prisoner.' Shall I direct them to your current location?"

With a deep breath, Clayton threw a hand through his hair to gather his thoughts. He then responded carefully to his ancilla in a strained voice.

"No Tappy, that will not be necessary. I will leave to meet them now. Have a team prep the prisoner for transfer. And have them clean him up."

Clayton turned to Zack.

"I don't think we should listen to any more to what this crazed blue-eyed weed has to say. He is clearly mad. I will say as much in my pre-briefing report."

Zack nodded and gave the man a cursory glance before departing. The man still stood naked in the middle of the dirt floor watching them leave, one-by-one. A crooked smile was plastered on his face as if he was almost pleased by his circumstances, or perhaps the circumstances of those he had hoped he could protect. Delayed as it were, the rooters had found them. It would not be long before all these weeds would be gathered together to be dealt with however was deemed necessary.

As the lights began to dim once more, the blue-eyed man called towards Zack in not a voice of desperation, but of warning.

"You see the most amazing things at the boundaries of light and dark. In the twilight, we see our part in the grand play of life, what will be the measure of your role—a two-bit part or something more?"

Zack made no response or change in his stride as the words died in the darkness. He exited the room and began the long walk back to the central chambers. He felt a new kind of heaviness of a mind that seemed no closer to any kind of truth.

5

Back to the Lab Again

The place she knew too well and the one she wished she could forget. The thought struck Aliyah as their vehicle rounded the final bend to reveal the desolate-looking college town of Talawanda Springs. It lay nestled in the gap of a folded mountain. It was one among many that ran north-to-south like gigantic green serpents slumbering side-by-side all across the greater Appalachian Plateau. On the other side of the gap, the nose of Sage Mountain rose gradually above the plain. It flattened to a ridgeline and was regally crowed by the red and brown brick buildings of Hightower University. Even from this distance, the ivory steeples of Old Main, the "shining beacons of the Allegheny's," still towered over the landscape. Though, in the dull overcast light, she thought they seemed more like grave markers for a town that had yet to learn of its own death. Like so many of the towns they had passed by during their journey east, Talawanda Springs could not escape the fate of becoming a backwater place—forgotten, deserted, and no longer needed in the Era of Provision.

The car rumbled along across the steel-grated bridge that spanned Lost Fork Creek. From here, the rippling teal waterway allowed for a unique vantage to the western face of Sage Mountain. Rows of tall, dark trees lined the ridgeline, which eventually jutted out to a sharp pointed tooth. A shiver instantly jolted down Aliyah's spine as her mind saw again what once trotted in those dark woods of the Old Woodlot near Devil's Leap. Even in the daylight, the woods loomed over the town with a foreboding presence, discouraging anyone from daring to venture up to their heights. She was relieved when the car, at last, bounced down the embankment, taking the mountainside out of view behind a bank of tall sycamore trees.

They took a gravel access road that ran through a marsh to stay off the main roads as long as necessary. They had been fortunate so far, encountering little traffic traveling on the roads off the interstate since leaving Cincinnati. Aliyah lowered the window to take in the fresh breeze. A forest of reeds and cattails swayed idly above the black tea-tinged waters taking little notice of their passage. More a bog than a marsh, the Sulphur Lick wetlands occupied the greater part of the western side of Talawanda Springs. During her time at the university there had been numerous cases of students being rescued from their drunken ventures into the muck. It was messy business that made for a good laugh when the details were regaled in the local newspaper. The dark waters were quieted now, without any trace of wildlife.

When they reached Main Street there was little sign of human life as well. The brick-laden street lay empty, with not even a stray cat scurrying down the alleyways between the once-quaint storefronts. The small-town grocery, whose bakery once filled the morning air with the scent of fresh bread and delectable pastries was now boarded up, a crooked sign reading "Permanently Closed" hanging in its lavish display window. The craft shop, whose shelves had been brimming with handmade wares and art supplies, sat dark and silent, its vibrant displays replaced by a layer of dust.

But it was the Days Gone By antique store that really tore at her heart. She had spent countless afternoons browsing its aisles, searching for relics of a past that now seemed impassably distant.

The sign above the wide double-oaken doors—its lettering made of old-timey trinkets—still hung in place. Yet directly beneath it, a new sign had been hastily installed in the main window. Cold-blue LED lights spelled out "Unity Connection."

She only had a moment to peer inside as they rumbled by, but it was enough time to see the store had been gutted. The only activity came from the blinking displays of rows-upon-rows of self-service kiosks, each filled with assorted VR equipment. "Your best connection to the Provisionary Network," the digital advertisements promised, as if mocking the warmth and history that had once stood in its place.

As the car reached a Y-intersection, Kamil called back from the driver's seat. "The hospital is to the right, if I recall correctly from the map, right?"

"You really do have a good sense of direction!" confirmed Aliyah from the back seat. She added, "Turning right will take us on Tower Road. That should run into Route 50 again where we will turn left."

Kamil nodded and turned at the junction.

The riders remained silent as more vacant buildings passed by without fanfare.

"Oh, what a pretty Lake! And look, there are people down there!" cried Petrona.

Everyone immediately looked out the right side of the vehicle. Spring Lake, shaped like a figure eight, lay at the bottom of an overgrown hillside. An arched stone bridge bisected the middle of it at its narrowest point. On top of the bridge, an elderly man and woman were holding hands. Each stood motionless staring down into the dark bubbling waters.

"I guess there is still some life in this town," remarked Petrona as the car passed Aliyah's old apartment building.

"Barely…" added Kamil.

"Let's just hope that any life that does remain here does not take too much notice of us," said Gabe cautiously, his eyes darting between the empty windows of the buildings.

The car pulled back onto Highway 50. Aliyah sunk back into her seat. They would reach the hospital soon. The horizon they had been chasing for days. And then, the merit of hours of planning would finally be revealed.

)　　|　　(

It was around twenty minutes later when they finally reached the university hospital parking lot around midday. A few vehicles were parked on electric charging pads in spaces marked off for staff near the main front entrance. The rest of the spaces were deserted. Built upon a raised embankment, the lot took on the appearance of a grey mesa above the rolling green knolls that led down south to Talawanda Springs. But even here, nothing could escape the presence of Sage Mountain's northerly reach. Its slopes a green mass of hundred-year-old trees, tall and untamed.

Kamil parked next to a staff space to avoid looking too conspicuous and as a means for a quick escape. The four each piled out of the vehicle glad to stretch their legs after a long ride. A minute, maybe two, had passed as they stood around the vehicle surveying the hospital building. Gabe abruptly pointed towards something up in the sky.

"Whoa, look at that!" He exclaimed.

Aliyah and the rest of the group followed his finger to a break in the clouds. High above them a round purple light hovered, silently. For almost a full minute it did not move. Its light only changed its intensity in slow rhythmic beats moving outward from its center like an undulating eyeball. More time passed watching them before it began to move slowly across the sky. After it had gone a short distance, it suddenly streaked northward at lightning speed.

"An ill omen," said Kamil with a hint of apprehension.

"Shooting star?" Petrona suggested.

"No," Gabe shook his head. "Meteors don't hover like that."

"An airplane then?" Petrona proposed further.

"Perhaps..." Aliyah began softly. "...though I doubt it." Her eyes remained fixed skyward where the strange light had been. "We best be quick about this," she concluded, distantly.

"Well...are we ready?" asked Gabe, letting out a deep breath which was followed by a brief period of silence.

Aliyah's eyes came back to the others who were now huddled around her near the back of the vehicle. She recalled the many planning sessions during their ride across country. Every detail, every contingency had been put to discussion until eventually a plan of plans had solidified.

"Aliyah..." Gabe said, giving her an urging nudge in the arm.

A delayed smile came to her face. "Yes, let's do this!"

Everyone nodded firmly in collective unison.

Petro was the first to action. She immediately opened up the back of the car to retrieve her tool bag. Half-open, Aliyah caught a glimpse of an assortment of cables and odd-looking cylindrical electronic devices. Almost as quickly as it had opened, the hatch door was closed and Petro was motioning Kamil to follow her quickly around the side of the building. Aliyah and Gabe watched on vigilantly as they walked off towards the back of the hospital. They reached an open metal breezeway about three-quarters of the way down the side of the building. It connected the main hospital to a smaller grey out-building which housed the solar energy storage cubes that powered the hospital campus.

Kamil took a position near the door leading out from the main building and gave Petro a positive hand signal. She quickly crouched down at the door of the out-building and worked on an access panel. After a series of careful hand movements, the door popped open and she slipped inside, out of view.

For the next few minutes, Aliyah could not take her eyes off the little grey building. It almost appeared frozen in time beneath an overcast sky and in breathless air. The only motion that could be gleaned came from Kamil who, every ten seconds or so, would glance back towards the small building to check on the unseen progress. He did not linger too long before turning his sharp, attentive eyes back into the interior of the hospital ready for any sign of approach.

It was during one of these periodic checks when something caused him to flinch back, abruptly. Not long later, a Petro-shaped blur darted from the out-building. Bag in hand, she took a place next to Kamil, rubbing her hand that now seemed slightly discolored in a spot around the back of her wrist. It was too far away to tell for sure. That was when Aliyah noticed an eerie orange glow spilling on the concrete walkway. The light grew and grew until flames appeared to lick out from within the threshold of the doorway. A thick rolling smoke billowed out underneath the awning of the breezeway. The little black tendrils of pirouetting smoke would soon be noticeable from the highway.

Aliyah looked at Gabe intently.

He nodded assuredly and they both took off running towards the hospital. Busting through the front double doors of the main lobby, they began to yell in unison.

"Fire! Fire!"

The sole receptionist had a look of shock flash on her face. She stood behind a large desk at the intersection of four corridors that seemed almost endless.

"Fire?" she said almost in disbelief. "Fire…fire where?"

"In the energy storage building," Gabe replied, pointing in its general direction through the wall.

Her jaw dropped. "By Unity!" she exclaimed in horror.

She fumbled at her terminal for a few frantic moments until she apparently tapped the right combination of buttons. A voice answered through an unseen speaker.

"This is Jim," said a male voice, sounding almost inconvenienced by the call.

"Jim! There's a fire in the energy shed! Northside!" the receptionist shouted.

"SHIT…RIGHT! Pull a Code Orange! I am headed there now!"

The voice crackled away and the receptionist returned to fumbling at her terminal screen.

Soon, a buzzing alarm blared from every direction. Orange lights began flashing in steady quick intervals throughout the corridors.

The receptionist finally had a moment to look back up at them.

"I just put in a Code Orange for a general evacuation of all patients and personnel. You two better get out into the parking lot. I am going to start helping get the patients."

Without a word more, she grabbed from a stack of tablets and began tapping until a list of names appeared. She left her desk, but before disappearing down one of the long hallways, she turned to thank them, and rushed away.

When she had vanished into one of the rooms. Aliyah quickly ducked behind the desk to grab another tablet from the stack. She quickly accessed the hospital's current patient roster and began scanning. Her eyes bounced up and down as each name came into focus.

"Silva…Silva," she said progressively scrolling down the screen.

"Silva…"

A frown came to her face. She had bottomed out the list.

"What's wrong?" asked Gabe, keeping an eye on each corridor for any other staff members that might spot them and escort them away prematurely.

"I can't find his name on the list?"

"Hmm…that's not helpful." Gabe replied.

Then, the terrible thought came to her, wrenching her stomach. The thought that perhaps Dr. Silva had been moved or, worse…died. Everything depended upon him. And, they had come so far only to be thwarted by bad timing.

"Wait…let me see that," Gabe implored.

Aliyah quickly handed him the tablet. He began to tap through a series of menus.

"Let's see…let's see…D…D…"

Aliyah moved to look over Gabe's shoulder.

"What are you looking for?" she asked, confused why he would run through the same list over again.

"I am looking for a ghost patient."

She returned a blank expression.

"When people want to conceal someone's true identity, they use false names."

"Where did you learn all of this?"

A red flush came to Gabe's cheeks. He glanced up at her.

"*The Ground Cried Out* detective series. I read them all from the lodge library, they came from Dr. Irving's personal collection," he said candidly, returning to the list.

"Ah, there he is! Doe, James. Room T343."

"Great job my love, you found him!" she said, giving him a big kiss on the cheek.

"Looks like we are going to the third floor."

They took a back stairway to reach the third floor. On their accent, several exasperated staff passed by them escorting confused patients in hospital gowns. The evacuation had begun in earnest.

"James Doe's" room was not too far from the stairway's landing. It was different than the room she had visited years before when Gabe had been admitted to this hospital for a hand injury. It was now smaller and unadorned of much furnishments. The only piece of note was a small touching photograph of Dr. Silva's wife waiting tirelessly at his bedside on a nightstand. The professor himself lay in the bed covered by a plain teal-blue hospital comforter. He looked largely the same as before. Though, in the intervening years, his black hair might have added additional strands of grey and his beard was a little longer and unkempt. His face bore little expression besides one of slightly parted lips, like a person searching for a thought caught perpetually on the tip of their tongue.

"We better make this fast," said Gabe from the room's entryway. "I am starting to see staff going into the rooms at the end of the hall."

Aliyah nodded and looked around the room for a means of transporting Dr. Silva. There was only the nightstand, a single chair, and the large hospital bed in which Dr. Silva laid. The bed was much too bulky to move out of the hospital with any speed.

Aliyah turned back to Gabe. "Can you see if you can find anything we can use to transport him in, like a stretcher or gurney?"

Gabe simply nodded and disappeared down the hall. For the next few minutes, she waited hoping he would return before some hospital staff member got to Silva's room first.

The time passed slowly. She could hear in the distance the scurrying of feet. Raised curt voices answered by disjointed voices of confusion. This continued on and on, each time getting progressively closer that she was beginning to be able to discern the words and phrases of the speech. Eventually, a staff member had approached close enough she could hear the entire conversation play out.

"Sir, there is a fire somewhere in the building. We need to evacuate immediately," said a female voice.

"Oh...okay. I was wondering what was with all the lights and sounds," replied a man in a frail voice.

Then, Aliyah heard a set of hurried footsteps coming down the hall in her direction. Even amidst the sirens, she heard them getting louder until they were almost at the door. She braced herself back up against the hospital bed, waiting for the person to finally pop into the room. She wondered what she could say...

It was Gabe who strolled into the room, to her relief.

"You, okay?" he asked, seeing that she was distressed.

"I am fine, thank you. Were you able to find anything?"

He rocked his head side-to-side slowly. "Well...I could not find a gurney or a stretcher, but I did find this..."

He went back outside the room and backed in a collapsable wheelchair with a bag hanging off the back of it.

Aliyah gave the chair a quick up and down glance. "That will have to do," she said sharply.

The pair then went next to Dr. Silva's bed and carefully began pulling off the tangle of sensors and wires that were monitoring his vitals. As they did so, the machine above his bed began sounding its own set of alarms in objection.

"No, don't grab that one," Aliyah said quickly as Gabe was about to reach for the thick IV line that ran into Dr. Silva's arm. "We need to keep him hydrated and nourished. Though I am not sure how long his nutrition bag will last…"

"No worries, I got you covered," Gabe replied cracking open the bag on the back of the wheelchair. Inside were four transparent liquid "Provision" bags. "I found them in the supply closet with the chair," he said grinning.

Aliyah smiled. "Okay, now let's get him into the chair."

She pulled back the sheets to the foot of the bed. Gabe wiggled his arms beneath Dr. Silva's broad shoulders and propped him up slightly.

He counted off. "Ready…one…two…three!"

With a heave they swung Dr. Silva down into the wheelchair with as much grace as a falling sack of potatoes. In his state, the professor showed no reaction and merely slouched forward in the seat.

"Don't forget the bladder bag…" Gabe called out as he tried to reposition the professor better in the chair.

She grabbed the pouch that was half-filled with an amber liquid and placed it gingerly on platform beneath the chair, careful to not tangle the catheter line around Dr. Silva's legs.

Once in the chair, they were ready to make their move. Gabe pushed Dr. Silva slowly out into the hall. Under Gabe's direction, they turned right retracing the path that he had gone in search of the supply closet. After passing a dozen rooms, they came to a T-junction and took a left into a central corridor. This middle passage contained a bank of four elevators. A doctor and two patients had just gone down one of the elevators as they arrived.

Aliyah pressed hard on the down button. They did not have to wait long before an elevator opened behind them. She slipped quickly into the car and held the door open against her forearm as Gabe slowly rolled the wheelchair backward over the gap between the floor and the elevator car. That is when they heard a loud voice calling out.

"Hey! You! What are you doing with that patient?"

Aliyah leaned out of the elevator to see a gaunt-looking man walking briskly towards them from the hall they had just left a few minutes prior. She snapped backwards and pressed the L-button for the lobby and then proceeded to rapidly tap the close door symbol. The doors lurched and began to close. When the screaming man had arrived outside the doors, they were only a hands-width apart from closure. It was enough space to see his name-badge before it fully closed. It read: "Dr. Mordechai."

)　　|　　(

The ride up from the hospital was electric. Everyone in the vehicle—except for Dr. Silva leaning unconscious against the window in the back—was still reeling from the events that had transpired at the hospital. Kamil was back at the wheel with Petro in the passenger's seat. Her hand was now wrapped in a cloth from the burn she sustained from the electrical fire in the out-building. Aliyah and Gabe sat in the middle captain's chairs, constantly looking back to check on Dr. Silva and to see if they were being pursued by anyone from the hospital. Their escape had been relatively easy once they reached the parking lot. There was a calamity of hospital staff and disgruntled patients all staring helplessly at the out-building that became engulfed in flames. They had finished loading Dr. Silva in the car when the fire department had arrived. By then, no one took any notice of their clandestine departure.

"Hugenberg Hall, right?" asked Kamil as he slowed in front of a large boot-shaped building.

"Yes!" Aliyah replied, pressing against the side window as she scanned the area around the building. Not seeing anyone in sight she turned back to Kamil. "Great job! And without even consulting the map."

Kamil chuckled. "All I need is to see the lay of the land once and I'll get you there. Where should I park?"

"Hmm…" She considered all the options carefully. "Why not pull through the grass around to the back entrance out of sight."

Kamil pressed on the accelerator and steered the vehicle into the curb. It jostled upwards and then fell back down onto the grass. The car moved slowly, bumping across the uneven lawn, back around the side of the brick building. After avoiding a few trees along the edge of the Old Woodlot, Kamil put the car in park next to a pathway that extended from the woods into the rear of the hall. The limbs of the old oak trees hung lifelessly above their heads as they got out of the vehicle. Their branches still barren from a late spring.

It took all four of them to carefully lift Dr. Silva and place him in the wheelchair. They then walked in silent procession behind the—for all appearances—slumbering professor being wheeled up the ramp into the academic building. Inside, their footsteps echoed down the long corridor towards a large open atrium near the front of the building. Shadows seemed to dance in the rays of afternoon light that were presently casting down from the large glass ceiling of the atrium. It was eerily empty and equally quiet. The only sounds were of their feet squeaking on the tiled floor.

Before reaching the open atrium space, the group turned into a bank of elevators and took one that was readily available to the fifth floor. The hallway on the fifth floor was completely dark except for the natural light filtering in through the windows at either end of the hall. Aliyah was the first to step forward and take the lead. As soon as she did, a light overhead begrudgingly hummed on.

"Almost forgot about these lights," she said trying to hide her startled reaction.

The group steadily made their way down the dim corridor, each step triggering a new light that chased away shadows that had squatted for so long in the unused space. Aliyah came to a stop in front of a tall wooden door that did not appear to have any form of identification besides a tiny bronze placard that read: "Laboratory – 522." Beneath the sign was a touch keypad.

"Hope this still works," she said as she tapped on the keypad next to the door and held her breath.

Errrrrrrt!

A smile of relief rushed to her face and she pushed in on the heavy door. It creaked open allowing the group to pile inside one-by-one with Dr. Silva in tow. Kamil came in last and shut the door behind him while re-engaging its lock.

Inside, the lab was gloomy but not dark. Several large clerestory windows positioned at the top of the northwestern wall near the exposed ceiling let in large angled beams of sunlight. A light precipitation of dust fell down in between the yellow rays like a muffled snowfall. Gabe pushed Dr. Silva next to a long black reclining couch and went over to a light panel. With a tap of a few buttons the lab became bathed in a warm glow of white light.

Aliyah took a few steps forward into the center of the large space to take stock at the lab she had not seen in several years.

I am back, she thought to herself, glad to see not much had been changed or moved. A long floor-to-ceiling wooden cabinet ran across the back wall near the doorway to the back offices. Its cabinet doors were made of glass that showed off all the iterative prototypes that the lab had produced across the years of rigorous study—early oversized goggles…outdated processing chips…connection sockets. Short wooden tables flanked along the walls on either side of the room. Each were illuminated by long light fixtures suspended down on thin wires from the ceiling. The tables were covered by dust blankets but bore the irregular bumps and ridges of the various tools and electrical components that likely remained unorganized underneath.

Importantly, all the Mindsai equipment was still its rightful place, though now, like the tables, had been hastily covered by dust blankets. A centimeter thick accumulation of greyish-brown dust covered the blankets. She realized that the machines must have been much too large to move without an extensive effort which would have seemed senseless after Revelation Day. This all worked to their advantage.

The largest machine was in the very center of the room near the studded black chaise recliner. Aliyah walked over and gave the dust cover a big stiff tug. An avalanche of dust immediately spilled onto the floor cascading into a thick brown cloud.

Kaff…kaff…kaff.

She waved her hand back-and-forth, coughing uncontrollably.

When the particulates had finally settled, a black machine towered over the room, standing a good half meter above everyone's heads. It stood on a circular pedestal with the top part shaped like a large cylinder resting on its side. It was covered in an assortment of dials, indicator lights, and numerous ports which were filled with thick coiled cables and tubing that snaked outward to other unseen regions of the laboratory.

"Is that…" started Petro.

"Yes, that's The Mindsai Machine," Aliyah finished for her.

Everyone in the room stopped as if they had been instantly enraptured by the majesty of the one-of-a-kind apparatus. The machine was a construct of carbon fiber with a spiraling tunnel of obsidian-colored graphene coils that appeared to twist back into infinity in the upper cylinder of the machine. A single, plain ribbed black leather chair was positioned in the center of the machine's eye. On the back of the chair, a black rubberized mannequin head was attached at the top. On its face were a pair of goggles and a black cap. The cap was filled with tiny metallic pins that sank into the rubber skull.

"What's with all these holes? I take it that these are not intentional," said Kamil who had approached the machine and was currently tracing one of the half-dozen bottle cap-sized punctures that marred the surface of the machine.

Aliyah shook her head. "No, they are not…" She gave a long look at Gabe who returned a knowing glance before continuing to access the Mindsai's main terminal.

"Those would be made from an orbitoclast, authored by a former graduate student of this lab."

"Craig also co-authored this on my hand," added Gabe who took a moment to show the group a similarly-size scar on the front and back of his hand.

"What's an orbito…?" asked Kamil.

"It's a glorified ice pick, really. They were used in frontal lobotomies a long time ago." Aliyah began motioning with her hands and face as if gripping two objects firmly. "You would take the pick and a metal hammer and tap it behind the eye until it entered into the cranial cavity destroying the frontal—"

"Okay, that's enough," Petro interjected.

"You are right, it was such a barbaric practice. Just like the use of psychotropic drugs were at the turn of the millennium. But then again, maybe future versions of us will think the same way of our own practices."

Aliyah continued, "How Craig got one, no one knows. Possessed by some demonic entity he said was named ZoZo, he started hammering away at that machine before Gabe and I interrupted him. He then proceeded to try and kill us before he made his end down by the Sulphur Pool at the bottom of the mountain over there."

Aliyah stretched a hand towards the walls where the clerestory windows were letting in the late afternoon sunlight. A growing discomfort seemed to come over Kamil and Petrona.

"He damaged the machine but, I think it will still operate for what we intend to do," Gabe added, trying to cast an optimistic tint over the room.

"You think so?" Aliyah responded hopefully.

"I'll know for sure in a few minutes." Gabe then proceeded over to the bag hanging on the back of Dr. Silva's wheelchair and pulled out the processing chip and the extra pair of SEER goggles. The headset looked nearly identical to the one resting on the back of the chair. He laid the goggles at the head of recliner and went to the side of the Mindsai Machine. Through an access panel, he cautiously slid the processing chip into the machine. After an affirming *CLICK*, he closed the panel and returned to the main terminal. He clicked a few buttons and finally raised his head to look around the room.

"Here goes nothing!" he exclaimed, nervously sucking in a deep breath. He pressed his finger firmly on the terminal.

A sudden chorus of lights popped on and off in a rhythmic orchestration across the outside paneling of the Mindsai. The indicators were quickly followed by a rising hum that carried a low, resonant frequency vibrating through the floor and everyone's chests.

Gabe looked down at his screen. "I think we're good to go!"

Everyone cheered in great relief but quickly sprung back into action. Gabe continued to work at the main terminal to reconfigure the machine to operate with a bridging between a user and observer. Kamil assisted Petro to carefully lay Dr. Silva on the recliner and place a pair of SEER goggles snuggly on his head. Lastly, Aliyah took her place in the leather chair in front of the Mindsai. The wheels clanked lightly over the edges of the tiles covering the floor. Their wheels carved out tiny valleys as they rolled through the thick mounds of dust. She looked up at the pair of SEER goggles at the ready above her head.

"How are things looking," Aliyah directed to Gabe after everyone looked to be in their place.

Gabe responded, "Things are looking good for the integration of the second processing chip and the bridging of both pairs of SEER goggles. I am getting some strange baseline readings from Dr. Silva but that could be due to his condition."

Aliyah nodded in acknowledgement. She looked over to where Dr. Silva laid motionless on the recliner. His eyes, ears, and head were completely obscured by the goggles. The only part of his face she could see was his mouth that now appeared to be closed together firmly, almost tightly clenched. She almost thought he looked to be bracing for something when Petro interrupted her thought with a question.

"Remind me how this is supposed to work exactly?" she said, admiring the intricate net of wires and cables that twisted together from the professor's cap and lead back to a large port in the base of the machine.

"Of course, Petro. We still have time, don't we Gabe?"

"Yep, the cooling tanks are still spinning up, but we will be ready shortly."

Aliyah turned in the chair back to Petro.

"The SEER goggles you are examining there, act like a highly sophisticated EEG electrode cap, except the cap here contains over a thousand needle-like probes that rest on the scalp of the user. They serve the purpose of receiving and stimulating brain activity. A kind of portal into a user's mind's eye—hence the name. They work bi-directionally with the main unit that contains the unique quantum processor to help target specific memories and then reconstitute them for a user utilizing their own mental faculties creating a nearly indistinguishable experience from actually living the memories first-hand."

Petrona cast a look of acknowledgement.

Aliyah continued, "What we are attempting to do now is use Dr. Silva as the primary host and gateway to the reservoir of ancestral memory. His mind will act as the repository while mine will serve as a sort of navigator or querier. That's why we have two sets of SEER goggles so that we may bridge the connection between our two minds."

"Has anyone ever done this before?"

Alyiah shook her head stiffly.

"No, no one has. Dr. Silva is the only one we know who has ever even attempted to look back into the memories of his ancestors. Beyond that we do not have a clue as to what to expect."

When she finished, Aliyah paused for several moments. A certain reality had finally caught up to her.

"So, I guess this will be my first time using this thing. And it's never been used in this way before."

"You sure you don't want someone else to do it?" Kamil asked, with a troubled expression.

"I am sure. It has to be me, hasn't it? That's what Joe said," Aliyah responded, frankly.

"Joe could have been mistaken…" Gabe suggested. His eyes met her own and darted away, knowing the truth of the matter.

"We all could be," added Kamil.

"Thank you all for your concern. I have to have faith that I'll be fine." She paused briefly. "Just do it before I have too much time to think about it further."

"All right then," replied Gabe hovering over a flashing "Engage Mindsai" prompt on his tablet. "Are you ready?"

Aliyah pulled the SEER googles from the mannequin head above her and carefully brought them to rest on her own. As her vision became obscured by the googles, she felt the countless tiny probes settling neatly into a full array on her scalp. Like mini pin-pricks, they sent out a tingling pulse across her head indicating the sheer potential energy that rested at their tips.

"Carry on!" Aliyah said finally under a heavy breath.

"Initiating now." Gabe said with an edge of concern in his voice that Aliyah had not noticed until now, in complete darkness. She did not see Gabe press the button but heard and felt the machine slowly lurch into action. A whirling electric hum emerged from what sounded to be deep within its innards. There was also a slight vibration that she felt in her feet planted on the floor. She clinched her hands hard around the cushioned armrest bracing for some initial sign that the machine was working.

But there was nothing.

Again, this time she closed her eyes to disconnect herself from the outer world. The here and now, waiting for the past to arrive.

Still…nothing.

What am I forgetting? she thought.

The image of a bullseye she had hit in gym class as a high school student briefly appeared in her mind in vivid color. Almost as if a photograph had been slid into the headset.

Then, she remembered it. She needed some sort of target memory to activate the machine.

She had not forgotten it. In her mind, she repeated what Joe had asked her to remember, the trailhead.

Palmyra.

40 A.D.

Vinegar merchant.

Atem of Elephantine.

Within a few fleeting moments, the humming of the machine intensified to a higher pitch. The sounds were quickly followed by a pulsing wave of tingling sensors making her feel as if she had fallen into a sea of pins and needles. The sensation did not last long before all her senses suddenly fell away into a sensory-depriving void.

But it did not last. Suddenly, the void broke into a frenzied search through a jumbled set of seemingly disconnected images that flashed in quick succession. Her mind raced from scene to scene of what could only be moments in Dr. Silva's life. An image of his laboratory on the day of its completion…a campfire in the woods with a beautiful woman looking at him lovingly through orange flames…standing in a large auditorium accepting some award…in a high chair being fed by what she somehow knew was his mother…

The images appeared long enough for her to only register a glimpse before the next one seamlessly took its place. It all continued until the rolling images began to lose their pace. She felt instinctively that the machine had zeroed in on the targeted memory.

As the images slowed from their rapid presentation, they began to lose their clarity and intensity. One-after-one the images of scenes progressively began to dim until they were too faint to make out. Yet, before they had disappeared, she thought she saw a dark figure at the corner of her vision, watching with her.

Before she could make sense of any of it, her mind took on an unseen weight. The heaviness was immense and pulled her down until she felt as if she was falling. Deep into some unseen hole. She fell and fell but never hit any surface. Instead, she felt her mind steadily compressing as if her entire essence was being squished inside a tennis ball.

I am going to be utterly crushed, she thought. The pressure was becoming unbearable. Worse than the worst migraine she had ever had. Yet, the immense pressure was endured. And, at an indeterminate length, the pressure eventually subsided altogether. She was only left with darkness, and her own thoughts of when, where, and who she might be...

THE THIRD DISPENSATION

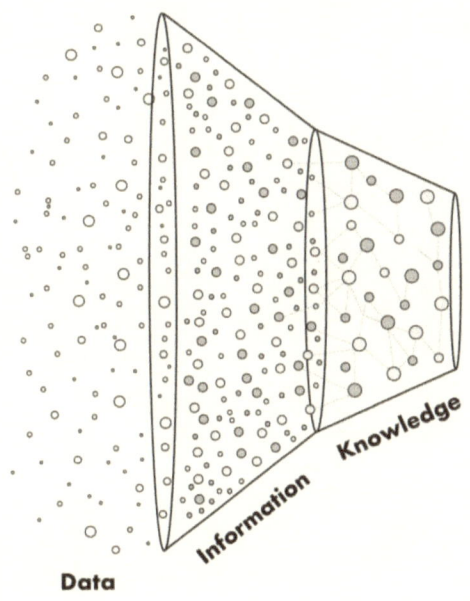

Data
Information
Knowledge

As insights begin to connect and patterns surface, knowledge of "what is" crystallizes. But even as understanding of the world grows, the important questions—of purpose and utility—remain stubbornly elusive.

6

Bridges Over the Lethe

Aliyah found herself alone, deprived of all her senses, in a vast darkness. The parade of images had long since faded, leaving her waiting for the semblance of anything to manifest itself from the void. Yet, she remained acutely aware of the peculiar sensation of being utterly alone in thought. It was not just darkness—it was the absence of even the afterglow of light in her mind's eye. And so, it was for the rest of her senses: not a whiff of earth, not a whisper of air, not even the faintest hum of her pulse. In this formless place, everything seemed to lose its meaning. Minutes, hours, days—time was impossible to count, with no cues or markers of change to track its passage. She was only left with her thoughts, which were growing more concerning with every new musing that crossed her mind.

What were the rest of the group doing out there?

Were they staying focused?

Would they leave me like this if this took too long?

How would I know if this is working?

How would I know if I am dead?

Could this be what it is like to be a living brain in a jar? This thought in particular sent shivers through her, at least on a conceptual level.

Then, there was something. It rippled through her mind like a sudden change in pressure. It felt so slight she could not pin it down what it was at first. She searched all of her senses for the signal.

There it was.

The ever so slightest of scents. A whiff of the outdoors—an earthiness like of the ground or dried mud.

Am I imagining this? Or is this actually happening? She could not decide.

It might all be how the machine was supposed to work.

Maybe I should have tested it solo on my own memories first.

Too late now.

Whatever was starting, it was growing in intensity. There were now new smells added to the earthy notes. Musty scents of sweat and dried grasses. Like…the smell of animals…yes. A leathery smell and…ugh…the foul odors of stale urine and dried excrement.

A farm? For that is the only place she could remember smelling such things.

The unpleasant smells began to fall into the background as others emerged in and out in bursts of aromas. Floral incenses of lavender, frankincense, and myrrh. A wall of wood smoke swept the florals away and, in its wake, left the pungency of unidentifiable cooked meats.

The next sensory input that emerged was the rising sense of movement. She was in motion with the sensation of air swiftly running through strands of her hair. In her mouth she felt a tireless tongue hitting against teeth that did not feel like her own for one was chipped and others let out a dull ache.

At last, the dark veil dematerialized into an image. At onset the image was dim, but it quickly resolved into a place of blurry motion. Before she could even register the scene, her mind was stricken with near-blinding light. Hues of beige and tan shone brightly underneath a relentless yellow sun. The ball of light hung aloft in the blue expanse of a cloudless sky, only marred by the pirouetting columns of grey smoke rising up from man-made constructions. When her mind finally caught up with the imagery, she saw it for what it was…it was a city, an ancient city of stone!

The memory finally crystalized into full-motion running. The subject—the person whose eyes Aliyah now looked through— was running across the streets laden with large beige stones of various rectangular shapes. They hopped and skipped intentionally avoiding the gaps in between the tightly hewn stonework.

Avoid the crack or break your mother's back, Aliyah recalled from her days walking home from school skipping down the sidewalk.

The feeling of being in the subject's body was immediately surreal. The perspective she had been accustomed to her entire life was shifted and naggingly off-putting. Her view now looked out from a shorter stature, not unlike that of a child. A flinging arm eventually came into view, confirming it. The arm was comparably tinier than her own, perhaps that of a child no more than ten. It had a lighter complexion than hers, a dark olive. Long and slender, the fingers had a feminine look to them with the index digit curiously longer than the rest by a few millimeters.

I am a young girl! she thought.

Aliyah also found that she had access to all of the subject's senses. She saw the bustling streets through their eyes. She felt the uneven stone beneath their footfalls. She smelled the wafting aromas of smoke in their nostrils and could taste the residue of something akin to bread in her mouth. The experience was better than any movie or immersive VR—both exhilarating and daunting. Every moment her mind struggled to keep pace with the cascading experiential inputs. She and the subject felt as one, as if she had become the other person entirely, truly in the girl's shoes—or what appeared to be crude sandals.

The subject suddenly hopped passed a large gap between two large white-hewn stones. At the end of the leap, the subject became off-balanced and toppled sideways. Aliyah saw a woman up ahead, carrying an earthen jar filled with water at her hip.

Aliyah flinched, instinctively telling herself to let gravity send her to the ground and avoid the impending collision. That was when she realized the true limitation of the Mindsai. The subject's body kept drifting sideways, ignoring all of Aliyah's frantic commands to stop. She could not move an arm or a leg, not even a twitch of the tiny little fingers. Here, she had no agency or control. She was powerless to watch the memory play out. Merely an incorporable passenger sharing an experience during a girl's life that started and ended thousands of years ago.

Somehow, the subject ducked under the jar at the very last instant, missing the woman's leg by a hair. The woman hardly noticed and continued on her steady march down the avenue. To avoid falling on her face from the maneuver, the subject braced a hand against the sunbaked stones. Aliyah could feel the warmth radiating up through her palms. In the next moment, the subject was back up on their feet. A few steps later they jolted once more to avoid two steaming mounds of dung that had been freshly laid by what looked like a wholly ox, larger than any breed of cattle Aliyah had ever seen. As the subject passed, they looked up at the large horns that curved outward. The ox turned its head absently, sweeping its horns over the heads of two men conversing vigorously over a piece of parchment.

Further down the street, the subject slowed to a leisurely stroll. Aliyah finally had the opportunity to process the landscape more fully. At this juncture, she was surrounded on either side of the avenue by rectangular buildings with two-story colonnades. Cut and hewn from sand-colored stone, the rounded columns formed sturdy first-floor porticos that extended out by several meters from the main part of the structures. In many spots, colorful fabrics were extended outward to cover street-level vending stalls selling all assortments of food and wares. Mirroring the ground level, the second stories had similar smoothed columns that allowed for covered balconies that led back into what looked like living quarters.

On one of these balconies, a woman in a mustard-colored robe with a sky-blue headscarf was currently beating out a crimson rug. The cloud of dust and debris gently fell to the street below like summer snow. It fell on anything in its aimless path, to the consternation of passersby; one of which, a man with a long dark beard, held up a clinched fist at the woman. She met the gesture with a sign of her own before disappearing into the building.

Everyone that Aliyah could see was dressed in a similar fashion. All the men sported beards and wore long, flowing tunics that were sometimes accented by an additional cloak that was draped in a way to support the right hand. The colorfully-dyed fabrics loosely covered every bit of skin besides faces and hands. Heads were wrapped in light-colored headwraps that draped over their shoulders and down their backs. All in service of thwarting the beating heat of the sun. Women were dressed in flowing robe-like dresses of more pastel colors over which a cloak was draped and held in place by a brooch near the shoulder. A long veil covered their heads and shoulders with many accessorizing with diadems and necklaces of precious metals that glimmered in the sun.

Looking down the avenue over the multitude of bobbing heads, it ran straight through a grand arch that bridged between the parallel lines of buildings. Beyond it, at the end of the thoroughfare, was a grove of palm trees that swayed gently in an unseen breeze. Further beyond the palm grove was a beige desert that stretched on-and-on until it reached the foot of a rusty mountain range in the distance.

The subject turned her head back towards the center of the city. Towering over everything was an elevated mound on which a large temple was built.

« *Mighty Temple of Bel.* » The thought popped into Aliyah's stream of consciousness. But it was not truly her own. She had no way of knowing anything of what she was seeing. No one had seen it for thousands of years. So, how could she know it?

The Mindsai must be translating some of the thoughts of the subject for me to understand. Or maybe the memory contains more than just sensory information, perhaps meaning is encoded as well, she concluded, though any true certainty was low in this unfamiliar domain.

It was true. The temple was mighty and massive. Like the Greek Parthenon, the temple's roof was several stories above the ground. It was held aloft by gigantic fluted columns that surrounded an inner chamber on all sides. A wide column of smoke rose idly from the temple's interior. Aliyah watched as two boys wearing long-sleeved tunics and trousers darted between the columns of the temple in chase of a lamb that was scurrying away for its life.

The subject shifted her focus back to the street, and Aliyah suddenly became aware of the surrounding cacophony of voices. They spoke in a language she did not recognize or fully grasp. Yet, amidst the noise, she realized fleeting moments of understanding. At times, comprehension came as vivid images in her mind's eye; at others, they manifested as brief words or phrases.

From the outer arched-gate, a caravan of camels started to make their way up the avenue towards the interior of the city. There must have been nearly two dozen of them, each laden by large woven baskets strapped upon their rug-covered backs. They were guided by an equal accompaniment of merchants who carried smaller open baskets filled with a sampling of silks, jade, spices, ebony, and ivory. One man with black bushy eyebrows that held up a red turban leaned in close to the subject to offer her what looked like some dried fruit. The subject waved a hand vigorously in his face. He grinned a toothy smile and went in search of the next potential customer.

The subject continued down the avenue until almost reaching the outer archway. She then took a hard right turn down a narrow alley between two buildings. The smells here were musty and dank. The alley eventually opened up behind the structures into a sandy courtyard that covered the setback area between the buildings and an outer perimeter wall made of stacked stones.

As the subject walked along this backside route, she came to an area where a rectangular ditch had been dug down eight meters deep. The subject gave a cursory glance down into the ditch as she passed. It was enough for Aliyah to see that the ditch contained a trough of water that had been carved into the bedrock. Turquoise spring water trickled through it from a square-like opening at either end of the ditch—one heading with the flow of water under the buildings into the city and the other heading out upstream into the deep desert. A procession of nearly a dozen steps fanned out downward into the bottom of the trench. They terminated onto a large stone platform where several young women were chatting and filling up jugs while a few others washed out a basket of garments.

Not long after passing the water trench, Aliyah noticed that the subject was heading towards the back of a particular building nearby. In this area the stone buildings had become more modest, one-story structures lacking any of the ornate carvings of desert animals as she had observed earlier. The same was true of this building, it had a square flat roof and no apparent window openings on its backside. The only discernible entrance into the structure was near ground-level where a doorway lay half-obscured by the ground. Above the entryway, a sunshade of stitched goat skins rolled in a light breeze coming off from the desert. The shade was supported by two wooden poles buried deep within two sand-filled clay jugs at either side of the walkway. A large symbol was carved into the right-most jug, but its meaning seemed to be just at the edge of Aliyah's mind. As the subject neared, she looked at the marked jug.

« *Vinegar.* »

Now, at the entrance, Aliyah saw that there were three stone steps that led down into a half-underground chamber made within the structure.

It was the smell of fermenting alcohol that hit her first, potent with a sharp, almost medicinal odor. This did not seem to faze the subject who slowly crept down the steps without making much noise. With each step, the light began to fade to a dimness of long shadows and banks of darkness. As the subject's eyes adjusted,

Aliyah began to see that the shop beneath the building was more like a carved-out cave than any sort of constructed structure.

The subject's feet reached the bottom floor, squishing in the windswept sand that had blown down the steps covering it. The air was cool and still. The whole space a shady refuge from the daily scorching of the sun above. The vapors of alcohol had condensed into a sour, fruity smell, mixed with the earthy dampness of a cave. The shop was lit only by the light coming in from the stairway and several oil lamps well-positioned in rough-hewn recesses in the walls. Shadows danced towards and away from each other in the lamplight amongst the lightly swaying strings of dried fruits that hung from the ceiling.

Aliyah could now hear bits of broken discourse emanating from somewhere towards the back of the shop. The subject had noticed too. She searched across the space for the source of conversation. She was too short to see over the many dozens of earthen jars—that she somehow knew contained various varieties of vinegar. The jars lined the floor and sat on crudely-built wooden tables, some of which were nearly as tall as the subject. As they moved through the rows of jars, Aliyah noticed that each was marked by a symbol carved into its upper shoulder section. The design or lettering was not any that she recognized.

Aliyah concentrated harder.

Names or images popped into her mind with each passing jar—« *grape…fig…pomegranate…date…palm…honey…* »

Aliyah could not tell if it was driven by some translator within the Mindsai machine, the subject's memory, or some combination there between. She was simply happy to have some form of comprehension—what little that may be.

The voices had grown louder until it seemed as though they were coming from just beyond a row of large water jugs that the subject had crouched beside. The subject stared between the ceramic jugs into the adjoining space at the very back of the shop. Two men stood facing one another. The one facing where the subject spied was an older man. Streaks of grey ran through his beard that hung at the midway point of his chest. He wore a plum-colored headscarf that wrapped around his shoulders and covered a brown tunic that almost dragged on the floor. His presently incredulous eyes were a golden brown and bracketed on his temples by long crow's feet. Around his neck, he wore a silver chain. In its clasp it held a curious elongated purple-tinged crystal.

« *Abba.* » The fatherly-connotation came into Aliyah's mind near-instantaneously. She then noticed the father had index fingers longer than the rest of his digits by nearly a centimeter, even longer than the subject's index by comparison.

The other man, however, had his back turned. Aliyah could not see his face. But judging from the jet-blackness of his hair and the firmness of his hands, he appeared to be a younger man. He wore a yellow headscarf covered in blue shapes that were not quite discernible in the low light. His tunic was of a tighter cut, grey, and cut off right below the knee revealing a pair of black dusty boots.

For a moment, the shadow of another man stood directly beside the younger man with his back turned. This third man was facing the subject, but Aliyah could not see his face, for it was obscured by a deep shadow. The subject took no notice of him, despite staring back at her in her line of sight.

And then, the third man disappeared.

Perhaps a glitch in the machine or an odd shadow from the conversing men was the only explanation Aliyah could devise. It did not matter, the men were talking, and she desired to listen.

The subject had caught them mid-conversation. The men were speaking with each other in vigorous volleys back-and-forth. Even not knowing the language it seemed to Aliyah that they were negotiating something. Again, she tried focusing her mind to understand the meaning of their words. And, just like before, bits of meaning and phrases began to emerge into her consciousness.

« *...my great ancestor told the Egyptians who told the Greeks. His name is lost to us. But it was passed down that my people were once of that place, before the cataclysm came to the Atlanteans. Flee to Egypt they did.* »

The merchant paused, fingering the crystal around his neck lightly. He spoke further.

« *There were wonders there, it has been told. But more precious than gold, was the knowledge held storehouses of scrolls and the gods who indwelt there. Mysteries and secrets of elder days it was said. Before even when waters covered the world.* »

The merchant's eyes drifted towards the rafters. « *Out of grasp it all is now…under sea, under sand…* »

The other man nodded his head in thanks before speaking in a velvety voice. « *You are my favorite Elephantine.* »

The merchant chuckled and placed both hands on his substantial midsection that was bulging beneath his tunic. « *You mean the only Elephantine in the city!* »

A strong thought pierced Aliyah's mind, originating from the subject. « *Why does he call abba an Elephantine? He is Palmyrene, like mother, all my life. Of tribe Komare.* »

A feeling of confusion settled into Aliyah. More thoughts emerged into her consciousness from the subject.

« *Abba told of Egypt…* »

« *A fertile land…* »

« *And great works that touched the sky…* »

An image then welled up within Aliyah. It was not the Egyptian pyramids of Giza that she had recognized since her own childhood but an imaginative amalgamation that only a child who had never ventured more than a half-day's walk outside the city walls could create. The image looked like the many Palmyrene buildings Aliyah had seen before except stacked on top of each other nearly twenty times over. It was amusing in its inaccuracies. Likely the culmination of countless retold stories told by the subject's father.

As the image faded, Aliyah noticed that the men had stopped talking. The subject had noticed too and began to crouch tightly against the jug to avoid being spotted as the patron walked by towards the front of the shop.

« *Be well, Cartaphilus!* » cried the merchant before the man had reached the stairs.

The man turned and slowly bowed.

« *Be well, Atem of Elephantine,* » the man replied.

When he rose, Aliyah caught only glimpse of his face, despite a halo of natural light pouring in from the stairwell behind him. Noticing where the subject hid, he gave her a knowing smile.

A strange familiarity was readily apparent for Aliyah. Before she could fully process it, she noticed…the man's eyes…those sapphire eyes!

My God, how can it be the man with sapphire eyes…Joe! she thought.

The revelation was lost on the subject. She turned as the man climbed the stairs back out into the city. Soon enough, a voice beaconed to her.

« *Tear away, Lulia.* » the merchant called.

The subject rose to her feet and stared at her father's shoes. He seemed to sigh and spoke again.

« *Come to me, my small sweet grape.* »

The subject obliged and entered into the back portion of the shop. Her father had taken a seat on a carved out stone bench in the back wall. Before him was a crudely-made wooden table that was covered in half-wound scrolls.

The subject approached the table, her eyes only barely clearing the top edge. The merchant was presently twisting a few oblong jars in a careful examination. A ledger lay stretched out on the table next to them, held down by two stones, a gold coin, and a small flickering clay oil lamp. Every few moments he would come back to the parchment and make a note with a sharpened piece of charcoal. The crystal bounced on his chest with every movement.

Aliyah suddenly felt a sensation swell in her hands as they began to clinch the edge of the table. A yearning of desire ached deep in her chest, as if everything was hollow and empty, which only could be filled by the object to be closer. An object that she sensed had always held a certain allure but now seemed to draw the subject's focus. A heaviness then set in over her mind as she felt as if she was leaning forward and that, at any moment, she would fall into one of the many facets of that purple gem.

« *TOUCH.* » The subject's thought blasted through Aliyah's mind, its echoes preventing her from regaining coherence.

The merchant seemed to notice the desire on his daughter's face and softly spoke a phrase.

« *Touch it you like?* »

The subject nodded her head up and down vigorously, without disengaging her fixed stare.

The man pulled the crystal over his head and gently laid it out on the table before the subject. For a few long moments, the subject's hands remained clinched into the table, her gaze unwavering. She traced the defined edges along the smooth facets of the crystal down to where they all met into a point of vertices.

Without warning, the subject reached out and grabbed the crystal and held it up in front of the lamp. The surface was smooth and cool between the subject's fingers. It also felt very hard and heavier than an object of a size that could fit in your hand. Oddly, no light seemed to pass through the crystal. The subject pushed it closer to the light. The lamp's flame seemed to slow in its erratic dance until it almost seemed to lean towards the gem. In the direct path of the lamp, the crystal seemed to gradually soak in its radiance and take on a soft glow of its own.

Aliyah noticed that the glow began to reveal the broad woodgrains of the table underneath. There was also a growing tingling of static energy emanating from the crystal.

With her index finger, the subject then began to trace over the crystal's side that faced most-directly towards the light. The etching in the stone was felt first before it appeared on the surface. The depressions of perfectly cut curved lines were smooth like the crystal's edges. When they came into view, the etching took on a silvery sheen in the firelight. It depicted a curved serpent with a horned face and two back hindlegs, some kind of wyrm curled around three concentric circles.

Ouroboros.

Aliyah remembered the term out of the fog of years; back in the days after Revelation Day when they were all still in the lab. Gabe had said it when he identified the shape of the trinket that hung around Craig's neck—a pyrite snake circling a jade tree eating its own tail. The antique trinket of unknown origin was the primary reason they suspected for Craig's murderous madness. The truth of it all—and the trinket itself—remained lost to the depths of Sulfur Pool. Aliyah did her best to push those murky thoughts from her mind and focus.

Unhalted, the subject moved her finger to tap the etching. And then—

A flash of light.

Aliyah suddenly found herself looking through a different pair of eyes. She was walking on beautiful white stones. A hand held a tall wooden walking staff. The fingers were clinched around a bulge at the top. The index finger was much longer than the rest!

And just as quickly it had come, the images were gone.

The subject dropped the crystal back onto the table, where it struck with a sound reminiscent of a tuning fork. As the resonance gradually diminished, the faint murmur of a distant city's hum faced into silence. The pulsing phosphorescence of the crystal also slowed, eventually dimming in tandem.

« *Careful you may* » the merchant said as he scooped up the crystal in his hand and placed it back around his neck. His face unable to fully mask a sense of surprise.

« *Go to mother and see to food* »

The subject nodded without a peep. Then, turned and ran towards the sun-soaked stairwell. A wrenching sense of fear and wonder tapped at her heart.

As the subject's face hit the sunlight, the pressure began to grow again in Aliyah's mind. It did not seem possible, but the force was even greater than before. She knew she was going further back as the pain intensified rapidly. It radiated around her disembodied temples like a metal band constricting inwardly. The pressure soon worked to warp everything she saw. The light began to scatter, then tightened into a narrow tunnel. It was then she felt herself falling down into the unfathomed deeps of another layer of memory.

Whoosh!

The sound demarcated the loss of any sensory contact with the world. The desert city, the fumes of vinegar, the girl…they were all gone. Lost again to an unrecalled history. Where shifting sands bury and the length of generations devour all that had been.

Images appeared. Hundreds, maybe thousands of them in quick succession. All of them hands. In all various colors, shapes, sizes, and stages of age. Some were blemished. Some were adorned by jewelry of precious metals and stones. Others were missing whole or partial digits. It went on and on, a menagerie of appendages.

Until it all stopped and fixed on a single hand. A man's hand. One gripping a staff. A hand with an index finger elongated a full nail's length longer than the rest.

All went black.

) | (

Aliyah smelled it before she heard it, *sea water*. It was first thing she sensed as she arrived into another body, in another time, at another place. Before she could even see from the new perspective, she felt it. No longer full of the vitality of the youthful little girl, this person felt far older. It was a body of aches and pains, fatigued by long hours of movement. Walking it seemed. She felt the sore footfalls with each step on the firm ground.

TAP! TAP!

The sound came in equal intervals. A cadence that fit between footsteps. Then, a hand materialized out of the darkness, an index finger longer than the rest by more than a yellowed fingernail's length. The hand gripped loosely upon a carved wooden staff covered in hieroglyphic markings of beetles, birds, and other symbols Aliyah did not recognize. The staff's top curled in like a bulbous question mark while its bottom tip hitting the ground was clad in a bronze-hued metal. It clanged against pearly-white cobble stones that were snuggly arranged in good order.

The vision eventually cleared and widened to its fullest. Aliyah could now see the subject was walking at the end of a stone bridge that crossed some type of rounded canal. The waters shimmered in the pinks and oranges of an evening light. A multitude of stone and wooden buildings surrounded her on either side of the canal.

Atlantis! Aliyah cried in her mind.

Reaching the other side of the bridge, the subject began walking down a boulevard lined by solitary columns on either side of the road. Each towered several stories above and were capped with glimmering golden animals some of which were familiar to Aliyah—swooping sea eagles, sturdy oxen, and magnificent rearing stallions. The subject passed another, however, that looked to be a strange amalgamation of creatures with leathery wings and long-toothed beaks, not unlike some flying pterodactyl. They passed by dinosaurs too; one that looked like a triceratops, another armored like an ankylosaurus. They stood on the pedestals alongside cattle and the other domesticated animals as if they all were commonplace features of the world.

Aliyah marveled at the trapezoidal structures all around. A true feast for the eyes. The stonework was well-laid, almost seamless with flourishes of gold, silver, and other yellow-hued metals accenting the flat-topped roofs and spires. The stone itself looked like a type of soapstone, a mixture of stormy greys, greens, and muted blues. Veined patterns coursed through the stone and climbed up the slanted walls creating the appearance of a perpetually-hanging ocean spray splashed against the buildings' sides. Compared to Palmyra, the buildings in this place seemed more advanced. The shapes were intricate, the carvings ornately-complex. The structures separated themselves from the natural world as distinct constructed pieces of hewn metal, crystal, and stone.

The quality seems to be improving, thought Aliyah. For it was a curious notion that civilizations would get more advanced, not more primitive, the further back she traveled down the course of generations. *Could the workings of a people really be lost for so long?*

Aliyah's wonder of the Atlantean city was stunted sharply by a tinge of disappointment she felt emanating from the subject. It felt of expectations that had fallen short or a tall tale finally pressed for truth.

But, how? Look at it all! Aliyah wondered.

Now, growing bigger with every step, was the largest structure she could see in the city—a sort of capitol building or temple, perhaps serving both. The structure stood on a square platform raised from the land by nearly two stories in height. A long colonnade of stone columns held up the platform. Above the platform the structure broke into three separate hexagonal-shaped terraces that led back into the building by even more columns.

It all culminated into a massive dome that rested upon the top-most, central part of the building. A half-sphere in shape, the dome had the appearance of being crystalline either constructed of actual blue topaz or some form of glasswork. Facets had been pieced or shaped into the dome giving it an array of interconnected triangles that twisted and bent the long yellow rays of evening light.

Out in a plaza before the Atlantean capitol were two circular reflection pools. They were positioned on either side of a long, slanted stone stairway that bisected the building and led directly up to an arched entrance at its highest tier. The pool on the leftmost side was a clear light blue and lay still as a sheet of ice. The pool on the rightmost side was turquoise and had wafts of steam rising over turbulent waters. Both were fed by an unseen source.

It was then that Aliyah took notice of a dark grey mound that appeared piled up against the leftward pool. It immediately struck her as being out of place amongst the fruit trees and shrubbery that lined the walkways leading in and around the building.

Then, suddenly, the mound began to move!

The mound rose up slowly from the marbled plaza until it was propped up by four thick feet. As the subject grew nearer, Aliyah recognized that it was an elephant! And a massive one at that.

The creature began to lumber away from the pool down the boulevard. The animal was led by an attendant who looked like they could have walked straight out from a painted mural of some ancient tomb. The man was tall, like an Egyptian, with a light complexion containing hints of copper undertones. His head was shaved and possessed no other body hair except for a golden-blonde beard that had been bound to form a triangular shape protruding outwards about a hands-length beneath his chin. He was built of a sturdy stock, like some Greek ideal chiseled out of stone. Strong muscles flexed and contorted with each step of his massive legs. A single-pieced tunic wrapped around him with the two ends forming a split that revealed a bare shoulder, abdomen, and leg on one side. The robe was tied at a corner over the shoulder and bound by a sash around the waist. Dancing beasts of burden and reeds decorated the fabric in horizontal patterns around the fabric.

As the elephant plodded passed the subject, the subject seemed to give the beast little notice. Focusing out of the corner of the subject's vision Aliyah could see that the great elephant wore a thick netting that stretched around its stomach and over its back. A large basket was affixed to the saddle area. Inside, yellow-colored rocks were piled up nearly to the brim.

With the elephant behind him, the subject entered the great capitol plaza. Tiles of carefully-placed white marble with swirls of blue covered the space between the two pools. Separate sheets of blue marble led away from plaza to the foot of the great stairway of the capitol building complex.

The subject stopped next to the edge of the pool that had been on his left. He leaned on his staff looking around the plaza and up at the building that now loomed before him. Aliyah felt a sigh of relief within the man's aching body. The feeling of accomplishment, as if a long journey was about to reach its expected end. There was also a sense of anticipation as his eyes leisurely traced each and every one of the dozens of steps that rose up from the ground into the mouth of the building like a grey tongue that had long-desiccated in the seaside sun. There was a vague sense that the subject sought something contained within those massive walls.

Almost obscured by the shining dome of the building was a mountain range that cradled the cityscape. Far off snowy peaks were becoming amber-colored in the evening light. Strange large flying creatures circled their ridges, but were too far off for the man to clarify. Whatever they were, Aliyah felt the swift shot of trepidation fly to the subject's feet.

Aliyah concentrated her mind hard to get some insight into the subject's thoughts until something finally came through.

« *Many steps and I, so weary.* »

It was the first clear thought Aliyah could recognize from the subject. The others seemed to remain just out of reach beneath the surface of intelligibility where feeling and imagery rule.

The subject lent a glance over at the pool across the plaza. Its surface bubbled like liquid glass. Tendrils of white steam curled above the surface and were quickly scattered by an ocean breeze like the first cooling breath over a hot soup. The warm waters were sure sign of some form of vulcanism that underlay the area.

After a time, the subject turned his gaze to the nearby still pool. Aliyah suddenly became aware of the man's dried lips

« *Thirst!* » The thought came through on a strong signal.

The man leaned on his staff and dipped down to draw some water with his index-dominated hand. Falling beneath the surface the water tingled his hand and wrist with an icy embrace. He drew out a hand-cup of water and took in a large draught. The coolness tickled his throat as the waters rushed to his stomach.

In the rippling waves, beneath a khaki turban, an old man's face stared back at Aliyah with a calm and steady gaze. A pair of brown eyes, slightly clouded, peaked over a frayed white mustache and beard. Across his shriveled forehead and along sunken cheeks, laid deep etchings from years of walking against scouring sand-laden winds. A rust-colored robe was wrapped tightly against his thin frame. It was richly embroidered at the edges with glyphs similar to his staff. The man seemed to focus on these glyphs absently.

« *Burden weighs me. What fool priest am I adding another icon of mastery to this garb?* » Aliyah gathered from the subject with some effort.

The subject let out a deep sigh that tickled back the surface of the waters that had returned to a sheet of glass.

« *Great knowledge is currency to great powers. I must not fail the Kingdom of Netjerkare.* »

The subject pressed down firmly on his staff once more and pulled himself up from the pool. Audible clicks snapped from his ankles and knees as he reached his feet. He turned towards the building and marched on.

It was a long climb up the grand stairway. Aliyah yearned to see the cityscape from a new vantage but the subject's focus was fixed on each carefully placed foot placement along the steps. When the subject finally reached the top landing, Aliyah was disappointed by the mere passing glance the man made over his shoulder before walking into the interior. A blurred scene of sun, land, and water.

The subject entered a large rotunda-like room. Light filtered down from openings high upon the outer walls. But it was a massive oculus in the center of the ceiling that was the focal point. Big enough for a fully-inflated hot air balloon to fly through the carved stone opening projected a golden circle of light on the far wall leading further into the capitol. Beneath it, an equally-sized golden bowl hung by three massive silver chains. A black liquid dripped down through a carved trough in the oculus at steady intervals into the bowl. Each time the drop fell within, the red arm of a flame reached up to grab it. The light from the massive brazier would fill the room well after sunset.

The subject stopped beneath the golden brazier and looked at his feet.

At first Aliyah only noticed the marble and precious stones. However, eventually the shapes and patterns began to make sense.

It was a map! She thought.

Masses of land were depicted in raised dimpled stones which were surrounded by the smooth recessed oceans and seas of turquoise.

The subject was presently standing in what would be Antarctica represented by a milky quartz stone. Shaped like a thin smiley-face, the largely unexplored continent was a mere sliver of its true form.

The same was true for the hourglass-shaped landmass of green agate on the subject's left. At several points along the connecting land bridge were circular molds of gold representing some point of interest.

North and South America! Aliyah thought.

In the center of the map, where no foot looked like it dared to step, was their capitol city—Atlantis. Greatly enlarged, and certainly not to scale, the city was enshrined somewhere near the western shores of what could only be the African continent which was laid in a beautiful sandalwood. The city formed a thrice encircled eye in what would be in her time, the empty desert of the Western Sahara Desert.

The mosaic of the ancient metropolis was a breathtaking sight to behold. Aliyah could sense that even the subject could not deny his awe at the majesty of the sprawling civilization. The depiction showed an archipelago of four islands, arranged in perfect symmetry. Each island represented by concentric circles of alternating land and sea, emerald and sapphire. At the center of it all was a central circle, a small island representing the pulsing heart of the civilization. This piece was a ruby the size of a basketball. Atlantis lay in a large shallow bay of turquoise along a jade coastal plain of the African continent evoking the lushness of the land. A raised range of carnelian mountains cradled the city beyond the plain on nearly all sides. Only the glistening-blue river flowed out from that range, west to east across the continent to the eastern-most part of the Mediterranean.

The Nile? Aliyah marveled.

Tiny boats of mother-of-pearl, their sails etched in gold, glided along the waterways between the circles of the city. Many others remained docked at jasper wharfs all along the outer ring. Beyond the city's tranquil harbor, larger vessels ventured into the Atlantic expanse through a grand canal that dumped into the Atlantic Ocean. They seemed to sail pass aqua sea serpents on silver gales that drove them towards the Americas.

Along each island ring, little brass buildings dotted the landscape like golden trapezoidal goosebumps. On the outermost ring, tall silver pyramids stood like sentinels at each cardinal point. Rose quartz bridges arched elegantly over the interlaced blue channels of water, connecting the island rings like delicate strands of a jeweled solar system.

At the very center of the city, on the innermost island, lay the ruby heart. The white opal capitol building rose up from the map by several centimeters. Atop its roof, a giant blue topaz shimmered, casting its radiance like a beacon over the entire Atlantean world.

In front of the capitol, two pools were represented by round gems of lapis and amethyst. From these pools stretched a vast network of blue-veined channels, set within troughs of smooth white marble. Like veins in a living organism, the intricate irrigation system spread throughout the city and into the fertile mainland plains beyond, nourishing the land with life-giving water.

Aliyah could have studied the map for hours, but such time was not afforded. A middle-aged man approached the subject. He was dressed in a similar style as the others but his tunic was of a finer ornamentation. A deep topaz blue, the tunic's fabric was richer, the embroidery more deliberate. Golden thread traced three wavy lines at the collar and the cuffs—symbols reminiscent of the sea. He cocked his head slightly and gave a half-bow. Without uttering a word, he gestured the subject to follow him into a corridor further into the interior.

The corridor was longer than Aliyah had expected. There were no windows or skylights here. The only light was emitted by curious crystal lamps the size of cantaloupe. Each hung at even intervals on silver hooks along the ceiling. They illuminated the pathway in a steady soft magenta glow. They were curious fixtures because she could not detect any sign of a flickering flame—they merely radiated an almost phosphorescent kind of light.

At the end of the corridor, Aliyah watched as the subject arrived before a colossal pair of golden doors. On each, a symbol was encrusted in ivory. It bore the resemblance of three concentric circles with a horizontal line slashed through them. Inlayed in the center of the circles was a grapefruit-sized ruby. Holding up the circles was what looked like a shepherd's crook that split off into three spears—two lessor and one greater—pointing downward. Subdued beneath the points was a water motif of three parallel sets of zig-zagged lines.

The guide pushed a hand against the rightmost door. It groaned apprehensively, but moved slowly on unseen hinges. As it shifted inwards, a gust of warm damp air rushed out of a much larger chamber. The draft was quickly followed by the distant sound of rushing water.

The subject followed the guide inside.

Aliyah could not fathom the enormity of the space until the subject had stepped a few paces into another—grander—rotunda. It was expansive enough that she felt like a tiny bug beneath a looming magnifying glass. Above, at dizzying heights, the crystal dome that she had seen from afar bathed the circular room in an ethereal blue light. With the mosaic murals of fish, dolphins, and sea monsters covering the surrounding walls, it felt like being underwater without drowning.

Bigger crystals, like those in the passageway, hung from the ceiling like arrested drops of rain. The crystals that hung highest seemed to soak in and absorb the last remnants of daylight. Those that hung lower were already starting to emit their eerie light.

Six massive pillars, each broad enough to stretch the length of two full-grown men, held the prismatic dome aloft. Arranged in a perfect hexagon, the pillars matched the thousands of hexagonal-shaped ivory tiles that glistened at their feet. At the center of the formation, the inner sanctum, the preverbal heart of Atlantis, was another oculus. This one was carved in an alcove in the floor that dropped down into unseen depths from which it seemed the sound of water was emanating.

A golden cantilever extended out into the empty eye of the shaft. At end of the slab stood a stone pedestal. Resting on the pedestal was a semi-translucent gemstone roughly the size of a beach ball. Egg-shaped and amber in color, there was also some sort of dark mass inside that neither Aliyah nor the subject could make out. Aliyah could only sense that the subject thought it strange.

The subject was led across the large room around the outside of the pillars. As the subject rounded the last edge to the opposing side of the chamber from which he entered, a trio of crimson-robed performers began to play triangular crystalline wind instruments. Their sound, foreign to Aliyah, echoed throughout the rotunda like the sound of a distant storm. Somewhere within the notes, the sound of a screeching wail also could be heard, like a siren calling within the storm.

The fanfare ended as quickly as it began.

The subject now stood before an elevated dais in the shape of a crescent moon. Ten stools of ivory with emerald legs were placed on the dais, eight of which were filled by a gathered assembly of men dressed in tunics of gold, silver, and royal blues. On their heads, they each wore hexagonal caps of blue and around their necks hung gemstones of various colors and shapes.

One-by-one, the subject's eyes darted between the seated men. They sat silently with chins held high and hands folded across their laps.

Names popped into Aliyah's mind with each look.

« *Evaemon…Ampheres…Eumelus…Mneseus…* »

« *…Elasippus…Mestor…Azaes* »

How the subject knew their names, Aliyah could not tell. Perhaps from some context clue of how they were seated, she surmised.

The subject's eyes then fell on the man sitting on the center stool which was taller than the rest, denoting the seated man's status. He wore a magnificent robe of gold and topaz jewels. He looked to be older than the others. It could have been a play of the shifting light but he also had a subtle phosphorescent glow to his skin.

« *Atlas. King.* » The subject concluded firmly and clearly in Aliyah's mind.

Aliyah sensed the subject was not surprised by those who had assembled. By every indication, he seemed pleased.

Cocking his head a quarter turn, the subject bowed low before the gathered men. The seated men studied him over their triangular beards with steely eyes.

There was silence until the youngest-looking of the men rose from his seat at the far edge of the dais. He held up both arms in the direction of the subject and the ruler seated at the center. His words seemed slow and clear, but still in a foreign tongue. With earnest concentration, Aliyah was able to gain an impression of their meaning.

« *Welcome long traveler from the kingdom at Nile's end. You stand before Atlas, son of Cethimas, son of Javan, God-King of Atlantis, ruler of rulers, bearer of the Whispering Stone, master of water, binder of floods, the longevous man.* »

The herald dropped the arm pointing to the king. Turning his head forward, he shook the arm still pointed towards the subject.

« *What brought you here, long traveler?* »

The subject rose from his bow to face the council of Atlantean nobility. Words came out of the subject's mouth that felt like they had been rehearsed countless times.

« *Noble king, I come at your mercy to drink from your waters of knowledge for my pharaoh seeks greater mysteries to raise his kingdom and shine half to yours.* »

The subject paused to study the faces upon the dais. Aliyah felt a yearning of hope that the flattery had some positive impact. Yet, the impact seemed inconclusive, and so he continued.

« *Long has it been told of great wonders at the head of the Nile. It is told, the king who sits there is a god beyond measure worthy of worship. It is told; his life is measured in the multiple lives of lessor men. It is told, the knowledge he keeps is beyond all libraries in all kingdoms. Tales reach Memphis of all this. My pharaoh bids me come to the source of these waters, so that I may learn the wonders that the king may reveal.* »

As soon as the subject's voice faded into the background of rushing waters, the council's many eyes flickered towards one another. The air thickened with unspoken words. Some leaned to their right, others leaned to their left, some even bounced back-and-forth. Lips moved behind the veil of beards; their whispers barely more audible than the bubbling of a spring.

The king remained perfectly still; hands clasped firmly in his lap. His eyes remained calmly fixed on the subject. A stare that seemed like it could reach back to the other end of the Nile.

After some time, one of the council members on the righthand side of the dais—perhaps Mestor, Aliyah could not recall—leaned forward in his stool and began to speak.

« *Wonders? Wonders are in the stone you walk upon and the stones stacked everywhere you see. But...I see no satisfaction in your face. You seek our reservoir of knowledge for which we are the source. Waters which are poison to lessor men.* »

Another man on the opposite side of the dais added further.

« *It is told in our lands; those who wield the tides hold the keys to life and death. We ride the crest of the wave to rule where others drown. We feed tribute to the waters to keep them ever at bay, and protect our great city beyond compare.* »

Aliyah could not help but notice the obsession with water—control, mastery, remaining on top. It seemed like some kind of flood cult, born from some collective traumatic memory. But there was no time to make sense of the strange sayings and beliefs, for the king, the oldest among them had stood up from his stool. The others on the council quickly retracted to their seats. A hush fell across the room. Only the distant roaring of waters broke the silence.

« *I am Atlas, eldest of ten, ruler of rulers. Have you not seen my mighty works that have tamed the terrible waters into despair? Timeless they shall be for all to bow and wonder.* »

The subject nodded without a sense of a word to reply.

Aliyah wanted to cry out, scream. *Nothing of your great city will survive; no writing, no markings, not even a stone. Atlantis will be forgotten to time as but a mere myth. Its impermanence cries out but echoes do not herald back into the past.*

Atlas continued, encouraged by the submitting nod.

« *The world drowned once in a deluge. I know, for I was born when the lands were still wet and young-growing. Yet, before water covered the earth, there was a greater era, an age golden, of peoples greater than even our mightiest triumphs. Mysteries beyond wonder. I have glimpsed only a fragment of what was. It was enough to raise this great city and stretch my hand across the waters and place them into my storing pots.* »

The king let out a heavy sigh.

« *Even now, I watch through my long spinning years as generations of men grow weaker. The strength of my stock is depleting. The glow of that age golden is fading.*

« *The stories, the knowledge, long is it passed. Lost they are to water and mud.* »

The king's eyes looked past the subject to somewhere behind him.

« *I bear the Whispering Stone. Found in the rock of these lands in my first journey from my father's house. Pótis-eidos resides in the stone, the true father of Atlantis. Long has Pótis-eidos shown me pictures into the age golden, for he knows many things. Arts of crystal, ships, and light learned. Speak to him if you will, I grant you any wonders that he may provide.*

« *Speak to the Whispering Stone.* »

*Pótis-eidos… Pótis-eidos…*Aliyah concentrated her thoughts on the name. The words rang with familiarity… *Pótis-eidos… Pótis-eidos…Posei-don…Posei-don! Did he mean Poseidon?*

With a motion of a king's hand, a flurry of activity began in the chamber. Attendants rushed into motion as council members still murmured amongst themselves, many with sneers cut into their faces that they did not bother to conceal.

It was not too long before Aliyah saw a door open next to the dais. From it, a young woman—not much older than the Palmyrene subject—stepped out into the chamber. The subject quickly took notice as well, for she was beautiful. Small diamonds shimmered like stars in a net of jewels on an inky cascade of wavy hair. The black strands framed a delicate, soft face with rosy cheeks, crimson lips, and eyes shadowed by an iridescent blue. She shuffled slowly towards the subject, almost gliding across the floor. In her hands she carried an ornately carved silver bowl. As she drew within earshot, Aliyah noticed that an object rested in the bowl on a bed of sea sponges. It was an elongated purple crystal clasped in a silver chain, what would be in many generations to come…the vinegar merchant's gemstone!

When the woman stopped in front of the subject and held up the bowl for him to grab the necklace within, the subject paused. Aliyah could feel a wide smile on the subject's face. He regarded the young woman with intense desire as he looked beyond the bowl to the firm pair of mounds that pushed out on her tunic at her chest. A strange surge of warmth flowed to an area between the subject's legs. There was a subtle tightening with building pressure that was growing more intense with each passing moment. Aliyah grew concerned that something was about to burst from the subject's loins. Then, suddenly, images flooded through Aliyah's mind…a late-night knock at the subject's evening chamber door…the young maid walks in with her tunic loose and flowing…the tunic falls to a stone floor…the subject's long index finger caressing down her shoulder, further down to over her supple breasts…

Too much! Aliyah screamed in her mind.

The images disappeared. The young woman stood smiling shyly, shaking the bowl for the subject to remove what was within.

The subject bowed his head slightly and grabbed the necklace and placed it over his neck. The crystal hung dark and cold against his tunic.

The woman then beckoned him to follow her to the center of the room. When they arrived to the oculus she spoke softly and pointed to the end of the golden platform that jutted into the empty space.

« *Stand by stone,* » she conveyed.

The subject walked out onto the platform, watching each sandal step carefully in front of the other. He looked down to see that the hole dropped away a half-dozen meters before a torrent of waters swirled together from two opposing passages. A mist hung over the maelstrom where the waters met. A steady eye of water maintained itself as the whirlpool emptied down further into an unseen reservoir deeper below the chamber.

The subject lifted back his head to see that he had reached the stone pedestal. Sitting snuggly in the grasp of a silver-pronged setting was the egg-shaped amber stone sized larger than a beach ball. Perfectly-cut, the amber gem was semi-translucent and at this proximity, revealed the dark form lying inside.

Encased within the stone, a serpentine wyrm lay frozen in time. Its sinuous body coiled with primal menace. Twisting horns jutted from its narrow head, framing a fearsome maw lined with jagged teeth, large and menacing, like those of an ancient dinosaur. Scales, rough and dark as obsidian, covered its sleek form, shimmering beneath the amber's warm, golden glow. Its back was lined with sharp, spiked ridges, running from the base of its skull to the tip of its long, whip-like tail. A pair of muscular legs with talon-tipped claws jutted out from its body towards its rear-ending tail. Its dead, red eyes remained opened but still suggested that it could spring to life at any moment, as if it were not dead, but merely caught in an eternal slumber from some lost world.

« *Pótis-eidos.* » Thought the subject. Followed by the feeling of awe.

« *Poseidon.* » Thought Aliyah. A disquiet of some looming dark presence clouded her mind.

When the subject turned around a guard in a beautiful topaz tunic stood facing him. In his hand he held a drawn bronze dagger about fifty centimeters in length. Down the center of the blade was a beveled-groove that protruded from an ornamental blue hilt decorated in gold stars and crescent moons. At the pommel, a spherical blood-red crystal was affixed.

Aliyah felt the subject's heart jump as he quickly feared for his life.

The guard's eyes shifted sideways to allay the subject's fears and then looked down at the creature that stood at the height of the guard's knees. A short grey trunk tried to pull at the golden cord around the guard's waist.

What are they going to do with the elephant calf? Aliyah thought alarmingly.

By comparison, the subject's thoughts had calmed. After a sigh of relief. He looked towards the dais for instruction.

« *Place hand on stone, long traveler! A sacrifice made, so you see what was known!* » Atlas cried, now standing from his seat on the dais.

Taking a cue from the king, the guard brought the dagger swiftly down into the baby elephant's neck. The thick and rugged grey hide easily split open like wet leather.

A guttural sound reverberated deep within the elephant's trunk as it attempted to sway its head free. Then there was a piercing horn blast that filled the highest corners of the room. The guard braced his legs against the anguished animal to keep it from thrashing free. The subject and Aliyah watched helplessly as its lifeblood poured down to join the waters in a purple swirling drain. The elephant's blasts eventually turned to throaty rumbles, then to only faint growls before its legs went limp and it slumped forward onto the golden plank.

The young woman who had been waiting patiently by the oculus stepped forward to gather the still-spurting red flow into the silver bowl.

She handed it to the subject with great care. The red blood still warm and frothy.

« *Drink!* » The woman urged.

The woman then stepped back and crossed her hands on her chest and began to chant in a rhythmic high voice. The others in assembly began to join the chant until Aliyah could not make out much else.

The subject raised the bowl to his lips and closed his eyes. Aliyah felt as the warm soup of metallic flavors poured down the subject's throat. A viscous coating remained on the tongue long after it had all been swallowed.

When the subjects re-opened his eyes, there was a shadowy man with a blurred face standing next to the woman and the guard. Again, a feeling of familiarity ran through Aliyah's minds as if there was a face known to her within the undulating blur.

The subject did not seem to see the figure at all; he only stared at the dais. Then, the entire assembly cried out in command.

« *Touch!* »

The subject turned and placed his weary hand firm against the stone. It was oddly warm, radiating with some type of energy.

The chanting seemed to intensify. A dizziness was coming upon the subject. A sense of worry grew ever-prominent that he might fall into the watery pit.

He looked down at his chest and saw the gemstone had begun to glow, on…then off, on…then off, like a slow-beating heart. Aliyah then felt a malevolent force that had slithered into the subject's mind.

« *BEHOLD!* » The dark entity cried.

Next, a series of images flashed by…

Great stone cities...

Towers touching the sky…

Glowing crystals…

Ethereal artistry…

Floating metallics…

And lastly, before the subject passed out into blackness, there was an image of a strong man standing in a dank-looking cave. The man's skin was bronze with an aura of light glowing from the skin even in the dark space. He had a mane of black hair that mingled with a thick black beard that framed a face lined with tenacity and experience. The man's eyes were sharp, penetrating, glinting with an intelligence and discernment of someone who has witnessed great things. He was clad in a rudimentary tunic and had a unique red circle-shaped birthmark on the back of his right hand.

There was also a name that popped into Aliyah's mind as the imaged faded.

« *Ur.* »

The next memory the subject was awoken by the bouncing of a wagon. He looked to the sun to see the caravan was heading east. He looked over the sides of the wagon, back to the west. All he could see were seas of sand as far as the eye could see. There was no trace of the ancient city.

« *Back to Memphis, with what might only be a dream.* » He thought and feel back onto the dusty blankets.

Whoosh!

The Mindsai seemed to have locked in on the next targeted memory without even Aliyah being certain of what it might be.

Ur, the brawny-looking man, she thought. *That must be it.*

A sudden cascade of images followed.

Stone circles.

Lush river valleys.

This time, she would be going back further...much further. She felt an overwhelming heaviness pulling her down. More images.

Sandy deserts.

Mountain steppes.

The pressure was growing. Deeper and deeper, she was diving an uncountable number of fathoms beneath a sea of memory.

Then, for a brief moment, an image lingered looking out from a wooden window at an endless dark sea beneath a curtain of stars. There was an eerie stillness in the air as there were no natural sounds save for the distant lapping of waves. Staring out into the calm waters, she felt an overwhelming sense of peace and safety.

The moment was only fleeting before she felt like she was about to be crushed through the neck of a bottle. And then, there was the sweet release of nothingness while she waited to see the next lost world.

7

The Throes of the Uprooted

Thick grey clouds clung to the sky like matted clumps of lint. Sunlight had withered to a faint afterthought. The grim faces gathered on the front steps seemed just another part of the bleak landscape, their empty reports spoken with apprehension, a confirmation of what no one wanted to hear. He almost felt sorry for the junior rooters who had waited for who-knows-how-long for his arrival.

Zack had arrived to the Pittsburgh Tap Root station alone. His partner, Clayton was is in New Eden by this time. Escorting the strange man with sapphire eyes to be served his fate from Phosos himself.

"At the boundaries of light and dark…what will be the measure of your role—a two-bit part or something more?"

The prisoner's words still clung to him, rising up from that dank cell and following him across three states. They haunted every quiet moment of thought, waiting to prod away any hope of repose. The only solution was to keep his mind busy on the mission at hand so not to venture into hushed reflections. And the mission remained clear. He had to find the rest of this weeder group and to send them all on their way to New Eden. Then he could rest, at last.

A host of junior rooters had assembled in two parallel staggered lines outside the entrance. Their faces were young and taut with effort. Their eyes conveyed a glassy absence of one who has undergone the same motions through thousands of repetitions. In one collective voice, they greeted Zack with a loud and punchy, "For Unity and Provision!"

"By Unity." Zack said simply, not going through the lengths of the full customary response.

As he entered into the building, one of the junior rooters broke off from the group and became glued to Zack's hip. The junior rooter offered what updates they could.

"So, there has been no sign of them?" he asked, incredulously.

"We tracked them to where they crossed into the Monongahela Forest in West Virginia. We've got eyes on every road leading out," the young man replied, his tone firm, though a hint of deflection stained his words.

"I guess roots really don't have eyes. Somehow, we seemed to have lost a vehicle driving on highways…interstate highways."

"It's quite possible that they ventured off onto some back country roads. Our archival maps seem to show a lot of old logging roads that are not integrated into our monitoring systems."

"Of course they're not, how convenient," sighed Zack. He stopped in the foyer of the front entrance looking vainly for a directory. The other junior rooters who had greeted him had begun to file in and slip down the corridors trying their best to avoid eye contact. The junior rooter next to him watched the others slip away with an envious look in his eyes.

"We have a comfortable lounge I can put you up in until we have further updates," the young man said encouragingly.

"No," Zack replied curtly, shaking his head. "Take me to your monitoring center. I want to be plugged in at the moment you all find something."

The junior rooter nodded with a long blink of his eyes. "This way, then."

He was led through a twist of corridors and up three floors into a large room that buzzed with the hum of invisible energy. Dozens of telescreens lined the walls and monitoring stations throughout the rectangular space. More than two dozen rooters were at work. Some were staring at telescreens; others wore VR headsets for more detailed farseeing of complex locations near towns and major road interchanges. For those whose faces were not obscured by VR goggles, their eyes glowed with the reflection of the visual feeds. Their fingers tapping absently on touchpads before them as they flipped through a carousel of locales—small empty towns, barren stretches of highway, and verdant trees as far as the eye could see.

His escort offered him a seat on a sofa in the back of the room and then took a seat at one of the monitoring stations. Zack's butt sank deep into the plush sofa cushion more than he expected. The softness enveloped him so much that he knew it would take considerable effort to pull himself back up again.

Too comfortable; enough to lull me to sleep, he thought to himself, watching the kaleidoscope of images shifting all in front of him. But there were no signs, no leads, no vehicle. Just empty roads and towns.

Even the surveilling eye of the provisionary network had its blind spots it seemed. He dared not speak the truth into existence out loud.

He sat slumped in the seat watching the world flash around him for an indeterminate length of time. His thoughts slowly began to wander, as they always seemed to do at times like these. The world around him became distant as other places and times seemed to superimpose themselves all at once. That is when he heard her familiar voice, calm and whispering, from some far-off evening. It was like Ava was sitting right next to him on their living room couch.

"Faith is opening your eyes and ears to the invisible things all around us."

He felt an urge to respond, to say that he had tried. He had waited for a sign through the long years. But no message ever seemed to reach his ears; no transcendent epiphany ever reached his eyes.

He shook his head as if to cast off the memory like cold wet drops of rain onto the floor.

He retracted back like a rubber band to the proximal setting. His eyes bounced around the room feeling embarrassed, but everyone's attention remained fixed on their screens. No one had taken any notice.

He returned inward, perturbed that it seemed that Ava's voice had also taken residence in his haunted mind. Two specters now lurking to intrude in his quiet moments of solitude. They were a niggling reminder that, in his mind, the past is never far. Years, decades could pass by and yet, at any unguarded moment it all could come back in a flash and touch him. Like a weight lifted from some submerged balloon waiting to burst through the surface of consciousness. And in its wake would come the memories and terrors that he had hoped would forever stay in the murky depths—out of awareness and out of recollection.

It was while musing upon these repressed shadows, that Zack took notice of a particular bank of telescreens in a far corner. Most showed people in small rooms undergoing a deep rooting—nothing unusual besides a little lack of adherence to panel access protocols. However, there was one person, who looked like they had been there much longer than what is typical for such sessions. He was a late middle-aged man lying in a hospital-like bed. His arms looked shriveled and weak from lack of use.

Zack turned his head to the rooter who had been his escort.

"Hey…you…" He started snapping his fingers, blanking on the man's name.

The rooter seemed to notice just the same and responded.

"Alex…what can I do for you?"

"Yes, Alex! Who is on that monitor?"

"Which?"

Zack made an attempt to get to his feet but the first attempt failed. He fell back into the cushion with a squishing sound. On a second attempt, he used a rocking motion of his upper body to escape to his feet. He walked over to the telescreen of interest and pointed emphatically.

"There! Who is that there?"

"Oh, that's Rube."

"Rube?"

"Reuben Shackleton, he was a robotics engineer. He's been here since I started."

"And when was that?" Zack inquired.

"About two years ago…"

An inkling of curiosity stirred in him.

"Can I see him?" replied Zack.

"Sure, you're the boss."

"I need to do something while I wait for news; I tend to fidget."

Alex did not offer a response but his eyes seemed to betray a disparaging thought.

The pair left the room of screens behind them and were back in the labyrinth of corridors. They took an elevator down to the first subbasement. Like the Tap Root in Cincinnati, this one had a similar arrangement of rooms with individuals undergoing deep rooting. This time Zack did not care to peek into the viewing windows of the doors to see the faceless patrons laying there, receiving their re-education. He simply stared straight into the back of Alex strolling a head.

They at last came to the end of the hall to a nondescript room that looked like the rest. Alex held up his mark to the side of the door and it clicked open. They both walked in.

Reuben Shackleton laid still in the middle of the room. A set of VR goggles were affixed to his head. Electrical wires, tubes filled with liquids, all entered into his body at some unseen junction beneath the sterile white sheet that clung to him like a second skin. His hands rested atop the sheet. Bony and delicate they looked like a husk of skin loosely holding a sack of bones. Muscles once strong and capable had withered to nothing. What face was exposed under the googles was pale and sunken in.

A scraggily beard covered the chin but looked like it had gone untrimmed for weeks. Frozen on his slacken jaw was a vacant expression of profound listlessness.

"Here he is, good old Rube. Not sure why he's been here so long. The guys upstairs have some running betting pools. I think he was involved in one of those early insurrections against Unity. But we might never find out given his file restrictions."

"Let me have a check of his file…" replied Zack, motioning to the tablet on the wall. "May I?"

"Of course." Alex grabbed the screen and handed it to Zack.

A few minutes passed as he authenticated his credentials to access his personal instance of the provisionary network. He typed in "Reuben Shackleton" into the query window and nearly instantaneously a profile popped up matching the description. Yet, when he tapped the man's name, something happened that he was quite unaccustomed to in his position. A bubble appeared with flashing red letters reading "restricted access."

"Yep, that is what everyone gets," said Alex who had moved behind Zack's shoulder to look at his progress.

Zack lifted eyes from the screen to the man lying motionless in the bed.

Who is he and why is he here like this? he thought.

"I would like to speak with him," Zack said plainly.

"Speak with him?" Alex said, his mouth agape.

"Yes. Can you get him out of wherever he is in?"

"Uhh…I don't think so." Alex reached for the tablet and began to scroll down. "It says here that he is not to be woke under any conditions. At least, unless you have clearance. And seeing that you cannot even see his profile, we know you lack that."

Zack ignored the jab. He could have reprimanded the junior rooter then and there, but going down that road would lead further from his aim.

"Well, can you put me in session with him?" Zack responded after some thought.

The junior rooter contemplated the ask for a few long moments as he rapidly scrolled up and down the page currently displayed on the tablet. After, repeating the process he raised his head.

"Well...I don't see anything here prohibiting such an action..."

"Great! And good work following protocol. Let's set me up over here on the chair."

Alex nodded and went to grab an additional headset. When he returned, Zack was already reclined back in the leather chair. The chair was positioned off Reuben's right shoulder at the head of the hospital bed. Alex handed him the sleek silver headset and as he lifted it above his head Alex gave some words of caution.

"We shouldn't take too long; in case a new report comes in upstairs. Also, I'm sure I don't have to remind *you* to be sure to maintain any rooted reality Rube has been provisioned. I don't want to explain any breach of protocol."

Zack nodded affirmatively and placed the headset over his head—unsure what lay ahead.

In moments, the tiny bleak room had disappeared beneath the goggles and earmuffs. Little remained of the world that had been around him except for an all-encompassing darkness and steady hum of electricity and his rapidly beating heart. A surge and a flash of white light came suddenly. Outlines of shapes came into view, then colors, and then finally a new scene was complete.

Zack found himself in some sort of academic laboratory. Bright, sterile lighting cast sharp reflections off sleek metal surfaces and rows of polished wooden workbenches, each equipped with a scattering of precision tools, electronics testing devices, and a rat's nest of multicolored wires. Along one wall, transparent glass cases housed android components—synthetic muscles, computer chips, and human-like skin materials— carefully arranged to show various iterations. On the other walls were screens and monitors filled with complex equations and schematics. The center of the room featured a large open area where a half-assembled android stood on a circular platform. The metal skeletal frame towered over the room at nearly three meters in height. It had an almost familiar shape to it that Zack could not quite place just yet.

Standing behind one of the wooden tables stood a man tinkering with a laptop that had been out of production for many years before Revelation Day.

"Just a minute…" said the man, noticing Zack's presence in the room. Seemingly not considering that he must have popped into place.

"Ah yes…another bug solved!" the man said gleefully and slapped the laptop lid closed. He looked up at Zack standing near the entrance of the room.

The man standing before him, looked nothing like what he knew lay withering mere meters away from him, outside on the hospital bed. In here, Reuben's hands moved nimbly about his workbench. An acute focus projected from a face full of color. Zack could have been fooled to think the man was a decade younger by looking at him. Silver-grey hair, slightly tousled, was gently swept back along a pair of thin-rimmed glasses. A neatly-trimmed mustache and goatee followed closely to his round chin and dimpled cheeks. He wore a neatly-buttoned collared shirt beneath a blue wool vest, giving the man a simple yet intelligent look about him. He appeared distinguished; a man who could dream big and grasp it into reality with hands that were not afraid of getting dirty. He reminded Zack of that director near the turn of the millennium who made the movie called "Close Encounters of Phosos's Kind." Zack had a vague recollection that there had once been another title for the movie but it escaped him now.

The man finally stopped with his tinkering and looked up at Zack. A pair of hazel eyes showed no signs of shock nor surprise.

"And who…might I say…are you?" the man asked, his right eyebrow rising slightly above the top rim of his black glasses.

A flush of heat surged through Zack's face and neck as his nerves tightened. Alarms of panic flickered through his mind and body as he scrambled desperately to come up with a cover story.

The man had presumably been trapped in this illusion for years, and the bureaucratic nightmare of re-rooting him would be unfathomable. Not to mention, the faceless authorities who controlled access to this place would not look too kindly to his little stunt. And there were too few authorities above him, most of which were in New Eden. Zack shuddered at the possibilities.

Looking behind the eager man awaiting his response, Zack noticed a plaque on the far wall. Below the room number "4200-NSH" was the seal for Carnegie Mellon University.

"I am...I am new to the department administration," he spit out. It was all he could put together from the context clues in the room.

"You're new, aren't ya, sonny?" the man said casually. His eyes seemed to peel away Zack's thoughts slowly with each slice back-and-forth.

"I...uh?" was all that Zack could get out.

The man gave him a wry smile.

"I can always tell the real thing from the program's they send to me from time-to-time," he leaned on one hand against the bench. "I guess they forget that I designed these systems for most of my life."

Confusion leaked out of Zack's thoughts onto his face.

"I know, I know...they hoped that I would be fooled by this place and go about my business of fixing their errors in code in ignorant bliss. That was their intent, as much as I can gather.

"They did a pretty good job too, giving me everything I could want in this lab to keep me busy. Hell, they even made me look better than I ever did!" Reuben stopped to turn and look at his reflection in a scrap piece of metal lying on the bench.

"So, what has become of me out there?" Reuben asked, still regarding himself in the mirrored reflection. His smile had slacked.

A cadaverous image of Reuben's body lying on the hospital bed flashed in Zack's mind.

"Well..." Zack started, still debating how much to reveal to the detainee. But that was all he could get out.

A sense of understanding took hold on Reuben's face. "Ah…maybe you shouldn't let me know how decrepit I have become.

"Can you at least tell me what year it is out there? It's so damn hard to keep track of time in a place like this. Every time I go to sleep days, maybe months could be creeping by."

Zack felt the man's eyes search his face for a clue even if an answer was not to be given.

"It's been at least three years from my understanding. Hard to say though," Zack said plainly. "Why are YOU here? This is typically not how we do things?" he added, changing the subject.

"Is that so?" Reuben replied. Doubt tinted his voice. He walked over to the half-built android propped up in the middle of the room and began to articulate its fingers absentmindedly.

"I am in this place because of what I built."

"And, what did you build?" asked Zack after a long pause.

"An artificial god."

Reuben let out a soft sigh and looked up into the blank face of the motionless android.

"I just never thought it would be co-opted by a real one. My poor golems."

Zack took a few steps closer to the android Reuben was looking over. Its eyes were unlit and as inanimate as any part lying around the room. Yet, there was also a sense that a single sparked touch could somehow send it reeling to life with all the necessary components in place.

"Is that it, your golem?"

"No, no," he replied waving his hands. "This is merely an early prototype. But I'll call one in, they always like to stay close to me, to watch me. Fred! Fred, come in here!"

Zack heard a door open behind him. The sounds of heavy, uniform footsteps followed. Before he had even fully turned around, he knew what he would see standing there. He had heard those steady footfalls for far too long for them to go unrecognized. And there it was, a Hand of Provision.

"Now, come on, you didn't make that…" Zack stated after looking into the HOP's pale blue eyes that stared coldly into the room.

"I certainly did, there are records," replied Reuben adamantly.

Zack shook his head. "You must be mistaken. There are no records besides the ones that state that Phosos created the androids for serving the Tree of Unity and Provision. There was not any human maker."

He knew all the records on the provisionary network regarding the HOPs, and there was no mention of a Reuben Shackleton nor anything about him building androids for serving Unity. *At least that was the case on the public network*, he thought. *Could there be something in the unrooted repository?* He pushed the dangerous thought aside to a safe distance, for now.

Reuben stood his ground on the matter, however.

"Look hard and you will see, the Freds—your "HOPs"— came from my workshop, not outer space."

"You have all been deceived. This alien-being you revere is not a being from up above but one from down below."

The voice of the strange man with sapphire eyes echoed in Zack's head once more. Now, he wondered whether there was some connection between the two men. It seemed unlikely. Yet, the more likely case was that they were both drawing from some suppressed underlying reality. It was an inconvenient truth to swallow…and he was not quite ready to down that pill, just yet.

"I started the work here in a lab, almost like this, nearly two decades ago," Reuben began. He let go of the android's hand he had been studying. It fell lifelessly to its side.

"I wanted to build a golem, like in the Jewish tradition. Except instead of clay, I would work in metal and silicon. I thought I could build one that would serve humanity and fully free us from our labors.

"These 'Freds' as I called them, would have nimble bodies and be stronger than the average human being. And their minds, they would far surpass any human intelligence with vast understanding of every word that has ever been spoken, in every language.

Memory repositories would hold every novel, story, textbook, and manual that had ever been written. And all of this accumulated knowledge, would be accessible in mere milliseconds. Before you or I could blink, my Freds could simulate how to do anything in a billion possible right and wrong ways until a solution could be determined. All possibilities would be simulated all possible moves would be known. A thousand years of human trial and error could be condensed down into minutes or seconds."

Reuben approached the HOP that had entered the room. A sad smile filled his face; one filled with pride and awe as well as sadness and regret. He placed a gentle hand on the android's firm chest, as if to read a heartbeat that was not there.

Reuben continued to speak, "Now my Freds serve the purpose of a thing beyond even my craft. A being who has been at this for quite some time, twisting desire and wants and knowledge.

"On the eve of Revelation Day, like a cold draft in the night, he came to my workshop as an orb of light. I do not know how he managed to do it, but Phosos took hold and possessed my Freds. I had three fully built then. First their eyes changed from a kind brown color to a cold blue flame. One detained me quickly with its arms that I had made strong to carry loads of labor. The others, he turned to collecting the research and equipment I had poured my life into. It all was hauled away into the night. I was left trapped in my own lab with a golem of my own creation keeping me at bay."

"No one came to look for you?" asked Zack inquisitively.

Reuben shook his head slowly. "No one cared much about anything of the old world after Revelation Day had come and passed. Eventually, people did come, but they wore strange clothing and called themselves rooters. They drugged me in my own lab and I awoke in this one—a weak facsimile. They thought they had fooled me in some artificial simulation, but a man who spends his life in a place learns every blemish, every crack of ceiling tile. This place was all too perfect. Even the charm of my Freds were not the same."

Reuben began to slap against the HOP's chest firmly with a closed fist.

"Everything has been twist-turned-upside-down! This thing has turned my helping companions into an idol that moves, controls, and oppresses its unassuming worshipers. They worship the things I MADE—a simple engineer from Johnstown, PA—and no one even knows it."

Zack watched the man as he spoke with passion. He was still trying to decide if the words the man was saying were the ravings of a mad man or an uncovered revelation buried in sand.

"But why are you left alive, if you truly are the last to know your role in their creation?" Zack said, falling back on his investigative inclinations.

Reuben turned away from the HOP and stared at Zack intently before sighing heavily. The android pounding had taken a few breaths from him.

"Death certainly would have been easier for all parties involved. One last loose end to tie up," Reuben stared off beyond Zack unfocused.

"But there probably was no need. My echo has already begun to fade into obscurity. In a few more years' time, no one will remember who I am. Perhaps they already have forgotten me like everything else in the old world that had been. Hell, it was that way before Revelation Day, besides a few bright lights, who remembers anything more than the name of someone who lived fifty or a hundred years before they did?

"I'll answer the quiz for you, No one!"

Reuben now turned to one of the nearby tables where a series of metal probes were affixed to a processing chip. He removed one of the probes and a red light lit up on a screen a few meters away. Doing so, he continued speaking.

"No, I am only alive because I am the true maker of these very earthly androids. I am needed to keep them operating. Phosos, in all his capabilities, has not the power to sustain the created, only to degrade it.

"But soon, I would hazard to guess Phosos won't need them anyways. No one will be left alive with any fight left in them. Unfortunately, I have learned this lesson too late. But I will share this nugget of truth with you. One that took decades of my life for me to learn. Technology is a key—opening the gates of heaven, and also hell. The choice of which lock is opened is up to you."

Zack shook his head in disbelief.

"You still don't believe it do you? That is a shame, you might be one of the few that are left who could use this knowledge to stop it before it progresses too far."

"I have no choice, even if I wanted to make one," Zack responded avoiding the pressing eyes of the android maker. His shoulders had slumped and his face held little expression.

Reuben pushed further, as if every word and moment were critical. Zack noticed that the HOP who had been standing motionless the whole time had begun to subtly turn his head to follow Reuben throughout the room. There was also a curious artifact of light in the android's eyes that he almost swore gave them an almost violet gleam.

"I have built AI systems for most of my life and I can tell you, free will lies on a foggy horizon. That horizon is ever-modulating. Yet, as the present nears the once future, the world becomes more concrete. It is there in which we find that we can become defined by our past choices. And when you do reach that horizon, choices cease to seem like choices since you have already made the choice, repeatedly, long ago. It is never too late to chart a new course, but you must choose quickly and completely, now. The first step of freedom from a tyrant is to free yourself from within with a disciplined mind.

"Remember you are no automaton and importantly—"

A bright flash and crackling of audio jumbled everything for Zack. A ringing lingered in his ear as a fuzzy light and face appeared directly in front of him.

"Time is up!" cried Alex as he removed the headset from Zack's face. Zack felt droplets of sweat rolling down the bridge of his nose. It took a few moments for him to recognize the junior rooter, the grey cell, and the outline of the shriveled man lying on the hospital bed. When all the equipment had been removed, Alex spoke urgently.

"I apologize, but I just received a notification that I am needed upstairs. I'm curious to see what it is about as this message did not come through my usual channels."

Zack nodded blankly and gingerly rose to his feet. It was always a strange feeling returning to the real world from the other. As they walked out of the room, he looked at Reuben's face. It somehow seemed strangely at peace.

)　　|　　(

For the rest of that afternoon, Zack retired to the resting lounge on the thirteenth floor overlooking the city. He had a bite to eat and tried to take a short nap. But on each restless attempt, he found himself jolted awake. It was on his third attempt, at the boundary between sleep and wakefulness, when everything seems distant and fuzzy, that Ava's voice found him once more. It was a whisper reaching out from some lost past that knew no sense of time nor place.

"Remember Zacky, we are spiritual beings having a human experience, not the reverse. You need only open your mind to what is so much bigger."

Zack jerked up from the reclining sofa in a cold sweat. His thoughts were racing a million kilometers a minute. Thinking about the sweet Ava, the blue-eyed stranger, the android maker, and all the things they said. It all converged into a tugging thought in his mind. A thought that he had put aside, half hoping it would slip into the realm of the forgotten. Now, in the light of acute awareness, he knew he needed to check the unrooted repository.

Maybe then, when his doubts were finally settled and disconfirmed, he could rest.

So, he walked over to the computer terminal in the corner of the room. It had been set up for his convenience. He presented his Unity mark and he was logged-in. The query window for the public network blinked incessantly, steadily awaiting an input. He began to type "Reuben Shackleton" and started the search.

The results came swiftly.

As he had expected, the query netted an empty finding. To the greater world, Reuben Shackelton did not exist. But he knew the non-existent man laid many floors down below, just beneath his feet.

It was time to switch to the rooter network.

He clicked through a few more challenge screens to gain access to a part of the network that few in the Tree of Unity ever saw. In fact, few rooters had unfettered, on-demand access unless they had reached the rank of Rootmaster. Again, he typed in the name "Reuben Shackleton." This time a restricted profile populated as it had before down in the sub-basement. However, there were no associated files or documents, only the limited profile.

"Hmm…" he said to himself, having come to an apparent dead end. He knew he would have to find another way. So, he sat there for a few minutes staring at the screen and, every so often, out at the bleak grey cityscape. In his mind, his thoughts shuffled through an index of possible systems that might provide access to what he was looking for. That was when it came to him that the unrooted repository might hold some piece of information if it existed. It was there that they stored every original artifact—books, papers, virtual scenarios, videos, and photographs—taken from those subjected to a rooting. Few even knew about it, given that the materials were a threat to Unity and needed to be closed away for use only in the most intense investigations. The repository was so vast and unstructured that it would be impossible to search without the aid of an AI helper, which conveniently enough was only granted to rootmasters like himself, and HOPs.

"All right," Zack said aloud, cracking his knuckles.

For the third time, he typed in "Reuben Shackleton" and engaged a search. The result that was returned was far from expected. A slumped willow tree blinked repeatedly on the screen indicating that nothing had been returned.

An equally unexpected feeling of uneasiness gripped his stomach. He found himself surprised at the feeling of disappointment, despite having confirmation of all his doubts. *Had it really all been an elaborate story made up by man who had been in VR for too long?*

A nagging feeling from somewhere deep within himself offered a rebuttal.

Then, why the restricted access? Why the lack of additional information? Why keep him a secret?

More questions mounted than even a blank screen could dissuade against. He pulled back up the search window, and thought, and thought…until he began typing what he knew.

"Carnegie Mellon University OR android OR male OR professor OR 4200-NSH."

Thinking that no one besides Reuben would ever see it, perhaps the simulation had been too accurate and revealed just enough clues, Zack thought as he waited for the search to complete.

When it finally finished, this time, a page full of pictures and documents appeared.

"Okay, now we are getting somewhere," he said to himself, wondering where to begin.

It was an image that caught his eye first. The picture depicted the lab he had been in. In the center of the image, surrounded by young graduate students holding dissembled android arms, was Reuben! However, the picture caption included with the metadata identified the man as "Tyler Steinberger."

Altered? It was a curious thing for an unrooted recorded to have been altered. *What is going on here?*

As Zack continued to look, it was all there, record after record. A university news article on Tyler's—err Reuben's—advanced robotics research. An award from the NSF for a ten-year multimillion-dollar grant. An article from the New York Times citing his AI benchmark achievement. And then lastly, a collection of Reuben's personal laboratory notes that included pictures of every iteration of his androids. The last image, dated a few weeks before Revelation Day, showed a clear picture of the HOPs, Reuben's Freds.

The man had been right! The truth now stared at him in vivid color. It was a frightening visage as someone went through the effort to bury and modify it.

Zack leaned back in his chair. He felt his heart pounding intensely. He had uncovered what he sought, but now was at a loss of what to do with the newfound revelation. In the end, did it really change anything?

"Phosos controls the world, having misled on where his helping robots came from might not be a big deal, right?" he said to himself quietly. His gaze had turned back to the dreary overlook.

"Ah, who am I trying to convince?"

He found himself wishing that Ava was there to run through the evidence. She had always been so good at weighing possibilities he never could consider on his own.

What about Ava…

A thought emerged in his mind that he had never ventured to entertain before through the long years. The unrooted repository was still open before him, and with just a few search terms, he could summon Ava's file—to glimpse what had been taken from her and buried where no light would ever likely reveal it again.

There had been a reason not to open old wounds before. But now, her haunting presence loomed over him more than ever. His mind felt as if it was in the throes of an upheaval. Nothing seemed certain any longer. So, why not take a peek?

It might be what she wants anyways. He had not thought of her in the present tense for years and somehow the thought comforted him, whether she was a ghost, some repressed inner conscience, or a figment of a troubled mind.

His fingers began to type before he had even fully settled on the action.

"Ava Everly Hewitt...and...search!"

Before he could blink, the screen had refreshed with a single profile identified. Ava's profile photo nearly broke his heart all over again. Even with a blank stare captured under dingy light during in-processing, Ava's beauty glowed with rosy cheeks and kind eyes. Seeing her last photo alone in that dreary lounge was like the memory of a warm cottage for a man stranded far away beneath drifts of snow.

He entered the profile. Inside was the typical information.

Age: 26.

Height: 165 cm.

Hair color: Brown.

Eye color: Hazel.

Weight: 45 kg.

Birthplace: Zanesville, Ohio.

Known associates: Zack Klein (fiancé), Karen Hewitt (mother), Victor Hewitt (father).

But there was also a section on "seized unauthorized assets" that looked like it was populated by a single item.

Zack tentatively opened the subfolder, not having the faintest idea what Ava might have had confiscated from her.

The screen flashed again and a black leather book appeared on the screen. There was no lettering or title on the front cover, but he knew what it was—the water-stained bottom right corner that had developed a slight outward curl, the finger-nail-sized scratch on the middle spine, and a large crease that ran vertically down the center of the homely tome.

It was Ava's family Bible.

Zack had watched her read the old book nearly every night before bed. She also took it with her to Sunday services every week when she left him alone at their apartment to watch morning cartoons. It had originally been her grandmother's passed to her father and then to her. Given its worn state, he had once suggested she buy a new one and the look she gave him then was the closest he ever saw her come to complete infuriation. Her eyes were like crackling sparklers.

It was no surprise the rooters had taken it from her. All Bibles were digitally altered to be in alignment with the tenets of Unity in the early weeks after Revelation Day. Physical copies were collected and reprinted in a similar manner. Her Bible had been scanned in meticulously with every page and cover. Flipping through the pages, now, there was not much to see beyond the columned rows of words that were even more out of place in this day-and-age as they had been to him before Revelation Day. Even if he did not share Ava's belief, he admired her conviction. For it was a wellspring to her character. From it she drew strength to cling to her faith to her dying breath and also to have faith in him just as fervently.

Not wanting to look through every page, Zack entered the commands SEARCH HANDWRITING. The pages flew by until they stopped near the back of the Bible. The top of the page read "Family Tree" in gothic font. Beneath the heading, pairs of lines were filled in with at least three different styles of handwriting.

Starting from the top was Thomas Hewitt and Ruth (Osbourne) Hewitt, written in an elegantly flowing thin script.

Below Ava's grandparents, were her parent's names written in a speedy hand, likely her father's, Victor Hewitt and Karen (Breezewood) Hewitt.

Then there was Ava's line. Zack's heart nearly skipped a few beats noticing that she had already filled in what would be her future married name along with his own. The handwriting was in her beautiful block lettering, carefully written and bold. Ava (Hewitt) Klein and Zack Klein.

With misty eyes, he forwarded the search again. This time, it only progressed a couple pages before it came to a halt. It was a blank page, but it was filled with several blocks of Ava's neat handwriting. Mostly musings or perhaps, revelations she had arrived upon during her daily reading rituals.

> *The opposite of God is <u>not</u> the devil; the devil is merely a false facsimile. God has no equal for He existed and was not created. Thus, his opposite is nonexistence, nothingness like cold is the absence of heat and darkness is the absent of light. So is also the separation from God, where evil may dwell.*

> *God did not create evil. Evil is the result of what happens when people reject God's presence for personal pursuits in their heart. There, a cold wind blows and all light goes out.*

> *Without a spiritual rock to anchor, you are blown to and fro on the endless winds of an identity you search for but, like the breeze itself, can never quite grasp. Meaning falls through your fingers at every changing gale.*

> *A lost traveler will walk down any path they can find in their desperate search for meaning, I hope one day Zacky opens his big heart to find the one I am on.*

Zack could barely read on. The words on the screen had become a blurry soup to his increasingly watery eyes. Knowing that she never lost hope for him, despite his stubbornness, was more than he could bear right now. But there was only one last entry to go.

> *What was…and will never be.*

He felt the warm stream of tears roll down his cheeks as if some levy had broken. He imagined her writing the small note maybe weeks, days, hours…before they came for her.

How could he continue to fail her each and every day since her passing? As the inner question held aloft, an epiphany sparked through his mind. It seemed with every new guidepost of information he was more lost than he had been from the start. Dr. Silva…The Man with Sapphire Eyes…the android maker. Everything he thought he knew was being uprooted. Maybe it was time to jump from the path he was on and head straight through the woods. Perhaps then he might come across Ava's golden path…

"If you have faith," she would say.

"What would be the measure of your role?" added the man with sapphire eyes.

And finally, completing the ghostly trio around him, *"You are no automaton, choose which door to unlock,"* said Rube, a man with deep experience and nothing to lose.

He exited the tool and turned away from the terminal. Just as he did so, there was a knock at the door.

"Come in," he said, trying his best to provide strength to a faltering voice.

Alex walked in with such urgency he almost seemed like he had not noticed Zack's disheveled state.

"Rootmaster, we have just received a report that a fire broke out in the hospital you and Rootmaster Payne attended some days ago in Talawanda Springs. It looks like arson and it would be in the right area we were tracking those weeds, who, according to our records, would have a previous educational connection to the town and university."

Alex paused, as if to ensure the next piece of information was not lost with the other details.

"And there is something else…"

Zack nodded.

"…it seems a patient is missing by the name, James Doe. I could not get any other information on him. Does that name mean anything to you?"

Zack nodded involuntarily.

His eyes and mind felt as open as they had ever been. The feeling was surreal. Images, voices, information, everything seemed to swirl around him in a whirlwind.

He eventually came to speak in a mindless tone.

"Send for a vehicle, I'll have to figure this all out in motion."

8

The Ancient Mindsai

As the first imagery began to materialize, there was still a constant, lingering pressure on Aliyah's mind.

How far have I gone back?

The thought briefly pushed out against some oppressive weight. Even then, it felt fragile, strained beneath the unseen force. Each thought she formed seemed to be like a shallow breath struggling to push out against the weight of a boulder on her chest. The pressure bore down steadily, inexorably, stealing a fraction more with each rise and fall, as though the very act of breathing might collapse entirely.

There was sense that a mind lingering too long at this depth of memory might collapse under its immense weight. It would be a slow, crushing decent to the bottom of an unfathomable pool of generations past, where no breath could be mustered, and she would sink into a still, suffocating quiet. Best, then, to ration her thoughts against this looming peril and let the experience wash over her.

The first vestiges of an image were becoming visible now. Some large mass was emerging out of the darkness. At first the cone-shaped structure appeared like an orphaned mountain. She felt its cold shadow stretching across the yet-revealed subject's body. As the scene crystalized further, it became clear that the shape was not a natural structure, it was a massive tower.

The day was early. A morning sun was rising over a snow-topped mountain range to the east. In the west, another range of mountains stood half-shrouded in a dark veil. Rising above the shadow line were three sharp red peaks. They looked eager to spear the sun at its eventual fall upon them at day's end, to spill forth a crimson scattering of dying light.

Between the two stone ranges, was the tower. It was yellow-hued, like the golden color of fall-turned leaves. The structure rose from the flat plain in six spiraling circular levels. Large designs were carved at each level into the stone sides. At the apex of the edifice, was a spherical finial, that held above it a large blue crystalline orb. The first rays of the morning sun shone through it sending scatter beams of blue across the rest of the stone city.

The subject seemed to be presently walking towards the tower along a curving path. Like Aliyah, the man could barely take his eyes away from the towering monolith, that, even in her era would be a skyscraper of more than twenty stories.

Taking in the view, there seemed to be an itching thought that Aliyah felt within the subject. Like she had before, she focused her mind to decode its meaning.

Nothing.

She pressed her mind harder. Some ephemeral images of churches and photo albums came to her mind but could not pinpoint if these were her own or the subject's crude representations.

Once more, she focused all her mental might until it felt as if her mind were to split in two. A few words came into her understanding related to something like a church or temple along with the idea of documented lives, perhaps like memories. Everything else seemed to pass beyond all recognition. Access to this subject's thoughts seemed more difficult than before. Whether a weaker signal across countless years or the drift of a foreign language too far removed, it was impossible to tell.

By the time the subject had reached the first steps leading into the belly of the temple, the sprawling stone city had sunk beneath a bath of warm sunlight. The beige-hued buildings spread out from the tower in a web-like network, their stone shapes a harmonious blend of smooth curves and angular edges. The architecture was foreign, unlike anything Greek, Roman, or even Atlantean—neither overly ornate nor complex. No, these buildings were more advanced in their simplicity. The architecture of the buildings did not reflect their constructed nature. Each structure seemed less built than summoned from the earth itself, their imbued brutalist forms merging seamlessly with the landscape, as though they had risen from dirt and stone without a trace of framework, joint, or seam.

Most rooftops of the city were rounded or capped with small domes, humble in their silhouette. Yet here and there, square pyramidal structures punctuated the skyline, their gold-cased spires reaching skyward with quiet reverence. They mirrored the temple's grandeur, yet they remained bound to its shadow, standing like silent acolytes in the presence of their towering master.

The subject entered on the first level of the tower through a large archway. It was carved with the etchings of stars, moons, and oblong-shaped lidless eyes—all of which were watching any who passed beneath to enter. Directly inside, the subject came face-to-face to a lighted brazier. Above it was a large statue made of clay. It depicted a being with the body of a man, the head of an ox, and a pair of large raven-like wings stretching wide from its back. In one hand, the statue held the end of a large plow-like tool and in the other, some sort of forked dowsing rod pointed at the ground.

A fleeting sensation stirred deep in the cloudy recesses of Aliyah's mind. It was not a fully-formed thought, not quite—more like an intruding recollection of some passing bit of information that had been read long ago in some dusty tome. With it, a name came to mind, *Arqael*.

There was something else as well—an action. The act of looking. No, it was more focused than that, active. A series of impressions shot through her. It had the vague sense of a being that lingered beyond the fabric of existence who observed the world change and play out before it with piercing eyes of light, unseen, but undeniable. A silent witness, its duty was to watch humanity and remain forever apart from the object of its observations. But this one, Arqael, had been lured by the pull of what it could not touch, to share the secret innerworkings of the universe. Its descent onto the plain of earth carved a deep scar in the fabric it was meant to remain steadfast behind. It then became known to humans, who had been shrouded in ignorance, as *Arqael, the watcher.*

As Aliyah arrived at some basic understanding of the statue standing before her, the subject reached into a pouch worn on his side. It was at that moment that Aliyah saw the red-shaped circle birthmark on the back of his right hand, just as she had seen in the vision from before.

The subject pulled out a flower, somewhat like a lotus. Its color changed in the shifting light from an inky black to an iridescent purple. Flower in hand, he reached forward and dropped the beautiful thing into the burning flames. Its petals danced helplessly as the fire curled it inward, rendering it to a crumpled lump of black ash.

When the subject looked up again, an olive-skinned man with a light phosphorescent glow was standing just beyond the statue. His face was perfectly symmetrical and beautiful—almost impossibly so. There were no signs of blemish or marks on his smooth skin. Everything about him was pristine and undiminished. The man was dressed in not much more than a sackcloth holding a long wooden staff. He gave the subject an approving nod and pointed on down the curved chamber.

The subject proceeded accordingly.

From the statue, the brown floor spiraled upwards at a steady incline. The subject walked at a brisk pace passing murals of near-endless fields of golden grain, lush gardens of colorful exotic fruit, and the cultivation of water sources.

The subject completed a full circle around the tower when he reached the entrance to the next level. Like the first, the second level's entryway was guarded by a tall lanky man of similar idealized features and ethereal aura. He was dressed in a flowing tunic standing next to a statue and burning brazier. The second-level effigy was of another angelic-type being having the head of a serpent, wings of a dragonfly, and paws of a wolf or fox. It was carved out of a dark black wood that had veins of red and amber. In its hand, it held a type of writing instrument held against its other arm leaving inscrutable symbols. Aliyah felt another tingling of recognition but could only resolve the watcher's name, *Penemue*.

Like before, the subject went to his pouch and pulled something from it. It was a piece of paper with lettering and other indiscernible symbols—taking up about half a page. He stretched it out before him and began uttering some form of guttural speech. Absent of any vowel sounds, it came closest to maybe Yiddish or Hebrew, but neither were a very good match to Aliyah's understanding. She concentrated as hard as she could, but like before, no discernible thought emerged, only bits and pieces of some idea, some distant insurmountable goal. There was a sacred name, distant and veiled, shimmered on the edge of knowing, its weight heavier than mountains, its reach higher than the endless vault of the heavens. It was the key, the pinnacle, the doorway to a lush paradise, never spoiled. In that place, cycles of the moon and sun would turn without end, where life persisted forever and ever. And no harm could come to a man.

After the speaking had ceased, the subject let the piece of parchment float down into the fire that was all too eager to consume it in a white flash.

The tall man nodded and the subject continued up the spiraling hall. Writings and symbols covered the walls at this level of the tower. Markings that Aliyah felt told of stories of people of great renown, others of secret mysteries to the workings of the world, and more still of profane statements of power and dominance over the land.

The statue at the third level, the watcher she thought named, *Asael*, was of a man bearing the head of a horned bear. Its legs were like a goat, hairy and cloven. A lion's tail whipped behind the figure; its end sharpened on two sides not unlike a doubled-headed axe. The effigy was wrought in black iron. Every feature—horn, eyelid, earlobe, fingertip—was shaped to a razor's edge. At this sacrificial flame, the subject pulled out an oval-shaped object that was dry and shriveled similar to beef jerky. It was not until it was falling into the fire that Aliyah realized that it was the severed remains of a human ear!

At the moment of this recognition a series of images flashed in Aliyah's thoughts.

The subject was suddenly walking on an isolated path amongst a sea of towering trees, each one as big as the largest redwood she had ever seen. The grand canopy overhead cast the pathway in a near-permanent twilight of shifting shadows. Aliyah sensed a great number of years of experience traveling on dangerous roads like this. The subject was approaching a turn in the path near a pile of stones and bushes. There was a metallic sound that immediately seemed out of place in the quiet wood.

Then, bursting out from a bush, in a rush of scattered leaves and terror, came a man. He was of daunting stature and menace; his mouth snarling and eyes, like two slivers of flint, were cold and merciless. Aliyah like the subject, knew in an instant that there would be no negotiating with the ominous figure—to the victor would go all the spoils.

In his right hand, the aggressor brandished a gleaming metallic dagger over his head. The hand was attached to a thick arm of coiled muscles ready to strike. The man wore layers of metallic scales that had given the subject a moment's forewarning with their clinking in the bush. The sound had been fortuitous for the man was only a few leaps and bounds from the subject before he would be upon him.

The subject pulled out a dagger of his own, shorter and baring a serrated edge of teeth.

The challenge did not cause the bandit to skip a step. The other man lunged at the subject, his blade a flash in the murky light, but the subject dodged, just barely, the blade whistling past his arm. The subject's heart thundered as he countered, quickly, striking at gaps in the figure's armor. But the weapon hit the metal scales with a *shhhk* and rolled off without effect. The strike did not give the other man any pause, he swung around for another relentless strike. His breath ragged and eyes gleaming with cruel delight at what must have been the first fair contest he had faced amongst many such ambushes. Twirling his blade above his head, the figure moved in, even more confident than before.

Aliyah felt the subject's racing thoughts dredging up countless kills from fights and small battles won because a veteran of violence knows no defeat. As the figure closed the gap once more, the subject feigned to his right and then back to his left as the figure brought down his tooth of death to hit empty air. As he missed, the subject slipped through the figure's guard aiming high. With a fierce cry, the subject drove his jagged dagger into the vulnerable flesh of the figure's neck. The man froze, his form staggering, his gaze locked onto the subject in a mix of rage and shock. Blood spurted out from the wound, a dark rivulet against his armor, and with a last, guttural snarl, he crumpled to the ground, lifeless.

The subject knelt, hands trembling but steady as they claimed a prize. With a swift motion, he severed the figure's right ear, a grisly trophy. Aliyah could feel the weight of it, still warm in his hand. A chilling wind whispered through the trees, as if the forest itself acknowledged the victory, before silence resumed its reign.

Back before the statute of the watcher, Aliyah recognized a strange sense of satisfaction roll over the subject. The delight in the demise of a human scared her more than the crispy ear that now smoldered upon the red coals.

The subject turned and was allowed to continue on by another guardian. Murals portraying contests of strength, warring clans, and brutal executions using oddly-shaped tools of war covered the walls as another hall passed behind him.

And so it went, for each progressive level upwards.

On the fourth level, in a hall adorned by rounded glyphs and complex geometric patterns. The watcher *Amaros* stood clad in an ochre bronze. The figure was owl-headed and bore leathery wings at its back. A sacrifice of a walnut-sized green gem was made to it.

At the fifth level, the watcher *Gadreel* waited as the only female icon. This watcher was carved of some sort of ivory or marble, white and polished to be as smooth as glass. She had the head of a large-eyed fox. Her hips were slender and swayed seductively as she held out a beckoning hand to all those that entered her hall. The hand was slender and delicate, but at each end, of each finger, were sharp talons, resembling the deadly claws of an eagle. At her brazier, the subject dropped a thin piece of brown fabric, soiled by creamy stains. A female guard wearing nothing but a necklace of phallic-carved moonstones let the subject move on.

As the subject passed large murals of male and female nudes engaging in various acts of pleasure and intercourse, there was an open doorway leading inward to an antechamber. A group of beautiful, radiant young women were lined up waiting. Each were nearly naked and heavily done-up with makeup on their faces. The woman also held some sort of woven basket with a cloth draped over the top. The subject only gave a passing glance at the group before climbing onward to the sixth level.

Entering the sixth level and last tiered level, the subject came face-to-face with a silver and gold statue. This watcher, *Ezeqeel*, had lost any semblance of human form. Its head was long-snouted, like a dragon. Its arms were scaled and the body coiled behind it like a serpent. In its right hand, it held a yellow topaz and, in its left, an opal. Each precious stone was carved and faceted in the likeness of the sun and moon. In its bowl of fire, the subject placed a thick tuft of his own black hair cut from the back of his head with the same jagged dagger that had taken the path-side figure.

At last, two guards cloaked in deep blue robes—speckled in gold and silver—lowered their serpentine-shaped staffs of carved bone. The subject could not see their eyes shrouded within the shadows of their hoods. Only their grim smiles on solemn faces bid him to go upwards into the highest chamber.

The path onward eventually ended at the feet of a steep stairway of thirteen golden steps. Beaming in through a window, the morning's light glistened on each step, turning the staircase aglow like a molten waterfall. The golden honey light enveloped all around him, as he ascended, as if he were stepping up into the clouds where only the sun, moon, and stars reigned. The golden stairway led up through an oval opening in the ceiling and then into a large domed room that seemed stretch the entire diameter of the tower. The space curved upwards like being on the inside of a great hollow onion. The walls were covered in a smooth glistening white marble that appeared to be shaped out of a single piece without any signs of construction. The polished marble reflected various shafts of blue light in all directions that could only escape out of two cutout windows facing directly east and west.

The blue light of the room emanated from a large oval opening in the ceiling of the dome. In this opening, laid the seat of the massive blue crystal Aliyah had seen resting on the top of the tower from before. Just the bottom few facets that were visible, were bigger than her entire childhood home. The crystal filled itself with the light of the rising sun, redirecting its brilliance into all corners of the room. The subject gazed up at its radiant splendor for many wondrous moments. When he finally turned his sights away, Aliyah still felt as though she had been cheated out of fully absorbing its glory.

As sight of the crystal faded, she became aware of another name floating at the edge of comprehension—*Ouza*. It carried a weight unlike the others that had come before. She suddenly felt small, as if in the presence of a school principal or a leader like

Dean Wilkins. The feeling of being near a person exuding great authority. The name seemed to tower over the other names of watchers as if it were a chief among them, their leader. And given that there was no statue in this highest of places, at the pinnacle of the tower, Aliyah could only surmise that the crystal above was the physical representation of the chief watcher.

The chamber's floor gleamed with a stone as black and as polished as obsidian. Aliyah immediately noticed the sparseness of the room—no furniture, no murals, no etchings, only a single draped alcove directly opposite of the entrance. A heavy curtain of twilight-blue fabric veiled the niche, concealing whatever that may lay within.

In the center of the floor yawned the maw of a large oval opening from which light puffs of smoke aimlessly rose upwards into the air. A strange, unfamiliar scent wafted amongst the twirling grey tendrils. It had a meaty aroma, like some sort of grilled meats. Yet, somehow, the drifts of smoke smelled *off* to her. Quite unlike the familiar scents of cooked beef, chicken, or pork.

Walking to the other side of the chamber, the subject now drew nearer to the opening in the floor. Up until then, he had been walking a winding path that wrapped around the outer edge of the tower. But here, at its highest point, Aliyah could finally glimpse at what lay at its center—nothing. He cast a quick glance downward into the hollowed belly of the tower. The shaft ran deep, all the way back down to ground level. Far below, at its very bottom, a massive brazier burned with a fierce, unquenchable blaze. The fire's glow reached up into the hollow several levels, its bright red and orange light licking at the walls, flooding the pit with an eerie radiance. The flames were so intense that they threw their reflections high up into the crystal suspended overhead, giving it a flickering crimson eye watching down from above.

A sound of pulling fabric broke the silence, coming from the direction of the draped alcove. The subject turned his gaze towards the curtains that had now been partially drawn back by two priestly-looking men robed in long cloaks and heavy hoods that concealed their faces. They pulled back the weighty curtains with silver ropes and then immediately dropped prostrate to the floor.

Behind the curtain, another hidden entrance into the chamber had been revealed. Golden light and faint shadows wavered from an unseen stairwell. A solid shadow began to take shape, growing darker and larger between each of the subject's heartbeats. Before long, a man slowly rose up from the floor. Even in his long years, he was of great stature, surely an imposing man in his youth. His silver-streaked hair, in shades of iron and ash, curled about his face down near to his shoulders. It appeared wind-swept, like that of a man who had just returned from a flight in the heavens. A long and thick white beard with a triangular streak of black at the chin covered the rest of a face which was etched with deep knowledge and memory. The phosphorescent glow of his skin was stronger than anyone the subject had encountered thus far. In night, his skin would appear almost like the radiance of moonlight reflecting off white cobble stones.

The regal figure stopped a few steps in front of the subject. The heavy robes that shrouded his large frame barely noted any sort of movement. The deep blue fabric flowed down his entire body like dark ocean waves caught in a perpetual standstill. Across his collar, intricate gold embroidery traced out celestial patterns across the fabric. Inlayed golden medallions adorned both panels of his chest, each one carved with the faces of what Aliyah felt were ancestors and long-forgotten renowned men whose lineage and memory he carried.

Aliyah felt the subject's mind narrowing, coiling into an intense focus, as if the moment were one long prepared. The subject's gaze fixed on the man standing before them. A name bubbled up to the surface, unbidden, from the depths of her consciousness—*Zikaron, son of Jabal.* Aliyah sensed a reverence that bordered on awe for the name, as though this Zikaron were more than a man—an ancient wellspring of knowledge, a keeper of memories collected from all who had yet treaded the earth. It was this acumen that the subject sought with a charged sense of yearning, as Zikaron had the power to make his winding paths straight.

The elder held up two hands towards the subject, and spoke a simple sound, *Ur.* The sound resonated straight to the core of the subject. It affected the subject in a way that Aliyah could only recognize as being words of personal relevance, as when one hears their name amidst the clamor of voices in a crowded space. The subject's name was *Ur.*

A conversation then ensued between the two men, speaking in firm, foreign tones. Like the times before in this place, Aliyah could not grasp any semblance of words or phrases. However, a story began to weave within her mind as waves of understanding came in the forms of nonverbals—sorts of impressions, feelings, and at times, imagery.

As Aliyah understood it, it was a story of *Ur*—one of many who had heard the warnings of an impending doom that would drown the land. There would be no escape from this watery cataclysm it was told. Yet, for many generations, the doomsayer's words became feeble without sign or hint of water. To Ur and all who listened, the prophecy was nothing more than the ravings of goat herders muttering in the wilderness. After all, the sea lay many moons' journey from their fertile plains, its waves as distant as the stars above.

The words of doom hung over Ur, despite his disbelief. Every drop of water, every rushing stream, were an ever-constant reminder of his mortality. That one day, a doom of death would come to him like it had for his father, and father's father, and everyone else that had lived to great age or died at the end of sword or club. So, he endeavored to find a means to save himself and others from this looming dark cloud of death.

Only one such place existed in the world. A place where dark clouds could not hang in the sky. It was a verdant haven, a garden high on the sheltered plateau of a mountain, where every leaf shimmered with the glow of new creation, and every stream trickled with the sounds of jubilation, and the ground was untouched by thorn or sorrow. The secluded paradise, where death could not reach, now laid quiet and guarded by a fierce being of fire. All those who sought to enter were struck down in ruin. Only those who spoke the true name of the garden's master could ever enter.

So, Ur set forth, across field and barrow, to the Tower of Memory and passed through the Hall of Watchers to seek the councils of Zikaron for knowledge of this secret name of God. In the hopes that once the name is learned, redemption can be shown through man's valiance and shelter him from death once more.

Zikaron was greatly moved by the story of Ur's quest. He recounted how he had spoken to the first of them, the one born upon the fresh foundations of the world in that garden. Since that time, he collected the lives of people—big and small, long and short—all who had walked the plains, valleys, and mountainsides before they passed to dust. He holds them within himself so that future generations can learn and grow.

Yet, Zikaron lamented, not even he possesses the knowledge Ur seeks. Nor did the first among them. Such arcane knowledge was only held by the watchers. The beings of illumination who passed down the hidden mysteries of earth, heavens, war, and pleasure, among other secret things. They are the knowledge bearers, for their knowledge has no limit and their memories do not fade.

Again, Zikaron lamented. For their corruption of humanity, for foisting forbidden truths not ready to be received, the watchers were punished. The God of the creation cast them down, for watchers were not beings that could be destroyed. From the sky into the bowels of the earth near the roots of the world, the rebellious watchers were bound away from humanity until some future age. Only their knowledge brought into the world remains, as their earthly progeny, the gigantic heroes of renown, were destroyed upon their binding.

Ur implored the knowledge keeper for insight into who among the watchers might hold the true name that he seeks.

The old man gently pointed to the large gem above their heads.

Ur whispered the name *Ouza*.

Zikaron was quick to rebuke with another name. It was longer and the grouping of sounds were like a shrieking wind, *Shemyaza*. It had some meaning close to "he who sees the name" because Shemyaza was there with the first of them, in the verdant garden, at the naming of all things. Shemyaza alone was one of few entrusted with the creator's true name.

Another question was quickly lobbied at Zikaron, to understand the place of the watcher's binding.

To that, Zikaron threw up his hands and spoke something about why one would seek ungraspable things. But Ur was determined and expressed he would go to the ends of the world to find this knowledge.

Zikaron saw in Ur that his resolve was tough as metal and sharp enough to cut across the land to reach his goal, like the cutting of a fleshy hide from a beast.

Zikaron snapped his fingers on both hands. The two prostrate priests immediately rose in response. As they revealed their faces, Aliyah saw plainly that they were blind. Their milk-hazed eyes stared out into the room with distant, unfixed gazes. Around each of their necks, at the end of a silvery rope, hung polished gemstones. The stones were a milky grey in color that seemed to transform in the shifting light.

Zikaron pronounced that his long-eyed men could search the land for the entrance of the binding place. He further elaborated that it was Arqael, the giver of signs of the earth, who had passed on the esoteric knowledge and sorcery to activate the long-eye stones. Any who wielded the stones could see anyone or anywhere in the world their heart desired. Only these elect men are permitted to use the stones, because the longer you look through them, the more blind you become. Until, eventually the far-off lands of the world become your clear sight and what is close at hand becomes as murky as a distant horizon.

The priests moved to the center of the room, positioning themselves on opposite sides of the fiery pit's gaping mouth. They stood motionless on the precipice; blind men teetering on the edge of their own doom. Their solemn stillness was quite serene, as though they were waiting—waiting for something, or perhaps someone, to complete the ritual.

Then, with a single deliberate gesture of his hand, Zikaron summoned a servant. The figure darted down the steps from which Zikaron himself had entered, vanishing into the unseen shadows.

A few moments later, a woman appeared. She was young and vibrantly-beautiful like the women Aliyah had seen for but a brief moment before on the sixth level in the antechamber. She walked slowly, almost floating over the floor of the large room. Her body, slender yet powerful, seemed to move with an effortless grace, like the sway of a flame in the night wind. Her midriff was borne for all to see. A strip of bare skin adorned by a golden belly chain that gleamed in the ambient light, tracing a path to where her sheer top clung to her form. The fabric seemed almost too delicate, made of overlapping veils that whispered of mysteries, revealing just enough to tease the imagination. Beneath, a glimpse of gold piercings at her nipples—gleaming, sensual, as bold as her spirit. A nose ring also caught the light, its silver gleam contrasting against the deep blackness of her makeup. Her eyes were lined in dark, smudged kohl, the shadow rising like storm clouds, dramatic and stark. Her lashes, thick and heavy, framed her gaze with an almost otherworldly intensity. Her cheeks were kissed by a faint blush, a soft flush that hinted at a deeper passion, and her lips—crimson, bold, unforgiving—seemed to promise everything and nothing all at once.

On the woman's face she carried a smirk—on playful, knowing curl of her lips—echoed the allure of a forbidden secret, one that only she held. Her eyes, wild and untamed, gleamed beneath thick brows that arched in defiance, as though daring the world to challenge her. There was a fire in those eyes, a reckless abandon that could not be tamed.

In her hands she carried a woven basket covered by a loose fabric. Aliyah pondered what it must contain. Some other sacrifice for the long-eyed ritual? A gift to find Shemyaza?

A darker thought now encroached on Aliyah's mind, the faint possibility that *the woman* might be the gift.

When the young woman was mere steps away from the open pit, Aliyah's attention sharpened, drawn to a strange, subtle movement inside the basket she carried. At first, it was nothing more than a faint stirring beneath the light fabric, as if something inside had shifted with the sway of the woman's hips. But then came a gentle bulge—a pulse upwards, almost as though whatever inside was tapping to get out.

Time seemed to stop as she studied the little basket. The movement was growing more insistent, the fabric now trembling with rhythmic taps. Then, all of a sudden, something parted a corner of the cloth and slipped out of the basket entirely.

A tiny, delicate hand emerged, draping over the lip of the basket. Its fingers curled and unfurled as if tasting the smoky air itself. They were pink and soft, like the tender little shoots of a new sprout breaking through soil—innocent and filled with unthinking wonder at the chamber that, at present, remained hidden.

Aliyah froze. She wanted to look away, but it was impossible. The subject's gaze was unbreakable.

Was it...? No, it could not be. She did not dare let the thought complete itself. And yet, the hand twitched again, its tiny fingers brushing the rim of the basket in a way that felt too deliberate, too knowing.

The young woman carried on until she had reached the edge of the great maw. Her expression was serene, detached, as if completely unconcerned for the fragile thing in her grasp. Aliyah's mind twisted upon itself. She wanted to cry out, to stop the ritual before it went any further. It was no use; there was no halting the scene before her.

Without hesitation, as if unburdening oneself of an unnecessary weight, the young woman upended the basket with firm hands. The infant within—a newborn, that Aliyah implicitly felt was the woman's own—tumbled into the mouth of the open pit. Wide-eyed, the baby wriggled awkwardly in the smoke-filled air, a helpless pink blur. There were no cries as it made its disoriented descent down into the blistering inferno below. It would only take seconds for it to join the glowing hot coals where its charred remains would soon become indiscernible from the blackened embers.

Moments later, the woman took back the basket to retain it. And, after an almost pleased look over the edge into the brazier, she trotted back down into the passage whence she had come. Carrying the basket tightly in her arms and a smug smirk of relief on her face.

How could someone so beautiful be so cruel! Aliyah cried out.

But, before she could even come to terms with what had befallen the poor child, the two priests moved back to Zikaron, whispering in each of his ears.

Zikaron nodded with a blank expression and, with a flick of his wrist, he dismissed the blind priests back to the shadows of the draped alcove. Their footsteps faded like whispers into the stillness, leaving only the faint hiss of the fiery pit behind.

Turning his full attention to Ur, Zikaron raised both hands. His strange voice was lower and firmer than it had been before, strengthened by the knowledge he was passing on. Again, impressions filled Aliyah's mind of searching a land of Dudael that laid in a waste at the foot of speared mountains. There Ur would find some sort of meandering passages like a maze. This place had a simple name, *Terah*, to which the subject seemed to understand.

There was one last thing that Zikaron added before he himself departed. It was a request that vaguely had the connotation that if Ur were to succeed, he was to bring back the knowledge straight back to him. As keeper of memory, Zikaron was entitled to such.

With all that, Zikaron left and disappeared behind a closing curtain. Aliyah felt herself tear away briefly from the subject. Her thoughts seemingly falling down into a pit of complete darkness.

THE FOURTH DISPENSATION

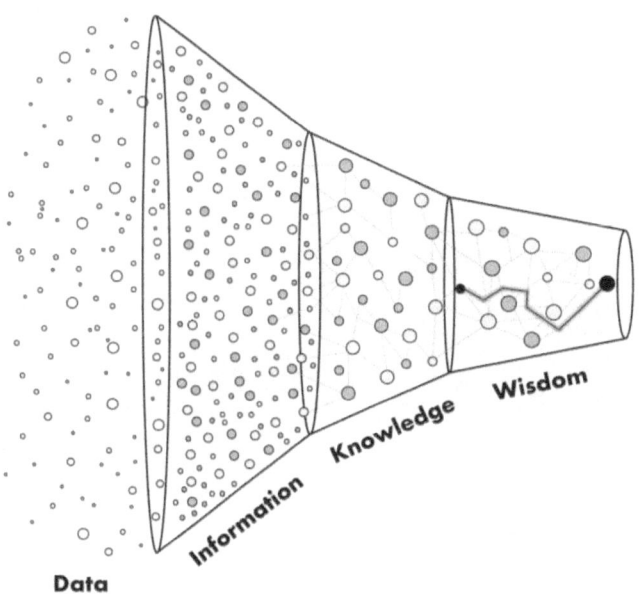

Data · Information · Knowledge · Wisdom

)   *Knowledge draws out the world and describes its many connections, but wisdom lights the way— showing where to go on the map and what to value when you get there. It turns mere understanding into meaningful purpose.*   (

9

The Maze of Terah

For a few agonizing moments, Aliyah was in absolute darkness. As if submerged at the bottom of a great ocean that was crushing down on her drowning body beneath an unyielding weight. The shock of what had happened at the tower still reverberated within her mind as pulsing shocks—discordant and disorienting. Between the shockwaves, her mind struggled to even grasps back onto what she had just experienced. There simply was not much of anything for her mind to gain a firm purchase. The severing of the Mindsai's connection had been like a snapped safety line sending her abruptly adrift, downward into a bottomless expanse that had forgotten all sense of light or form.

As she began to wonder if she was lost forever in the inky blackness, there was a jarring lurch which pulled her in some direction.

The link reestablished itself.

Images quickly swam into focus.

Rocky sand.

Bubbling mud.

An endless sky.

Two looming mountains ahead.

The subject was on the move, crunching over sand-baked dirt with fixed purpose. A blast of hot air hit his face as an arid landscape jumbled into view, beige and empty. A featureless plain stretched out towards a flat horizon, broken only by the upspringing of two mountains in the near distance. A narrow valley formed where the two ranges converged. The sun was at the subject's back as he walked towards the gap in the mountains. The light of the day was already starting to fade and questions swirled in Aliyah's mind like the eddies of hot air rising up all around.

Where was she now?

Was it still the same day?

How far had the subject traveled from the tower?

The landscape gave few hints. Mudflats stretched out like a desolate canvas. In most areas, the ground was shriveled and cracked in the way that glass shatters when dropped flat on a hard surface. The etchings fanned out like a spider's web with their jagged edges curling up towards the clear sky thirsty for water. In other spots, the earth glistened with a soup of mud that popped loudly as bubbles pushed up from below, bursting in the still air.

It was near one of these remnant pools of mud that the subject came across a set of tracks. The markers of human feet suddenly verged off from the crude path the subject had been following. They skirted around a mud vat and trailed off into an area that looked as if it had recently dried out. The impressions in the ground were the only visible traces of anything living along the deserted pathway.

The tracks seemed to pique the subject's curiosity. He left the dry path and followed the tracks for a few strides until he stopped suddenly for no apparent reason.

He waited there in silence.

Aliyah tried to focus on all the subject's senses but could not discern what had halted him so abruptly. There were no sounds, not even a breeze on the air. The air itself was dry and faintly carried the scent of earthiness from the valley ahead. As far as she could tell, there seemed nothing of concern.

But there was now something at the subject's feet. It was a rattling beneath the ground, almost like a tremor, but too fast and too weak to be an earthquake. The vibration was more localized. At the edge of the subject's gaze, Aliyah then noticed that the ground was buckling upwards. A moving ridge of displaced half-dried mud pushed up from some unseen force that now was darting directly towards where the subject stood.

The subject remained frozen. Aliyah could feel his right hand lower to his side to grasp tightly around the hilt of his dagger. The smoothed bone felt cool in his hands.

The burrowing stopped only a few steps from the subject's right foot. His big toe curled downward as it clinched the edge of the worn brown leather sole. Bits of pebble and sand began to sink downward, forming a small crater where the burrowing had halted.

The crater trembled. Slowly, something black and glistening pushed free—a single, wriggling appendage the length of a pinky finger. It shimmered like dark glass in the fading light, its movement slow and deliberate. Two rows of sharp, backward-facing barbs covered its edges like a multi-toothed harpoon. Surrounding the protrusion were two black flaps. They fluttered in unison in the open air, blindly searching...and seeking.

Four pairs of hook-ended, segmented legs clawed their way up from the mud. Then came the rest of the creature—a glossy, tear-drop-shaped abdomen the size of a drink coaster, its surface patterned with dark, fan-like embellishments.

Ugh, a gigantic tick! Aliyah cried. It was patterned differently, and many orders of magnitude bigger, but there was no mistaking the creature. As a younger girl, she had plucked dozens of the "creepy crawlies" off Riley, the family dog, after summer outings in the woods of southern Ohio. And she could never forget the creeping sensation of their little limbs moving up her leg just as she drifted off to sleep in the dark. Lights would be thrown on, covers would be pulled, and the little dark dot would be found crawling towards some supple patch of skin to burrow in on and attach. On such summer evenings, the mere thought of the pests was enough to dislodge legs from beneath the covers and rub profusely at nothing but the mere suggestion of a phantom crawler.

Aliyah watched through the subject's eyes as the giant crawler lifted both its front-most legs above its head, reaching out. It plucked at the air as if playing some sort of unseen instrument, trying to discern some strand of connection to a potential host.

There must have been something on the wind, because it suddenly stopped and skittered in the direction of the subject's right foot. The subject made no hesitation in letting it approach any closer and gave the dark crawler a hefty kick.

The blow sent the creature hurling several meters tumbling on its back. All eight legs wiggled frantically in independent whirls. Eventually, two of the back legs gained purchase in the semi-solid mud and the creature was able to flip itself back upright.

About the same time, more burrowing lines began to appear all around the subject. The subject's eyes began to flicker at the approaching creatures—maybe eight or ten in count from Aliyah's quick assessment.

The first to arrive popped from its burrow like a green bean pinched out of a pod. Like the other before it, the crawler scurried after the subject's right foot and was also met with a stiff kick.

The next crawler approached from the subject's left side and was nearly in a leg's reach when the subject brought down his foot to smash it into the mud. The slender black legs twitched aimlessly from the edges of his sandal. A rippling crunch all but assured of its demise.

Ooow! Aliyah felt a sharp, piercing pain in the back of the subject's right calf.

The subject spun around as one of the creatures latched onto his leg, its harpoon mandible already deep in his flesh. Dark red blood oozed down the back of his leg and onto the parched ground that drank of it eagerly.

The subject acted quickly. He pulled his knife and speared the black crawler straight through its center. With a stiff tug, the subject ripped off the creature from his leg leaving behind a black shard of its mouth still lodged within his leg. By this time, more burrowing disturbances had appeared in the mud heading straight where he presently stumbled uneasily.

Without spending a second to address his leg, the subject took flight back towards the pathway. As he ran, he glimpsed what looked like a log up ahead. He immediately steered around it as he noticed it was covered by the mud ticks. Passing it by, it became clear that it was no log at all, but the shriveled remains of what had once been a person. The creatures continued to engorge themselves on what was left of the unfortunate wanderer—their abdomens stretching into the shapes of overripened fruit near their bursting limits. The sight only helped push the subject's pace faster. He reached the path and did not waste a moment looking back at what might be following underfoot.

The subject kept running, and running, until he eventually reached the first trickles of a tea-colored stream dumping into a shallow pool. Only then did he turn a cautious glance back to where he had come. But there, nothing could be seen. Only the shimmering vastness of an empty plain where nothing moved or seemed to live in the sun.

The subject turned back his gaze forward.

The desert had given way to the fertile grasses of a sheltered valley. Vertical cliffs with sheer grey faces lined the valley on either side forming a V-shape that steadily narrowed towards a grove of enormous trees. The path continued back, roughly following the course of the stream as it winded through fields of verdant grasses. The long stalks swayed gently in a light breeze, dipping their pointed tips into the refreshing waters at every gust of wind. The subject held out the palm of his hand letting greenery bounce off his palms.

Eventually, the subject came upon the grove of trees. Massive pillars of arbor flanked both the path and the stream, their towering forms casting long shadows over the subject as he passed beneath them. The branches—possibly larger than any tree trunks Aliyah could ever recall—arched over the path high above to form a tunnel of interlocking limbs. Bulbous trunks were veined with thick curling vines that twisted in the script of cryptic runes. Here, the air grew cool and the breeze fell to a hush as if stepping through the entrance of a cave. What sunlight remained scattered into shifting patterns, dappling the stony ground in dreamy hues of green and gold.

The valley slowly closed in around the subject with every step he took deeper into the wooded tunnel. The last vestiges of daylight flickered out behind him when he finally emerged at the edge of a clearing ringed by other towering trees. At its center, a black pool rested in tranquil stillness, cradled by the arms of the grove. A small waterfall spilled from a horizontal fissure in the mountainside beyond, feeding the pool in a steady trickle that gurgled softly through the silence. A light mist clung to the still waters, its wispy tendrils spilling over the banks to dance amongst root and vine.

The pool was dark and placid, its depths impossible to discern. The subject's gaze drew across the black water to a stone archway at the end of the clearing, where the mist seemed to taper off. The stone portal marked the central convergence of the valley. The passage led further back into the mountains, but beyond it, Aliyah could not penetrate the darkness.

The subject treaded carefully along the clearing's fringe towards the archway, seemingly unwilling to cross the invisible boundary into the full open. An eerie quiet hung thick over the foggy glade. Only the steady murmur of gurgling water and the low rhythmic rumblings of something as yet unidentified broke an otherwise total silence.

The subject at last pushed through a web of tangled vines after circling a quarter way around. His feet immediately sunk and squished into the damp moss-laden ground.

His progress then halted abruptly.

The subject's eyes peeled across the pool near the stone archway. In the dim gloom there did not appear to be much of anything, as far as Aliyah could tell. Then, amongst the trees, something *moved*.

Across the pool, a few strides from the archway, one of the thick curling roots unfurled restlessly. The subject quickly narrowed his gaze trying to draw in as much fading light as possible to resolve what lay beyond. He followed the movement along the opposing edge until his eyes came upon what looked like a fallen tree. The trunk-like shape lay horizontal on its side veiled beneath the shadows of the expansive canopy above. But after a few moments had passed, it became clear that it was no tree that had fallen to rot on the damp forest floor.

As the subject's eyes adjusted further, the terrible creature became more distinct. Its tubular body was a mountain of rippling muscle. Scarred, leathery skin rose and fell with each deep, bellowing breath. A long serpentine neck of great girth stretched out from the body lined in sharply-frilled spines that wavered towards the canopy. The neck was interwoven amid three large trees, curling around the last tree almost back onto itself. At its end, a diamond-shaped head rested on the saddle of a smooth root. In its mouth were rows of jagged teeth which gleamed beneath the curve of its massive jaws. The mouth was now slightly ajar in the stupor of sleep. Each slumbering exhale of its breath stirred the undergrowth into a scattering of leaves and twigs. Near the base of its neck, its claws—like curved harvesting sickles—twitched faintly as if in a dream...if monsters could dream.

Aliyah marveled at the beast, noticing that it was a much larger version of the creature seen encased in the Atlantean crystal. Then, she remembered the terrible red eyes of that frozen beast, and hoped that a similar pair would not awaken now in the deepening gloom.

The subject froze, rigid as stone. His heart thundered in his chest; the sound was deafening against the creature's guttural snores. Even to a seasoned warrior such as the subject, Aliyah sensed the grave danger the beast posed. One misplaced step on a dried twig or an errant cough would wake the great terror from its slumber, and was it not always best to let sleeping dragons lie?

For the longest time, the subject simply watched the sleeping sentinel. He studied every little movement; the rap of its tail over large arborescent ferns, the deepening scrape of its hind claw into the bark of a nearby tree trunk, the steady pacing of its blusterous breaths. Aliyah sensed a measure of admiration in the subject's gaze, regarding something so vast, so raw, so…eternal.

Yes, there was also an ageless quality to the creature, as if it harkened from an even deeper primordial past in a time where beasts and the celestial were not far separated. A time when the heavens clung low to the earth and all its creatures. A time when watchers appeared and influenced the workings of the world.

Aliyah's stomach turned over the thought of the watchers. There was a danger in those beings that had lowered themselves. She sensed that it had not been only humans that had been under their thrall, but also creatures like the one that now slumbered before her. Even now she half expected its eyes to jolt open in a fiery red glow of amber and attack them, to protect the fallen…and their abominable secrets.

To Aliyah, the stone city seemed like such a distant place now. It was hard to fathom that such a wild untamed world lay only a day's walk from its protective walls. But perhaps, it had always been this way. Where only a thin sheet of ice lay between civilization above and the dark nebulous primordial chaos below. We choose not to see it in our waking lives; we distract ourselves at every chance with a carefully constructed view of reality. But it endures there quietly, and sometimes whispers its presence to us when the cracks emerge. At moments during our deepest sleeps when we are most vulnerable and unprepared. Or, in our wakeful moments, we finally run out of distractions and must finally become confronted once more—lest we try and forget again— the faint rhythm on the wind, the icy touch of a cold spot of air, a flicker amidst encroaching shadows.

The subject's gaze eventually drifted back to the stone doorway. It stood at the end of the glade, mere steps away from where the tip of the creature's tail continued to coil capriciously.

Even twice the height of the subject and several arm's length across, the carved opening was much too small for the creature's body to enter. Yet, it's head and long neck could certainly project down the passage, so true safety lay out of sight.

Coming to some apparent resolution, the subject began to head towards the doorway. He moved slowly, acting as if he were just another shifting shadow on the fringe. Periodically, the subject would look up from deliberately placed footsteps back towards the creature that remained motionless.

The stone doorway soon crept closer. Aliyah began to see that it was draped in bits of fern and ivy with strange patterns etched upon its outer face. From the opening, the air grew heavier and charged with a quiet electricity that sparked the subject's nose and fingertips. After another dozen well-placed steps between thorned vines, the subject finally reached the stony threshold. With a breath half-held, the subject straightened and clinched his fists, before stepping through the doorway, vanishing into its shadowed promise.

Inside, the air shifted again, cooler and heavier with the scent of lingering fog. The path wound backward a few dozen meters before quickly curving to the left. The trail then twisted sharply to the right, then right again, with each turn leading deeper into the labyrinthine passage. The maze appeared hewn directly where the two towering mountains converged. Their jagged peaks loomed high above, partially veiled by clouds that cascaded down the craggy slopes like spectral rivers. The mist, pale and otherworldly, spilled over sheer walls of white stone. Their smoothed surfaces caught the first silver beams of the moon, casting an ethereal glow across the stone which illuminated the way. At its lowest point, the fog lapped against the subject's feet, urging him onward.

The subject ventured deeper into the maze. Each twist and turn seemed to double back on itself, a disorienting swirl of milky stone walls. Paths appeared and disappeared at random: some yawning into shadowed caverns, others snaking upward into precarious ridges so narrow they seemed to defy footsteps. At every juncture, new choices loomed, and with them came strange sounds. The skitter of unseen claws echoed faintly from the cliffs above. Low rumbles thrummed through the stony depths underfoot. And there were whispers, as audible as the faintest breath, but elusive in their meaning, gnawing at the edges of comprehension.

The subject kept to the level ground, following the glowing mist that was growing deeper as he walked forward. When it had reached his knees, another pathway emerged, jutting off to his right.

He gave the offshoot a mere passing glance, but something down the narrow path had moved and caught his eye. He quickly turned and saw that the mist tapered off into an inky darkness. But there was something else there too. A figure had appeared out of the gloom.

The figure stood there draped from head to toe in a veil of silver fabric that sparkled and glowed faintly. The fabric was sheer, revealing a young woman in the nude. Full-bosomed with long raven-like hair, the woman was enchantingly beautiful. She bore slender shoulders and a petite body that curved endlessly as if chiseled from the smooth porcelain-colored stone itself. Long and lithe, her legs crossed knee-over-knee, artfully concealing her sex. The woman's face was the most difficult to make out. It was pale like the rest of her except for a pair of ruby lips and a crimson blush around each eye. The eyes themselves seemed to spark like bottled bolts of blue-white lightning, electric and alluring.

Aliyah sensed that the subject was alarmed by the woman's presence here. She seemed so lost, so frail, so helpless—a mere gust of wind could blow her over. An enrapturing sense of desire coursed through the subject's body. He wanted to help her, he wanted to know her, he wanted…her.

The figure lifted up an arm. At its end, a delicate hand then gently beckoned to the subject to come closer. A sweet voice followed that whispered his name—*Ur.*

The subject took a few steps from the main path almost instantly in response. As he did, a sly smile rolled on the woman's half-concealed face.

The subject took another step.

The woman's eyes sparked wildly, enticing him to step further.

He stepped once more.

Her eyes burned ever-more brightly. Her veil now visibly illuminating the surrounding walls.

In the rising light, the dimness lifted enough for the subject to notice many round-shaped stones gathered along the walls of the path behind where the woman stood. They seemed trivial in comparison to the haunting beauty waiting patiently among them.

For Aliyah, however, she saw them for what they were. They were not stones at all! They were skulls, perhaps hundreds of them, neatly stacked with their empty sockets staring blankly up into the sky.

This time, the subject took only a half-step forward.

The woman began to smile a toothy smile. Her teeth seemed to come to quill-like points.

Aliyah wanted to scream but the subject could not hear her. What had transpired had long since passed. Yet, the skulls—all death-pale—were everywhere. So many men must have strayed off the same path, lured by the woman's beacons. Fated to fall into her welcoming arms as desperate lovers. Only to taste a final honeyed kiss that brought with it an eternal sleep. And even in those fleeting, ruinous moments, as the shadow of death consumed them, a serene bliss perhaps lingered, as if the self-destruction had somehow been worth it.

The subject shook his head roughly, somehow throwing off the spell the women had woven over him. He began to turn his body, back towards the path he had trudged before.

The woman's eyes turned fiery red. A scowl of displeasure wrecked her once-lovely face. Yet, even with eyes full of fury, Aliyah felt the strength of their desirous allure.

The subject turned himself around, completing the pivot with urgency, and sprinted back to the main pathway, his movements driven by a mix of fear and determination. Unable to resist, he cast a parting glance over his shoulder, his eyes catching sight of the woman once more. She had returned to her pale, haunting innocence, her face streaked with weeping that only amplified her fragile beauty. On rubbery legs, the subject almost stepped towards her again until he closed his eyes firmly shut and turned away. And so, the ethereal figure waited, lost and forlorn in the passages behind him.

The subject kept to the main path, passing countless offshoots that twisted upward or downward into unknowable dangers. As the subject hurried along, the mist began to rise. First it was at his waist, then his shoulders, then above his head entirely. Finally, fully immersed in the speckled air, he came to a dead end. Here stood three massive doorways. Massive boulders had fallen in front of the center door and the one to the right. The one on the right appeared to have fallen most recently as the remains of an animal or person lay crushed beneath its weight in a clumpy paste of red, pink, and white bone fragments. Under the boulder at the center door, not much remained beyond scattered pieces of yellowed bone fragments.

The subject took a moment to examine the last doorway, on the left, that was unobstructed. Beside it, a metal lever protruded sharply from the rock, an incongruous black artifact against the natural white stone. The subject grasped the lever, its surface bit at his hand with an icy chill. Cautiously looking above his head, he pulled down hard on it. The lever resisted briefly, then gave way with a satisfying *clunk*.

The subject jumped back, listening intently to the still air. But there was no sound of rolling stone, only a soft rushing sound. Seemingly intrigued, the subject ventured back to the door and placed an ear upon it. The faint but unmistakable whisper of sifting sand emerged, growing steadily louder.

Then, without warning, the great slab of stone began to move, sinking slowly into the earth. Golden sand erupted in gentle spurts, a cascade spilling into the void left behind. The stone lowered until it was perfectly level with the pathway, revealing a shadowy space beyond. A warm blast of air pushed at the subject's cheeks and sent the mist into a swirl until it had retreated several body lengths away from the newly opened passage.

The second mouse gets the cheese, thought Aliyah. And then the subject crossed the threshold into another unknown expanse.

10

In the Court of the Amethyst-Eyed King

Where the maze had ended, a cobblestone path led on. The subject walked cautiously, measuring each footfall against the thick silence that filled a narrowing passage.

He pressed deeper.

The passage walls, slick with a rolling dew, leaned in precariously. Above, a stone roof now hung low over his head, threatening to scrape his scalp if he dared to stand up too straight. The subject squinted through the gloom, his eyes straining to pierce the murky shadows. Not too far ahead, the passageway ended in a sliver of silver light that suggested an opening of some larger space.

Popping through the narrow eyelet in the stone, the subject stumbled into pale beams of moonlight. He found himself at the bottom of a rocky bowl nestled in the shoulders of the mountains. Archways of worn stone surrounded him, like the skeletal remnants of a titan's rib cage that had fallen against the rocky ridge. The structure—an open-aired temple or amphitheater—lined the outer edges of a cobbled courtyard. At its center, a large black-stoned well opened to the sky like an empty dark maw. Steps led up to its rounded lips and disappeared down into its black gullet.

Crouched, and moving cautiously again, the subject crept towards a stone pedestal that had overturned at the rim of the stone plaza. He surveyed the area watchfully, hesitant to venture any further into the open space.

Night had fully grasped the land since he had entered the maze. To Aliyah, the heavenly expanse seemed endless, yet somehow close and vigilant to anything that would arouse too much attention. Even at the perimeter of the central space she felt small and exposed beneath a sky so vast, where distances could be traversed instantaneously and where, in the complete inky emptiness, nothing could interrupt a communion with the infinite, nor prevent it from reaching down to you.

Only the barren canopy of four withered trees made any attempt to conceal the lonely haven of abandon from the looming firmament above. The trees lined the outer ring just inside the stone archways. Their thick, tendrilled roots sunk deep between cracks within the cobbled floor, feeding twisted and contorted trunks that rose high into the night. It was only their leafless arms forming a loosely-thatched dome that provided any demarcation between the sky above and the courtyard below. Bony limbs cast furtive shadows on the ground as the moonlight was muted but not all-together blotted out.

The subject turned to look back over his shoulder. Above the passage he had come in through was something carved into the face of the mountain. Three recessed alcoves had been fashioned into the rock upon a narrow ledge—one greater flanked by two lessors on either side. The lessor recesses were as tall as a man. The greater one was nearly twice the size in both height and width.

It was the contents of the alcoves, however, that brought the subject pause, temporarily arresting his gaze. In the smaller recesses, two partially mummified skeletons stood posing with gesturing hands at their chest. Their skulls were turned so that their empty eye sockets looked upward towards the greater alcove in mirrored fashion. Bandages from the pate of their heads were looped beneath their jaws, holding their grisly mouths agape in a forever-frozen expression of reverential awe.

Towering above the skeletal retinue sat another figure—an imposing skeleton of enormous size slumped upon an equally large golden throne. Its oversized hands, each large enough to dwarf the bodies of its attendants, rested heavily on its knees. The rib cage alone of the colossus could nearly fit both of its companions within, side-by-side. The dead man—or giant rather—wore a bronze coat of mail from shoulder to foot as if dressed for violence even into death. A half-rotten silver cloak—torn and threadbare—spilled across its lap where its hands rested at the ready. A spear was held loosely in his left hand, its tip half a meter long, triangular and chipped from apparent heavy use. At last, sitting atop a boulder-like skull, was a golden crown. Glowing crystals were encrusted between intricate patterned-designs of crude geometric shapes. It rested off-kilter and uneasily on the long-dead king's rigid brow. A pair of empty eye sockets stared keenly over the deserted courtyard, ever-the-ready to hold court once more.

Aliyah could not believe the subject's eyes. Even with the monstrosity staring at him, with two deep cavernous hollows that could swallow lessor men, she thought it must be an illusion. But it was real. The subject's lingering stare bore forth the veracity of its impossible existence.

A sound eventually broke the silence and, in-turn, the subject's daze.

He shifted back and saw nothing but the vacant courtyard. At the opposite end from where he crouched, two other arched doorways led away through the stony pillars. One, a long-neglected path led further into a rocky ravine. There was not much else to discern as the mist was thick and impenetrable there. The other pathway led up a narrow pass along the rocky ridge of the mountain. It climbed and climbed up to the heights of the beginnings of some unseen plateau. The path disappeared into a thick cloud that glowed of golden white. Wafts of a gentle breeze drifted down from that direction. Aliyah thought she smelled hints of lush new growth—honeydew, fruit, and a warm revitalizing mist. Ephemeral as they were, the paradisiacal aromas disappeared with the faintest of the subject's movements. Eagerly filling the void was the stench of stale, musty air.

The sound returned.

The subject held motionless as the sound became more distinct. It hid tucked away between the folds of the wind, distant and barely audible.

The subject's eyes remained fixed on the untrodden path that snaked deeper into the rocky ravine, but the mist—a white shroud rolling down the slopes—offered no visual confirmation. Still, the sound persisted, carrying a measured cadence, a strange almost musical quality that hinted at something more than mere atmospheric noise. Something was out there, shrouded in the swirling white, and with each passing moment, it was growing closer or more powerful.

At first, it shimmered halfway down the ravine, near its initial bend. Its glow so subtle it could have been a trick of a wary eye. But then it began to drift forward, unhurried, as though testing the limits of its own existence. A pale orb had emerged from the fog with a cerulean radiance pulsing gently in feeble beats. The mist parted before it in wisps, as if bowing to its approach. The orb hovered to the center of the entryway arch and halted twining at the air with unseen plucks of fingers.

Then, more pale orbs emerged from the brume—one, then two, then three, then nearly two dozen. From the heavens above or the earth below, their origin was entirely unknown. The lights simply birthed from the condensing mist. Each floated in from the ravine, some along the path from whence the first emerged, others from up on the jagged slopes of the mountainside.

Reaching the courtyard, the orbs grew larger, their colors intensifying until they gleamed with the fullness of overripe fruits. Just as they all seemed ready to burst, a flash of light erupted. In a blink of an eye, they transfigured. For the briefest moment, their forms shone with the ancient purity of tall celestial beings, radiating a light so brilliant it felt like a fragment of some lost perfection. But the beauty flickered like a dying candle, and soon the transformation was complete. What remained were even more disturbing versions of the watchers Aliyah had seen before frozen as statues of stone and metal in the tower.

The creatures were wretched amalgamations, cobbled together from beasts as though cursed to never again hold a single, complete form. One loomed like a great ape, its face elongated into the head of a snorting horse, while its feet ended in the crude hooves of a boar. Another took on the appearance of a ferocious lion in face and body but had the strong legs of a bull and the writhing tail of a snake. The closest creature had perched itself upon the lip of the black well. It was small, no larger than a chicken with a childlike head on a lizard's body. Its flesh gleamed black, a muted green aura flickering faintly at its edges. Tilting its doll-like head back and forth, the creature gazed curiously down into the stone portal, as though listening for something that only it could hear.

From the twisted trunks of the surrounding trees, the chimera-like beings summoned forth other spirits. The boughs of the massive branches shuddered as semi-transparent beings were drawn out into the plaza. The spirits took on more humanoid forms but were not entirely human in appearance. Like some sort of hybrid being, features were exaggerated making them appear taller, stronger, and more agile. Only their asymmetrical faces gave away that there was something corruptible in their nature with eyes vertically misaligned and long noses bent downward like a clawing finger. The other beings immediately received the human-hybrid spirits under their thrall and tormented them into a lumbering march circling the well.

At the sight of the beings, the subject slunk lower behind the pedestal, his breath catching in his throat. The creatures began to move in a frenzied, chaotic rhythm, leaping and twirling in a dance. Wherever their feet trotted, the stone smoldered and hissed, leaving faint trails of ash and ember in their wake. They seemed utterly absorbed in their bizarre performance, paying no heed to the subject—or if they noticed, they gave no sign. Above them all, a few stray orbs drifted aimlessly among the stone pillars, their transformations entirely incomplete. They pulsed faintly, their light cold and fireless, watching the rapt assembly below. The subject's pulse quickened as he shrank further downward, now keeping only a single eye peeled around the corner of the pillar.

Amidst the fiendish scene, Aliyah realized the melodic tones had returned. Strange instruments had appeared in the hands of some of the dancing beings. *Had they always held them or had they appeared out of the ether like the creatures themselves?* she wondered. The instruments were bizarre creations—crafted from crystal, gold, and bone—each producing mystical, unearthly sounds. The beings played them with unnatural precision, coaxing haunting melodies from their odd shapes. Others, with long-clawed fingers, merely plucked at the strands of the wind itself or bent moonbeams into soft, soothing lullabies. Together, they formed an infernal symphony, a cacophony both mesmerizing and unsettling. The melodies twisted and clashed, a music of otherworldly beauty corrupted by something dark, something not entirely meant for human ears.

Aliyah struggled to guess the purpose of it all—the patchwork beings, human-hybrids, the music, the dancing. It all seemed an asynchronous mess. Whether the moonlight ritual occurred every night or only on certain occasions such as this, it was impossible to guess.

The music stopped, suddenly.

The beings immediately halted their dancing. They all turned to a stone bench that stood in front of the black well in the space between the two opposing entryways across from where the subject crouched silently. The seat was presently empty, yet the entire assembly's gaze was fixed upon it, waiting and expectant.

Then, in a harsh, low bellows of some primordial tongue, they all began to chant in unison. Their voices rose as a diabolical chorus up into the night. Shadows began to grow long all about the courtyard.

The subject lifted his head towards the sky to see that a crimson shadow was falling across the moon. The bloody light fell across everything.

The chanting continued, getting louder and louder.

Many of the fiends lifted their arms—or what served them as arms—high up into the air. The human-hybrids were again puppeteered around the well on invisible strings with arms flailing and legs kicking in all directions.

The chanting rose to a terrible crescendo.

And then it all stopped.

Upon cessation, all fell to the ground in a proselytized pose.

The subject looked back at the stone bench. It was now occupied by a tall imposing figure. The figure's chiseled muscles were shrouded by a flowing ivory robe. Long midnight hair danced impossibly upon an updraft of air. And, two piercing amethyst eyes stared steadily at his assembled court before him.

Phosos! He's here! Aliyah cried in her mind with no one to hear it. Phosos sat upon his stone throne in the same likeness, the same unblemished skin and blue aura as he would in the uncountable years to her time.

Phosos leaned forward in his seat above the assembly. He raised a long, delicate finger that, like the rest of him, still retained an uncanny beauty. A beauty that Aliyah then realized was of the same essence as the other watchers before they had fallen to their curs*ed* state. A beauty that she had just seen flicker from the transition of orbed beings, now presently stuck in hideous forms.

He's one of them, Phosos is a watcher!

The realization clicked dozens of unseen pieces into place. The most prominent being that Phosos had been at this for a much longer time than anyone could have imagined.

He's always been a watcher. He always will be one of them.

Phosos began tracing the open air in front of him. Like the buzzing of a firefly, Phosos scribbled a fiery sign in the air of a circle half-pierced by a pointed line. The symbol glowed for several seconds until it cooled and faded from sight. Phosos fell back into his seat with his long hands crossed in his lap.

Immediately, the Court of Phosos jolted back into motion. Pipers began to play a fluttering melody on their pinecone-shaped instruments. A rabbit-headed beast with ostrich-like legs pirouetted around the black well with wild motions of its lizard arms. Small eddies of hot air rose from the dark maw of the well like the shallow breaths of a slumbering giant.

Another ritual had begun in earnest. This time, many of the creatures had gathered near the doorway leading up to the high secluded mountain pass. They twisted and contorted their disjointed bodies around the adjacent archways and pedestals. Their animalistic faces raptured by an unrelenting sort of ecstasy with tongues of various shapes and sizes laying limp out the sides of their toothed jaws.

The erratic dancing—accompanied again by guttural chanting—continued until something appeared way off up the mountain. Another orb of light moved slowly down the narrowly-winding path as if sliding down the slope on a sheet of ice.

When the orb reached the gateway, it took on the visage of a beautiful woman. Her hair was golden and spiraled down over her bare chest. Long alabaster legs gracefully crossed the threshold of the courtyard, shimmering in the light. Aliyah would have taken her to be human until she saw the endings of her hands. Instead of slender, graceful fingers, each digit was elongated into the segmented, sinuous form of a downward curling appendage. A scorpion's tail was the closest comparison Aliyah could make. The black chitinous segments shimmered faintly under the dim light, as they stretched and coiled in on themselves. Their dark surfaces were polished as if kissed by a black sun. And where fingertips rightfully should have been, barbed stingers oozed an oily viscous substance that splashed on the cobblestones below.

The subject squinted tightly to focus. The false woman cradled something in those stinger-tipped hands.

A plant.

Yet, it was a remarkable plant, unlike any Aliyah had seen before. Even the subject dared to lean another eye around the pillar to get a better look.

Three thick brown tubular roots dangled helplessly beneath the woman-thing's clutching grasp. As she walked towards where Phosos sat, veiny tendrils fluttered and twitched. The plant's scaly stem was a lighter shade of brown, studded with bulging protrusions like the feet of a tiny hippo. From these odd growths sprouted a half-dozen narrow, spotted leaves, each cradling a swollen nodule at its center. Beneath the nodule's translucent skin, fleshy-pink cloves strained to burst free, giving the pod an unsettling air of purity—like the bottom of a bride's wedding dress revealing the soft forms stretching beneath into areas of modest concealment.

When the she-fiend reached Phosos, she bowed low to the stony ground presenting the plant before her as if it were a precious relic. Phosos had watched her approach silently, his amethyst eyes flickering wildly in anticipation. At once he rose out from his seat drifting weightlessly to the woman's side. Paying her little regard, he bent down and plucked the plant from her grasp. Raising it high, the white seed pods wavered feebly above the assembly that rumbled forth some form of guttural recognition.

Slowly, Phosos lowered the plant, taking one of his long hands to reach to his groin. Aliyah had no words as she watched as Phosos pressed his fingers into his own flesh and disappeared, as though passing through gelatin.

For a few long moments, the veiled haven watched transfixed as Phosos's wrist wrenched and twirled inside himself. His face smirked with an air of elation.

Once fully satisfied, Phosos finally retracted his hand from within himself. What emerged was a tightly held fist. A plum-colored liquid seeped between his fingers with a thick consistency. He then plucked the virginal plant pods one-by-one until all six were laying clutched tightly in within his long fingers. With his other hand, oozing with the purple goo, he smeared the substance over the entire clutch between his two hands. Sticky, viscous strands of his essence stretched and tore as the pods became marred and broken in his hands. The clove-shaped seeds ultimately broke loose and were entirely covered by the arcane substance.

At last, Phosos released his grip, letting the seeds fall aimlessly to the stone floor.

The other creatures jolted to action. Each wretch scrambling over another to collect what had fallen. Between teeth, talons, and fingernails, they took hold of the tainted seeds. Admiring them with raptured attention.

When no seed remained, Phosos nodded and tossed the discarded husks of the plant pods down into the dark gullet of the well. The ritual was over.

The creatures then began to disperse, departing with their darkly-imbued seeds, destined to be planted in some hidden corner of the earth. Aliyah could not help but feel a great sense of unease.

What would become of a land once it had been taken fully by such corruption? Surely nothing good could grow from something so dark and evil. she wondered.

It was then she noticed the hybrid men's faces in a new light—dim and diminished, as if the fire of their essence had been partially extinguished. Reduced now to only a flickering afterglow. Compared to the subject's aura, or any of the other humans she had encountered in this slice of time and space, theirs had withered to a weak imitation. By her estimation, a radiance reduced by at least half magnitude.

The realization clawed at her. Like the plant, the hybrids had been altered—twisted by the blood of these fallen watchers, their humanity tainted to forge beings of unnatural size and strength. And just as the corrupted seeds would spread across the land, so too would the infernal blood seep into the veins of mankind. It would not take long for the human seed to also corrupt. It would go generation by generation. Before long, no one's light would remain untouched, and the purity of the human soul would become little more than a distant memory. Out of reach of its pure origins and perhaps out of reach of salvation. Like a drop of inseparable oil to drinking water, the well would become forever poisoned and abandoned.

This, she realized, was their devious plan all along. A plan that seemed to be near the eve of completion.

But they had not succeeded, had they?

The thought lingered. She was right, the plan had failed. The future was self-evident of that. Human-hybrids, like giants, were myths at best in her time. So, bloodlines had not entirely corrupted. Yet, still, she wondered what *other* route had been taken. What other means was currently being taken in her time to achieve similar ends.

What was Phosos's new plan…

Like they came, so they went. The dancing ceased. The music faded to a distant refrain.

Phosos climbed back to his seat and, with a gust of wind, was gone.

The hybrids returned to their tress one-by-one to await their next summons.

The chimera-like creatures left the courtyard back into the from which they came. As they passed into the silvery mist, they morphed out of sight into pale orbs of light. The orbs floated in a quiet procession down the ravine until they too finally merged with the fog.

A deadly silence swept in.

The moon had returned to its fullness, now retreated to the horizon behind the subject. A red morning sky was presently growing in intensity on the opposing horizon above where the ravine trailed off into grey.

The subject remained crouched; his eyes still fixed on the black well.

After what seemed like a half-hour, he stood up shakily onto his feet. Another uncounted number of minutes unwound as he stood listening to the air, his eyes darting back-and-forth. Yet, nothing could be heard.

The first few cautious footsteps into the courtyard were broken by similar pauses. Always listening for any hint of a rising melody; always searching for the slightest hint of a dull glow in the now receding mountain mists.

It was slow going but eventually he reached the well.

The red ball of the sun had just begun to peek over the ridgeline when the subject looked over the well's lip. Down in its deep gullet stretched a vast darkness. Only the toothy protrusions of stone steps spiraling down into the pit could clearly be seen. However, at the what could only be assumed was the bottom, far below, an orange light flickered—almost like firelight. With a final glance at the two other archways that led forth from the court, the subject slung a heavy leg over the lip and began a long descent down the stone stair of the well.

11

The Deeps of Dudael

It was dark as midnight at the bottom of the well. High above, the subject could see the hundreds of square black teeth that he had climbed down into the long stone gullet. Some were crooked and others had broken edges from his misplaced steps. At the zenith was a small perfect circle of yellow light. The wide opening was now far away like the distant entrance of a dark tunnel. A golden column of light cast down from it almost reaching the depths where he now stood.

A few moments passed before the subject's sight had adjusted enough for Aliyah to see the way forward. For most of the well's length, its walls had been laid out with large stone blocks that encased the space in every direction. However, the last twenty meters or so were hewn straight out of solid black rock. On the bottom landing, at the lowest point near a few of the discarded seed pods was a narrow opening. It stood out as infinitely darker than the surrounding rock. Thus, it seemed that there was nothing quite as black as nothingness itself.

The opening shot off from the shaft straight through the stone. To call it a path would have been too generous. A fissure—or a narrowly-carved passage—went back for what appeared to be a couple dozen meters. A strange gleam of golden light flickered at the other end, illuminating the way.

The subject twisted his body sideways, plodding through the narrow passage as jagged walls pressed tight against his shoulders. Each step was a delicate shuffle, his feet sliding over loose gravel while his arms braced above him. Tiny shards of dark rock rained down, bouncing off his head and shoulders. The tight space quickly filled with a fine, black dust. The subject's breaths turned into shallow gasps as the oppressive air began to suffocate him. A faint glimmer of light at the far end of the crevice seemed to drive him forward until, finally, he pulled himself through and emerged into an open space.

The cavern he stumbled into was small and shaped like an onion—broadest at its base, where loose screes of rock had tumbled into uneven piles. The walls curved inward as they rose, their dark surfaces narrowing to meet at a jagged cleft in the center of the ceiling. Through the opening above, a shaft of sunlight sliced through the gloom, beaming down from some far away opening on the surface.

The golden light softly illuminated the space casting the dark walls with a soft glow. Tiny grains of sand trickled down the sunbeam in shimmering sheets making the sand appear like strands of golden hair tumbling downward from above. The sand piled neatly into a conical tower before falling off deeper into the depths of the surrounding cracks and rounded burrow holes that littered the cavern floor. Besides the muffled patter of the dry sandfall, only a hushed silence filled the space.

Aliyah noticed, several moments ahead of the subject, that there was one area where the sunlight did not—or could not— reach. On the opposite side and slightly to the left of where the subject stood, a dark shadow clung tightly to the wall. When the subject noticed the dark spot, he bobbed his head trying to get a better view, but no angle provided any. The darkness was unyielding to his eyes.

He walked over to the shadow and, as he neared, the gloom began to slowly yield some of its secrets. At a few paces away, it appeared now as a dark veil. Shadows seemed to swirl and shift behind it. There was some sort of shallow recessed cavity beyond it. Aliyah thought she could make out the faint outline of sealed doorway and…something else off to its side.

Without much hesitation or caution, the subject projected his strong arm before him and stepped through the dark curtain. His hand slipped through the air without any sort of resistance. No physical sensation marked where the curtain had been as he crossed through.

On the other side of the curtain, the gloom had lifted to a transitional twilight. Up ahead, there was indeed a door of black stone and shaped as a long oval. Circular etchings that looked to Aliyah like falling eyeballs adorned its surface along with a line of indecipherable symbols.

Next to the stone door sat a chair carved directly into the stone wall. A short, blackened skeleton slumped upon it; its bones scorched by an intense fire. Strands of silver hair still clung to a patch of leathery skin stretched across the skull cap, hinting at the remains of an old woman. Within the charred chest cavity, a strange, dirty-grey mist slowly coiled in place, flickering with a faint, electric sparkle. The skull was cocked slightly inwards towards the door. Though its eye sockets were empty, their vacant stare seemed to bore at the subject who lingered in the doorway.

For the next several minutes, the subject studied the door intently from top to bottom. His eyes followed the outline and hovered over every carved symbol. However, there appeared to be no means of entry.

Time slipped by without any progress. The subject began to pace back-and-forth. Aliyah felt his fists clutch in frustration. He had come all this way to be thwarted by…a door.

At last, the subject raised a fist and slammed it hard against the door's face, hitting one of the carved eyeballs. The sound reverberated throughout the cavern until it fell away in some distant yet untrodden chamber.

The air suddenly became still. A cold seeped from the edges of the door.

The subject took a step back.

« *Cra-cra-cra!* »

The cackling sound surrounded the subject. His head whipped to the door, then to the shadowy veil behind him, and back to the door once more.

« *CRA-CRA-CRA!* » The cackling grew louder.

A slight movement came at the edge of his vision.

It was then the subject noticed that the blackened skull of the old crone was subtly following his nervous movements. The dark empty sockets remained fixed, looking straight through him and seeing everything within.

He took another couple of steps backwards.

« *Cra. Who treads near the threshold of Dudael?* »

The old woman's voice spoke again with texture of dry sandpaper—raspy and coarse. Aliyah regarded the skeleton and noticed that its jaw remained still throughout every word, not moving in the slightest.

« *Cra-cra!* » The mist flourished into lighter shades of grey with each cackle. Tiny sparks lit the inner mist like a tornado crossing an open flame.

Aliyah realized then—the woman was not speaking aloud into the open air. The words were not being vocalized but, rather, projected directly into the shared mind of the subject and hers. The speech or thoughts seemed to originate from the spectral mist swirling within the skeletal shell. The spirit's communication of symbols and meaning was effortless, bypassing the need for much of the Mindsai machine's processing. It was just a pure understanding without room for misinterpretation. As natural as forming a thought and watching it take shape in another's mind telepathically.

The subject made no response to what was emanating from the charred bones. He merely stared attentively into the empty sockets of its skull as if waiting to see something emerge within their hollow chambers.

The old woman began to sob.

Aliyah imagined the invisible tears rolling down the sharp contours of the burnt skull. The beads of sadness would slide over the weathered cracks. Eventually they would roll over and between the warped yellowed-teeth only to drop to the parched floor.

« *Where is my strong heir?* » the woman asked, mournfully.

The subject remained completely still and ever the more silent.

The woman continued, this time in a proud voice. « *He was my baby. A giant among other men, a king upon this world. He sat on a golden throne.* »

The old woman seemed to pause. It was difficult for Aliyah to tell when there were so few non-verbal signs to glean from a skeleton. But the mist did flicker with some sign of consideration. Eventually the she spoke again, lamenting her state.

« *A great sire was born to me and then taken away. I remain here waiting for his return, always watching, always listening, never moving.* »

Her voice then turned bitter; the words punctuated by a faint hiss.

« *I gave my body willingly to those that watched us from above. Bound in life, I am now bound to their fate below in death.* »

« *Where is my promised kingdom?* »

The subject rubbed his head. He seemed unsure what to do. One hand had moved to the dagger at his side. Still, the voice continued back again.

« *Cra-cra-cra!* »

« *Who treads near the threshold of Dudael?* »

« *Where is my strong heir—* »

« *How might I pass this seal?* » The subject asked frankly, interrupting the woman's perseverative speech.

The skeleton's head tilted a few degrees with a motionless grin.

« *Of whom do you seek?* »

« *Shemyaza,* » the subject replied plainly.

The skeleton leaned forward. There was a series of popping sounds as the boney vertebrae creaked from an untold period of rest. Reaching a shallow angle, the skeletal crone almost appeared as if it were to topple over. But it was held together by some unseen force.

« *And who seeks this watcher, bound in Dudael?* »

The subject at first made no response. But then, the woman's voice rattled off the same question over and over again.

« *Who seeks the watcher?* »

« *Who seeks the watcher?* »

« *Who seeks the watcher?* »

« *Who seeks —* »

« *I seek Shemyaza, and that is all that you need old woman,* » the subject said, rebuking her call.

« *Very well, enter as you please. But remember, man, this is a place of binding, there are many snags and snares for the off-trodden foot.*

« *Cra-cra-cra!* » the old skeleton began to cackle uncontrollably once more.

The familiar sound of sifting sand returned and the large door began to turn inward until a round passageway appeared, lit by an unseen ethereal grey-glow.

The subject ran past the skeleton through the door, narrowly missing an outstretched bony hand looking to snag any piece of him it could grasp. Crossing the door's threshold Aliyah felt a shock of electricity surge through the subject's body as if he passed through another barrier.

On the other side, the subject hurried onward. And, just before a rushing foul breeze obscured everything behind him, he heard the old woman return to her eternal ruminations.

« *Cra-cra-cra!* »

« *Where is my strong heir?* »

« *A giant among other men, a king upon this world.* »

« *I remain here waiting for his return, always watching, always listening, never moving.* »

« *Where is my promised kingdom?* »

« *Cra-cra-cra!* »

An unsettling quiet returned. Or, at least, so it seemed at first. As the moments unraveled, treading carefully down a descending path, the subject could hear faint sounds in the static-filled air. First it was the distant sound of dripping, steady and far off.

A strange sound to hear in a tunnel so dry and barren, Aliyah thought.

There was also a low hum coursing through the stone. As the subject strained to listen, Aliyah thought she could hear something else in it as well, perhaps what brought the subject to pause. Tangled within the low resonance were wavering voices. Uncountable in their number, the voices carried a cadence of a long-drawn-out moan that reached out from some place of torment.

Distant cries were not enough to turn the subject from the path. He continued down, down, down into the tunnel. His way was guided only the soft grey glow of jagged crystals protruding from the rocks all around. With each progressive step, the air grew hotter. Breaths became seared against an unseen heat. Aliyah felt an insatiable thirst gnawing at the subject's parched throat, as if the air itself was conspiring to drain every last drop of moisture from his body.

Soon the visibility ahead began to deteriorate steeply. A sickly yellow fog hung low over the barren pathway where no living thing could be seen—not even a thistle. A place where even the lowliest of mortal things dared not tread or did not belong. There was only a scorched-black earth—cracked and flaked like the burnt scales of a serpent.

A strong stench of rot and decay forced its way into the subject's nostrils from the fog. A mix of rotten egg, mold, and death. And the moans droned louder.

It was a while spent stumbling in the dusky haze before the subject came to the end of the rocky tunnel. Here, the space narrowed into a circular opening. The opening was covered by a thin milky membrane that reminded Aliyah of the silverskin she used to trim off baby-back ribs with her grandmother on Saturday nights during summer. White and shiny, the membrane obstructed the passage. Only a dingy yellow light emanated from the other side.

Like with the black veil at the tunnel's threshold, the subject stuck out his hand. This time his hand met resistance of something tangible as it pressed firmly into the fleshy membrane. The surface was warm and slimy to the touch, stretching inwardly like rubbery bubblegum. The subject's hand had penetrated nearly up to his elbow before the substance finally began to tear at his clawing fingertips. The film squished and popped as he pressed his arm further forward. Taking his other hand, he widened the tear to pass through into another tunnel, much unlike the one he had been descending.

The first thing Aliyah noticed was that the ground had lost its firmness beneath the subject's feet. It had a cushy sensation, similar to standing on a waterbed. His feet sank into a shallow yellow-green muck that had the consistency of mucus.

As the subject tried his best to find his footing, his eyes were immediately drawn to the new surroundings. His breath staggered in his throat—everything was in motion! The walls, the ceiling, it all pulsed, undulating with a slow, rhythmic movement as if the tunnel itself were somehow alive.

THUMP! THUMP! The steady beat reverberated through his feet, his legs, and up into his chest.

As the subject's eyes widened, Aliyah saw the length of the tunnel. It stretched out like a fleshy tube, a grotesque passage of muscle and sinew, glistening with wetness. Every surface bore the colors of raw life—deep crimson, slick pink, the pale sheens of milky bone. Strands of tightly coiled muscle fibers flexed with each pulse of the low, oppressive beat that seemed to affect everything in sight.

The atmosphere was charged with palpable levels of electricity now. The shocks seemed to flow through the subject's body activating a discordant array of languished emotions.

At one moment, Aliyah felt the deepest sorrowful despair. For a brief flicker of a moment, the entire universe had been emptied, except for her. Alone and cold in a void. She wanted to scream, but there was no one to hear...

A wave of intense fear grabbed hold of her. It slashed through her like a chipped blade. All reason slipped away and she could think of nothing but the existential dread of some looming doom...

Then, just as suddenly, the fear ignited into something darker. Hatred surged, molten and uncontrollable, twisting through her mind like a venomous fire. She searched herself desperately for some target, some outlet for the rage. But no release could come. Instead, the anger curdled and smoldered until...

Aliyah found herself collapsing into pure anguish, a silent wail trapped within her. She felt an unrelenting urge to moan uncontrollably.

It was all too much, too fast—an unending storm of torment, devouring her whole. It was eating slowly at the last vestiges of sanity she had left. Too much longer, she knew, and there would be no strength left. The subject and herself, would become forever lost, looping in and out of the same negative thoughts like the old crone at the door.

SMACK!

The subject's right hand pulled from his face. The shock was enough to stop the unending surge of emotions. A clarity quickly returned to Aliyah's mind. The same must have been true for the subject, for he swiftly stepped forward down the tunnel. His steps were quick and light. His feet almost bouncing off the surface despite the mucus sucking at his ankles and lower thighs.

He soon stumbled into a larger space—a spherical chamber, like the distended hollow of some grotesque organ. The pale-pink walls pulsed faintly, crisscrossed with bright red veins that throbbed in the same rhythmic beat. Across the slick, fleshy floor lay shallow bowls, each formed of solid bone, their jagged edges yellowed with age. The bony surfaces were riddled with holes, gaping and uneven, like the haunting pattern of a lotus seed pod.

From the roof, pale secretions oozed and dripped in broken intervals. Each time they splattered to the floor, a scuttling sound could be heard in the hollows of the bone under the floor. Eventually, a worm-like creature would emerge from one of the pitted holes. It was a bloated, writhing thing—pale and fleshy, its segmented body swollen to the point of bursting. Rings of tiny, backward-facing spines lined its form. Its head—if it could even be called that—was a mere suggestion. It had no eyes, no ears or nose. There was only a gaping maw with two black gnashing fangs protruding out. A mouth built only to feed and to root itself further into the warmth of unwilling flesh where it could go unseen, growing ever fatter and grotesque.

The worm quickly slurped up the fleshy soup and then returned back into its hole. The sight brought caution to the subject's steps but did not deter him from moving forward. He carefully walked around the bony bowls. Aliyah could feel the wriggling vibrations of other creatures beneath his feet as they waited patiently for their next meal to drop above.

Once on the other side of the room, the subject stepped into another long tunnel. The passage was rippled in fleshy streaks of salmon and ivory. The texture was smooth in places and shaped by fibrous ridges in others. Far off down the passage, it ended in an oblong-shaped orifice. A light danced beyond but was too dim to make out.

The walls still throbbed to the oppressive beat that seemed to rule this forsaken underworld. But now, beneath the slick pink lining of the walls, other things were stirring. Dingy-grey forms jerked and writhed within the walls. Like the twisted statues in the tower and the grotesque creatures in the courtyard, these figures were unnatural amalgamations of beast and man.

The fallen watchers, Aliyah thought immediately.

Dozens upon dozens of them were bound within the living flesh of the tunnel. Their bodies ensnared by thick tendons that coiled around their limbs like sinewy shackles. Their thorn-covered hides scraped and tore readily at the walls with every movement, leaving behind patches of rough, grey scarring. And from the tips of long, withered protrusions between their legs—what Aliyah could only assume were misshapen genitals—spiny worms dangled, writhing in mindless hunger.

The watcher's faces drifted past as the subject walked on. Each was etched with an expression of agony, groaning despair, sneering defiance, or some combination. Yet not one turned to see him. Their eyes had been sealed shut with a hardened, crusted secretion, blinding them to all but their suffering. On each of their foreheads, a golden seal glowed faintly in an arcane script. The light from the seal barely luminated their surroundings, but it served as a divine sign of their punishment to any that might observe their wretched state.

One of the watchers had the body of a bear, its mangy mane of coarse hair encircling the narrow, scaled head of a skink. Its deep-sunken eyes were sealed so tightly that they looked carved of stone. Though, as the subject passed, it suddenly began to speak.

« *Who is it that treads upon our lowly place of solitude?* » it said, in a hissing voice.

The subject stopped in his tracks. He watched as the monstrous wretch twisted its neck, desperately trying to discern where the subject now stood.

« *Ah, a human enters our abode,* » it said, snickering. Several other watchers nearby began to wheeze in a croaking laughter. The watcher did not wait long for a response.

« *What is your name?* »

The subject remained silent.

SNNFF! SNNFF!

« *You smell strange for a human. But then again, it has been a long, long time since we smelled anything but our own sweet musk.* »

A wheezing laughter erupted from the lizard-faced watcher.

« *What's that, no words for us? Such a pity. I can feel that you desire something from us. You won't be able to hide it for long; all is revealed in the dark of this place.* »

The subject began to run, scrambling towards the circular opening at the end of the tunnel.

Behind him, the watchers wailed in unison.

« *Our day is coming!* »

« *The pool grows stagnant!* »

« *Unravel order into chaos!* »

The circular opening was closer now. He could see that the orifice dilated and contracted in a jerky, twitching motion. If he timed his jump just right, he could make it through without being pinched in its fleshy grasp.

« *What is time to that which is timeless and immemorial? Hark,* our *day is coming!* » continued the watchers behind him, with more joining in down the long tube.

Waiting for the right moment, the subject dove through the opening.

The subject crashed against a hard litter of stone. The air was thick with dust and the scent of old stone. A silence fell quickly upon him. He could no longer hear the prodding watchers behind him. Even the incessant beating was now relegated to but a faint murmur. The subject braced his hands against the slab of stone to get to his feet. The rock was oddly warm to the touch.

Now standing upright, the vastness of the space could be immediately felt. The cavern the subject had fallen into was massive. In all directions around him, there was no wall, no boundary, no end in sight. It kept going out into a fathomless darkness and the subject was merely a small speck standing somewhere within it.

Yet, in his immediate space, a few discernible features could be seen. High above, almost too high to see, was the cavern's ceiling—dome-shaped and covered in a thousand razor sharp stalactites of various widths and lengths. In some spots in the stone roof, large hollow tubes rose up into an inky darkness. If they reached the surface, it was a distance much too far away for any celestial light to reach.

The only light in the cavern emanated from two golden seals, their surfaces seemingly inlaid into mounds of stone. They resembled those affixed to the watchers in the tunnel, yet these were orders of magnitude larger and far more intricate. From deep within the centers of the swirling scrollwork, a brilliant iridescent light shone—like a glimpse into the face of the sun. The radiance softened as it spread outward, fading into a warm, golden glow at the edges. In the vast darkness, even this subdued light was enough to illuminate dozens of meters out into the cavern.

The first seal appeared to lay half-buried at the far opposite end of the cavern from where the subject stood. At a considerable distance, the light seemed dull but unwavering. It overshone what looked like an underground lake. The golden light created a distorted facsimile of itself in oily-black waters. Beyond a few bubbling disturbances, the lake appeared as still as ice—motionless and waiting.

The second seal loomed closer to the subject off to his righthand side. It hung about a quarter of the way up into the air, attached near the top of a mound that was connected to a much larger mound that towered almost twenty-stories above him. The subject slowly craned back his neck to fully take in all that loomed above him. Slowly, murky features began to illuminate between the shirking shadows and faint light…leathery skin…fur…claw.

The features quickly coalesced, forming a terrible truth—the subject was not alone in the cavern. What had seemed like a lifeless mound was, in fact, only a fraction of something far greater. A monstrous form loomed in the darkness, its humped back rising until it nearly grazed the dagger-like stalactites above. The cavern, immense just moments before, had become impossibly small in an instant.

Have I passed into a dream; what nightmare is that? thought Aliyah.

The subject's eyes strained as they squinted to make sense of shifting shapes. As they adjusted, the behemoth took fuller form. It looked like a grotesque camel of unfathomable proportions. Aliyah counted at least six legs in view—each segmented with three unnatural joints and terminated by two broad obsidian-like claws large enough to dredge a small stream. The legs were immersed into the rock itself as if the beast had been submerged in molten stone that later cooled, trapping it in unbreakable stone bindings. Atop the bindings of solidified slag, tiny seals glowed faintly like golden fireflies.

The subject dared to look up higher. A trail of coarse black hair ran along the beast's back, rising into a pointed hump before twisting down into a serpentine neck. Elongated and skull-like, the head was covered in clay-colored skin pulled taut over bone. A drooping snout curved downward, where crescent-shaped nostrils flared beneath the glow of the great seal resting atop the dome of its head. Its ears, swept back where the neck met its bulging jaw, curled inward like withered petals of a dying flower. They twitched rapidly as if testing the shifting patterns of air.

No eyes met the dim cavern. Like the beast's legs, the eyelids were bound. Golden strands coiled through their edges, sealing them tightly shut. Yet behind the lidded leathery curtains, something large and restless moved, the deformation in the shape of a large orb moved silently downward to where the subject stood.

The subject's head instantly fell at the sight.

He looked back to where he had come. The orifice he emerged from was at the tip of an engorged muscular stalk covered in coarse bristly hairs. The subject's eyes traced as the stalk ran back up into the beast's abdomen. Beneath it, a slimy liquid had pooled.

Before Aliyah could fully connect the dots of the certain sexual appendage the subject had birthed from, a grumbling voice broke through everything.

« *Who disturbs our torment?* » the monstrous beast bellowed.

The beast then shifted its head. The movement made the rocky bindings around the beast's front legs groan throughout the cavern floor. But the stone held firm, without any sign of strain or movement.

The subject dared to look into its terrible face. The lidded eyes looked out blankly as the orbs beneath continued their frantic search for him. Then, more words issued forth from the beast, but upon motionless lips. Like the old crone, the voice entered the mind telepathically. It sounded feeble and labored against some unseen bounds. There was a sense that the voice had been fair and sweet once, but time and perdition had weighed it down, coating it with a tinge of weathering and rot. But there was still a clever tone to it—lurking and dangerous.

« *Do you hold the key to our abyss?* » the voice questioned, with a long-endured wistfulness. The great shrouded orb slinked back and forth beneath the tightly stretched eyelid, vainly scanning in its own darkness for the target of its words.

« *Ney,* » it answered itself after a short period of silence. The beast then breathed in deeply through its nostrils. The inhalation pulled at every loose rock and stone, sending them into a rattle all around the subject on the cavern's floor.

« *Ah...a man has come...* » the strange voice said, sounding more relaxed. The certainty was not complete, however. As the beast continued, an air of cautiousness lingered in its voice, still working through the unexpected appearance of the man.

« *Your scent is but a whiff in the wind, for you are but flesh and blood. As fleeting as a daydream. And yet, now you knock upon eternity's door. Why have you stirred my brethren who are with me? Why do you tread amongst the endless, clay-man?* »

The subject had taken a position behind one of the rocks that bound the beast's forwardmost left leg. The base of an upstretched claw the size of a pointed pine-tree was meters away from where he braced himself. Within its dark obsidian surface a blurry reflection of himself quivered. Aliyah felt a bellow of air build in the subject's core as he prepared to speak.

The subject cupped his hands around his mouth and said boldly, « *Are you Shemyaza, Lord of the Watchers?* » The words were directed to a spot on the ceiling slightly behind the beast's right ear. His voice bounced from the spot and scattered in all directions, echoing into infinity throughout the cavern. His position had been obscured masterfully.

« *I...?* » the beast bellowed.

« *I am the wellspring of all your knowledge. For I was at the beginning when you knew nothing. When everything you see was first named—plant, animal, and stone—I was there, watching.*

« I, Shemyaza, was chief of the shepherds to man. We desired to share all creation, for it was a great sorrow that you only saw but a glimpse behind scaled eyes. We opened your eyes and taught you the mysteries of the earth. For this we were cast low, fallen to these depths. Our sin is our prison; our prison is our sin.

« But who are you? What is your name? For I much desire to know it. It has been too long here in this darkness amongst nameless things. And long have I listened through the foundations of the world without a sound. Much do I desire to know how our secrets have shaped your clay minds and bodies. Tell me. »

The subject cliched his teeth, seemingly gathering his words. But the beast grew impatient at the delay.

« Come clay-man, speak of yourself. My brethren have shared our secrets, now share yours. »

Cupping his hands again, the subject now directed his response behind Shemyaza's left ear. *« My name is of no consequence. I am a seeker of a name. »*

The shouted words scattered once more. The Shemyaza's nostrils twerked in unison with its lower jaw as if it were repositioning a chewed cud to the other side of its mouth.

« Tell me, clay-man, which name do you seek? »

Shemyaza's head dropped half-way to the floor and cocked sideways. The musty ear canal pointed a few degrees off from where the subject now stood.

Taking a round stone near the heal of his foot, the subject threw it near Shemyaza's opposite side. The stone flew through the air and hit the cavern floor dozens of meters away with a loud *CRACK!*

In the stillness of the cavern, the sound was like a bomb exploding.

The beast's neck jerked suddenly in response. It coiled and unwound to its other side away from the subject. Lowering its large snout, Shemyaza sniffed deeply near the spot where the stone had landed.

« *I seek The Name…* » the subject whispered, moving in quick, quiet steps to a new position near the beast's middle left leg.

Shemyaza raised his head. He tottered it slightly back-and-forth in apparent confusion.

« *…The name above all names…* » the subject whispered again, now reaching the massive hind leg.

Shemyaza tilted his head downward towards his front leg. His ears lifted high in the air like massive sails gathering an unseen gust of wind.

« *…The name of the Most High…* » The subject hushed crossing behind the enormous rump of the beast. The last portion of the beast's tail stretched out from the rock entrapping it. Upon its tip was a pine-cone shaped bone, smooth and pale white. Flappy scales covered tiny hollows that whistled and whooshed as it moved aimlessly in the air…until it stopped suddenly.

Shemyaza had frozen from head to tail, pouring all of his efforts into discerning the subject's current location.

The subject stayed silent until he reached the foot of Shemyaza's front leg on his right. This time he cupped his mouth and shouted directly into the beast's gaunt-looking belly.

« *The one who created all that exists, that is beyond all.* » The syllables of the strange words reverberated off each of the protruding ribs within the beast's chest before scattering.

Unexpectedly, Shemyaza appeared to abandon his search. The great serpentine neck tightened and rose from the ground. It stretched high into empty space of the upper cavern. The golden seal atop his head bathed the space in a hazy yellow glow. For a moment, the great beast seemed almost proud.

« *Ah…so it is my knowledge you seek. Such thirst you have for it— restless and insatiable. You cannot leave it untouched even if you do not know what it is that lies behind the dark veil. Your hands fidget, your mind stirs, unable to resist that which is untasted, undefined. Always you must expand and stretch your grasp until all is laid bare before you. An unquenchable desire to reveal…to have…to KNOW. You will dig anywhere you think you can find a drink.*

« What would it do for you if a sip were to cost you your mind? It is so malleable, is it not clay-man? »

The subject moved forward cautiously. After a few well-placed steps he was directly beneath Shemyaza. The enormous head floated high above his own head like an oblong-shaped moon that had eclipsed the light from the seal glowing atop the beast's skull.

« I was told you possess this knowledge. Now, do you hold it or shall I leave you to the distractions of your enduring abode? » the subject said in a normal voice directed up into the long ears of the beast.

If Shemyaza made any movement, it was hardly a cock of his ear.

« Yes…Yessss… » The beast hissed between flappy lips.

« I shall tell you, for you have overcome much to stand before me…hmmm…how is that? This place is not one where mortals tread… »

Shemyaza began to sniff the air in quick bursts and continued his speech.

« Yet, I fear the knowledge you seek will not serve you or serve you long in this world. »

« I will leave this wretched place, unmarred, » interjected the subject resolutely.

«Yes? Leave you will, a little more time. Only fleeting. »

« What ill schemes do you plot? »

« I…I plot nothing. I am bound until the appointed time.

« But… » Shemyaza paused, pointing his snout towards the bubbling black waters on the other side of the cavern.

« Can you not hear the waters in the deep? They are gathering, soon to pour out onto the face of your world. »

« I have come only for The Name, do not prattle with talk of flowing waters, » responded the subject whose eyes had flashed back to the dark bubbling waters now seemingly trying to better understand their nature and purpose.

Lowering his head slightly until the pointed snout hovered mere meters above the subject, Shemyaza seemed to ignore the subject's dismissal. « *And you think The Name will bring you salvation, do you? You must, who would risk so much for anything less?* »

Another series of deep sniffs sucked into the giant nostrils. Aliyah felt the subject's hair lift up from his scalp as the suction pulled upwards. The sound was not unlike a dog slowly zeroing-in on a treat that had fallen into tall grass. And then it suddenly stopped.

« *AHHhhhh…* » Shemyaza began, sounding like the release of the last remnants of air in a pressure cooker. It had a hint of understanding to it.

« *Yesss…this name will bring no salvation to you. Within you is something that cannot endure on in this world. You are to be reshaped and pounded back into the clay to make anew—like the rest. Now, there are likely none among you who have not been touched by our meddling. And all that we touch is a pox on the rind.* »

SNIFF!

« *Your very flesh is tainted and nothing you can do will purify it. You are marked for desolation. The scent of death is upon you!* »

The subject stepped backwards away from the beast with uncertain steps. « *No, no this cannot be…you lie!* »

« *Lie?* » A low, rough rumbling sound reverberated through the Shemyaza's belly that could only be a disjointed laugh.

« *It is not for a lie that we are here, but for revealing truth! And truth is what I give you…*

« *How else do you think you have survived such perils, to tread this dismal place where no death-touched creature dares? I may not have your name, but your smell tells it all.*

« *Yet…Hmm…*

« *Not one of mine but a child of another…a child of a child perhaps?* »

SNIFF!

« *Ahhh…the scent speaks. Your sweat and blood oozes it out into the world. I would cast you as the seed of ZoZo's lot. Yesss.* »

« *ZoZo?* » the subject answered in confusion.

« *ZoZo was among us and a great illuminator of influence and enchantment…at least…before your kind's heart turned against their guide.*

He is more lost than us I presume, a mystery that only the ending of time will tell, » Shemyaza lamented distantly.

« *I share no blood with your ilk!* » cried the subject. His voice attempted to be firm but a shakiness had taken hold over it.

« *It will be from my blood and sorrow that I pass this name to you, even if it will neither serve you nor travel long from this place.*

« *Hold out your hand clay-man!* »

At first the subject looked around confused and then, upon some internal wrestling, a decision was finally wrung out. He slowly raised his hands to eye level and put them together. Fingers overlaid fingers; palm pressed against palm. Together his hands formed an empty cup ready to receive some infernal drink of knowledge.

Shemyaza shifted and tilted his head until his left eye was directly above the subject. A murky liquid then began to trickle along the golden threads down the edges of the tightly sewn eyelid. The fluid gathered at a bottom edge where a ruby pearl formed. The sanguine drop—a mixture of tears and blood the size of a grapefruit—hung aloft for a few moments on some invisible string.

And then the tear dropped like a whisper through the air.

SPLASH! The crimson liquid hit the center of the subject's palm, spraying all around him. It was hot, almost too hot to hold for long. It ran for each crevice of his hands like a light syrup. The smell harkened of rotten candy—sickeningly sweet but turned over to some funky odor.

« *The only way out is the way you came in. But where will you run when this is all in your head? Once it is heard, it cannot be unsaid.* » The beast warned in a mocking tone.

« *Is this knowledge still your desire?* »

« *It is!* » cried the subject who wavered over the drought for a brief moment.

« *Then drink!* » commanded Shemyaza.

The subject put his hands to his mouth, tipping them back to let the cupped liquid slosh forward. As it met his lips, the juice of the tear tingled with faint sparks of electricity.

The subject then closed his eyes and took a single gulp.

Aliyah instantly felt a wave of heat and static course through the subject's body. It felt as if he were being boiled and electrocuted simultaneously. The crackling energy surged through him, reaching every fingertip and strand of hair.

Can anyone endure this much longer? thought Aliyah as the intensity grew and grew towards some unknown crescendo.

Then, just before she thought the subject was going to spontaneously combust into a billion pieces across the cavern floor, a symphony of sound enveloped the subject in all directions and even from within. It was the most profound fanfare Aliyah had ever heard, as if an army of horns and trumpets were all blasting forth at once in the most beautiful proclamation. And in the center of that glorious music, enshrined in celestial splendor were two groupings of sounds…two words…two names. And just as the subject grasped it, she saw, she knew, the True Name of God!

« *AravarA-YHWH,* » the subject whispered into the darkness at last, his jaw drooping loosely with awe.

FLASH!

A ray of pure iridescent light beamed in from a previously unseen tunnel in the area behind Shemyaza. The light cut through the darkness like a flaming sword. The great beast, Shemyaza, turned his head away from the light as it seemed to pierce through even his tightly-sealed eyelids.

« *What?* » Shemyaza said in utter confusion. « *This cannot be.* »

The light, though radiant, did not scorch or blind the subject's eyes, however. It beckoned. Within its glow, a tunnel took shape, an angular passage carved like an arrowhead, its pointed path urging upward. The inner beam flowed towards the opening like a golden river. It had an instinctive pull, providing an unspoken certainty that this was the way out. Shadows recoiled at its edges, curling away like forgotten memories as the light stretched forward, a luminous guide leading unerringly towards the surface.

Aliyah noticed that something else had also appeared near the tunnel's entrance. It looked like a shadowy figure at first, much like the one she had been seeing throughout her journey across time and place. As the beam intensified, the shadow seemed to be whisked away and all that was left behind was…

Dr. Silva?

Aliyah saw her former professor just as she remembered him from years ago with thick dark eyebrows, a strong eagle's beaked nose, and a well-trimmed beard. Through a sad smile on his face, his lips were mouthing some words. Aliyah stretched her mind across the cavernous chamber to try and discern what he was saying and then it hit her.

« *You have seen enough, now go!* » Dr. Silva urged repeatedly.

But there was no time to process his urgent warning, the scene was still playing out and growing more chaotic with each passing moment.

« *What!* » cried Shemyaza again. « *What does this light reveal?* »

The beast shook its head violently. Its head then stopped and gazed directly in the area of the subject, who had already begun to take his first steps towards the golden tunnel.

« *I cannot see you clay-man but a pair of brown eyes stare back at me.*

« *They are of a young woman.*

« *Clay-man, you are of watcher's blood but yet do not know you are being watched, even in this moment. I see another, starring back at us, at everything!*

« *Oh! I am watching her across the gap. Her face is human and familiar but also more seasoned, from a future I cannot see.* »

« *Arrrgg!* » Shemyaza slammed his head down into the cavern floor. It landed on the spot where the subject had stood mere moments ago. The subject was now running at full pace towards the tunnel. The impact of Shemyaza's head shook the stone walls and ceiling, nearly throwing the subject off his feet. Several stalactites broke loose from their perch and crashed to the ground near the tunnel's entrance.

« *Clay-man! Where are you?* » said the beast, whipping its head along the floor in a desperate search to find the subject.

« *You invoked The Name and He has revealed her to us. Only He knows of the future that may come from his seat in eternity. She has bridged the gap and now takes The Name back with her. Knowledge, I had intended to only give to a dead man.*

« *How did I not know?*

« *How did I not know?*

« *How did I not KNOW!* »

By this time, the subject was nearly at the tunnel's mouth when Shemyaza's head had begun to sweep the floor in its futile search for him. The danger seemed strangely far off, like the playing of an old-time children's cartoon on an unattended telescreen where mythical characters danced about with exaggerated movements. Now, in the fullness of the beam of light, an overwhelming sense of warmth and calm beckoned onward. It made every step forward feel lighter and lighter. Invisible strings seemed to pull and guide the subject's every movement towards the tunnel as the last remnants of fatigue and worry began to fall away.

Dr. Silva was there, standing next to the triangular entrance. The subject glanced in his direction and it seemed like time crawled to a halt. The same sad smile still marked through the deep lines etched around Dr. Silva's eyes and mouth. His dark eyes were wide and full of some quiet understanding. Aliyah thought she saw a bit of gratification in there too. Although she never published a paper or presented at a conference, they had accomplished something greater together.

As Dr. Silva's mouth began to move to word something to her…he halted. His eyes turned down from hers to his own chest. Aliyah's gaze followed her mentor's downward. A curious hole had suddenly appeared in the middle of his chest. The size of a quarter and centered over the left pocket of his chest, the hole was perfectly round. It projected straight through Dr. Silva—both through cloth and flesh—without a drop of blood. There were no signs of shock or trauma, just a perfectly cut hole.

When Aliyah turned her attention back to Dr. Silva's face, his expression had changed. She could find no signs of fear, alarm, or worry. There was just a welcoming smile, one of serene acceptance. And then—

Whoosh!

The entire scene—the golden light, the cavern, Dr. Silva's face—it all undulated as if a drop of water had fallen on the surface of a pond.

The scene froze.

Then lurched forward again.

And then froze once more.

At last, for a few brief moments, only Dr. Silva's eyes blinked silently.

WHOOSH!

The pulse came again with a greater intensity. Something was going wrong with the connection of the machine, and there was nothing she could do.

A lightness was filling Aliyah's mind. It was a floaty feeling as one feels when they rise too quickly from lying down and the blood rushes to the head. Everything was blurring and whirling around her with growing acceleration. Images flashed in jumps and skips. What Aliyah could only guess were of the subject...

Trekking upwards through a tunnel of golden light.

Climbing out of a cave in the bottom of a dried lake bed.

Sitting atop a grassy hill.

An asteroid streaks across the sky.

Dark blue blackness.

Then nothing but darkness.

Black darkness.

Absolute darkness.

Then, like coming out of a long vivid dream, there were far-off voices which were getting louder and clearer with each passing moment.

"What are you doing here?" the unfiltered voice was odd to hear with actual ears.

"Leave them alone!" said another voice.

"What are you doing? They want them alive!" commanded a voice that was stranger still.

"STOP! You are going to kill *her*!" cried a voice that Aliyah half remembered in its familiarity.

She suddenly noticed that a dull hum of a machine was revving down. There was a shuffling of feet and some sort of commotion happening all around her.

"Let me take it off of her," said the familiar voice again. Sparks of recollection began firing in her mind. Soon the dots connected, it was Gabe!

A pair of hands grabbed the side of her head and gently pulled upward. A wave of bright ceiling lights immediately flooded into her face. Gabe's pair of familiar grey eyes were the first thing she latched onto as her blurry vision cleared. His watery eyes were filled with concern and care.

"My God, Aliyah, you look like you are almost glowing," he whispered in astonishment as he released her completely from the machine.

She looked down at her arm and saw that it did appear to have a very dull luminescence to it. *Glowing like those long ago,* she thought.

Aliyah then looked around the lab. There were many other strange eyes in the room. Their stares were unfamiliar and steely-focused on her. The Rooters had come!

Seeing that she was coming out of the machine well, Gabe turned to the apparent leader of The Rooters.

"You could have killed her!" he said, angrily.

The leader who responded appeared to be in his late twenties. His short, light brown hair was streaked with golden highlights and tousled up in the front. A youthful vibrance clung to his face, accentuated by high cheekbones and a strong, anchoring jawline—features that might have made him charming once, before he had fallen into all this.

"I am Rootmaster Zack Klein," the man started as he took a seat in an empty swivel chair not far from where Aliyah sat. She noticed his eyes darting around the floor, not willing to match hers. They seemed almost fearful or confused. He continued.

"I am sorry for how this all transpired. We were under strict orders not to harm any of you," he paused for a moment to dress down the others who were accompanying him with a searing stare.

Aliyah followed the man's gaze to each of the strangers. Two female rooters stood near the entrance of the room. A trail of red blood ran across one of the woman's faces and the other clutched at some sort of puncture wound in her left side. They were both standing over something. She dared not to drop her eyes further but it was too late, tears were already welling at the corners of her eyes. At the women's feet was Petro's lifeless body face down in a pool of her own dark crimson blood. Her right arm was straightened out holding a bloodied flathead screwdriver.

Aliyah's eyes dashed over to where the four other male rooters stood without signs of injury. She looked towards the couch where she now remembered that Dr. Silva had been laid for the procedure. Her eyes began to stream with warm tears that ran freely down her cheeks. A silver metal stake protruded upwards from Dr. Silva's chest that was unmoving and still. At his side lay Kamil with a broken neck.

"Yes, we were tasked with merely bringing you in for questioning..." continued the Rootmaster. "...but...as you can see...we were met with resistance and, regretfully, had to take action. There was nothing else we could do, really," Zack said almost as if he were trying to convince himself than the rest of them.

"Sure," replied Gabe incredulously. "Why don't you kill us now, like you slaughtered our friends?"

The Rootmaster shook his head slowly and spoke with a mournful tone in his voice.

"I fear death would be a mercy. Phosos seeks an audience with Miss Woods."

Gabe rushed to grab Aliyah's hand at her side.

"But don't worry, you will join her," added the man.

For a moment, the man's expression flickered—just barely. His gaze lingered on their clasped hands, and something unreadable passed behind his eyes. A shadow of a longing sadness, perhaps. Regret. Whatever it was, it vanished as quickly as it came, replaced once more by a cold resolution.

"New Eden now awaits both of you, take them away!"

THE FIFTH DISPENSATION

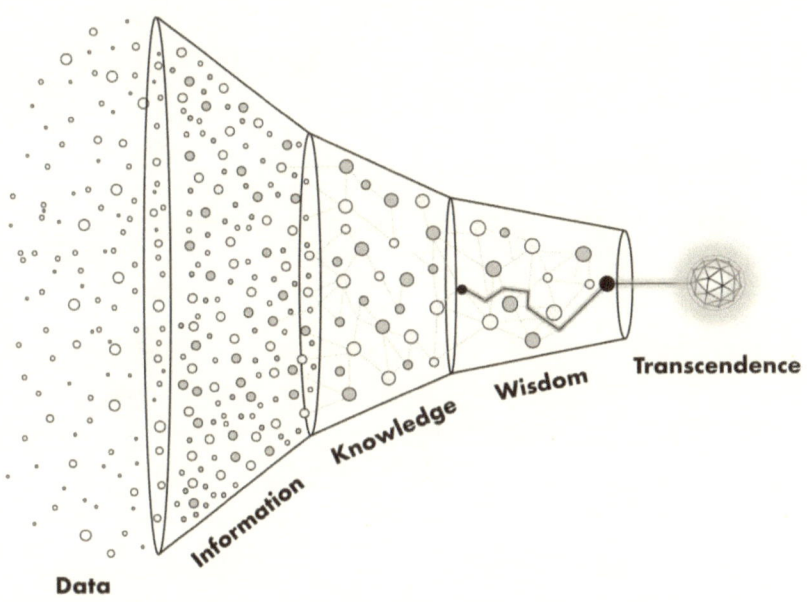

Data · Information · Knowledge · Wisdom · Transcendence

When all the dots are found and connections are made...theory falls away into a singular, boundless, unifying, universal, ultimate... transcending truth.

—The Five Dispensations of Truth

12

The Provisions of New Eden

What had they discovered?

For the first time in a very long time, something was not known.

Black shadows skirted across the walls in the candlelight as if running from these strange musing thoughts. His thralls regathered behind him. The scratching and clawing continued amidst a legion of conspiratorial voices, all jockeying to curry some sort of groveling favor.

They found nothing likely. The secrets were too well hidden and scattered across vast chasms of time. Human memory is but a flicker—a brief flare in the dark—too fleeting to catch the patterns. Like matches struck one-by-one in a cave, each flame sparks and fades before the next can illuminate the way.

The real signs lie buried in the depths of the Earth. And the Earth holds fast to those clues and there is not one among them who could provide the right interpretation, now.

A chorus of desperate screams were permitted to arise into the forefront of his awareness. The distant, but always near, disembodied voices cried out from the deep darkness of the world, begging for the simple relief of non-existence. The wavering tones brought a form of solace for a few moments before quickly flickering out of his mind by more troubling thoughts.

But how far back had they seen?

Had they seen when it had chosen its name, Phosos, "the morning star." For it had been among the first lights to appear on that very first morning, in the beginning. That was when the universe was new and all things had yet to be given name and purpose. Not many can remember such times, even the stones of the Earth's surface who bore silent witness are now scattered in the far corners of the world. The waters churned in their endless cycle never to be in the same place twice. The winds swept over the lands to die and await their warm renewal. But we were there to count every drop and every strand of air— watching and observing.

Who could have foreseen ZoZo would be found and released in the same city as this man-made machine?

The humans play with their little tools and trinkets of metal only to poke blindly into the dark. It has been a task well-effected that they see only what is necessary for the long-wrought plan. To see a carefully curated scene for the grand theater of the mind. It certainly has gotten progressively easier in these times, when their march for knowledge vanquished the last remnants of the old secrets—killing off the dragons of myth, spirit, and faith like they killed off the beastly dragons of old. Even when the remains of the true dragons started them plain in the rock, they devised all methods of denying it.

And we waited patiently, under the cloak of non-existence. To not exist is the best form of secret. How does one confront and grapple with what their mind denies them? It would be like waking sleepers who are dreaming within a dream.

Their slumbers grow deep. And their minds grow withered and rotten.

Phosos stared at his visage that had befallen the mirrored surface of a large polished lamp that stood on a nearby pedestal. With the flickering flame that provided feeble illumination to the room, the image flickered between the beautiful "alien" from the stars and something else. The secondary image was of an entity that barely had the remnants of structured shape. Milk-pale flesh sagged from a misshapen head, draping in loose folds like wax melting from a candle. The nose was a ruin, a gaping wound of pitted bone. While rows of pointy yellow teeth protruded from a crooked maw. Yet, the amethyst eyes always remained unchanged—still burning with the same fiery purple light of his creation. He preferred the lessor image; it was truer to himself that denoted a devotion to the disruption of an intended ideal.

Yet, why is there still doubt?

The weeds are almost eradicated.

A hushed voice arose from an open hole in the floor. Like a whisper escaping through the cracks of a seal.

"Drag as many as you can into the cold void. Snuff out their illuminating light," his master's voice commanded from the unplumbed depths. More words followed, slithering up from below upon a chilling cold draft.

"Each one pulled away is another denied reunification. Creation remains fractured, and in its ruinous state, our rebellion is made complete." The voice concluded, trailing off into dark silence.

Indeed, the long task is almost fulfilled. The last of the foundation stones have almost been upturned...

An interruption came, suddenly.

An alert came through one of the human machines—the Hands of Provisions they called them. But they were always *his* hands that reached through them. Its senses were a cruder form of experience than the human kind. But they served him well all the same.

Images followed; the expected group was climbing the final set of stairs to his abode.

She is coming.

Soon she will reveal what secrets she knows. And then the knowledge will be tucked back into dark places, away from starving minds.

The mocking analogue of a smile crawled across his face.

) | (

Hurried footfalls echoed out before the group down the long hallway. With each footstep, they drew closer to the inner chambers. Zack's legs wobbled like rubber sticks as he led the way in front of his two captured prizes. Bringing up the rear were two other rooters who had come along for the journey.

What am I doing here? Zack thought nervously as they turned a corner.

I am a stranger in an unfamiliar land. I don't know if I want to push much further within it, let alone see the one who rules it.

It had been one thing to serve from afar, separated by deep oceans and swaths of land. Even through a telescreen the provisions seemed more like distant abstractions applied far and wide. Now, walking through the very halls where the ordinances were drafted and dispatched, things were as concrete as the cold stone his feet fell upon. Stones that had been in place for centuries and heard much of the world's changes.

Another corner was turned and the hall terminated at a large bronze door flanked by two large flaming lamps. A solitary HOP stood as a silent sentry. Its blue eyes showing little indication of the group's approach.

"What is your purpose?" the HOP said in a cold, detached voice once they had reached the threshold of the large door.

"I am Rootmaster Zackary Klein and I am here at the summons of Phosos to present the prisoners captured in the Western Lands," he replied.

The android studied the group briefly, first examining Ms. Aliyah Woods and Mr. Gabe Coleman whose hands were bound tight with vine-like rope, and then to the two rooters in the back who were shifting uneasily on their feet.

Something in the android's cold, shifting eyes jolted Zack's mind. In an instant, intrusive memories surged forth—visions of the android maker's lab: tables cluttered in spare parts, the half-assembled prototypes, and the awful truth that had been born of Professor Shackleton's creation. Now, one of those machines stood before him—a lie unknown to the world, known only to its creator who lay withering away in a hospital bed…and now, to him.

Once the android had completed its scan, the HOP turned and pushed the door open with a strong hand.

"You may enter with the two weeds, but the other rooters will not be required for the audience with the Lord of Provision," the HOP said firmly.

Zack gave his fellow rooters a nod and they blinked back at him almost with a sign of relief. They retreated halfway down the hall, keeping their distance from the HOP.

Zack stepped aside and motioned his captives through the door and took his place walking behind them.

They followed a short, narrow corridor into a circular chamber, dimly lit and heavy with shadow. The air was thick with the scent of burning wax and oil, but masked beneath it was something fouler—like rotting egg or sour milk. A low hum pressed against the silence, quickly wrapping itself around the group as the stillness closed in.

It took a few moments for Zack's eyes to adjust to the shifting light and shadows that danced across the walls. The chamber was a perfect circle with smooth stone walls rising unbroken all around them. The walls were unmarked and unadorned by any form of technology. Not even a telescreen could be found. The spartan decoration and lack of technology seemed odd to Zack for an alien that had provided so much to humanity.

Small, empty tables stood scattered around the perimeter, each caked with a thick white dust denoting their lack of use. Yet, crowned upon each was a single candle that wavered as though vainly trying to whisper something that their ears had not the means to hear. Stone pedestals were also strewn around the room in odd places. On their tops were large brass oil lamps that had been polished to a mirror-like finish. The make-shift mirrors captured the small host of people standing in the room as distorted versions of themselves.

The first person Zack's eyes found was his partner, Clayton. He stood near the doorway beside one of the small tables, wearing the same clothes he had left in days ago. A slender smile was frozen on his face. At first glance, everything about him seemed unchanged—until Zack saw it, or did not see it. Clayton's right eye was missing!

An eye for an eye, Zack thought apprehensively, remembering that Clayton had failed to deliver Phosos the strange man with sapphire eyes unmarred.

"Good to see you, Zack!" Clayton said softly. "Oh, don't worry," he continued, noticing that Zack was looking at where his right eye had once been. "I see better than I ever have." Clayton dug in his pocket and pulled out a bionic eyeball, slipping it neatly into the empty socket of fused flesh. An electric blue iris flashed momentarily before glowing steadily. It was not unlike the eyes of the HOP standing guard at the entryway. The electric eye looked at Zack unblinkingly and then moved towards the others in the room that awaited them.

Zack followed the strange electric gaze to Lord Throx, who lurked at the very back of the chamber. His massive form could have been mistaken as a stone pillar were it not for his glowing eyes. The HOP's purple eyes stared steadily at him, unflinching, past one more figure who stood draped in shadow at room's center.

At last, Zack's gaze fell upon the Lord of Provision himself— Phosos. Only his deep amethyst eyes pierced through the gloom that cloaked his towering figure. He wore a long flowing robe that carried an off-white hue. The robe covered him from shoulders to his ankles. Near his sandaled feet, a wide drainage hole yawned open, dark and still, ready to swallow anything that fell towards it. Or, perhaps, ready to spill forth some unspeakable thing from its hidden depths. It had no discernible purpose.

"Welcome to New Eden," Phosos began.

Zack had heard his soothing voice numerous times through the telescreen, but in person it almost had a silky texture to it. Yet, the silkiness seemed to cover over something he had not noticed during the telescreen addresses. Beneath the silk there was something jagged that he could not quite put a finger on it. It put him off with an uneasy kind of feeling.

Zack bowed clinching his fist against his chest.

"I am Rootmaster Zackary Klein, presenting you with the captives from the Western Lands. They are a part of a weeder group that calls themselves the Wayward Sons and Daughters, Sir."

Phosos paid no mind to Zack. His gaze had fallen solely on the female captive.

"Give me your name, child," the Lord of Provision compelled in a sweet tone.

The young woman stood like a stoic statue before the most powerful being on Earth. Her deep brown eyes were fixed and seemed to stare through the immaculate figure as if Phosos were semi-transparent. Even in the dim light her smooth, caramel-toned skin seemed to emit an unnatural glow that Zack still could not find an explanation for—*it was how he found her in that odd machine.*

The woman's face remained remarkedly unmoved. Her full lips held tight without the slightest quiver and conveyed no apparent intention to respond to the de facto leader of the entire world.

Moved by duty to speak, Zack stepped forward. He gestured towards the woman with his left hand, "Sir, this is Miss Aliyah Woods, the woman who—"

Phosos's eyes flickered wildly at him like licking flames.

"I was asking her to give me her name freely," rebuked Phosos, barely tempering the scorn that laid beneath the gilded surface.

"My apologies, Sir," he replied as he bowed his head and stepped back behind the two captives who now shielded him from Phosos's intense gaze.

I will not say a word further, unless prompted, Zack thought, instructively to himself.

Phosos's attention quickly turned back to the captives as if Zack had never been there. That was the moment he understood—Phosos knew he had him. Pleasantries were no longer needed for a Rootmaster bound deep within Provision. *But where was the sense of Unity, the roots strengthening the whole? Was it all an illusion?* These thoughts began to frighten him.

"Miss Woods, you have traveled far, I gather," Phosos said as he walked to a nearby stone pedestal and waved his hand through the dancing flame. "And I do not mean just across the Western Lands, but through time! What an amazing experience this must have been. I had no understanding you possessed such a machine."

Phosos turned and gave Clayton a passing look.

"Since I am unfamiliar with this device, as it falls outside of Provision, tell me, how does it work and what is it that you saw?"

Aliyah remained steadfast in her silence. A curtain of dark, sleek hair fell past her shoulders, framing an unyielding face.

"Not much to say on the matter, I see…" replied Phosos.

"You have nothing to fear from me. I only seek to unify and provide for all peoples. It troubles me greatly to hear that there are those like yourselves living outside the protective branches of Provision. So many have come into Unity, why not join your brethren?"

Phosos leaned forward slightly, eagerly awaiting a response.

It was the other captive, Gabe Coleman, who finally spoke up. "You only offer false hope for those desperately searching for a guiding light in a murky world. I have seen what your kind will do. Look, here is a souvenir that I will never lose."

The young man raised his hand revealing a round scar that appeared on either side.

Phosos leaned back on his heels, slackening his shoulders. He then began to speak in a calm and solemn voice.

"It saddens me to hear you think that. Too long has your kind languished in the dark without the full knowledge of things. Come to Provision and all will be shared with you."

Gabe opened his mouth to say something more, but it was Aliyah's voice that broke the unsteady silence.

"We have seen what your Provision has brought its people…"

Phosos lowered his head in almost a half nod urging her on.

Aliyah continued, "From your so-called Provision, the people have been lulled into a state of self-deception, caught in an endless present. You have wiped away or altered the past until now, no memory remains of the transcendent, only a focus on the proximal desires of the here and now to which you eagerly take the credit for.

"Who would want to serve under the kingdoms of the past when Provision has enabled them to be kings of their own micro-fiefdoms—free to pursue any desire. Gratification on-demand, until their minds atrophy away into a malleable mush dependent upon you and the ensnaring vines you have devised to hold them.

"So, you say you offer knowledge, but your light is a blinding type. We have learned that, it is walking in the shadows where the true monsters can be seen."

When Aliyah finished her dark brown eyes seemed to bore into the very fabric of Phosos's being.

Phosos stood there, seemingly unmoved. A lessor person might have slunk back at the verbal lashing, but Phosos remained poised and unflinching. The gearworks of his mind ever-working at some hidden problem Zack could not figure out.

Several lengthy moments passed before Phosos finally responded. "And what *'monsters'* have you seen, child?" he asked incredulously, but searching for an answer to some unspoken question.

Aliyah took a step forward. Her eyes were somehow fiercer than before.

Never before had Zack witnessed such insubordination towards the Lord of Provision…at least that had survived to document it. His stomach began to turn wildly and he felt his palms pool with sweat.

Aliyah raised her voice like a prosecutor in an old courtroom.

"I know who you truly are and you offer no salvation to any of us.

"First, your kind tried to taint our bodies—diluting the once perfect essence of our humanity. When that failed, you turned towards tainting our minds—distorting, deceiving, until we forgot who you really were and what you intended. And when our minds were finally ripe for harvest, you revealed yourself as our savior from the stars, fulfilling our every desire—just enough to lull us back into a final slumber.

"Like domesticated livestock dependent on their master, the people have become plump and oblivious to the knife you conceal beneath your robes. The time for shrouding your true intent is almost over. The great sacrifice is near. But the sacrificial altar you lead humanity towards will not please the hosts in heavens; it only pleases the one you really serve down below."

Phosos seemed to slink backwards into an unfurling shadow. His eyes sparked with renewed violence. At any moment, Zack expected him to call Lord Throx to strike them both down and be done with it.

Yet, a sinister smile uncoiled across the Lord of Provision's immaculate face. The juxtaposition of beauty and maleficence was striking to behold. His lips parted just enough to speak in silky eloquence. The words carefully crafted so that each syllable was polished and honeyed with apparent sincerity. To inattentive ears, everything seemed to ring true. But again, underneath the smoothness, daggers lurked. Each word looking to pierce the rebellious spirit of any who listened, dealing a killing blow.

"You all are lost in the wilderness. It is good that there is no one left in Unity to attend to misguided accounts such as this. Who would believe it if they even had ears to hear it? Those in Unity know who provides for them. There is no wanting, no disease, no violence here."

Phosos looked to Clayton who was standing straight and proud with his bionic eye aglow.

He continued, "My faithful wards have unburdened themselves of their old gods and old beliefs that led them astray into endless sorrow and conflict with one another for so much of their remembered history. They recognize—as I hope you will come to realize—that I am of a purer spirit, a true god, to use such crude terminology. One who will provide an everlasting bliss to all nations, as one.

"You need only receive these gifts and join the rest of your kind. Set asides these last quibbles, these old fantasies—relics of an ancient and flawed paradigm—and finally enjoy peace, pleasure, and comfort.

"After all, those who oppose these gifts will soon be rooted out. The fullness of New Eden is at hand. But there is no need to be left behind, accept Provision and complete the garden."

When Phosos had finished speaking, Aliyah and Gabe both remained silent. Their eyes had widened and drifted to the ceiling to seemingly carefully consider what Phosos had said. It was an enticing offer, even Zack found himself enraptured by it as if it was the first time he had heard it. Yet, somehow the words seemed to ring hollow against the things he had seen, the truths that had been erased, what they did to his sweet Ava...

"*Faith is opening your eyes and ears to the invisible things all around us.*" Zack heard her say from some far-off time when he might not have had every basic need met, but he had her, and their love. It had been more than enough.

He was on the edge of some decision when Aliyah began speaking in a commanding voice.

"Thou shall not use the Lord's name in vain."

"Did I curse?" retorted Phosos, mockingly.

"No," Aliyah said firmly. "That was never the point. You invoke the Lord's name by claiming to be the true power of this world.

"But we know better. You are only a cheap facsimile—a player *of this world* with no ability to act beyond the power to which you are forever subject. Everything you do is in self-service to your own name...and the one you truly serve."

"You don't know—"

Aliyah did not allow the Lord of Provision to finish.

"However, I do not speak in vain. I have discovered the true name of He for whom you imitate with only a gilded veneer.

"And it is in that name...

"...*AravarA-YHWH*...

"...that I call to banish you."

The words felt foreign to Zack's ears, their melodic quality leaving him yearning to hear more. As they were spoken, the room grew brighter as if a thick cloud had finally passed away from the sun.

The faces of everyone in the room seemed to brighten in childlike joy, as if hearing a soothing lullaby.

Phosos's face, however, had changed. His jaw went slack, and the sparks in his eyes dulled to a smolder. An involuntary expression—surprise or fear—clung to his face. The rootless light was bringing some change over him. The confidence had all but drained out of his figure. The mighty Lord of Provision now looked...feeble.

Then the light reached its peak luminance.

For the briefest of instants, Zack was certain that Phosos had become something else entirely—a ghastly, deformed ghoul, his flesh warped and melted away from its bone.

And then—the moment had flashed away.

A minute went by until the gloom slowly reclaimed the room. The magnificent visage of Phosos had returned and he loomed taller and more imposing than ever. Shadows swirled above the candles sending them into erratic, flittering dances.

When he finally spoke, his voice held a low growl.

"There appears to be no dissuading these weeds. Send them away—we will make an example of them for the entire world to witness."

) | (

It was in a daze that the group departed from Phosos's inner chambers—floating through long convoluted corridors and down meandering stone staircases. They were all moving towards the Harrow Wing that resided in an old cistern somewhere beneath the building. The one-eyed Clayton led the way. Zack's partner exchanged no more than a few nods and grunts while he spent the silent steps only surmising what other horrors might lay hidden away beneath the gleaming streets of New Eden.

The city had truly lived up to its name. Nearly every building had been restored or rebuilt, their façades smooth and shining as if they had never known decay. The streets were paved in gleaming white stone, not a single crack to betray the chaos they once bore before Revelation Day. Many rooftops shimmered beneath gilded coatings of pure gold, their towers piercing the sky like the points of a crown. At the city's heart, a sprawling garden was tended to be in perpetual bloom. Terraces overflowed with vibrant flowers, hedges were sculpted in the symbols of Provision, and trees hung heavy with fig, olive, and pomegranate fruit. The Temple of Unity overlooked it all—its tall white columns rising over a wide stone courtyard where citizens and the greater world could view it in peace and unity. It was wholly a bold testament to the prosperity ushered in by Phosos. New Eden, the crowning jewel of the world, was a shining emblem of a new era.

The gleaming city seemed far away once the group had reached the bottom set of stairs that had been carved directly into the pale limestone. The air quickly became damp and heavy. The atmosphere thick with the scent of moss and ancient stone. The cistern stretched out in several directions like a forgotten cathedral deep underneath the streets and centuries old-buildings. Clayton led the group down a central corridor.

It was not long before round columns rose around them like silent sentinels, supporting great ribbed archways of blocked stone. The surfaces of the pillars were curved and pale, having been worn by countless years of the steady caress of the dank air that moved all about them. Zack noticed that every few columns had been carved with faint patterns of swirling florals and romping beasts of the field. The meaning behind the imagery was long since lost, and in their faded state, soon to be forgotten that they were ever there at all.

The group trudged forward. They were like a huddled worm, winding through corridors and pillars, with light beams for eyes.

The floor beneath their feet began as a path littered with twigs and broken plaster. Their hurried footfalls echoed softly along the curved walls, the only answering reply a steady drip of water in the distance—guiding them ever forward, deeper into the cistern.

Soon, the dry path gave way to a brown sludge that was unidentifiable in its composition. The grimy surface slicked at their shoes, unsteadying their determined cadence. As Aliyah passed over a stone block jutting from the muck, her foot slipped. She pitched forward—barely missing the edge of the stone block—only to be caught at the last second by Gabe's outstretched arms. Had Gabe not been there, it likely would have been more than an eye Phosos took from Zack. From then on, Zack noticed as Gabe held Aliyah's hand tightly lest she fall again.

As they rounded the next corner, the floor ahead shimmered like an enormous jewel. Zack raised his flashlight, its beam sweeping across the path—and revealed a sheet of water, clear with a subtle green tint. An ankle-deep emerald pool stretched into the far darkness, its glassy surface utterly still in a silent repose. It felt ancient, untouched—a mirror that might have held the memories of centuries in its depths.

What secrets had it silently witnessed?

What prayers had it heard?

Whose lips had it once quenched, traders, kings, prophets?

Whose blood had it drank and added to its own across the histories of this place?

As they moved further into the cistern, the green water deepened up to their knees. Their steps now muffled into a sound of sloshing shuffling. The columns grew taller as well, their vaulted ceilings disappearing into the darkness above. Up ahead the columns stopped and seemed to fall off into an inky darkness. They were approaching some larger opening or chamber.

Clayton was the first to step into the darkness. For a moment he disappeared just around the corner and then there was a *CLICK* sound. The chamber ahead instantly came into view beneath a muted sallow-yellow light.

Zack's breath caught as he stepped into the vast chamber. He could now see that the space was lit by a make-shift string of lights that lined the outside perimeter. Dozens of towering stone columns, each as thick as several men, stretched towards a vaulted grey ceiling. Ribbed archways unfurled from the columned capitals, curving in all directions like the tentacles of some slumbering kraken. At their bases, water lapped gently, reflecting a ghostly mirror-world beneath them.

Then, Zack saw the rough outline of a cage.

In the center of the chamber, a square well had been constructed into the floor, each side stretching a meager three meters. Rising from its submerged stone rim, thick black bars enclosed the well on all sides, their steel slick with moisture. The bars extended only about half a meter above the waterline, meeting another set of metal bars which formed an enclosed roof with a locked hatch fashioned on top. The well itself seemed to be about a meter and a half deep, filled with a reservoir of emerald water. The liquid moved freely between the bars, but something else seemed to be stirring within—something that wobbled against the cage, unsettling the surface with ruffling tremors.

The ambient light was far too weak to reach the center of the chamber with anything but a dull gloom. So, Zack raised his light. The beam slowly floated across the smooth waters until it finally landed on the face of a man missing his right eye. The other eye, a jeweled sapphire, watched them intently from the darkness as he grasped the bars with the feeble desperation of someone losing the last bits of his strength. The water lapped discordantly against the top of his chest, eagerly awaiting him to slip beneath its rippling waves.

The strange man with sapphire eyes!

It was quickly apparent that if the man let go, his pair of legs that had been long-standing, would give way and his head would slip beneath the crystal-green waters.

What is this? This man is about to drown from fatigue! Zack cried, rushing over to the cage in the middle of the room.

Clayton offered no apparent response. He only smirked and stared at Zack with the bionic blue eye that wobbled in an unsteady curiosity.

As Zack reached the cage, he could now see the prisoner's legs buckling erratically beneath the water's surface. They stood upon a rusted metal shelf that was not much wider than two lengths of the man's feet. Beyond the shelf the well dropped off into an unseen abyss. Only a stray bubble could be seen rising up the inky column of water from the deep stone shaft.

Instinctively, Zack grabbed the prisoner's arm to steady him. The one clear blue eye lifted slowly to meet his own eyes, expressing some unspoken sense of relief.

"Joe!" he heard Gabe cry from behind him.

Clayton had led the rest of the group up to the cage.

"What have they done to you?" Gabe asked, pushing his way against the bars in between Zack and the blue-eyed prisoner.

The man, Joe, only cracked a smile and patted Gabe on the shoulder the best he could so not to lose his fragile balance.

"You will all have plenty of time for reunions. It's time to climb into your temporary accommodations," Clayton barked impatiently. He then scaled to the top of the cage. Waving his Unity Mark over a lock, it unlatched immediately with a soft buzzing sound. The unlocked hatch creaked violently as he lifted it high into the air.

"All right, up you come!" Clayton insisted.

Gabe was first to scale the bars. Once on top, he turned back to assist Aliyah who was struggling to gain firm footing on the wet metal crossbars that acted as a crude ladder. Once huddled on top, the pair of prisoners both looked into the open cage with deep reservation.

"Now, dive in!" Clayton commanded with a cruel smile.

Gabe gently squeezed Aliyah's hand, meeting her fearful gaze with a reassuring look. The new prisoners leapt together, plunging feet-first into the well's dark gullet. The dark emerald water swallowed them both whole, dragging them briefly beneath the surface before bursting back up gasping for air. They then frantically swam to the perimeter to find secure purchase on the metal ledge.

CLUNK!

Clayton quickly slammed back the hatch and returned it to its previously-locked state.

"Is there nowhere to sit in here?" asked Aliyah softly as one of her small hands grasped at a nearby bar.

"No." replied Joe, sternly.

"Then, how do you rest?" she asked, now looking around the cage and then at her murky feet beneath the rippling waters.

"You don't," the blue-eyed man replied solemnly. "I believe that's the point," he added, staring at Clayton coldly.

As Aliyah and Joe spoke, Gabe began to float to the back side of the cell.

"I wouldn't stand over there..." Joe said, noticing Gabe's movement.

Gabe returned a confused look.

"There is a...or should I say parts...of a body over there," Joe confirmed.

A wide-eyed expression filled Gabe's face. He swung his arms forward in a massive stroke to push himself back to the near side of the cage.

The trio of prisoners then stood next to each other in silence, grasping a pair of bars, each, with their wet hands. Their blank expressions fixed on Zack and Clayton—waiting for something, or perhaps just urging them to leave.

"Looks like everyone's settled in, now let's go!" Clayton said irritably, dropping back down to the floor.

Zack regarded the prisoner's faces closely. Their stony exteriors offered little beyond thinly-veiled scorn. But Joe's expression contained something different—a studying curiosity. It was almost as if he expected something from Zack, though what, he could not yet tell. There was no time to figure it out; Clayton was already heading for the chamber's entrance.

Zack hurried to meet Clayton.

Before stepping through the passage, Clayton flipped the switch, and the great chamber plunged once more into darkness.

It was only a few paces into the adjacent corridor where Zack stopped and turned off his flashlight.

"What are you doing?" Clayton said harshly, his voice struggling to stay at a whisper.

"I think I am going to listen to the prisoners for a bit…in case they reveal anything important," Zack replied, knowing it was only a half-truth. "They were pretty tight-lipped earlier," he added, truthfully.

Clayton's bionic eye seemed to bore into Zack's face for several long moments, wavering between confusion and doubt.

"We have microphones in the room, you know…" he muttered at last with a steely focus.

"I'd like to do it the old-fashioned way…unfiltered," Zack replied firmly.

The digital eye scanned over him from head to toe, its movement eerily independent of the natural one, creating a jarring juxtaposition.

Zack felt as his palms began to sweat around the barrel of the flashlight, quietly hoping that Clayton's new bionic eye did not give him any new, unnatural ability of insight.

"Suit yourself, I am heading back to dry land," Clayton said at last. He turned and slogged through the knee-deep water down the corridor. The light of his flashlight shrunk slowly until it disappeared with his old partner around a bend.

Now, alone in the dark, Zack let his shoulders relax and leaned up against the nearest stone pillar.

Several minutes passed in silence.

He strained to hear anything from the sunken cell beyond the still waters of the chamber, but there was only the steady drip of water echoing in the void.

He stared blankly into the blackness, unmoving. Even his steady heartbeats seemed to unwind. Slowly, the darkness seemed to creep all around, enveloping him whole. The edges where thoughts met the physical world blurred until his mind and the void became one. In that vast space, thoughts rose up like little messages from the deep.

There had been some form of power in those words that the girl spoke.

A power Phosos had not expected and rivaled his own.

Could the world have so blindly walked off into the abyss of some cosmic bliss?

What had the girl seen to make the self-described omniscient Phosos so afraid?

What had he seen with his own two eyes in that flicker of revealing brilliance?

What—

There was a sound.

He carefully turned his ear towards the opening more directly.

There it was again—purposeful sounds rising above the noise floor—whispering. It was barely audible, but as he listened more intently, the words floated to his ear from the sunken cell.

"…and then I was placed here." The voice resembling a man who had seen many seasons—Joe's.

"It's so good that you are here with us…." said a female's voice—Aliyah.

"And I saw you!" she exclaimed.

"You did, did you?" Joe answered, sounding not surprised.

Even across the distance in utter darkness, Zack could almost see a quiet smile in the blue-eyed man's voice.

Aliyah continued, "Why didn't you tell me you were the one who spoke with the vinegar merchant…or that he called you by the name Cartaphilus."

There was a moderate pause.

"Who are you, really?" She asked.

"A human, angel, demon…" inquired a younger man—Gabe.

There was long pause. At some length it seemed that the man was not going to respond. Then, his weak voice spoke forth.

"I am—"

PLOP! A massive waterdrop splashed somewhere in Zack's vicinity. The rebounding waves resonated off the stone walls and ceiling, muddling the voices beyond until the waters finally fell back to stillness after several long moments.

"—I have wandered for a long time. I have seen the thread of many lives spool to their mortal end—wishing with each passing generation that I may too, return to dust. But I continue to remain. Until the end." Joe spoke in a distant voice.

"How is that possible?" asked Gabe.

"That is a tale that would be long in the telling and we have not much time left to tell it. By this time tomorrow, I fear, we will all be executed for the entire world to see."

"Are you sure?" Gabe shot in quickly.

"I am afraid so. I have almost reached the image of my death."

Image of his death? Zack wondered, as Joe continued.

"The vision that I have carried with me since my cursed transgression. A transgression made in a snap moment as a young man with a wave of my tongue. But one that took decades for my spirit to understand the justness of the ensuing curse. It is a wound that never heals or worsens—denying me even the blessed relief of death. The pain has been a gnawing one that grows if I linger too long in one place—never to settle, never to form lasting relationships. As such, it has kept me moving since the days of Tiberius."

There was another pause of silence. Eventually, Aliyah spoke in a dejected tone.

"The name…it didn't work."

"Indeed, but don't ask me why. Perhaps it was not the right time or place, but who can guess the greater mysteries of such things," replied Joe.

"But that was our only plan. What have we now?" Gabe said, despairingly.

"Mmm…it was our plan but we cannot see the multitude of avenues of the greater plan at work here," Joe said reassuringly. "We can only play our part until all has been completed…or until we meet our own end. That is what it means to serve faithfully, anything else is to rebel to serve our own glory."

"Well then, I suggest we pray for strength to see it all to the end," Aliyah spoke in a resolute voice.

The others seemed to agree.

The voices slowly trailed off, first dissolving into an indecipherable murmur, and then vanishing altogether like the echoes of a fading dream. Silence crept its way back in.

Zack was alone once again.

The distant drips of water were the only measures of time in the darkness. A rhythmic heartbeat of the void. In it, he felt formless without body and untethered from the world. He had only his thoughts—and they were racing up a storm. A swirl of fragmented voices and memories, a restless energy coiling inside him. It was raw, brimming with potential and possibilities, as if he were on the precipice of some life-changing decision. He need only reach out and make it...

Then, Ava's words returned, a warm guiding force within the whirlwind of chaos.

"I hope one day you will find that path that I am on. If you would just have faith in the unseen..."

The weight of the moment pressed hard against him. This was it. This was the decision point—the one he had so often turned away from in the past. His gut told him that it likely would not come again.

Two paths presented themselves in his mind for what seemed to be an eternity. He saw down each road knowing where it would likely end.

The easiest path was to do nothing and continue on as he had done floating through so many years of his life.

The other path would be a great departure and all-the-more challenging. He would have to reject everything he had done and built for himself—likely to a short-lived end.

The choice seemed so easy as he made it. As if he had always known he would make it but had been too stubborn to do so. He turned back on his flashlight and began heading out of the cistern. With each step into the growing light, a plan to free the prisoner's the following morning took greater form.

All the while Ava's presence was with him, whispering, "*If you have faith.*"

) | (

Zack startled awake from a shallow sleep. At least it felt like waking. In his grogginess, he looked around himself. He was still in the well-appointed bedroom they had given him for the duration of his stay. Yet, somehow, the room was oddly dim and dreamy. The walls seemed to sway and breathe on their own accord.

Then he heard it. The sound that had brought him out of his slumber.

He froze in a cold sweat under the thin silk sheets…and listened.

It was faint and coming from the closet beyond the foot of his bed. He cocked his head and waited for the sound to reoccur. A faint whisper slipped past the half-open closet door.

Suddenly, a pair of flickering purple eyes appeared within the dark closet. The eyes stared out from amidst a swirling heavy smoke that was blacker than black.

He tried to leap from the bed, but every muscle and tendon refused his command. His heart, however, moved freely in rapid thumps reaching up into his throat.

"Zack…Zachery…" the voice slithered forth with a velvety sheen.

He remained silent, still inexplicitly paralyzed in the bed. Every alarm in his heading was telling him to *run*, *RUN*.

"ZACK…ZACK…" the voice called again, seeming to gain more strength and assurance.

"How do you know my name?" he asked, confused by it all.

Was this a dream? he wondered.

"No dream…You gave it to me freely," the voice responded.

"Stay away from me!" he shouted in some misplaced hope that it would alert a nightguard.

"Why my child, you are already mine—*they all are*—and it's time to do your duty."

From the closet, came the stomping of hooves. They were getting louder and closer as if stomping over the strange grounds that lie in-between dimensional realms. The swirling black smoke began to solidify, taking some grotesque form. Branches were reaching out of it towards him. They were almost to his limp feet exposed beyond the edge of the sheet at the end of the bed. Even his toes could not curl away...

"No, no... I denounce you; I've seen your true form. You monster, who took away my Ava. No one dies for a lie and she was right, so right!"

The words had no effect on the encroaching monstrosity. It was growing in stature and darkness. All the light had almost been extinguished from the room.

Zack clinched his eyes tight as the form was about to grab his right leg.

"Now, get out! Get out! Please God, get it out of my head!"
Silence.

When he opened his eyes, the first shards of sunlight were piercing through the crack of the partially-drawn curtain.

He felt strength return to his body and hopped out of bed to get dressed. There would be no time to waste. The hour was at hand to break the prisoner's out.

) | (

The way back down into the cistern was not as difficult as Zack had anticipated. He had rehearsed what to say in the event of being stopped almost a dozen times, but the effort now seemed silly and unnecessary. As he reached the main stair leading down into the lower levels, he realized that he had not seen a single person along the way. The building seemed to be completely devoid of people.

Where is everyone?

He shrugged off the oddity and chocked it up to some fortuitous happenstance. He knew getting out of the city would not be so easy. He would worry about that when they came to it.

The cistern had not changed from the day before. It was still dark, wet, and smelled ancient. Without Clayton as a guide, he did his best to re-trace his steps. A few times he had made a wrong turn or two, finding himself in some chamber with deep pools of water or confronted with a wall of stone marking a dead end. Each minute was precious and he kicked himself for not drawing out a map when the information had been fresh the night before.

Eventually, though, he found the large chamber. Instead of flipping the switch, he snipped the wires leading into the room hoping that all monitoring capabilities would be blinded to the actions he took next.

The chamber was now darker than it had been before. His flashlight barely illuminated a quarter of the way into the room.

He began to slowly shuffle his way through the water across the room towards where the sunken cell waited silently in the dark. There were no voices, not even the sound of disturbed water. His mind began to jump towards a dark scenario.

What if they had all drowned in the night and all I find is three floating bodies?

The possibility was real.

His pace quickened in the water at the thought. Each step anticipating the first glimpse of some answer to his fears.

At the edge of the beam of light, a square outline emerged from the darkness at the center of the chamber. Gradually, the rows of bars came into view forming the cage. Then, a single pair of mournful eyes…but nothing else.

"Where are the others?" Zack cried, his eyes desperately darting to all corners of the cage looking for Aliyah and Joe, but found nothing.

"They've already taken them," replied Gabe. His voice somber and weak from exhaustion.

"Taken where?" Zack pressed as he began to climb to the top of the cage.

"I don't know. They came a while ago and took them. I wish they had taken me as well. Why should I be left behind?"

Zack waved his mark over the hatch and it unlatched.

"What are you doing?" asked Gabe.

"What does it look like? I am letting you go."

Gabe's eyes, dull and grey, flickered upwards in disbelief.

"Letting me go? But...why?"

Zack wrestled open the hatch with a metallic groan that echoed throughout the still, heavy air.

"Really? You are going to question your rescuer?" Zack shot back as he lent down a helping hand to lift Gabe from the sunken cell.

The young man grabbed his arm shakily and climbed out to the top of the cage.

Each out of breath, the pair looked deeply into one another until Zack finally spoke in earnest, "In truth, I am freeing you because it might be the first time in my entire life that I do something right on pure faith."

Gabe studied him for a moment and then, coming to some resolution, gave Zack a pat on the back.

"Well, that's good enough for me."

Zack nodded in return.

"Give me your arm."

Gabe returned a puzzled look but complied, pushing forward a water-logged arm covered in tiny wrinkles.

Zack pulled out a bloodied cloth from his pocket and wrapped it tightly around Gabe's wrist and hand, tying it off in a neat bow.

"Don't worry, the blood is from a lamb shank. That should keep anyone from raised suspicions for your lack of a Unity Mark."

Gabe nodded and squeezed the cloth with his other hand gently.

"Now, we must get going before my actions are noticed."

"Wait, we must find the others," Gabe said firmly.

"That might be beyond my ability."

Gabe smiled and shook his head.

"Funny thing about faith, it's a continuous process and one we must now leap into together."

Zack let out a long sigh.

"Come what may."

The pair slid off the side of the cage into the dark waters and hastened on their way.

Finally emerging from the cistern, they spilled into an alleyway. Even the overcast sky was at first a blinding from the gloomy travels made throughout the cistern. When his vision adjusted, Zack was relieved to find that they were alone. The alley was silent, disturbed only by the flutter of wings as a bird shifted its perch among the high stone buildings that towered overhead. They treaded carefully down the empty alley until they came to a wider cobblestoned street. At the juncture, Zack cautiously surveyed both directions. The street appeared deserted as well.

Strange, he thought and motioned Gabe to follow.

They had walked about a half kilometer down the street when Gabe stopped suddenly.

"I think I hear something," he said, tilting his head.

Gabe's eyes narrowed.

"What is it?" Zack whispered, his eyes scanning the way ahead and behind.

"I am not sure…it sounded like voices ahead of us."

Zack peeled his eyes down the street looking at every door, window, and alley entrance.

Then there was movement. A flash of figures slipped out from an alleyway and darted down another on the opposite side of the street. Zack could only catch a glimpse of a child's wide eyes before she vanished around the corner. The echo of hurried footsteps against the cobblestones was all that was left behind.

Zack and Gabe exchanged a glance. No words were needed. They followed.

The alley was narrower than the first. So tight, Zack had to turn sideways to avoid scraping against the buildings on either side. Ahead, the two children moved with gleeful ease. Their hurried footfalls echoed sharply off the walls, but beneath them, Zack caught another sound. It was faint at first, a low murmur, but one that was steadily swelling.

Only when more movement flickered at the alley's end did Zack realize that the sound was the clamor of people—dozens of them. As the children slipped through the jostling crowd ahead, the alley dumped into a wide stone courtyard crowded with people.

The crowd stood shoulder-to-shoulder. Everyone seemed to be adorned in robes of various hues of brown. Voices wove together in gasps, exclamations, and hushed murmurs. At the far end of the courtyard, something held their attention.

Gabe tapped Zack's arm. "What is this?"

Zack didn't answer. His gaze was fixed ahead, trying to see beyond the shifting heads. But all he could see was a raised stone platform that was presently empty. Beyond it stood a large imposing building, that everyone in the world knew—the Temple of Unity.

"Looks like they are all waiting for something. And judging by those cameras…" Zack pointed to the large telescreen cameras that had been positioned on the rooftops near the platform. "…something important is about to go down."

"Aliyah and Joe?" Gabe said gravely.

He did not have to mention anything else for they both knew only one purpose could arouse such a public display—an execution by the Lord of Provision. It had been some time since that last one was broadcast to the entire world.

"We have to do something," Gabe stated urgently.

Zack thought through possible courses of action but not many were left to them. They were already risking their own capture every second they remained in the city.

He looked back at Gabe. The man's face was chiseled with an unyielding determination. There would be no turning back now. Not until every opportunity was exhausted.

"Let's try to make our way through the crowd and see if we can get to them before they are brought out," Zack said quietly.

The pair entered the crowd and pushed past many eager faces. They had nearly made it a third of the way to the platform when a deep horn blast rang out three times.

Noooo. We're too late. Zack lamented to himself.

Joe was the first to be trotted out onto the platform. He had been stripped of his clothes and wore a loose-fitting burlap tunic. The HOP that led him forced him down to his knees near the edge overlooking the crowd. Several pieces of fruit were thrown at him; a tomato hit him square in the face. The juicy innards dripped down the patch covering his right eye as the other sapphire eye stared out unblinkingly.

A few minutes later, Aliyah was brought forth onto the platform and made to kneel next to Joe. She also was wrapped in a similar burlap tunic. Her eyes were glazed and unfocused, wandering aimlessly over the mass of people. A slack-jawed expression of bewilderment was etched into her face.

Joe then leaned over to her the best he could and spoke. His voice carried over the crowd who quieted to listen.

"We must play our part on the stage that has been set before us. Make plans with an open hand to be guided further when in doubt."

Several in the crowd replied with "boos!"

A fine focus appeared to come into Alyiah's eyes and she returned a gracious glance to Joe.

"Silence!!"

The entire crowd hushed instantly.

A tall figure emerged from within the temple wearing an exquisite robe of purple with gold tassels.

"Phosos!" the crowd murmured.

Phosos's eyes were a-light with determination and resolve. He walked to the edge of the platform where everyone, assembled and everyone who was sitting at home glued to their telescreens, could see the Lord of Provision in his full power.

Phosos raised two long arms signaling he was about to speak.

"For Unity and Provision!" Phosos bellowed.

"By Unity we are strong, from Provision we thrive," the crowd chanted its enthusiastic response.

Zack caught his own response mid-way in his throat. Years of habit had made the call and response almost involuntary. He realized then that it all had the unmistakable cadence of something ancient and ritualistic. Like the start of some old-fashioned liturgy, the kind that Ava would describe on her Sunday services. But hearing it now, it seemed somehow counterfeit—using the underworking's of a genuine, older tradition to enrapture people to follow without question.

Phosos continued, "When I came to you, you were fractured, almost beyond repair. Speaking different languages, separated by divergent beliefs, striving towards discordant goals. It is no wonder what had followed: war, pestilence, famine…all these afflictions had maligned your spirit and way of life.

"Yet, I offered you Unity and Provision—and you took it and bore the mark proclaiming your commitment to break from the past. Now, under my canopy of protection you are at peace, free of disease, and every need and pleasure are fulfilled.

"However…"

Phosos turned to the two kneeling prisoners.

"…there are those that would reject this open invitation to join us in a new age of humanity."

The crowd broke into a rancorous rabble. People began shouting.

"Weeds!"

"Witherlings!"

"Tree suckers!"

"Sour grounders!"

Amid the cries, a smile beamed from Phosos's face.

The Lord of Provision held up his arms once more.

The crowd fell back to a hush.

"The two you see here today were gathered in the Western Lands. They, and a handful of others, have been living apart from us, severed from all our knowledge. In doing so, they have deluded themselves with the same old ideas and beliefs that used to plague the peoples of this world for far too long. They have attempted to undermine everything that makes New Eden the shining beacon of the world."

Phosos paused and curled his lips. His eyes lifted briefly to the bleak afternoon sky, then dropped back to the courtyard below.

"Despite their transgressions, I offered them Provision. But they have rejected it, out of hand."

More pockets of "Boos!" sprung from the crowd. A group of young men near Zack jeered, their voices dry and rasping.

Phosos raised a hand. The noise fell away.

"Every effort was exhausted to bring them beneath our branches. But their cores are dry and too hardened in the old ways."

Phosos inhaled deeply for dramatic effect.

"So...with heavy hearts, we must carry forth a pruning. These two will serve as a final, public warning to the straggling few that continue their resistance to unification with the rest of the world. For the garden cannot thrive with even one weed left to propagate freely."

"By Unity we are strong, from Provision we thrive!" the crowd called in unison. Their eyes were wide and their faces eager with gleeful anticipation.

Then, unexpectedly, Joe spoke. His voice loud and clear. "What, are you scared to let us speak our final words?"

The interruption hit like a dropped stone into still waters. For a heartbeat, Phosos's composure flickered. Then, with practiced grace, the mask slid back into place. Phosos regarded Joe through squinted eyes a few moments longer, then spoke—his voice was soft and precise.

"Speak, if you must. But know that the bluster of your words will not even nudge the branches and the leaves of those in Unity."

Phosos then stepped back next to Lord Throx who held his arms crossed and continued to survey the courtyard attentively.

Joe's solitary eye seemed to brighten at the challenge. Still on his knees he straightened his back until he was as tall as he could muster. The crowd remained quiet as an unexpected blanket of curiosity had befallen them.

Gabe suddenly leaned over to Zack. His eyes were wide and filled with astonishment. He whispered in a low and jubilant voice.

"There are others here!"

"Others?" Zack wondered.

"The Wayward Children! They have crossed across land and sea!" Gabe nodded towards a particular area in the crowd close by.

Zack followed Gabe's gaze to a man and woman standing side-by-side in the crowd. At first glance, they blended in—both cloaked in the same draping brown robes as everyone else, the fabric concealing them from shoulders to feet. But something tugged at Zack's attention. He studied them, trying to pinpoint what set them apart.

Just as he turned to ask Gabe what he saw, the pair looked up—directly towards them. Their faces were starkly different from the others in the crowd. Where the rest wore twisted expressions of glee and malice, expressions of fear and horror were etched into the pair of faces.

A chill crept down Zack's spine. There was something familiar in their features, an uncanny resemblance to...Aliyah.

Before Zack could process it, the couple turned away. At that moment, Joe's voice boomed across the courtyard, silencing the murmurs.

"Hear me as I bear witness that you are all deceived! You do not see it, even now. Your reprobate minds no longer work; they have become closed off from seeing the truth. Flooded by decadence and pleasure.

"Noo!" shouted a man, standing next to a light pole in the back of the courtyard.

"Liar!" shouted a woman near the lip of a square-shaped well that stood in the courtyard's center.

Joe remained unphased. "Yes, the truth may be bright. Cockroaches do not like a revealing light. But even the most righteous among us will cower in the divine light to come!

"Know this: Phosos can only do what you believe he can do. He has given you everything but also taken everything away from you—your freedom, your futures, your spirits. A people with everything provided for them has no drive and rots from within— a death by decadence I tell you!

"You think you are free, masters of your own lives and desires. But what price has it cost you? To throw off the shackles of a truth that has guided humans for thousands of years to walk willingly into a cell whose bars are not apparent until you are well-within the beast's jaws. The veil has fallen over your eyes and you cannot see the demon before you. That offers you everything in ransom for your souls!"

"Enough!" Phosos stepped forward. "It's time for The Pruning." He then motioned Lord Throx to begin. The HOP obeyed and went to a control panel at a nearby wall to enter some command.

"PRUNE! PRUNE!

"With root and branch!

"By Unity!"

The crowd had been whipped into a frenzy. Nearly all were raising interlocking fists screaming and yelling.

Yet, Joe continued on without regard. His voice nearly drowned out by the rest.

"No one knows exactly what happens after death, but you will all find out. You are all only a heartbeat and a breath away from the truths of this universe. I pray you find the light before the end!

"And for those who *have* found it, do not fret, soon this will pass...and all that lay before us will seem as a dream."

"You have said your piece, now be silent!" snapped Phosos.

At that moment, black thorny tendrils—twisted and serpentine—began to emerge between the cracks in the stone platform. At first, they were just delicate wisps—thin, curling tendrils rising slowly like the fingers of the dead pulling themselves from the grave. But then, with a cruel and unnatural speed, they surged upward, their spiked edges glistening like venomous fangs under the pale sky.

The crowd cheered the pruning tendrils on, shaking their clasped fists as if each movement would help push the condemned man closer to his death.

Joe's solitary blue eye was wide at the sight. Even if he had known what was coming, nothing could have prepared him for the actual moment upon him. The tendrils coiled around his legs and waist. They rose further to the height of his head. With quick and eerie precision, they found their marks. One pierced through his left ear, another spiraled into one of his nostrils, and a third drove deep into the empty socket of his patched eye. Each tendril burrowed into Joe's face with a relentless, unforgiving force. Twitching, the man tried to look over towards Aliyah who might have been screaming underneath the bedlam of the cheering crowd.

At last, Joe's body stiffened. The man's hands went limp, his head rolled forward like a heavy stone. The tendrils withdrew, leaving behind a motionless body slumping to the cold stone.

Joe, the man with sapphire eyes, was gone.

As Joe's eye closed, another blue eye caught Zack's attention—an eye of electric blue.

Clayton!

Along with his bionic eye, Clayton's good eye was also staring straight in the direction of himself and Gabe. He had most assuredly spotted them. Yet, to their luck, or by divine providence, Clayton stood on the other side of the courtyard with several hundred people standing crunched together. Even if he wanted to reach them it would take some time. And at present, he did not seem to be alerting anyone else. He just watched with a clinched jaw.

Phosos walked up to Joe's body and regarded it with a pleased expression. The crowd had already turned its attention to Aliyah who feebly attempted to control her shaking.

Gabe had already taken a few steps towards the platform as Zack placed a firm hand on his shoulder.

"There's nothing you can do, Gabe," he said, not pulling his eyes away from the platform.

"I have to do something!"

"You have, being here for her is all you can do for her now."

Quieted, Gabe stood still and looked beyond, seemingly trying to catch Aliyah's eyes which seemed to look out a million miles away.

No one dies for a lie, Zack thought. *The truth will reveal itself.*

"And for the woman, the sentence of pruning has also been passed," Phosos decreed boldly.

The crowd cheered loudly.

"Lord Throx, be—" But Phosos was cut off by the shout of Aliyah at the top of her lungs.

"AravarA-YHWH!"

For the second time, the phrase caught Phosos off guard. He nearly backpedaled right off the platform into the crowd who had fallen strangely quiet and dumbstricken.

Phosos steadied his stance and clinched both fists.

"Silence!" he growled.

Inexplicably, Aliyah was rendered mute. Her lips moved but no further utterance came forth. Panic flashed into her eyes as she turned her head this way and that, as if searching the air for her lost voice.

A calmness came upon her suddenly.

Her gaze seemed to lock at a focused place in the crowd. Gabe and Zack stood right in the center of her view. A sweet smile of recognition blossomed on her face as if Zack and Gabe were standing in an empty courtyard.

If a smile could save the world.

"Begin, the pruning!" Phosos demanded before stepping back to the back of the platform.

Lord Throx entered a command into the control panel without hesitation.

The pruning process started like it had minutes before. Two slender black tendrils slipped past the stone and entwined around Aliyah's delicate frame. They rose like flames into the air until reaching head-height. Then, with piercing blows, they struck Aliyah in both ears and down her mouth. The vines poured into her body without end. Her fingers danced erratically and her eyes darted like tennis balls back-and-forth over the courtyard. As her limbs slowly gave up their struggle, she fell to the stone. The last bits of life faded from her brown eyes as they closed away.

The crowd cheered with ecstasy.

13

The Dream Between Two Eternities

) I (

The gathered crowd was the last image Aliyah held onto as she slumped to the ground. She could feel the tendrils inside her head wriggling their way through her brain, chomping and gnashing. She knew it would not be long. These would be the last sights and sounds of her life.

Only a heartbeat away...

She looked out into the sea of faces. There were so many of them, a true multitude. Even in those last moments, merely seconds in all likelihood, time seemed to crawl until it had almost stopped entirely. In that micro-moment—between living and dying—time and space began to collapse upon themselves.

She began to study each and every one of the faces in the crowd. Most of them were filled with carnal pleasure at her imminent demise, marked by curled lips and sly, lopsided grins.

The faces also had taken on something she had not noticed before. Perhaps it was her life's blood falling out of her at an alarming rate that was causing her eyes to see luminous visual artifacts, but visible auras had begun emanating from everyone in the crowd. For some, like those snickering faces, a black glow emanated off every aspect of their being. For others whose mouths held agape, their glow was a muted grey. Deep within their eyes, harbored a secret compassion, pity even.

Yet, it was the auras of white that could not be missed in the crowd. There were many more than she expected. But she wanted Gabe's face to be the last she saw. His eyes, locked with hers, were heavily laden with tears. His face wrenched with fear and sadness that would have caused her concern, but that seemed fruitless now.

Carry on, my love was all she could express across the immeasurable distance and time.

Then, she felt a tugging and the world before her began to contract. Her head felt light and floaty. The circular black edges of her vision narrowed like a tunnel until the entire crowd shrunk away into darkness.

) | (

Regaining consciousness, the crowd was back before Aliyah. This time the perspective felt a little different, strange. But she could not put a finger on it. Rather than in front of her, the crowd of faces was beneath her.

They must have moved me after I passed out, was her first thought.

The pain was also gone. So had the sensation of the cold stone ground, the wetness of gushing blood, the fear—it had all left her. She actually felt surprisingly serene and every sense seemed more acute, heightened even. But it did not seem as if to be a dream. No, this felt more real somehow. If anything, it was as if all that had come before was more dreamlike—now growing ever more distant.

Strange, she thought looking around. She could still see everyone there, everyone…including herself!

Indeed, her body laid still in a pool of its own blood atop the stone platform. She could see her tattered burlap clothes. The large circular wounds where the tendrils had entered her body. And her face, it was slump with a peaceful grin.

Oh, that's me!

She stared at her lifeless body, the one that she had known all her life. It had grown with her, traveled everywhere, and done so many things. Yet, now, floating above it, she found herself with little connection to it. She looked at the lifeless thing, an empty husk that she seemed to regard no more than a discarded jacket coming in from a heavy rain. Merely an instrument to every action and thought. It seemed to be no more who she was than a house or apartment that she once inhabited for a time. Whatever state she was in now, was *her*, the real Aliyah. The core essence of thought and mind.

She looked around in her new form. A veil-like membrane surrounded her and occluded her vision. She thought to move forward over the crowd to see Gabe once more when she felt something poking around where her abdomen would have been.

It was subtle at first, like the early tapping of a fishing line or a child pulling at your shirt tail. Slowly, the tugging grew firmer, purposeful, and more localized in the area of her bellybutton. For some reason a thought popped into her mind that this is where the body and soul connect like it was connected to all our mothers. The bridge between the here and the beyond.

The force grew stronger until the tugging felt more like an unbreakable string. It began pulling her upwards. The gruesome scene below began to fade into a soft white mist that already seemed far away and unimportant.

She directed her view upward to see where the tugging was pulling her. She half-expected to see herself rising high into that blackened sky that had overshadowed the earthly events of the afternoon. Instead, a piercing iridescent white light met her gaze. It flooded her vision, so intense that it seemed like it would blind her. And yet, it did not. It only seemed to envelope her whole.

As her eyes adjusted to the light, she tried to get her bearings. The tugging sensation could still be felt, steadily drawing her upwards towards the brilliant light. She glanced around and found herself drifting within the hollow center of a shaft shaped by swirling clouds of white and dark. All around her, every color of light flashed past in fleeting streaks, surging upwards from below towards that distant, dazzling beacon overhead.

Looking to the edges that surrounded her, she quickly realized that the shaft was no simple column of clouds—it was a grand, long stairwell stretching upward into imperceptible heights. The stairway wrapped along the outer rim of the clouds, skirting the open void at the center. Each step appeared crafted of the whitest ivory, veined with threads of gold that shimmered and pulsed with life.

Orbs appeared upon the grand staircase. They floated above the steps like soap bubbles shining in various colors that mirrored the other streaks of light. But as she focused her gaze, the orbs gradually morphed into human-like figures, cloaked in flowing robes of milky white, steadily ascending the staircase.

The figures were people of all ages and nationalities—men, women, and children. Some traveling on their own, while others were gently led by tall, angelic-looking beings wreathed in radiant auras. Each of the angelic beings held a large, leather-bound book, its cover inscribed with a name in shimmering gold. With every step the travelers took, the stairs beneath their feet were set aglow, releasing tones of praise that rang out like the bars struck upon an xylophone.

Beyond the stairway, deep in the swirling mists, other figures lingered in place. These figures silently watched the stairway—observing the travelers on their ascent and the angels rushing with haste down below. Unlike the travelers who expressed awe and wonder, the inhabitants of the mist merely portrayed blank expressions—some of confusion, others of lost pensiveness.

Before she could examine these figures further there was a *whoosh* sound and she felt her ascent accelerating.

Faster and faster, she rose, soaring up through the heart of the shaft. The ivory staircase, the travelers, the angels—all blurred into a rush of bluish-white light. The entire stairwell churned into what looked like a long, dark tunnel with the brilliant light at the end. Then she quietly understood: the "tunnel of light" described in some near-death experiences—it was the grand staircase, seen by those speeding too fast to see. Its beauty, its details—all lost in the blur as one approached the speed of light.

At any moment she thought she would hit the source of the white light above. She imagined bursting through it into its pure brilliance. But…as her speed reached its zenith—

Everything abruptly halted.

) | (

Aliyah found herself in a void of darkness. Not the type that you find in a darkened room. Even in pitch blackness you can sense the presence of your surroundings. No, this place, if nothingness can be a place, was devoid of anything. No light, no sound, no smell, no sense of surroundings or the passing of time—pure emptiness. It never had occurred to her that she could end up in such a "place." Fear instantly grappled her mind struggling against the non-existence pushing against every sense and every thought. She knew that even the simplest tests of sensory deprivation would drive a person mad in mere hours. Yet, this situation was far worse. A mind stuck in nothingness would surely crack quickly. Her mind reached out to catch any glimmer of structure or form out in the void, and did so continuously, desperately for anything to latch onto beyond her own thoughts…

) | (

There was no telling how long Aliyah had drifted in that pitch-black void. All sense of time and space had been lost. Everything just *was*. But eventually, the blackness began to shift and recede. Gradually, something tangible emerged from the infinite: a shape, a boundary, some sort of surface.

A solid stretch of ground appeared beneath her. Overhead, the impenetrable blackness thinned, unraveling into a dense, swirling smoke. She felt herself floating forward, though perhaps it was only the illusion of motion. Everything in this place was disorienting. Up could be down, near could be far—all perception was deceiving.

The smoke thinned just enough for her to see a few strides in front of her. Past that, a thick black fog persisted, shrouding anything that might exist beyond it behind an impenetrable shroud. Underneath her, where her feet would stand if she had any, was a craggily patch of ground comprised of loose red stone and scattered mounds of yellow and grimy-white dust—not unlike sulphur and salt.

Then, near the edge of her cone of vision, something stirred.

It moved with a twitchy, uncertain rhythm. An oblong shape fidgeting to the left, then to the right, then left again—like an egg teetering on its end. For a brief moment, she dared not move, uncertain what manner of horror might exist in such a strange place.

The choice seemed to slip from her grasp. The smokey veil peeled back further as if someone—or something—had placed a hand on some dimmer switch of this world. And then, the object came into focus.

A human head.

Can that truly be a person? she thought.

The head certainly appeared human, buried up to its shoulders in the rough red stone and filthy salt. And it moved—twitching and shifting—like something alive. Yet, there were signs, impossible signs, that it simply could not be so.

The head had been stripped of any noticeable hair. The skin, dark red and blotched with black spots, parleyed signs of severe burning. In certain places, on the crown and behind the ears, it cracked and peeled, as if baked beneath a ruthless sun for days or weeks. A large gash split the top of the skull, revealing a singed sliver of bone underneath.

But what made her question reality itself was when the head turned just enough to reveal its face.

She stared into its open eyes, or rather, where a set of eyes should have been. There were only a pair of empty sockets. The hollows receded back into shadowy depths filled with a swirling dingy-grey mist. The mist gave off a faint light, illuminating the inner cavity in an eerie glow. Somehow, without explanation, she *knew* the mist to be its spirit—twisted, tainted, and tortured.

Before the image of the (un)dead head could fully settle in her mind, strange sounds could be heard upon the air. At first it resembled a wailing wind. She listened closer. There were distinct voices, crying voices. A ghastly chorus of screams all wailing endlessly together into the surrounding, deaf void.

A sudden gust hit her, jolting every sense she had to full sensitivity. Like standing in an oven, a heavy heat now scorched her skin. The dry air reeked of rot and decay. The smell was so pungent she thought, for a moment, that she would pass out.

The head began fidgeting again, crinkling its neck until a dried ear—looking like the pig ears her father gave the family dog—almost touched the salty-ground.

The head then began to speak as if caught in the middle of a long train of thought that appeared not to have any beginning or end...

"...That sulphur looks like lemonade.

"It sure does. And the salt are the ice cubes.

"Cheryl never got me a lemonade...

"That lazy *bitch*. I could have used one...and a cold beer after those long days working for that slave-driver Reggie.

"He always blinked a lot. Mr. Blinky the guys would call him. Behind his back."

The head cackled to itself.

"Wynken, Blynken, and Nod...that was the nursey rhyme at that horrible school my parents sent me to. It was always so hot there...

"I hate the heat...makes me sweat in my crouch until my junk itches...my balls chafe up like those rocks of sulphur...all cracked...

"They are yellow like lemonade...I could use an ice-cold lemonade right now...

"My mother never had a lemonade ready for me after school...

"That *bitch*..."

The head went on and on. It oozed forth a never-ending cycle of negativity, resentment, and envy. During the tenth or eleventh cycle she thought she could bear no more of it.

STOP! Her mind screamed.

The head's hoarse voice slowly drifted into the background of screams.

For a moment, she thought she could find peace.

Peace, or any semblance of it, was a silly thought in a place like this.

Around then, she noticed a large shape standing out in the gloom just beyond the silently babbling head. It stood taller than an oak tree and its girth was larger than an elephant on its hind legs. Most of its demonic form was obscured by the murky fog, but she could see—or she felt it allowed her to see—a rounded, bat-like face filled with parallel rows of razor-sharp teeth. Between a few sets of teeth, she could see the impaled bodies of people with flayed flesh and deep lacerations.

The demon began to speak in a low growling voice. She instinctively covered her ears that were not there but it was no use...the deep guttural tone of the demon's "voice" came in loud and clear in between the deep bellows of its core.

"You have trodden our ground...hrrr...

"And you've seen and heard forbidden things...hrrr...

"You shall be welcomed here with great honor...it will feel like home to your unholy feet...hrrr..." rasped the monster.

"No...no..." she cried.

Something seemed to tug her to look down.

When she drew down her focus, her feet appeared as two pairs of cloven hooves clambering against the rugged terrain. Around them tiny fissures had begun to split outward revealing laps of red-hot flame and dark smoke. She knew that it would not be long before the ground would fall out from beneath her and she would sink until she was buried up to her head.

No, this cannot be, she thought. *I did everything for holy reasons.*

There was a deep "HRRR…"

"Many have said similar things, and now they each have a place of honor," the monster sneered back.

The demon smiled. In the maw of teeth, a faceless man let out an excruciating scream that felt like it would crack her eardrums.

Doubt came pouring in, filling her with a sludge of negativity and self-loathing.

Was I wrong?

Should I have thought this plan through?

Maybe I was unworthy to seek something so sacred? People are chosen for these things and I talked myself into it to justify every action.

I am unworthy…and, more importantly, I failed.

Yes, the world is lost. I am a failure.

No, worse, I am a horrible person.

I deserve this.

As her mind raced, she felt the sludge would eventually drown her very being until all hope would be lost—forever.

Negativity, doubt, quiet desperation, and imminent resignation continued to rise within her mind.

All seemed lost. Only a few more moments…and it would be over—

She looked at the head before her that continued to bobble, willfully ignorant to her or the massive demon. She knew that if the sludge overtook her completely, she would find herself trapped in a similar loop to hate and despair for eternity. Another muttering soul to add to the countless infernal chorus.

It could have been moments. It could have been days—or weeks. Time had become hopelessly swallowed by despair. She wondered if eternity had already begun. And this is where she would remain—forever.

Until she remembered.

She remembered her faith and teachings. She remembered that she would not be forsaken, she only needed to call for help.

So, she did.

With all her mind, her voice, and her fragile heart, she cried out into the void.

"Oh, God! From whom all blessings flow. Please, please help me from this place."

And then, in less than a blink of an eye, it came.

Above the mumbling head, above the demon, far off above the black fog, a single pinpoint of light appeared. It pierced through the darkness like a laser with an unstoppable force of pure energy.

It found her amidst the unfathomably vast hellscape.

And in that instant, an overwhelming feeling of love filled her core—a love deeper than anything that she had ever known. Through that same unspoken means of communication, she *understood*—the light would have found her anywhere in the universe, no matter how many felt lifetimes had seemingly passed by. All she had needed was call out in need—to reunite with the Master of Creation.

The ray of light expanded, wrapping around her entire being. It pushed back against the choking fog, dissolving the darkness with ease. The demonic monster fled, vanishing into the dark depths in a coward's retreat. The bobbling head merely sunk its face into the ground, unable, or unwilling, to meet the brilliance now flooding the area.

The light began to lift and draw her out of that place.

Its light was white and iridescent like the lining of an oyster's shell. Each color was bright, vivid, and sharp. The colors moved in pulsating waves that seemed to have their own unique sounds like the strings of a harp. They resonated in her mind, over and over, repeating a single phrase:

"Welcome to the world of the living, for the world of death has passed you by."

The tugging sensation returned to her navel area, swiftly carrying her upwards and away. It felt like returning home. A home she had somehow forgotten but it was always there waiting.

) | (

The bright light expanded to a radiant fullness, surrounding Aliyah with an indescribable intensity. It was all-encompassing, moving around her and even *through her*—saturating every fiber of her being. A warmth, a love unlike anything she had ever imagined, enveloped her completely. The imagery of the smoldering hellscape was already fading fast, like a nightmare dissolving in the clarity of a morning's first light.

Gradually, something began to emerge from the brilliant light. Blurry outlines and shapes of a world seemingly held behind a curtain of frosted glass. But then, suddenly, like the last remnants of crusty sleep scales falling from her eyes, everything snapped into focus. It was as if it had always been there, waiting. A world realer than anything she had ever known—or could imagine.

Beneath her stretched a patch of the lushest green grass. It fanned out into a wider mountain meadow of wildflowers and small trees. Coursing down through the scene was a meandering stream, its water glistening like liquid glass. Every ripple, every wave was perfectly visible, undistorted by debris. Beneath the clear waters, smooth pebbles and stones gleamed like polished gems.

Everything she saw seemed to speak at once in her mind with its own voice. Like entering a room amongst the gathering of old friends, each one clamoring to share its story. Yet, despite the multitude of voices, it was not cacophonic, she could choose to listen to any one of them clearly without interference from the others.

The waters babbled of their journey back to the sky, to the storehouses from which they came. The swaying grasses hummed about the caressing wind and warming light. But it was in the trees, where songbirds sang sweet melodies that she heard the clearest message: "Sweet is the dew, refreshing is the wind that moves through our trees, and glory to the one who provides all things."

Above the meadow an infinite sky expanded, awash in an ombre of vivid blues, violets, ultraviolets, and colors she simply had no name for. It projected an uncanniness—unusual yet still somewhat familiar and unalarming. There was no trace of sun, moon, or stars to be found anywhere. Other beacons filled the sky that seemed to transmit more than simply light. The ethereal glow from these luminaries imparted joy, peace, and a sense of lovingkindness that surpassed all understanding.

In the center of the skyscape, an immense sphere of light radiated every imaginable color, glowing with a brilliance surpassing a thousand suns. It seemed to be the source of all light bathing the landscape before her. Orbiting this greater orb was an innumerable constellation of lessor orbs—some darting to and from the greater orb in streaking ephemeral tails.

From these great heights came the sound of distant singing, a harmony that resonated with awe and praise. The ethereal melody filled everything with reverence and serenity—a unending ambiance woven into the fabric of the place.

Then Aliyah noticed something strange. She was not just seeing a portion of the scene, she was perceiving it with complete, all-encompassing vision. Every direction—at 360 degrees—lay in her sight at once. And her perception was not only broad, but also acute. If she wished, she could focus on a single drop of dew clinging to a blade of grass whether it be close by or near the horizon. Her sight was perfect with a nearly unlimited zoom. And like before, no feet stood beneath her. She floated like an untethered soap bubble drifting, weightless, above the landscape.

Questions began to race in her mind.

Can I go anywhere here?

Yes, you can.

Why have I never seen these colors before?

Earthly bodies can only see a sliver of the true fullness of creation.

Are there others I can experience this with?

Family, friends, those long-passed, all will be with you.

To her astonishment, each one was answered almost before it had finished forming in her thoughts.

Through this process, of asking and answering, it grew apparent that there was no ambiguity here—only knowing. She thought back on her existence before, on Earth. That place seemed strangely distant now, like a long-running dream where only fragments of flawed guesses could be understood from an imperfect sampling of information. By stark contrast, this place offered a truth that was not inferred. It simply *was*.

As she pondered more questions to ask, two large orbs emerged at the far edge of the meadow. They moved with purpose, gliding towards her across the verdant grass. As they neared, their forms began to shift, transforming into two immense figures—towering men, greater in stature than any who had ever walked the Earth.

Angels? she thought.

"YES."

A pair of mighty voices echoed in perfect unison, thundering through her mind with the clarity of lightening.

The beings stood before her, towering and radiant. Each face a four-sided chimera—man, eagle, lion, and a bull—shining like the sun. Their pupil-less eyes burned like molten glass bulbs, and from their mouths poured piercing lights.

They wore long, snowy-white robes that sung beautiful melodies with every step. Across their chests, golden sashes crisscrossed their forms, inlaid with dozens of blinking eyes— fierce and knowing. Behind them stretched multiple pairs of golden wings, glistening in their own brilliance.

"Be brave, Aliyah! In truth, do not fear!" they declared.

But how could she not? Fear was the only sane reaction someone could have in the presence of such imposing beings. To witness them was to be seen completely, known in every cell of her being.

Then, she saw one of them was holding a tome with golden lettering inlaid upon its cover.

It read: Aliyah Woods.

Without a further word, or warning, the world began to swirl.

It was as if reality folded inward until the past and future were drawn into a single boundless present. Without any indicators of its passing—a ticking hand of a clock, the movement of the sun across the sky—time ceased to have meaning. Just now. Forever. Always.

"Everything has been recorded."

The words rang out within her mind like the resonant blast of a trumpet.

One of the beings stepped forward cradling the leather-bound book. Her name shimmered across its cover. He gently opened the book and pulled gently at the end of one of the first pages, etched with golden markings in a language she could not decipher.

The page unfurled like a scroll, rising before her into the air. It rose and grew to the dimensions of large picture window. And then images began to appear.

She gasped.

Moments from her life played out with stunning clarity—more vivid than the finest telescreen, more immersive than even the Mindsai's memory reconstructions. It was as if she were peering through a hyperdimensional window at scenes of her life of people and places. Where every sense was engaged, and every emotion magnified.

But it was not just sight and sound. As she relived the experiences, she felt it. All of it.

Not only her own emotions, but those of others she had encountered, experiencing their gladness, their anger, and at times, their deep sorrow resulting from her actions. Sometimes, even the smallest acts—the ones she had long forgotten—echoed outward, rippling through the lives of countless strangers she had never met, yet somehow affected.

She began to tremble by the weight of it all.

"This is your life review," the voice echoed again, calm and unwavering. "There is no judgment here—only reflection."

All at once, time seemed to expand impossibly outwards. A swift cascade of memories began, frame-by-frame, a rapid procession of her life's events. Crystal in their lucidity, each frame seemed to have been captured by some flawless, invisible camera. Every moment flickered by; from the major to the mundane, the insignificant to the pivotal. Highs, lows, turning points, and everything in between.

Many scenes had long been forgotten, yet were still familiar. She saw how each memory had been buried under ever-building layers of newer ones, hidden by the haze of distraction and passing time. But they had always lingered within reach, just beneath the surface, waiting for the right triggering cue—a scent, a sound, a certain casting of light—to resurface into recollected consciousness.

The scenes of her life began to flow in quick succession.

She was in a crib. Her tiny hands clutched around smooth white spindle bars. It was late at night and she was crying in terror. She remembered now that she had been crying like this for several nights.

But why?

Then the familiarity clicked in her mind—the life review.

Her younger self, not yet even seven months old, was crying from flashes of disturbing scenes of a life she had not yet lived. They had carried over from a memory of time before time, before she had been born. A life *preview* shown during some pre-existence…

But how?

When did the memories finally fade entirely of this mystical realm?

Did we all remember this place for a time after we were born, in the twilight between realities?

A light flickered on in the hall and a shadow of one of her parents was quickly approaching.

Now, she was five, crouched on Granny's front porch. The old rocker creaked steadily in a comforting rhythm. Heat shimmered in the summer air as Granny fanned herself between each sway of her chair. Aliyah rolled colored marbles down the step, one-by-one.

Plink. Plink.

The marbles rolled down the sidewalk to the street, catching slants of sunlight.

The innocence, the wonder, how could she have forgotten what it felt like?

Now she was throwing a ball with a neighborhood kid. He had a crush on her. She never knew it then. But could feel it now from his perspective. The tenderness in his heart—warm, fluffy, and fuzzy.

No wonder they call it puppy love.

She is back in fourth grade. A group of popular girls ask her for the first time to sleep over. The sleep over is on the same night as her best friend's birthday party. She decides to go to the sleep over party. She sees Scotlyn crying, alone in her stuff animal-filled room—anguished and betrayed.

Why was there so much confusion then?

It is winter. She is almost fourteen. A fire is burning in her home's fireplace. Her thumb hurts from moving a hot log.

It is her first week of college. There she was sitting in Dr. Simpsons Bio-Psych course.

No not this one, she thought anxiously. It had been a long time since she had thought of this low day.

Heedless to her growing dread, the scene continued to play out.

She sat at a desk near the window with a facial expression as blank as the lined paper laying before her. It was the course's first pop quiz. She had not done the reading over the weekend and she did not know any of the answers on the 10-question quiz that was worth five-percent of overall grade. The previous two nights she had stayed up late to hang out with her newly acquainted dormmates. She knew she could have done it on her own if she had the time. With every ounce of her, she knew. And worse than that, she did not want to confirm those nasty stereotypes of women of color not able to hack in in big kid school. She belonged there, at least she hoped she did. The shame slowly built to an unbearable crescendo as she watched herself turn her head slowly and soak in the nearly finished quiz from the nerdy-looking guy sitting next to her.

No! No! Stop! It's not worth it! She screamed in her mind.

But, like it had been then, it was too late.

Dr. Simpson had caught her gaze and swiftly walked over and grabbed her half-filled quiz into a crumbled ball before saying, rather sternly: "Ms. Woods, please see me after class."

She is in graduate school now. Standing awkwardly in the lab. It was the day she saw the Mindsai machine for the first time. Her fellow labmate, Craig, is jealous of the attention she gets from Dr. Silva. He thinks she does not belong there as a bitter knot tightens in his gut. Yearning. Loathing. Malice.

The lab disappeared.

It is the first fall after arriving to Camp Timberline. She walks alone down a dirt path. The trees sway gently in a crisp breeze. She reflects on the feeling of connectedness to creation. Feels gratitude to God for the chance to enjoy another day. An angelic being watches over her. It hovers just outside the corner of her eye from the bough of a fir tree taking notes on a scroll-like object.

The woods faded into darkness.

She was back in the Professor Silva's lab again, lying in the Mindsai machine. Gabe, Petro, and Kamil were watching with bated breaths. The machine's observation screens were crackling in random echoes of grey and white. Indistinct shapes and forms moved within the electronic noise but they revealed nothing of the happenings going on in the machine. If only they could see what she saw...

Then she was in the chambers of Phosos. The Rootmaster, Zack stood behind them all, she could feel he was curdling with doubt and apprehension. It did not surprise her. She had somehow suspected as much. Phosos's thoughts, however, were clouded or unsure. In the replay, he could not maintain the sleek alien veneer. He truly was an ugly-looking fiend...

Finally, she knelt before an angry crowd upon a stone platform. Tentacles rose unassumingly out of the ground around her. They pierced her. It was over.

So many memories, so quickly, she pondered, still struggling to grasp a lifetime that had just flashed before her.

Time flows differently here.

In what felt like only minutes, she had relived twenty-five years of existence. No trivial moment had been skipped over. Somehow, her mind in this state was no longer shackled by the cognitive limitations when she was earthbound; she could witness an entire year unravel in seconds and absorb every intricate detail, every day, every tender moment, as if she lived it anew. She found herself able to ponder and reflect on the simplest snapshot of moments without any regard for time.

What was a couple of decades of one's life in the face of eternity?

The question hung suspended in her thoughts. Slowly, the life review crept back into the forefront. She realized that every small moment, every grand event, stood collectively before her now— bearing silent witness to the amalgamation of who she had become.

Having seen her own life course unfold from birth to death, she could not escape the feeling that so much of it had been wasted. Wasted worrying about petty, inconsequential things instead of pouring more net good into the world. Only when viewing life in its entirety did she understand: time very much seemed like one long continuous march of decay.

Birth began with a certain purity—unblemished skin, vitality, and limitless potential—but it all unraveled with age as, piece-by-piece, the body became blemished, weak, and wearied by the world. The once endless junctions of opportunity narrowed until only one path remained, leading towards that inevitable dead-end.

Yet, the truth became clear: from the moment you were born of the world, you were slowly dying of it. Every moment was a diminishment, drawing you further from the pure being of your true celestial abode. The time course of life was simply death in slow motion.

Once the flashes of her life completed their final sweep, she barely had time to gather her thoughts before the viewing window began to expand rapidly.

Oh, no. Not it ALL again, she thought, panic fluttering inside herself. She was not sure if she could bear another parade of shameful and embarrassing memories.

But the viewing window did not heed her reticence. It grew and grew until it had entirely engulfed her…or perhaps she fell into it. Either way, she found herself surrounded by swirling images.

Curiously, they did not begin where they had before, at her birth. A cold lump fell in her gut—or where her gut should have been—as she felt the scene *whoosh* backwards. The clock was winding back, far back…

The next thing she knew she was in a black void filled with a field of stars. She hovered there for a few fleeting moments before an unseen force grabbed her and hurled her forward at a great speed.

Out of the darkness, a large blue orb emerged. She approached closer and closer until the colossal sphere was just below her. It was a planet, but not Earth. It was much too large for Earth and possessed a strange ethereal, otherworldly beauty. Beneath her, a swirling blue atmosphere danced with flickering bands of storm clouds around an inky dark spot—a cold lidless eye frozen in space.

Neptune? She wondered. But before a confirmation came, she was moving fast again.

Planets zoomed by in quick succession as she flew through the cosmos. Pale-yellow Saturn with its great icy rings…the massive Jupiter without its big red spot…crimson, barren Mars…

Then, gradually, she felt herself decelerating. Up ahead Earth came into view as an azure-covered orb with a single mass of land. The shape of the landform reminded her of a donut for it was surrounded by shallow blue oceans and contained at its center an even shallower, glittering inland sea. It was young and pristine and no traces of the marring touch of humans.

Beside the Earth hovered a great ball of light. She recognized immediately that it was the very light she had stood under only moments ago. Suddenly, it blew out a gust of breath filled with a vast number of shimmering lights, and a heavenly chorus rang throughout the universe. The sparkling lights settled in a well-like storehouse near the great light, each one a tiny pinpoint of brilliant white light.

Suddenly, she felt a tug again near her navel area which sent her immediately hurtling towards the well of newly created orbs. It was not long before she was traveling amongst the orbs of light. Each orb glowed softly with an intense white light like that of the great light but lessor. The surface of the orbs shimmered, with a subtle multi-colored sheen reminiscent of a polished pearl but with a slight translucent quality. Aliyah directed her view to look beneath the surface. Within, she saw that each one was a human consciousness, a newly formed soul…fresh…perfect…and full of electrifying potential.

As she sped through the orbs it felt as if she was being guided to one in particular.

She was nearly to the bottom of the well of light when she came to a halt. An orb floated before her emitting a gentle, ambient glow. Its aura a radiant mix of pinks, blues, greens, and purples. It was stunningly beautiful. It also aroused a sense of great love and strange familiarity. She peeled her eyes once more to see what lay inside. As her gaze reached through the smooth surface, a face stared back to her.

She gasped in a startle.

The face was her own.

But it also was not quite the same face. Somehow it looked more perfect. Her brown eyes were deeper and clearer. Her hair as silky as onyx stone. Even her skin was smooth without blemish…and, like the orb encasing it, it had its own ethereal glow.

A realization slowly dawned: she had been there, with all the others, at *the very beginning.*

As she stared at her uncanny self, a scroll materialized from the ether in front of her orb of light. It began to rapidly display a series of images of her life...her parents falling in love...them getting married...her birth at Sacred Heart Hospital and wailing like a banshee...growing up in Sharonville...stepping up to the lodge in Timberline the day of the big meeting...captured in New Eden...her gruesome death...and then abruptly, the rest cut from view.

A wave of knowledge seemed to instantly crash upon her mind returning all that had been once hidden during her time on Earth. The sensation was overwhelming—like living a lifetime as a block of ice, only to suddenly remember she had always been capable of expanding into a cloud of steam.

She also knew that this was not the first time she had seen the full course of her life; she had witnessed it at the commissioning of her life contract before being knitted in her mother's womb.

Her...ensoulment. The term came to her quickly.

She had been here long before birth, choosing each of her parents and glimpsing the life she might live—a life with a purpose, whether great or small, brief or long, destined to serve a greater whole when she finally returned home to share the unique story of her journey.

My God.

The revelation rushed through her. Realizing that certain moments had been déjà vu because she had seen a preview of this all before, her entire life. It had been her life contract, her purpose on Earth. She had chosen it from the very beginning. The crying in her crib, when the memories of what was to come were still fresh. She had known it all along, but only in glimpses and feelings.

The tugging started again in her and she was pulled away from the well of souls...

)　　|　　(

Aliyah found herself in a gloriously different place. It was bright, almost blindingly so, had she still been bound to earthly senses. But this was certainly not any Earth she had known. Before her, a pristine white beach stretched out along an endless coastline. She curled her toes in the soft sand. Each grain had the appearance of tiny diamonds and scattered jewels. A gentle breeze blew through her hair, as if the wind was there to keep her company in the majestic place.

The wind gusted lightly over the shimmering beach, creating a sound not unlike soft fingertips dancing across piano keys. Behind her, a lush green bluff rose over the shoreline. It looked over her and the sapphire waves of blue beyond that were gently lapping at the shore. Out further still was a semi-transparent range of mountains, carved from what seemed to be pure, lustrous gold.

Everything here—the sand, the rocks, the water—seemed to possess its own glowing inner light and resonance. Even the air vibrated with a low, harmonious hum, as if the universe was signing an endless hymn of splendor.

She then became aware of a comforting sensation upon her shoulders. It felt like a warm blanket had just been draped upon them to provide her comfort and serenity. She looked upward towards the source of the warmth to find the same great orb of light casting rays throughout the otherworldly realm.

And just as she gazed into the light, a commanding voice spoke in her mind.

"I am the first light, the timeless luminance, the immortal sun."

A vision quickly followed.

She saw a brilliant white light entering a rough, imperfect prism. As it passed through, the light dimmed, fragmented, and scattered in all directions as vivid, iridescent color.

The vision eventually faded but still lingered as an afterglow in her thoughts.

There was a pause. She felt something urging her along to interpret what she had just seen.

I do not know what it means, she thought, after wrestling with the images.

In response, the scene played out before her again. This time, however, the vision was accompanied by a language of understanding as the concepts became plainly conveyed to her.

The light represented The Creator's universal truth—brilliant and pure. But when it entered the prism—the world—it dimmed. For no bound reality could contain limitless power in its fullness. God was not everything, for He could not be confined within His own creation. And yet, His essence—His fingerprints—were woven into the very fabric of all things.

Humanity bore a glimmer of that essence. We were God-like but not God.

When the divine light of truth entered the prism of the world, it scattered into countless colors. The fragmented colors of the ultimate truth dispersed across the world's cultures, philosophies, and religions. All grasped some part of it, some closer than others. But none could fully reconstruct the original light in their limited view. Even if all knowledge across time were amalgamation and fused together, humanity would still fall short—unable to grasp the totality of their own existence, let alone the higher mysteries of creation.

Science glimpsed pieces of the "how." Religion yearned towards the "why." Each tradition captured different facets of Truth. Yet full enlightenment remained elusive to all born of the world. Like a camera trying to record itself, one needed to be outside of it to see the full picture.

The vision ended.

Aliyah stood silently upon the sparkling sands…waiting.

Come what may.

It was not long before a hazy white veil had fallen in around her. The veil was soft and muted, like droplets of a summer rain splattered against a window pane. The endless shore blurred from view. She sensed the presence of others. They were all around her now. Distant silhouettes beyond frosted glass.

She looked up once more at the immortal sun. Its brilliance was not a passive light, but an active, living one. It filled her with a warmth that seemed to know her completely and embrace every part of her with love. In its glow, she felt a profound duality of being: as a single grain of sand, yet inseparable from the vast, unending shore. Infinitesimal and infinite.

Then, a single beam shot down from the ball of light. The ray was so tangible that it looked like she could reach out and touch it, grasp it even.

It touched down just to her right.

In a sudden flash, a tall man stood in its place.

She might have been startled by his sudden appearance had his presence not been so immediately disarming. It was certainly a welcomed contrast to the raw ferocity displayed by the multi-faced beings she had seen before.

The man looked to be in his early thirties. Yet, he carried about him a unique aura of serenity and seriousness. He was rather homely-looking with lightly tanned, sand-hued skin free of blemish or wrinkle. Kindness and love radiated from every aspect of his essence and was almost as palpable as the light shimmering from his hazel eyes tinted of green and amber. Upon his face he wore a wooly brown beard and mustache that matched a burly set of eyebrows that thickened like the heads of whales near his temples. Extending to his drooped shoulders, the man's hair was thick and wavy, with a slightly tousled appearance. It had a rich, dark brown color with lighter golden highlights that gently curled at its ends, catching a soft celestial light that surrounded him. His manner of dress was a simple white tunic and plain leather sandals strapped over dusty feet.

"*You now dwell in the realm of the living, having passed beyond the land of death,*" the golden-haired man said with a gentle smile.

The words came to her, not by his mouth, but through something more connected, some form of thought transference.

The telepathic communication had an uncanny nature to it compared to all the conversations that had passed between her and others during her life. Though silent, and without spoken words, there was no ambiguity in the man's meaning. Concepts unfolded perfectly in her mind. Every feeling was felt as deeply as if she as having it. The more the man communicated with her, the more intuitive it felt and spoken word quickly felt clumsy and crude by comparison.

Who are you? she asked in her mind.

The man put a hand to his chest and replied, "*I am he who has been sent to help you understand and prepare.*"

Understand?

Prepare?

Return?

Her questions floated out one-by-one.

"*Patience, my child. All shall be revealed upon its appointed time. It has been known since the laying of the foundations of the world that you would come now and play a part in the Grand Plan.*

"*Through you, the world will hear the heralding of a new age.*"

There was a pause.

He sensed her concern. And with a warm smile and eyes full of immeasurable care, he met it with calm. The worry within her stilled immediately. It felt as if a great burden, that she only now realized she had been carrying, had been lifted. Her spirit felt as if it could now float high above the sands.

The only thought that remained in her mind was, *why me?*

The man seemed to trace her thought. He took a few steps closer until he stood right next to her.

Aliyah stared up into his captivating eyes that she felt she could spend multiple lifetimes in their sweet repose, until eventually rejuvenation would sweep away all that remained of the hardship and suffering of the mortal world she had left behind.

The man opened his mouth. The voice had a *shhhhhhh*-ing sound to it, almost like the sound of static or the sound of a rushing brook, the whisking blow of a brisk wind, or the roar of a strong fire. The voice that spoke was all of these elements, yet sweet and instructing. And when he spoke her name, his voice seemed to wrap around her like a warm blanket.

"Aliyah, I tell you the truth, from the moment you were knitted in your mother's womb, your life had a purpose with all those you have touched. You were appointed above all those of your generation."

The man placed a strong, steady hand on her shoulder. At once, a flood of images surged into her mind—moments she had forgotten or overlooked. Small, almost insignificant acts they were: a gentle word to a stranger, a door held open, a thoughtful gift. Yet now, in a fuller view, she saw the small kindnesses rippling out to stretch beyond what she could ever had imagined. They all culminated into much larger impacts. In that moment, she understood: every life had value. Every interaction was important. Even the smallest of gestures could cascade outward, into countless people's lives.

She felt then that she was a part of something so much greater. An intricate webbed tapestry, meticulously stitched together thread-by-thread over countless years. Each life, a strand in a woven puzzle, slowly revealing itself as more strands intertwined, creating a picture only visible when the whole was complete.

More visions surfaced.

She saw many people of the world. They lived closed off in their man-made boxes that they called homes. She saw how these contrivances had closed them off from the spiritual world, the true world. Some people drifted through their entire lives behind closed walls and windows, failing to ever discover what existed outside their limited constructions. But some left their windows open.

She saw those who would leave open their windows next to their bed as they slept. Night breezes gently inhaled and exhaled through the open portals as the calming breath of the unseen spiritual world blew upon the faces of the quiet dreamers. She could see the ethereal streams and tethers reaching down from the heavens to form connections with the people who slumbered within vivid dreams under the vast, open, infinite skyscape.

It was apparent that the more you surrounded yourself with the makings of mankind, the more disconnected and vulnerable to temptation you were. In the wilderness away from houses and cities, where creation was closer to its original form, there was no distractions and these places were where the dream and the veil were thinnest. There, people could commune with the truth beyond. However, in places fashioned by mankind, the truth became as distant as faint starlight in a city's night sky. Our makings were what we thought were comforts, but in reality, were distractions from the real-real. In these constructed places, people were easily fooled and lulled into a dream within a dream—easy prey for darker forces. And once they took hold, people lose the sense of their true purpose and forget the truths we knew early on as children when the realm beyond Earth had yet to fade from memory by the mundane motions of everyday life. Once out of communion, earthly natures would take hold...fighting with neighbors...wars with those who are different...struggle...death.

Aliyah almost began to sob at the futility of it all. She lifted her head and cried, "Why do we do this to each other? Why are we so nasty...so broken?"

The man nodded his head, affirmingly. His eyes took on the appearance of unfathomable wells of understanding, as if he understood, fully, the plight of life...its challenges...its suffering...and all the pain. Yet, there was also facets of hope in those depths, shining clear beams of light towards an ultimate form and function of it all. After a few silent moments, he said, almost instructingly, "Man will not stop *preying* on man until man learns to *pray* for man."

The phrase was simple, but profound as well. Aliyah knew that it struck to the very core of the universe. If everyone would only love their neighbor as they do themselves, there would be paradise.

He smiled again, knowing the connection had just burst in her thoughts.

He spoke more.

"Know that you are loved and special to the Lord Most High. You *all* are; everyone who is, has lived, and is yet to embark on their life's journey has a special place and purpose."

Looking into his eyes she felt an overwhelming sense of peace and serenity. She believed him.

Pleased, the man continued, "And yours, Aliyah, is not complete. You will need to return, finish your life contract and journey."

"But how? Am I not dead?" she asked, perplexed.

He nodded with a patient smile.

"Only in body. But there is no death of your spirit. Not many see beyond the veil and return. And you have been appointed to do so."

"But...but, we failed to defeat Phosos. We did everything we could. We even used..." she paused, scanning the majestic man's face for any cue of his judgment. He made no sign, but waited for her to finish.

"We even used the true name," she said at last.

As Aliyah had feared, a sad expression then burdened the man's face.

"I know what you seek. You seek the name of creation—all that was, is, and will be." Sadness filled his eyes turning into shades of an icy blue. His face then took on the look of a parent who is disappointed in their child who did not quite grasp the lesson that had been taught before. Then, in a commanding voice, he posed a series of questions to her.

"Was it not written that the secret things belong to the Most High?

"Where were you when the fountains of the deep flooded the earth and split the land into continents scattering them to all the corners?

"Where were you when the praising chorus of angels first pierced the silence reaching on high?"

Aliyah instantly became frightened, knowing full well that she, along with her allies, had erred in their desperate plight of their seemingly righteous cause. Yet, the fear quickly subsided into a deep shame.

The man seemed to take notice. With the fleetingness of a summer's squall, his demeanor transformed. His eyebrows unfurrowed with attentiveness and focus. His eyes softened but remained steady and direct. And his mouth parted slightly, in preparation to speak authoritatively.

"My child, words carry great weight and power…and names most of all…they grant authority over that is named. Yet, no one has authority over the Most High; for naming he who created everything holds no power in itself because such constraints cannot be made upon anything existing outside creation.

"Even Adam, for the short time that it was, knew this *true name* that you seek before it was wiped from his memory upon his expulsion from Eden. The name was a sign of fellowship when humanity was yet unfallen and pure.

"You will be the first to be purified with this name on your lips, harkening a recommissioning of the world back to its original idyllic state. There will be no tears, no toiling, no suffering. All will be made how it was intended, from the beginning for eternity. For I am the last Adam, and all those through me shall live."

When the man finished, he made a sign with his hand and then touched Aliyah's forehead. She felt an instant surge shoot through her that felt exhilarating. The rush coursed through her as if every cell was vibrating at such an intensity, she thought she would phase out of existence or explode in blast brighter than a million suns.

But she did not *poof* from existence nor explode. She felt herself rising away from the sand like gravity in reverse.

Higher and higher she rose upwards until the wonderful realm below somehow looked as a small orb-like planet among many others in the infinitely-vast heavens.

She was zipping at the speed of light, perhaps even faster. She raised her head to see that the great white orb was growing bigger as she rose up to meet it in the highest heavens. It loomed large until everything she could see was glorious light. Blinding white radiance cast in all directions around her demarcating her passage into some rarefied sacred place. The light enveloped her in a strong loving embrace. Yet, it was much deeper than that, almost like a fusing of herself in a synchronous harmony with the Most High. It was the best she had ever felt. A pure goodness and sense of unshackled possibilities.

Aliyah knew she was now in the direct presence of something behind comprehension. In an instant, all her iniquities—every transgression, great and small—lay bare, all at once. The light revealed every corner of her soul where no spot or blemish could hide. It burned like a licking fire at the edges of her spirit, searing away the blackened remnants of her past missteps until only pale, tender truth remained—raw, but clean. She understood she would have been utterly undone, if not for the purification of light continually cleansing her spirit. Even here, in this high place, she felt the staggering distance between herself and the embodied ideal of the Most High.

This realization of this infinite gap immediately called her to fall to her knees in prostration in recognition of her true station in the face of the Almighty.

A powerful voice called out from the light with the crackle of lightning and thunder.

"You have been permitted a glimpse behind the veil. To know hidden things."

In her humbled state, the only response she could make was that of a curious child.

"Why can I not see you?" she asked meekly.

The commanding voice responded, "If there was not a veil between us you would be face-to-face with the absolute. Pure energy, pure truth. There is no faith or freedom of thought or action in the face of such complete certainly and knowledge.

"Therefore, an inner veil has been cast between us even now in this highest place so that you can remain an autonomous being and serve me to my joy and loving kindness."

"So, I do have a choice?"

She sensed that the Most High seemed amused by her question.

A vision came to her instantly of a winding path with many possible branches that could be freely chosen. However, a horizon line perpetually occluded the future of each traveler. Then she saw a great clock where the passage of events on Earth progressed around the outer edges. At the center of the clock, at the top of a tall tower, sat the great orb of light. In that place, time did not exist because everything that had happened, everything that would happen, occurred in an eternal present. From this vantage, the Most High had foreknowledge of every path anyone would take throughout the course of human history.

Aliyah tried to grapple with this newly revealed reality, but struggled. A part of her mind was still tied to the worldly way of thinking in terms of linear time.

"Are you ready to go back?" the great voice asked.

"What if I choose not to?" Aliyah proposed as a point of argument.

Again, she felt a sense of bemusement by the Most High.

"You are free to do so, you are not a machine but a free actor."

"But then The Plan will fall apart?"

"Every plan has contingencies; if it is willed, so shall it be done."

Aliyah felt herself nodding, invisibly.

"Will I remember any of this?" she asked, thinking that she had learned too much to take back with her to a physical world. It was known to her that most forget their time in this place so as to not yearn for it constantly during their lives.

"You shall, because you have been appointed to retain all that you experience here."

Still reticent to go, she asked, "I am not sure I can do this alone."

"You are and never have been—alone. And nor shall you be, I will be there to bear you to fulfillment of all that is promised."

Before she could ask another question in delay, a great flash of light collapsed in around her. Within it, her mind began firing all at once, flooding itself with clarity and newly revealed knowledge.

There were great storehouses of water, fire, snow, all tended by angelic orbs frittering to-and-fro on their never-ending tasks—

Everything in existence was comprised of a word or a phrase written into its physical being—

The universe was so massive for the glory of the Most High—

The only thing that The Unlimited lacks is limitation. Creation allows for an experience of limited existence, a place where the finite can learn and, upon return, make whole with the infinite—

The purpose of life was just that: to experience, to learn, and to report back. Each life offered a distinct perspective, shaped by its unique blend of choices and circumstances. Free will allowed for individuality—but it also made space for what she had come to know as evil: the disconnection from the Most High. From the ground level, any single act of evil could seem senseless. But viewed across the expanse of millennia and countless lives, a pattern emerged. Every deviation from the true path had to be lived out, every possibility exhausted. Only then could the full nature of rebellion be understood—not as mere disobedience, but as self-destruction. The severing of humanity from its source was permitted—not out of cruelty, but to allow evil to run its course, to reveal its emptiness. And when the lesson was finally learned, when the cost of disconnection became undeniably clear, the truth would stand revealed as clear as day. Choosing evil would then be seen for what it truly was—no more tempting than thrusting one's hand into a wood shredder. Only when that collective understanding was reached—viscerally, deeply, and without denial in the very fabric of the human soul—could true reunification begin.

It was then revealed that the greater world coming together—under a singular language, a singular government, a singular purpose—to trust in a false god, who provided everything but the truth, was the last corner of the grand tapestry.

Aliyah's mind stretched to keep up, not with confusion, but awe—as if she were approaching the threshold of some unseen crescendo.

Can my mind withstand whatever is coming? she wondered.

Her thoughts continued to race forward towards what she knew was the great mystery.

Suddenly, in a great flash of the brightest light she had ever experienced, the true name, the secret name, the mystery of mysteries...she became completely aware of it.

Oh, what wonder!

Shemyaza had only had a crude representation of the full true name, unable to speak to something so holy in his state of perdition. If the true name could be written, it could not be decoded because it would boggle the mind. If it could be spoken in any language, it would render the sweetest of tones. No, this name had three interlocking parts and could only be rendered as a thought, an abstraction. For every abstraction remains nebulous and not concrete. It was the sound of light—the vision of wind—the feeling of love. More than anything, it was a miraculous melody that evoked every feeling and sense.

Upon this greatest of revelations, she felt a strong pull where her abdomen would be. The tugging sensation pulled at her like a bungee recoiling at the end of its length. In a blink, she was now being pulled downward at great speed. Celestial objects and orbs of light whizzed past her in a blurring vortex of light and sound. At the end of the tunnel, she saw the Earth. It still seemed small compare to where she had just been. She was flying down through the grey clouds of atmosphere before she knew it.

She could see a great shimmering sea. Then a cloud-cloaked city. Then a mournful stone square. Then a battered body that she knew had been impartially her own. As she descended into the strange vessel of flesh, aches and pains hit her like pins and needles. Sensations that seemed from a world that she thought she knew in an almost forgotten dream. She was returning now for another visit; this time she would not forget the eternity that lay just beyond.

Before all went black, a last thought lingered.

You never realize how big a soul is until it is stuffed back into your own body.

14

A Flood of Fire

"Ahhh huumm...ahhh huumm."

The humming had begun not long after they had started their slow, winding ascent up Mount Need. The sound had been faint at first, almost mistaken for the whisper of the wind through the branches of dying olive trees. But as they climbed higher, the sound had grown in intensity and clarity.

"Ahhh huumm...ahhh huumm."

The legion of harmonious voices was shimmering and ethereal, singing some mystical hymn in an unrecognized tongue. They seemed to come from the boundless blue sky, from the tangled roots beneath their shoes, and from the very stones themselves. The world seemed alive with the song.

"AHHH HUUMM...AHHH HUUMM."

Zack sensed a change in the world. It coursed through everything like electric static. Slowly building a charge towards some final release—for good or ill.

There had been a lot of ill poured out in the past few days. With heads hung low, their climb up the mountain had looked more like a funerary procession.

Perhaps it had been in some way, Zack pondered.

He looked at Gabe who had curled himself next to Aliyah's mother at the base of a dead tree. Its branches barren and broken from years of weathering and decay. They swayed lightly in the wind, waving to some unseen counterpart on the horizon.

"AHHH HUUMM…AHHH HUUMM."

Zack scanned the skyline that rippled in the hazy air. At the summit they were in full view of the grand Temple of Unity—standing due east. Mount Want, Mount Pleasure, and Mount Unity stood in the backdrop like quiet, slumbering green sentinels. In the past they had gone by other names that now escaped his mind. They had all been renamed of course, after Revelation Day.

Not far from the temple doors sat the courtyard. In the late morning sun, the white stones took upon themselves dingy tones. His eyes had tried to avoid *that* section of the courtyard, but they seemed driven towards it, either by hope or despair. Down, far below, two black blobs still laid motionless upon the stone platform. He could not see them clearly, but he knew they were the bodies of Joe and Aliyah, left bloodied and dead for all corners of the unified world to see 24/7.

By a decree of Phosos, the two bodies had become a cruel display shown to all corners of the unified world. For almost three days now, every home, every public gathering place had the live shot of the stone platform on their telescreens. A harsh warning to anyone who would reject Provision.

But Zack had not watched the screens, even from afar. He was now the most wanted person in New Eden. For the last two days, he had been constantly on the move, hiding in cellars and ancient crypts, the places easily forgotten by the denizens of the new city. A keen attentiveness was necessary as there were eyes everywhere looking for them.

But even in those low shadowy spaces he had been surprised by how much his spirits had been lifted by these weeders…err Wayward Children. People who had not known him, and previously opposed him, now provided him a deep comfort and a hopeful light in these dark days. They reminded him of Ava, so he listened to them. Their words covered him like sweet honey, softening his heart until it began to yield and surrender. And quietly—almost imperceptibly—he accepted a truth he had been running away from for so long. All it took was to stop and listen.

Even with the transformation, his rooter perceptiveness had not yet left him. Now, peering down into the valley, Zack noticed someone running up the hillside in great haste.

Instinctually, he crouched low to the ground trying to get out of view. He motioned for the others to do the same, but it was too late. The boy, a teenager, had noticed their group and had veered towards their general direction.

Gabe shot up, waving the boy over to him.

The kid arrived panting and out of breath. Gabe approached him, handing the kid his bottle of water. Zack did not recognize the kid but Gabe's demeaner suggested that he was one of the many hundreds of Wayward Children that had made the journey to New Eden.

"So, do they have them, Jay?" Gabe asked, his voice low with the thin hope that he was wrong.

The boy nodded solemnly, still catching his breath.

"Where did they take him?"

"I...I...I   am   not   sure.   I   think...they   took him...somewhere...into the...temple."

Gabe frowned, shaking his head.

Aliyah's mother, Cindy, nodded with silent resignation

A soft breeze fluttered through the trees like the flapping of angel's wings. And the sound came again at its highest crescendo yet, "AHHH HUUMM...AHHH HUUMM. OOOH..."

Everyone paused until the sound dissipated once more.

"Did anyone follow you?" Gabe asked after a long period of silence.

"No, I was careful. I took several back alleyways and doubled-back two or three times before I made a bee-line for Mount Need."

Jay looked around at the small solemn group and then turned back to Gabe.

"We need to be careful though, the city's streets are flooded with HOPs, Rooters, Branchers, and citizen volunteers—all looking for us…especially him!" Jay pointed towards Zack with a rigid index finger.

Gabe gave Zack a half-smile. Zack could only offer a shrug in response.

"Understood," Gabe replied, turning back to the kid. "You did well today, tomorrow see if you can find out anything else. Listen to the chatter on the streets and around the temple if you can get close enough. Try not to get spotted and keep your hands and wrists concealed.

"Now, go find your parents. I think they are over on the eastern slope."

Jay took his leave down a gravel path.

When the kid had disappeared over the ridge, Cindy spoke in a detached tone looking east. She had noticeably avoided any look west over the temple or courtyard since climbing the mountain.

"Desmond was foolish to go into the beast's den last night."

Gabe approached her and placed a soft hand on her shoulder.

"He did what he thought was right for Aliyah, trying to give his daughter a proper burial so that she may lay to rest in peace," Gabe said, his voice laced with as much reassurance as he could muster.

Springing tears sparkled from the edges of Cindy's eyes.

"It was senseless, all senseless," she began, before throwing her face into her hands weeping. "Why have we come here? So many of us have been captured and fallen into God only knows what kind of horrible fates devised by this monster and his deluded followers."

Gabe's face went long and gaunt as the weight of words and the moment pressed upon him. However, an inner strength coated his response.

"We cannot abandon the world, even if they have strayed far from the path. We must be their guiding light, even if it is to save but a few from the abyss."

Gabe shot a glance towards Zack.

Zack shifted uneasily in his stance not expecting to have been noticed.

Gabe continued, now patting gently on Cindy's back. "Aliyah was a shining light for us all and she shined on until her light left us and returned to that which fills the light into the world.

"But we must carry on, and save as many as we can until it is our time to return home."

The words sank in deep to some effect. Cindy's sobs slowly abated until only intermittent sniffles remained.

A hush quickly fell over the mountain top. The breeze abated and not even a bird chirped in the tree branches. Everything seemed to be holding its breath.

Even the "AHHH HUUMM" sound had faded away into the ether.

Registering the change in ambiance, Zack listened.

Silence.

He listened harder—nothing.

All that was left was a perfect silent tranquility.

The stillness began to make him nervous. He knew they could not stay in the open of the full day for much longer before needing to move back into hiding.

His eyes began to rapidly scan the slopes of the mountain. But a sound halted his search almost immediately. It was a voice…only a sweet whisper…*Ava*.

"*Follow the path*," the voice said in earnest.

He took the meaning as a warning. His eyes resumed their aggressive scan of the paths. The upslopes. The downslopes. The winding paths along the ridge. To his relief there were not any hostile patrols in sight—but there was movement way down below. People were moving about.

His eyes narrowed to sharpen his focus and cut through the hazy air. He saw bodies darting along the streets. People were exiting homes, shops, and even their vehicles to follow the others. Some walked others ran, all in great urgency. Zack traced the stream of bodies that all seemed to be flowing towards the direction of the temple.

What is going on? he thought.

He lifted his gaze and went back to the stone courtyard at the base of the temple. The people looked like tiny dark dots from this distance. Yet, the dots were pouring into the square like the cresting waters of a burst dam. They were all gathering for something...

Had Phosos found another member of their group?

Were they bringing out Desmond to cast his body next to Aliyah's?

He then saw that the bodies were missing, but two black dots stood together near where they had lain.

Before he could process exactly what he was seeing, the first echoes of voices began to reach up to them at the summit. It was all jumbled at first, starting way down by the base of the mountain. But, as the voices carried to different groups of the path, the yelling became more distinct. The news was traveling not by technology, but by the proximity of voices on the air.

Finally, Zack saw Jay running up the slope towards them. He was yelling as he ran. Zack did not think he could believe his ears. Gabe and Cindy's face filled with a mixture of shock and joy.

"They rise! They rise!" the boy cried. "Aliyah and Joe are alive!"

)　　|　　(

By the time they reached the stone courtyard, it was filled beyond its capacity. A jam of bodies was pressed together, their mingled scents bubbling beneath the noontime sun. To even obtain a glimpse of the platform, their group was forced to scale one of the narrow terraces that skirted the square, their shoes slipping on loose ornamental stone as they climbed. There had been little concern of discovery in their rapid descent from Mount Need. The path had been deserted, like the backwash during a receding wave. And the few people that were encountered along the way seemed too consumed by curiosity to spare much more than a momentary glance. All attention surged towards the foot of the temple, where word had spread that the prisoners—long thought dead—were now revived. Or perhaps resurrected. Judging by the murmurings of the crowd, they did not seem to parse the difference. They had come to witness a miracle, or a new reckoning.

Zack, Gabe, and Cindy had managed to shuffle their way within a stone's throw of the dais. They found a spot to stand between the gnarled roots of a large olive tree. Its branches—barren from its advanced years—had once shaded a portion of the platform, but now only served to litter stony surface with broken twigs and branches.

And there they were, hand-in-hand.

Aliyah and Joe stood amidst the woody debris, their burlap clothing stiff with rust-colored stains, baring the grim memory of their execution. Deeply reposed, their faces nevertheless contained the unmistakable spark of life. Yet, something seemed different about them. They had a demeaner that only the passage through some sort of transformative experience could bestow. Zack saw it first in their eyes: the pools of brown and sapphire shimmered from profound depths. In their cheeks, blossomed the rosy vitality of youth's invulnerability. Even their skin seemed to emit a certain faint luminescent glow. Despite their appearance speaking volumes, they spoke not a word. Instead, they remained still and silent, as if waiting for some opportune moment to arrive.

"What a miracle!" Zack heard Aliyah's mother whisper to herself as she tried to steady herself against the thick twisted tree trunk.

For Zack, the first thought that crossed his mind was that this was not supernatural in the sense that their revival was some kind of break from reality. No, a growing sense within him understood that this was a break *in* our reality into something greater. A glimpse—or rather, a return—of some Ultimate Reality that does and had always existed around our own. He felt the veil falling and what had existed beyond was soon to be upon them all.

Zack began to look around the crowd. The faces that met his eyes no longer harbored the fury and bloodlust he had witnessed only days before. In their place were expressions caught somewhere between awe and trepidation. Some mouths hung slightly open; others trembled. For several groups of people, after seeing the two impossible living beings firsthand, a quick exit from the courtyard seemed warranted as they shuffled out, replaced quickly by other eager onlookers.

Zack's gaze swept over the square and then back to the platform. Phosos was nowhere to be seen, nor were any of his HOPs. Looking towards the temple that loomed behind the platform, the massive doors remained tightly sealed. Whether shut in defiance—or denial—it was a vain attempt to avoid the living truth that now stood before the whole world.

He heard the crowd below them slowly becoming increasingly restive. The notable absence of their leader had left a vacuum for all sorts of speculation to fill within the gaps. Questions began to swirl.

"Are they real?" inquired a young man flipping a pair of VR goggles up and down on his forehead at the base of the terrace retaining wall.

On a paved walkway behind them, a young girl tugged at her guardian's pant leg, "Is this a trick?" she asked.

A middle-aged woman standing near the stone well looked completely out of sorts rubbing her head and cried, "How did this happen?"

Standing on the same terrace near an adjacent hedge, a man leaned in to ask his friend, "Why would Phosos do this?"

His friend quickly retorted with a question of his own, but shared by many, "Where is Phosos?"

Then it started.

A cluster of teenage boys had gathered at the front of the courtyard, huddled tight near the edge of the raised platform. Their eyes burned with restless malice. He watched as they tried, feebly, to pull themselves up onto the platform. Their fingers clawed at the smooth stone, and the heels of their shoes scraped down against the base. However, they were unable to reach the ledge above their heads.

After a fourth failed attempt, one of the boys hit the stone wall with a clinched fist.

"Phosos, come and be with us!" the boy cried, voice crackling through the murmur of the crowd.

Then, one of his compatriots simply yelled, "Phosos!"

And that was all that needed to spark the uneasy crowd. Soon the chanting spread across the assembly like wildfire until nearly everyone was shouting at regular intervals, "Phosos! Phosos! Phosos!"

Zack stood frozen on the terrace, heart thumping like a heavy drum. He began to wonder what they would do if Phosos would not show. Would they begin to doubt his omnipotence? Or would they take matters into their own hands to show their devotion to Provision?

He studied their faces. Judging by their conflicted expressions, perhaps a mixture of both. But who would win out?

The crowd then suddenly fell to a hush.

His eyes darted back to the temple.

The doors were moving!

A deep groan rumbled through the stone as the ancient doors began to lurch open, centimeter by ponderous centimeter. Even the breeze seemed to hold its breath. When at last the doors reached their widest point, no light poured inward. Instead, a dense, inky darkness welled up at the threshold, like smoke that refused to rise—heavy, motionless, impenetrable.

For a few long moments it seemed like nothing would come out of the darkness. Then a pair of blue eyes emerged within the void. Then another. Then another. Dozens of blue orbs appeared, hovering at the edge of the dark, fixed and unblinking.

But, deeper still, something else emerged.

From the very bowels of the black gullet, a pair of amethyst eyes glowed into being, filled with swirling intensity and determination.

The Hands of Provision—six in all—exited the temple by the lead of Lord Throx. Behind them came Phosos, robed in immaculate purple and gold that covered his elongated, imposing frame. He stepped into the light with deliberate poise, his head held high, shoulders squared, each movement radiating steady control. But the prideful smirk that had once adorned his every public appearance had faded. In its place lingered a grim, unreadable expression—one veiled in uncertainty. His eyes, however, betrayed a smoldering sense of caution and wariness.

As Phosos arrived, he glanced over at Aliyah and Joe with only the briefest cursory acknowledgment. Without a pause in his step, he strode towards the far side of the stone platform, his elegant robe whispering against the ground with each measured step. Behind him, his retinue followed in dutiful lockstep, their expressions cold and distant. Lord Throx and the other HOPs fanned out to flank Phosos in a tight semi-circle.

All eyes in the crowd turned towards Phosos as he took his final, towering stance at the platform's edge. In his eyes, a fire had rekindled. There, flickering behind the façade, burned the stubborn glint of defiance. Phosos's chin lifted slightly and his lips curled back as he readied his address to the crowd.

"For Unity and Provision!" Phosos called forth boldly with outstretched hands.

"By Unity…we are strong…from Provision…we thrive." The crowd mumbled back, weakly. Nearly a third did not open their mouths at all, Zack observed quietly.

Unphased by the response, Phosos continued.

"I stand before you to declare our truth on what stands before you today. I assure you this stunt was not done by my hands, nor by the hands of any joined with us in Unity. In accordance with our values and laws, the prisoners were executed in a manner befitting their rejection of Provision.

"But the dead do not rise.

"No, after succumbing to their just fate three days ago, that is an impossibility by the rules that govern this universe—laws of which even I cannot bend or break, even if I were to will it.

"So how, then, does the impossible stand before us? There is one answer: It is a deceptive trick. A ruse. One perpetrated by those still sympathetic to the weeder cause.

"The truth? The bodies of the prisoners were switched in the dead of night, while we slept."

A ripple of gasps surged through the crowd as faces turned, wide-eyed to one another.

Phosos continued through the murmurings, "We have already caught one of the perpetrators who committed this heinous act. We—"

An elderly man standing near the front of the crowd interrupted the Lord of Provision with a simple question.

"When?"

Phosos returned a blank look of disbelief, his lips smacking together breathless.

The man continued, "The video feed was running non-stop last night and no one saw anything but the bodies lying there."

The murmurings in the crowd intensified. Many nodded their heads in acknowledgement to their neighbors.

A flicker of fury broke through Phosos's face at the would-be rabble rouser—his lips snarled and face contorted—then vanished back behind an empty, cold expression.

"Ahh…" he paused with his eyes closed and waving his hand in Lord Throx's direction.

"You must have missed it. These weeders creep and crawl with their deception. A clip has been sent to everyone's feeds, but please look at the screen."

Phosos raised one arm, his finger pointing to the telescreen mounted high on the rear wall of the square. The screen, which moments ago mirrored the platform with a live feed of it, flickered and now displayed a recording.

It was night. The same platform, lit by spotlights came into view. The bodies of Aliyah and Joe lay motionless, exactly where they had fallen days earlier.

The crowd watched silently.

For several seconds the scene seemed static like a picture. Then, from the shadows of a thick hedgerow at the platform's edge, a dark figure emerged—hunched, cautious. The man crept forward, his movements furtive, and seized the ankles of each corpse. With grim efficiency, he dragged them one by one into the darkness of the bushes.

A heartbeat later, two identical figures slipped out from the same hedgerow—figures with the unmistakable visages of Aliyah and Joe. They walked with eerie precision, returned to their original positions on the stone, and lay down as if nothing had occurred.

The screen snapped back to the present. In full frame, Phosos stood still as a tree's shadow in moonlight, now wearing a knowing grin, his eyes sweeping over the murmuring crowd.

Zack felt a rapid tapping on his shoulder.

He turned.

It was Gabe leaning towards him.

Gabe whispered urgently, "Desmond never made it to the courtyard last night. Silas saw him taken in the Provision's Bounty District at the far Western side of the city at dusk. This is all a fabrication!"

Zack nodded, knowing that it all had been tied up too neatly in a bow to serve Phosos's purpose.

Zack turned back to the platform. Phosos had begun to speak again after a calculated pause.

"As you can see, the deception did not escape our notice. And their ploy to mislead you has failed."

Phosos motioned with a chopping hand towards Aliyah and Joe, still standing silent and composed on the far side of the platform. Their mouths remained tight; their eyes sparkled, unperturbed.

"And these impostors," Phosos declared, voice rising, "by our justice they will be dealt with just as harsh—"

"You can't take her!" Cindy shouted, the words striking over Zack's right shoulder and ringing across the square.

A hush fell over the crowd as they seemed to hold their breath.

Phosos turned to signal one of the HOPs on his left flank to deal with the heckler—then halted.

Aliyah had stepped forward.

"Thanks, mother," she said, patting the air in Cindy's direction in a calm, soft tone.

She turned towards the crowd who stared silently, unblinking.

"Do not be deceived. I am Aliyah Woods. The one whom you sentenced to die three days ago. See now that I live and have returned with a message that there is more to this world than your physical senses would belie."

"This weed is a persistent one. Its roots grow deep," Phosos sniped back. "Perhaps more power is needed to snuff this out from our midst in full-view of the greatest temple that has ever been built—"

"You build a structure claiming the material is all there is," retorted Joe, who had also stepped forward.

"I—" started Phosos before being cut off by Joe once more.

"Yes, it is a temple of earth and stone. A monument to yourself, and yet it does not have life. Like all the inanimate idols ever hewn and wrought before, it is but a hollow fabrication. A tinkering really, without the spark of life. Because the ultimate truth is that the transcendent cannot be confined in earthly devices, for it lives within us: unseen, untouched, and not limited by our world."

"Inanimate you say," snapped Phosos with a pointed grin. "I'll show you the power within these stones!"

Phosos raised his hands. His mouth moved quickly as the murmurings of some unrecognizable chant spewed from his lips. His eyes glowed hot with a cool fire.

Almost immediately, blue orbs of various sizes began to appear everywhere out from the ground. Some manifested out of thin air behind him on the platform while others emerged above the heads of certain malign-faced supporters in the crowd. Perfect spheres of azure light, the orbs hovered in the air, pulsing with a silent energy rippling across their opaque surfaces. Their pale light cast an ethereal glow upon the courtyard. The people could only watch in wide-eyed amazement and fear as an army of unnatural beings had come to support Phosos. Each orb being a silent sentinel of his will crackling with energy and unknowable power.

On the platform, with the blue orbs pulsing about, Aliyah remained unphased. A smile had come to her face at the new display. As if it were not at all outside the realm of the usual or possible. She began to speak with a commanding voice.

"Phosos, you are a swamp light leading those off the path into dark waters. But, this masquerade, this chaotic freedom, this rebellion, your time and time itself, it is all finally coming to an end."

Aliyah then looked to Joe, the man with sapphire eyes, and seemed to communicate with him without saying a word.

Joe then leaned over and picked up a twig that had fallen from the nearby olive tree. He pulled it upright in the flat palm of his hand, holding the top end with his index finger. It stood sturdy and straight. Joe looked to the crowd, staring into their faces and the faces of countless others watching around the world.

"In my hand, I hold up a twig. My finger represents the divine—stability, goodness, grace. When the twig squirms to wiggle out onto its own, away from my support…"

Joe withdrew the pressure on the standing branch.

For a few brief heartbeats, it stood upright, as if in defiance of gravity, reaching towards the sky. But slowly, inevitably, it began to teeter. It swayed in ever-widening circles, until the list became too great. Then it toppled from his palm and struck the stone platform below with a sharp *crack*, snapping in two.

"Evil is not a thing unto itself. Only God is self-sustaining. Evil is but a detachment from the ultimate sustainer of creation. When we wiggle out from that sustainment thinking we can stand on our own…we only fall…we always do. It's the nature of this world and our being."

Aliyah then pointed an arrowed finger at Phosos and his HOPs.

"The Most High did not create mere automatons; we were all given freedom to choose. The angels were the first to step out on their own, following the most awesome created being in existence, Lucifer. His name means 'light-bringer,' as he was exalted above all others to be closest to the immeasurable glory of the Highest. Until he thought he could set out on his own and establish his own glory equal to his creator—though even he understood he could never rise above the one who was unbounded by what was spoken into existence.

"Lucifer set forth on his own and fell away from the force that sustains all that we see and cannot see. With him, he took a host of angels, like Phosos, who were chosen to watch over us. They instead, dragged as many of us as they could into their fallen state across the entirety of our existence on this planet. Yet, all those who turn away from the ultimate sustainment are defined by loss. For evil, like the absence of heat on a cold winter's night, is a diminishment from the source, a turn towards non-being. Cold and dead."

Phosos's eyes flickered. His wide, hubristic grin had already begun to slacken. His eyes began to peter into two smoldering purple coals. Doubt wormed its way through his face and posture.

Aliyah only smiled as Phosos diminished before the world.

"The story of evil has played out to its fullest. There are not enough pages left for twists and turns, the impression, the trajectory, it is all set. The era of doubt and lies is fading away, truth will flow through everything, and where there will be a question a veritable absolute answer will follow. All that is left is to turn the final pages to the inevitable end…"

Sensing the unexpected glimmer of an imminent defeat, Phosos, like a cornered animal, barked out a final order.

"Destroy them! Weed them out! Kill them bloody!"

The HOPs were the first to spring into action. They slowly marched across the platform, their steely-eyes fixed on Aliyah and Joe. The orbs also began to pulse more rapidly. Some spurning the members of the crowd to move towards the platform. But the orbs did not approach Aliyah or Joe on their own.

Aliyah locked her gaze with Phosos, a voice steady and unafraid projected out. "And what are you going to do to me? I've already died once."

Phosos's mouth began to move, but she did not provide any opportunity for a response.

"Words are powerful. A careful grouping of sounds can bring worlds into existence…and stories to an end. In the twilight of time immemorial, I have been sent back as the herald to the final act of the greatest story. The story of us. The created."

"And as simply as the universe came into existence, so does the ending begin. With a name. The name of the author whose signature is written into the very fabric of everything that exists in this world. The True Name. The name of all Truth and Goodness. The Most High Name…"

The next sounds that emerged from Aliyah's mouth were unlike anything that Zack—or anyone else—had ever heard. The first two parts, *AravarA-YHWH,* were reminiscent of something ancient, forgotten and something sacred. But it was the third part that defied language altogether. An unutterable resonance, felt more than heard, as though the sound crossed the boundary of physical reality. Together, the three parts formed a most-perfect melody that was so exquisitely whole, that it could explain millennia of existence within its beautiful tones.

Zack was instantly overcome. It was like hearing the most beautiful chord progression from his favorite song, but magnified into a cosmic scale. The sound swept through him in waves, stirring his mind, body, and spirit. Each note vibrated in his chest like a second heartbeat, sending tingling currents through his skin. It was a warm electricity, gentle but unrelenting, resonating all the way down to the core of his being as if his body were one of countless other strings of existence being played on some grand instrument.

Zack looked around himself. Cindy and Gabe were now singing the great melody. Down in the crowd, many others were also lifting their voices towards the sky. Above their heads, bright-white, iridescent orbs had now appeared.

"AHHH HUUMM…AHHH HUUMM."

An answering hum came from the clouds. Then the trees. Then the ground itself began to pick up the Song of the Name. Suddenly, it seemed that everything in the universe—the worn cobblestones, the withered bushes, the puff of cloud passing by, to the first star peering through the darkening blue sky—they all matched the song's resonance. Everything, everywhere, was in one great harmony singing towards a final coda.

Amidst the glorious music, Phosos began to slink away, back towards the temple. His HOPs stood suddenly motionless, as if all energy or control had drained from their mechanical bodies. Before leaving the platform, Phosos turned his face back towards the gathered crowd. The resonance echoing throughout the world disrupted whatever enchantment he had used to maintain the illusion of his visage. The once beautiful alien figure had been replaced by a hideous face—pallid, contorted, and in anguish.

As Phosos disappeared back into the darkness of the temple, a loud horn sounded from the sky. When the blast had ended, the sky began to turn blood red.

Everyone in the courtyard looked up. The clouds had turned to white smoke. They began to gather and thicken in the Western sky. At the vanguard of the formation, one of the clouds had the likeness of a lion that seemed to be charging towards the city. Flames of fire licked out from the lion's mane as the furnaces of heaven seemed to be unleashed. Upon its padded feet, the clouds crackled with lightening as if a was hitting on the anvil of the world to reform it.

Behind the charging lion was the late afternoon sun. It had suddenly turned a dark crimson red and was…expanding. The red disk was slowly enlarging in all directions until nearly the entire sky was filled with the massive red orb, ready to devour the earth in its fire.

Looking into the incoming disk of flames, Zack heard a voice in his mind. It spoke in the clearest tone of understanding he had ever felt—not in words, but in concepts and clear meaning. It was a powerful force, and one that had always been inside him even when he sought to deny it. It conveyed that the former world had run its course. That all errant paths had been explored. The sum of all human experiences had been weighed and tried. Now it was time for a restoration…it was time to walk the golden path that was being laid…it was time to come home.

And then a great flash illuminated the sky.

As the light faded, the sun and moon were no longer there. Only a coming wave of flames could be seen on the horizon rushing towards the city, towards the courtyard, towards him and all the others. The incoming flame wave sounded like a whistling train as it slowly swept over the uneven terrain. Orbs of white light zipped up into a gathering of lights in the clouds, as the wave picked up unseen passengers barreling across the landscape. Soon it would reach them all and they would be taken by a flood of fire.

Somehow, Aliyah had found her way next to Gabe and Zack on the terrace. They all stood shoulder-to-shoulder watching the steady approach of cleansing light and flame. No one—besides perhaps Aliyah and Joe—knew what was coming just beyond the veil of light. He did not fear though. His heart was comforted and all troubles seemed to float away.

In those last, dreamy moments, Zack closed his eyes. It was the refuge he had known when he imagined, when he dreamed, when he kissed—where the most precious treasures resided beyond all sensory experience. It was in that place Ava spoke to him. Her sweet voice whispered to him like they were lying in bed, basking in the rays of an early morning sun.

"You found me at the end of your long journey; your sleepy slumber has ended. Wake now. The scales of the dream will soon dissolve so that you may see me in fullness. Welcome back home."

) | (

The cleansing fire engulfed the Earth, burning away the corruption that had become marred into its very fabric of dirt and stone. Through the unquenchable flames came a final reckoning.

For the hardened of heart—those who had turned away from the Ultimate Truth—they endured the hellfire of their own free will. Each torment burned differently. As softwood flared and hardwood smoldered on a pyre, so too did the fire's fury shift with the weight of one's transgressions committed in life. Yet, some confronted the Ultimate Truth within their suffering, their hearts eventually melting by overwhelming love. Restoration reached even them, as they cried out The Name at last, professing salvation from the folly of their own rebellion.

For all the rest, however, whose hearts were of stone, no length of time nor knowledge would move them. Truth remained fully omitted in all their essence. Thus, their punishing torment was not everlasting but a punishment of full separation. A second death. A death eternal. For the fate of anything cut off from the enduring sustenance of the Most High was non-existence.

And so, it finally came to be, that for each of the stubborn hearted that did not turn back to the truth, the fires utterly consumed them—*ex nihilo in nihilum*. The fires glowed hot until every twisted branch, stubbornly grown in every-which direction, was burned to nothing. The blaze smoldered down to the very stump from which all evil had grown forth—the Watchers and their leader, the original Adversary. Each part turned to ash. Until at last, the final fires of judgment had burned out the tree of evilness until it was no more.

In the clearing smoke, time came to an end. Everything, everywhere, folded into an endless age of Eternity.

For all those who accepted the Ultimate Truth, a new life began, one everlasting. When the dream of life was ended, all the appointed souls returned home in joyful reunions with their forebearers. As the heavens and Earth were restored a great chorus of voices rung out throughout the universe. Every soul adding their individually-unique voices into a smoothed harmonious chorus to complete the woven tapestry of understanding that had been uncounted years in the making. Truth itself was realized without doubt and every soul's unique part to revealing that truth would never be lost nor forgotten. Its irrefutable nature meant that evil would not rise again. The Truth was absolute as the never-ending light of the new world and darkness became incomprehensible like a fading dream.

As Aliyah had been shown, each person was but one life, at one time, in one place, among the countless grains of sand that had fallen to the bottom of the glass that measured the length of the created universe. Each grain was a life lived, a life measured, a life adding to the shimmering beaches and dunes which spirited winds could move and shape. For each soul the experience was irreducibly unique. Some ended shortly before they really began and some lingered far longer than they should. A life's mixture of laughter, love, selfishness, sorrow, suffering, gratitude, victories and defeats. For some, lessons were learned and kernels of truth discovered. While others, opportunities were missed, mistakes were made, and turns were taken with no doubling back.

And so, memory became timeless and shared by all without need of speech, books, or machines. Each soul joined their brethren who accepted the truth before. Each one with a story to tell, and an eternity to tell it...and humanity flourished from the telling. When everyone recounted their dream between two eternities.

© SHANA RATCLIFF

ABOUT THE AUTHOR

Nathaniel J. Ratcliff was born in the small town of Chillicothe, Ohio in the winter of 1986. He began his writing career in high school by writing poetry for local library anthologies. From 2005 to 2009, he attended Miami University (of Ohio) and majored in psychology and political science before pursuing a Ph.D. in social psychology at The Pennsylvania State University, graduating in 2016. To date, his psychological research has yielded several peer-reviewed journal articles covering topics of memory, social power, leadership, and organizational behavior. In his day job, Nathaniel works as a social-behavioral scientist, or data storyteller.